Golgren's rise to power during the Minotaur Wars was not the apex of his success. Now, with the help of the mysterious Black Talon, Golgren is taking control of the entire ogre race, finally forging a united nation from the chaos of the different lands and clans of ogrekind. But before he can be declared Grand Khan, the first in centuries, he must determine how to neutralize those who helped him rise to power.

The Black Talon. A secret sect of the ogres determined to bring back the glory of long ago, when ogres were not the twisted, crippled creatures they are now. When their empire was the talk of the world, and when they were known for beauty and power and intelligence. The Black Talon, guided by the ogre Dauroth, has a vision of the future of the ogres and will do nothing to stop their destiny.

And to them, Golgren is merely a convenient puppet. For now.

OGRE TITANS

The Black Talon

The Fire Rose
December 2008

The Gargoyle King
December 2009

THE BLACK TALON

OGRE TITANS VOLUME ONE

RICHARD A. KNAAK

Wizards OF THE COAST

The Ogre Titans, Volume One
THE BLACK TALON
©2007 Wizards of the Coast, Inc.

Published by Wizards of the Coast, Inc. DRAGONLANCE, WIZARDS OF THE COAST, and their respective logos are trademarks of Wizards of the Coast, Inc., in the U.S.A. and other countries.

Printed in the U.S.A.

Cover art by Aleksi Briclot
First Printing: December 2007

9 8 7 6 5 4 3 2 1

ISBN: 978-0-7869-4299-2
620-95965740-001-EN

U.S., CANADA,
ASIA, PACIFIC, & LATIN AMERICA
Wizards of the Coast, Inc.
P.O. Box 707
Renton, WA 98057-0707
+1-800-324-6496

EUROPEAN HEADQUARTERS
Hasbro UK Ltd
Caswell Way
Newport, Gwent NP9 0YH
GREAT BRITAIN
Save this address for your records.

Visit our web site at www.wizards.com

For those who wanted more Golgren.

BLOOD UPON THE LAND

Kern was a harsh, unforgiving place, especially in the drier, dustier regions to the southwest. The overcast sky this day did nothing to negate the heat and, in fact, seemed to amplify it. The parched ground and jagged hills of brown rock that made up the landscape looked almost as if they thirsted, so marked was the absence of any trace, any hint, of moisture.

That would soon change . . . but it would not be water that drenched the land. It would be *blood*.

The two armies were maneuvering into final position, their contrasts as striking as their similarities. Pride, as well as the harshness of the land, demanded that they move around in the open. Other races thought them nothing but beasts and butchers, but among *ogres* there was a brutal code of honor, a sense of what was correct and proper . . . and what was not.

And because of that, the battle had grown inevitable.

The higher ground belonged to what the Knights of Solamnia or any of the other human factions would have readily recognized as a horde typical of ogrekind. Hundreds of fearsome, tusked giants were brandishing their clubs, axes, and other weapons; at the same time they roared their impatience with those keeping them from charging forward. Squat, flat faces—like some parody of humanity—contorted horribly as their blood-lust rose. Under heavy, bushy brows and framed by mops of lice-ridden hair, jaundiced eyes glared at those on the opposing side.

Most of the horde's warriors were clad in simple, soiled cloth kilts. A few evinced metal-tipped kilts of the sort that had once belonged to Uruv Suurt—minotaurs—while others wore ill-fitting breastplates not only from the horned ones' empire, but from human sources. This armor reflected both the silver of the Solamnics and the black of the Nerakans.

Despite their inhospitable environment, nearly all of the warriors were barefoot. Having grown up in that dread realm, ogres who survived to adulthood had feet with soles like tough, tanned leather. Their toenails, like those of their hands, were long, curled, and yellow.

The heavy, repetitive beat of drums stirred the blood of the motley ogre horde, yet the three chieftains who had gathered the army together were not ready to let them loose. Their hesitation derived as much from mutual distrust as from caution against their despised foe. The three chieftains had no love for one another; their simple, agreed-upon goal was to destroy the leader who commanded the enemy, for he threatened not only their power, but all that was their way of life.

The three banners hung at a distinct distance from one another, each chieftain surrounded by his close followers. Crudely drawn images of dripping axes, savage reptilian heads, or birds of prey marked where one war leader's band ended and another's began. That was the limit to their organization, though. It was how their kind had fought for generations, in short-lived, makeshift alliances, and in their primitive minds, the chieftains saw no reason for change.

The roar of a giant beast momentarily drowned out all other noise emanating from the horde. The huge, furred mastarks—their prehensile noses swinging around like long, hungry snakes—had been kept in place as long as the massed warriors, and they were equally eager to get moving. More than two dozen of the huge beasts, each with a rider and guard atop, towered over the nine-foot-tall ogres. Their curled tusks were as long as their noses and often crisscrossed one another like two battling swords. It was all that the handlers could do to keep the bulls among the mastarks from jostling and trampling those in their path.

And just as eager for battle were the meredrakes. The size of a horse, the brown-and-green reptiles sensed the coming carnage and anticipated good feeding. Long tongues continuously licked the air as if prowling for blood. Handlers used whips to control the slavering beasts, but already two warriors had perished for the mere mistake of standing too close.

Whips and clubs also had to be wielded on many among the horde's ranks. Individual warriors were wary of each other, as well as of the rival bands who were temporary allies. Ogre alliances sometimes fell apart before—or during—chaotic battles.

In stark contrast, the troops lined up against the horde suggested a unity and discipline that was remarkable, if not unique, for ogres. Even Solamnic Knights would have been impressed.

They wore uniform breastplates that fit them snugly, and sandals on their feet. Their kilts were fresh and tipped with metal points. Many wore tight helmets that gleamed. Their weapons were the same as their foes' but newer and sharper. More important, these ogres were divided into specialty units. Those with spears led the ranks, followed by swords, then axes and clubs, then bows. The well-armored ogres were better groomed than their foes, although their trek had taken its toll.

The more organized force—which had marched from the northeast—also boasted mastarks and meredrakes, and those were as restless for battle as their counterparts. Yet their handlers kept better rein, aware of the punishment for failing to do so.

And where three banners fluttered over the opposing horde, only one showed here. On a field of brown, a severed hand clutched a crimson-soaked dagger. The banner was crisp and sewn with a skill that the tri-alliance couldn't imagine. It flew high over the one whom it represented, a slimmer figure nearly two feet shorter than those obedient to him. He was like no other ogre on either side of the coming battle, and there was in his features that which questioned the purity of his blood, for certain aspects of his appearance looked elf in nature. From the narrower structure of his face to a mouth that—other than the filed nubs that had once been tusks—was smaller and straighter than usual, much hinted at a lineage that might be entwined with that long-lived race.

Almond-shaped eyes of glittering emerald green surveyed the opposing horde with a calculating intelligence beyond the means of most ogres. The dry wind brushed back a dark, thick mane kept combed and clean. The unique ogre, commander of a disciplined army, wore a shining breastplate and kilt. His helmet included a high crest molded to resemble a griffon. At his shoulders was attached a long, sleek cloak of green and brown.

The drumbeats echoing from the other side grew louder, more incessant, he noted. Some of the ogre officers glanced up at their leader, who was mounted on one of the great muscled horses so valued by the higher castes of their race. But the smaller figure did not give any signal yet. His eyes continued to survey the enemy, as if studying each individual warrior.

Even the well-armored ogres grew restive. Despite their shifting and muttering, their leader acted as though he had all the time in the world. He took the reins from his left hand and wrapped them around his right arm. It was impossible to put the reins in his other hand, for that had been chopped off in battle long ago. In its place was, at least for the time being, sharp metal hooks resembling a bird's talons.

From a pouch at his waist, he removed a tiny vial. Practice enabled him to remove the cork with two fingers while retaining hold of the container. From the vial arose a sweet, flowery scent. The perfume did not remove the stench of so many hot bodies, but it did at least make the ogre leader smile slightly.

He snapped the container shut and replaced it in the pouch. His lone hand slipped to the long sword at his side. Attached to the saddle was a powerful hand axe.

"*Hasala*" the ogre leader quietly declared.

Around him, a score of closely favored underlings broke out into savage, toothy grins. They had heard.

They turned their own fierce beasts away and began to spread through the ranks, shouting commands in the guttural tongue of their race.

All through his army, trumpeters raised great curled goat horns, blaring out harsh notes. From the opposing side came similar calls. Drummers in both forces began beating louder, faster, stirring up the warriors. Mastarks took up the calls, their own roars echoing like thunder. Meredrakes struggled to plunge forward.

Then the Grand Lord Golgren raised his lone hand, bringing it down in a swift chopping motion.

With a unified roar, the armored ogres stepped forward—

And almost immediately ground to a halt.

It was clearly an incredible effort to restrain themselves like that, but they knew full well the punishment for failure. Meredrakes had to be quelled, and at least one mastark broke through the front, running several yards before its handler could calm it.

But the horde facing them from across a small distance did not notice those small disorders . . . for the moment that the grand lord had given his signal, even before his army had begun to advance, they, in turn, charged forward at their enemies.

Horns belatedly cheered their charge, with the three chieftains no longer able to hold their warriors back. With animal howls, the ogres from the southwest tore across the landscape. Behind them rushed bellowing mastarks and meredrakes eager for the kill. The sound of the horde's approach filled the ears of their waiting adversaries.

Golgren—sitting astride his horse, watching patiently, almost peacefully—gestured . . . and the sky filled with thunder and black lightning. His own followers gave a start at his sudden demonstration of magic, his command of the elements, even though they had been reassured that it would not be directed against them. The wicked, unnatural streaks shot down among the onrushing warriors, churning up ground and slaughtering scores. Some of those just beyond the reach of the terrible lightning strikes faltered, but the rest continued on, for it had to be a momentary quirk of nature. Their enemy's master surely could not call down the sky upon them . . .

The hint of a smile momentarily crossed the grand lord's face. He made another cutting gesture.

The lightning storm paused; then the very land beneath the horde's feet ripped open.

An entire advancing row of the ogre horde tumbled into a rapidly widening crevasse stretching across the plain. Behind it, the ground ruptured in a hundred places. Warriors sank out of sight. Others were tossed high into the air.

Several mastarks, frightened by the unnatural events, balked at the orders of their riders. Some tried to turn around. They wheeled and stumbled among those they served, trampling many ogres who could not get out of their way in time. One beast lowered his tusks as he sought escape from the terror, using them to barrel through the small figures in front of him.

And as the huge beasts ran amok in the horde, many of the handlers lost their grips on the meredrakes' leashes. Already driven mad by the destruction and scent of blood, the reptiles eagerly snapped at anything and anyone in reach. Two of the larger creatures brought down one screaming ogre, ripping apart his chest. Another swiped a warrior across the back, tearing away flesh and part of his spine. One meredrake, its senses overwhelmed, bit into the heavy, cylindrical leg of a mastark. The tusked mammal reared up—shaking its foolhardy attacker off—then stomped the lizard to a pulp.

"*Hasala* . . . " Golgren repeated. "Now it is time . . . " he added to himself in the Common tongue.

Three more bolts battered the quaking ground not far in front of his warriors, yet neither the lightning nor the tremors touched the grand lord and his followers. Golgren nodded with satisfaction. The sorcerers had obeyed the letter of his commands . . . so far.

He looked to the nearest trumpeter, who immediately blew another harsh note.

No more lightning fell. The monstrous quake stilled instantly.

Golgren pointed at the enemy, milling about in utter disarray, its beasts stampeding, some of the soldiers attacking each other.

His followers threw themselves forward. Even as the first ranks moved in formation, a row of archers in the rear opened fire. Ogres were not known for their proficiency with the bow, but they sent a hail of arrows that flew above their comrades and landed expertly among their targets. Screams rose anew and many of the enemy—some struck several times—dropped dead.

The archers repeated their effort, adding to the grisly pile of corpses already littering the ruined landscape. They began aiming at specific targets, such as the mastark riders and their guards. The archers were more cautious now; the Grand Lord Golgren wanted none of his own warriors to be slain from behind.

At last, the armored ogres reached the motley enemy horde, tearing into them with fierce, monstrous howls.

Heavy clubs shattered skulls with single blows. Keen-edged swords cut through thick, furred hides. Spears lifted impaled bodies into the air.

Ogre fought against ogre, and no ogre fought with as much fury and pleasure as the Grand Lord Golgren. Despite his slighter stature, despite lacking one hand, he had ridden at the head of his army, and although the first kill was not his, he was not far behind. With the reins still bound to his maimed limb, Golgren urged his horse deeper into the melee. His sword flashed left and right, cutting through the throat of one foe and leaving a ribbon of blood across the chest of another.

His face was frightening to behold; all vestiges of his possible elf blood gave way to something that, in its uniqueness, was even more terrible than the sight of an ogre. His emerald eyes gleamed brighter with each death. Golgren, baring his teeth, was a predator stirred by blood.

Senior warriors in the rear of the horde tried to beat those ahead of them into some semblance of order. The chieftains pushed their three bands into the fray. Although many of the mastarks had fled, a few still remained under control, and they were hurried to the center of the struggle, where the grand lord's adversaries would make their stand.

But Golgren's own great beasts, numbering twice that of the other side by that time, maneuvered toward the remaining creatures controlled by the enemy. Trumpeting roars accompanied the booming crash of giant bodies. Whipped on by their handlers, the mastarks grappled with one another using their tusks.

The grand lord, intent upon a shaggy warrior coming up on his right, suddenly found his horse twisting violently. With a helpless shriek, the animal fell, his rider barely managing to throw himself to the side before the bulky equine crashed to the ground.

Scrambling for his sword, Golgren saw out of the corner of his eye that two meredrakes had swarmed his mount. The animal was still struggling, but one of the huge lizards already had a mouthful of flesh and intestines, while the second struggled to remove a back leg.

The warrior attacking the Grand Lord from the right swung at him with a large club. Golgren stumbled back. The club raised a cloud of dirt as it struck the parched soil.

Before his foe could raise his weapon again, Golgren put a foot on the head of the club and used it to propel himself upward. As the other ogre gaped, the grand lord leaped up and slashed with his metallic talons at the enemy's flat face.

Blood splattered Golgren's immaculate breastplate. His adversary screamed. Dropping his club, the larger ogre clutched at his ruined face, which included one eye completely torn out.

Seizing his sword, Golgren ran the warrior through.

One of the meredrakes sensed the fresh bloodletting. It shoved past the still-shaking corpse of the horse to investigate. Unfortunately, that put Golgren in its path.

Brandishing his weapon, the ogre hissed at the huge lizard. Massive tail sweeping back and forth, the meredrake hissed in return. Blade before him, the grand lord took a confident step toward the beast, hissing again. At the same time, he weaved first left, then right, then left again.

The meredrake repeated its tail-sweeping motion with a more hesitant hissing. Still, it did not move toward the ogre. The reptilian eyes stared, its thick tongue darting out.

Golgren continued to hiss challengingly. He took another step forward, repeating his previous weaving pattern.

With a raspy call, the meredrake suddenly turned about, heading back to the easier fare offered by the horse.

The grand lord knew how to out-bluff those deadly lizards. But on foot, he was at a distinct disadvantage with so many on the field of battle bigger than he. Still, knowledge of that disadvantage had forced him, throughout his life, to excel at quick, clever warfare. Thus it was that the next warrior to come at him perished without much bother, his crude swordsmanship no match for the honed skills of the smaller ogre. The grand lord moved on even before the body finished tumbling.

An ear-splitting bellow presaged a giant shadow sweeping over not only Golgren but also several warriors from both sides. More nimble than his hulking brethren, the grand lord slipped between combatants just as two mastarks, their tusks tangled together, stumbled among the grappling ogres on both sides. Personal battles were forgotten as the smaller figures desperately sought escape. Many did not get away, the crushing of their bones drowned out by the mastarks' continued roars.

As he eluded the beasts, Golgren felt a fierce wind spring up. He nodded grimly, having already wondered when *they* would finally get around to that spell. They were tardy.

The wind grew to staggering proportions, but oddly, it seemed most focused on the grand lord's enemies. A dust storm quickly arose that threatened to blind those in the motley horde.

Alerted prior to the battle that such a thing would happen, the armored ogres kept their gazes fixed directly ahead of them. Their desperate adversaries swung wildly. Golgren's minions calmly picked their targets out and marked them for death. The battle grew more brutal, the outcome more and more apparent.

But that did not yet satisfy Golgren, who searched the collapsing horde for one particular individual . . . until he finally found him.

Slashing through the stomach of another opponent, the grand lord fought his way toward a gargantuan figure, who was busy chopping down one of the armored ogres under Golgren's command. Blood caked the giant's torso, and despite the fact his horde was in danger of being routed, his expression was one of murderous glee.

The gargantuan ogre wore a battered helm with a much-abused crest signifying that it had once belonged to an officer of the minotaur legions. Jagged scars covered his face, some of them aligned so perfectly they could only be ritually self-carved.

Golgren knew him as the most important, the most powerful of the three chieftains.

"Jari i oGolgreni, iTrangi!" the grand lord shouted to get the gargantuan chieftain's attention. "Come to me, Trang!" Golgren repeated in Common for his own amusement. No other ogre could speak Common so well, and the grand lord loved to flaunt his superiority even in the midst of such a pitched struggle.

The other ogre paused in the midst of throttling another victim. Like Golgren, he was on foot, but standing erect, his broad shoulders rose well above his rival's head.

Trang grinned like a hungry meredrake. He indifferently tossed aside his unfortunate foe and turned toward Golgren. *"if'hani . . . "* the vicious chieftain rumbled. *"if'hani iGolgreni."*

Trang barreled through two other fighters, knocking them aside. Golgren waited calmly, assessing each twist and turn of the other's charge. Trang had a reputation among all ogres; he had been, in fact, the one who had instigated the uprising, the battle, the insult against Golgren's primacy among the race.

Trang's dripping axe came down on the smaller warrior. The grand lord parried the attack with his sword. Their weapons clanged together, Golgren's entire body vibrating from the collision. Trang's incredible strength was no mere legend.

With a barking laugh, the giant brought up his axe for another powerful strike. Golgren immediately lunged in under his guard with his right. He intended to rip out the chieftain's throat with his metal claws, but Trang was more agile than most ogres and twisted away. Instead of the throat, Golgren's talons drew several crimson lines across the left shoulder.

The wounds were shallow, however, and did not elicit more than a grunt of annoyance from Golgren's adversary. The chieftain continued his assault, battering away with his huge axe. It was all Golgren could do to keep from being forced to his knees, so heavy and relentless was the rain of blows.

Trang's grin widened in anticipation of his enemy's demise. However, that grin and the smugness it represented were what the smaller ogre had been waiting for. Suddenly, Golgren dodged to the side of Trang's axe. He came up on the chieftain from the right, slashing quickly under the other's upraised arm.

That time, his blade sank deep.

Still, instead of slowing Trang, the wound seemed only to outrage the massive chieftain. He countered with a swift sweep downward of his axe, shattering Golgren's blade. The grand lord raised his talons to deflect the axe from his chest, but the blade's momentum—coupled with Trang's strength—enabled the weapon to rip off his well-secured false hand.

Golgren let out a cry as the tight straps and fastenings tore free from his maimed limb. He stumbled back just in time to avoid another swing. Trang chuckled darkly, his eyes red with bloodlust.

But his target still proved to be nimble. Three times Trang's axe shot toward the grand lord, and three times it found only empty air. Golgren fared no better; he had only a dagger, not yet drawn, available to him, so he was forced to duck and weave.

Around them, the rest of the combatants unconsciously gave space. No one sought to stumble into the path of two warriors of such reputation.

There was still only so much area in which to maneuver, and Trang was seeing to it that Golgren had less and less.

Yet again Trang brought his axe down hard, barely missing severing his smaller opponent in half. Frustrated at his near miss, the chieftain started to pull his weapon back up . . . when, with his lone hand, Golgren snagged Trang's wrist. Startled, the chieftain did not immediately react.

The grand lord swung himself up and over. Trang made a grab for him, but it was too late.

Golgren's legs had wrapped around the chieftain's thick neck. Despite the fact that he was bigger and heavier, Trang could not keep his balance and teetered backward.

The chieftain fell with a loud thud, but Golgren found one of his legs caught underneath his foe and his good arm slammed against the hard ground. Both ogres momentarily lay there, stunned.

It was Trang who stirred first. Growling, he pushed himself up on his elbows, and instantly Golgren slipped his leg out, struggling to find his footing. Fumbling with his hand, the grand lord drew his dagger.

Trang already had his axe gripped tight. Still rising, he spun around. His axe was aimed directly for Golgren's midsection.

The chieftain's target flattened himself on the ground. The axe swooped past just inches above his torso.

Golgren half crawled, half lunged.

His dagger lodged deep in the base of Trang's throat. Trang coughed and let out a long, choking sound. Despite his terrible wound, the chieftain tried to stand and renew his attack.

But his axe rose, then tumbled out of his shaking hand. Golgren shoved the dagger in deeper. Trang clutched madly at him, heavy paws groping for the grand lord's throat.

Fighting for breath, Golgren forced the dagger sideways, tearing open a huge hole in the throat.

The gargantuan ogre chieftain shivered and fell back, dead.

Golgren leaped atop the corpse. Continuing to work with his dagger, the grand lord cut through the rest of the neck until the ogre's head finally came off. Blood and other fluids dripped over his garments as he raised the grisly evidence of his victory high over his head, letting out a bestial howl of triumph.

Those nearest turned at the sound, noting the smaller ogre commander's victory over his mountainous opponent. The sight further disheartened and panicked the warriors of the horde.

An armored ogre on horseback fought his way to the grand lord. The moment he reached Golgren, the warrior leaped down and handed the reins to his leader. Golgren thrust Trang's head into the warrior's waiting hands then mounted.

"Do not lose my prize," he warned in Common. All those who would serve close to the grand lord had to learn the tongue, for Golgren felt it a part of "the fruits of civilization" he was bringing to his people.

"Will not!" grunted the warrior loudly, his round eyes showing his fear of his commander.

As his minion retreated to the back lines, Golgren procured a new sword from another underling. Armed once again and with the reins secured to his maimed limb, he let out a louder, more bloodcurdling cry and eagerly urged his steed into the struggle.

The slaughter continued.

II

WARY ALLIANCE

The mangled bodies lay strewn as far as the eye could see, and well beyond that. Severed limbs and other bloody parts could be found everywhere. Now and then, an island of brown fur rose among the ogre corpses. More than half the mastarks in the day's battle had been slain, as had many of the meredrakes, some simply because they had grown so maddened from the scent of blood that their handlers could not control them any longer and had to kill them to prevent unnecessary casualties on their side.

Although many bodies lay clad in the once-gleaming breastplates and helms, far more of the dead were easily marked as the uncouth warriors of the horde. Few had survived, as ogres are very brutal in victory or defeat. Those that still lived were marching along in chains, their fates possibly even more terrifying than that of their dead comrades. Examples would have to be made to emphasize the glory of the winning side.

The architect of that victory watched astride his

second horse as guards shoved the beaten warriors and as others ferreted among the slain, seeking spoils. Born to a land offering little, ogres were practical; if an item could be utilized in any manner, why leave it to rot with the dead? Even the mastarks were still of some use; warriors scrambled up, over, and around the huge bodies, not only skinning the beasts, but salvaging what meat there still was. The stomachs of ogres welcomed flesh long past what other races would deem safe.

Those who had died for Golgren were respectfully burned so they would not feed scavengers. There would be no pyres for the dead enemy, however, in contrast to what was often done among other races such as the Uruv Suurt or the humans. Fuel was too valuable to waste on the defeated. Besides, after the carrion eaters had stripped the bodies, the bleaching bones would present a monument to the grand lord. The other chieftains would be reminded of the consequences of defiance of his will.

With whips and swords to prod them forward, a new set of prisoners was brought before Golgren. His garments were still bloodstained, but his hair again was neatly brushed. He surveyed the sorry lot. Two figures immediately caught his attention.

"Wulfgarn . . . Guln . . . " The grand lord kept his speech in Common. His gloating grin was terrible to behold. "It is a sorry thing, this disaster into which Trang led you."

Wulfgarn, an older chieftain with one eye long gone to a sword slash, frowned as he tried to translate the foreign sounds. Guln, much younger and with a thick head of black, unruly hair, grunted bitterly. He understood well enough.

"It is a sorry thing Trang led himself into," added Golgren, gesturing to the warrior next to him. That ogre hefted the gory head of the dead chieftain. Trang's expression was one of astonishment, as if he were only then discovering that he was defeated.

Wulfgarn spit in Golgren's direction, though the missile fell well short of its goal. The older chieftain was rewarded with a savage whipping that sent him facedown on the ground.

The prisoners that were lined up behind those two— all subchieftains—looked anxious at the sight. They well knew the fate of most survivors. The grand lord might have them pulled apart by mastarks or bound spread-eagled among several meredrakes.

Looking past the two chieftains, Golgren picked out four ogres standing among the much-battered group. The guards undid their chains then kicked the hapless ones forward.

"Dakara i duru if'hani?" he asked of the chosen, eyes glinting. "Will you stand with or deny these dead?"

All four answered as he expected, falling down on one knee and bowing their heads to him. After acknowledging their submission, Golgren gestured for them to rise then had another guard present them with thick, weathered clubs stained with dry blood. The four ogres peered at one another, then at their captor.

The grand lord indicated the rest of the subchieftains, those he had passed over. Guards were already forcing those condemned souls to their knees. More than one had to be beaten down, for the prisoners knew what was coming. Other guards dragged Wulfgarn and Guln off to the side.

"F'han," Golgren quietly commanded.

The four moved in among the kneeling subchieftains. Clubs rose high and came down with savage strength. The thick skulls of the condemned easily gave way under the onslaught.

It took only one or two heavy blows to execute each, but wanting to show their enthusiastic allegiance to their new lord, the four subchieftains bashed away over and over at their targets, leaving most in piles of unrecognizable pulp.

When there was no more killing to be done, one of the four started toward Guln, but the grand lord waved him back. The subchieftain quickly retreated to stand close to his companions.

With another wave, Golgren dismissed the survivors, who were led away by one of his officers. Wulfgarn and Guln were also taken off elsewhere, their fates—it would have been Trang's, too, had he survived—already planned in advance. Golgren felt the need to set many examples for his people.

"A barbaric display," came an almost musical, cultured voice at Golgren's right. "But necessary, I suppose."

The Grand Lord Golgren did not turn to face the speaker. In fact, he did not even reply right away. While his guards shifted nervously, their eyes drifting in the direction of the new voice, he continued to gaze ahead, waiting. One hand retrieved his vial. The grand lord took a slow, casual sniff.

Finally, there came the light movement of sandaled feet and the faint swishing of cloth. Despite the overcast sky, strong shadows stretched before the mounted ogre leader. They were followed by one, then several more, such forms, each of whom dwarfed even the tallest of Golgren's warriors.

Each was one and a half times the height of an ordinary ogre but proportionately sleeker of form. They moved with an unnatural grace, almost gliding rather than walking. Their long, silken robes—dark blue with shimmering hints of red—flowed as part of them, accenting their wearers' perfection.

The giants wore crimson sashes that draped over their right shoulders and came down their left sides under the golden belts at their waists. Their left shoulders were covered by an armor plate more decorative than functional, with their arms unclad, save for red, silken bands on the wrists of their left arms and silver metal ones on their right arms.

But as elegant as their garments were, they paled in comparison to the faces of the ones gathering before the grand lord. No, *perfection* was not a word that adequately described the countenances of the newcomers. Their flawless features made the most beautiful elves look dull and drab in comparison. Several of Golgren's warriors stared, awed by what their eyes beheld and suddenly ashamed that they were lesser beings. It was hard for any among them to believe that those godlike creatures were kin, were also ogres.

The giants' skin was bluer than the open sky and without blemish. Their upswept, golden eyes seemed to glow from within. Their ears were long and pointed but in a graceful manner. Most wore their midnight-black hair bound in a thick tail.

Their leader, the one who had spoken in the cultured voice, gave Golgren a low bow. His lips parted, and suddenly the perfection gave way to something monstrous. The giant evidenced twin rows of savage, pointed teeth, reminiscent of a shark.

"The day is yours, oh Grand Lord," the figure pronounced in his almost musical voice, loudly and in succinct Common. "We give our congratulations to you on this great victory."

He bowed low again, the others behind him following suit. With the exception of a few personal touches to their garments, the members of the astounding group—all male—looked nearly identical to one another. Their leader showed a few peculiarities; his face was a touch older, wizened. A streak of silver—not gray—rose from the hairline on his back.

"Your words are most gracious, Dauroth," Golgren returned with equal ease of the tongue. He took another sniff from the bottle then returned it to the pouch. "And thus accepted by myself."

The grand lord noted a slight stirring among Dauroth's followers. They did not approve of his grandiose airs, he knew.

Golgren's hand casually grazed his chest, where a pair of chains around his neck indicated that more than one thing hung hidden inside his garments. "The Titans performed their duties adequately," he continued, ignoring the sudden darkening expression among those in the back at his careful choice of words. "Even though not all went in a manner so timely as might be desired."

One of the Titans emitted a low, angry mutter. Dauroth's head tipped slightly to the side, and the offending sound ceased. The lead Titan straightened to his full height. Even on horseback, Golgren was shorter and had to look up to meet his eyes.

Nonetheless, Dauroth showed nothing but subservience to the smaller ogre. "I must apologize for our missteps, oh Grand Lord. I promise that we shall endeavor to be of greater efficiency and value to you when next our services are needed."

"The tremor was a most amusing touch," Golgren commented offhandedly.

Dauroth smiled, displaying his sinister teeth. "I will personally see that we strive to enhance its effect in the future. This entire scenario was a first trial for us in such spell work, as you no doubt recall."

Golgren nodded once then pretended to lose interest. "We are done here, Dauroth. You and your Titans have my permission to depart."

"You have but to summon us again at your leisure, oh Grand Lord," the senior spellcaster intoned, golden eyes suddenly flaring bright with magic. "And we shall stand before you, ready to do your bidding, in the blink of an eye."

A whirlwind abruptly sprang to life around the Titans. Even though its reach did not extend beyond the magnificent giants, the nearby guards backed away. Only Golgren, his loose mane just slightly rustled by the wind, did not budge. The grand lord looked bored at their latest magical marvel.

Although they stood within the whirlwind's center, the Titans, too, were barely grazed by the magical wind. They huddled closer together, gleaming eyes narrowed in concentration. Dauroth raised his hands to the sides, revealing in that moment two other jarring discrepancies in the Titans' overall beauty. First were the bony, hooked spurs that sprouted from their elbows, almost five inches long. Yet more unnerving were their hands themselves. They were strong and sleek, true, but they ended in fierce, ebony nails—much like the claws of raptors—that stretched at least three inches.

As the wind rose, Dauroth looked to the sky and uttered certain words in a musical language.

As one, the Titans vanished.

The wind died down as soon as they were gone. Golgren let out a grunt that marked for all around him his lack of amazement at Dauroth's act. The other ogres quickly tried to copy his facial expression, wary of possibly letting the grand lord think that anything frightened them that didn't frighten him.

Golgren turned his mount around and headed to his tent. The rounded structure was formed from tanned hides and bone slats with a thick piece of mastark fur draping the entrance. Two guards stood near the entrance—one a typical Kern ogre like so many that comprised Golgren's following, the second a rounder, squatter figure in armor who hailed from the other ogre realm of Blöde. The two saluted him with equal fervor, their meaty fists banging hard against their breastplates. There still remained a grand khan in Kern and a ruling chieftain in Blöde, but Golgren was master of both regions in all but title.

And even that would soon change.

One of the guards took the reins but did not offer to assist Golgren down. The grand lord rarely ever accepted help from his own kind. An ogre who did not fend for himself was a fool.

Ignoring the guards, Golgren slipped into his tent. Inside was shade and warmth. The floor was covered by a wide mastark hide and softer skins, mostly from young amaloks, scattered here and there. There were also many colorful yet elegant pillows with intricate embroidery whose craftsmanship marked them as spoils from the conquest of elven Silvanost.

And even more important, another souvenir from that ravaged land, was the female who awaited the grand lord, a silver-tressed figure with eyes of crystalline blue and skin of ivory. Her form was slim yet appreciably curved in the ways Golgren liked; she appeared just a few short years into adulthood, even though she was a lifetime or two older than the ogre. Her hair was parted down the middle and flowed past her shoulders, down to nearly the crook of her back. Her somewhat narrow face bore features that were both delicate and yet toughened.

She wore the remnants of a once-grand gown whose color, green, almost matched the tint of Golgren's eyes. The bottom of her gown was in tattered shreds, while the bodice had been revamped and lowered—at Golgren's demand—to best display her charms. She wore only well-used, crude sandals of ogre make, sandals originally for a child of that race.

Her ankles and wrists were shackled in iron, providing her just enough mobility to perform her tasks but not enough to make an escape. In the past the elf woman—like her two predecessors—*had* tried to escape and failed miserably.

"Idaria," he rumbled.

She lowered her head. "My lord Golgren."

Assuring himself that the tent flap completely covered the entrance, the grand lord seated himself on the cushions. Idaria maneuvered herself around to her appointed place at his right. Without looking at her, Golgren held up the covered stump of his arm.

With practiced care, the elf undid what remained of the fastenings for his metal talons. Some of the stronger ones had dug into his flesh, causing bleeding that became apparent only when the wrappings had been completely removed.

"The weapon, it did not work to my satisfaction," the ogre commented more to the air than to the elf woman. "The device's making, it was crude. Not as I envisioned it. It shall need to be redone."

Idaria said nothing. If and when Golgren wanted her to respond, he would give her a clear indication. She continued to remove everything from his arm so she could see to cleaning the injured stump. Once, the thought of performing such a task would have affronted the elf woman, but Idaria had discovered that she was capable of enduring many worse affronts; she was a survivor willing to do whatever she must. That alone set her apart from those who came before her.

Golgren's ruined limb ended in a huge black scab with burn scars surrounding it. He had cauterized the wound himself in the midst of a high-pitched battle, long ago it seemed. Faros—then the leader of a band of escaped slaves that had been sold to Golgren's people by Hotak, emperor of the Uruv Suurt—had severed his hand. Faros had gone on to kill Hotak, and the former slave became emperor of the minotaurs.

Such a terrible injury would have ended the lives of most creatures—even most ogres would have perished from such a blow—but Golgren had managed to keep his head clear long enough to find a torch and sear the wound shut. Even then, he had nearly died, although he had recovered to fight on.

The singular drive that ultimately brought him to power had preserved him then.

Golgren's slave reached for two sealed jugs. From each she poured a small amount of liquid on a fresh cloth and began rubbing the mixed contents over the stump. The ogre let out a sigh when he was touched by the balm. His body visibly relaxed.

When she was done, Idaria replaced the jugs then wrapped the area almost tenderly. Golgren, who had in the midst of her ablutions shut his eyes, opened them and gazed deeply into hers.

"Wine," he commanded.

As silent as the night, Idaria retrieved the sack of wine. The environment of Kern was not suitable for keeping something as sensitive as wine for long, but the crimson liquid was still preferable to the brackish water in those parts.

As Golgren took the silver goblet—another elven prize—there came a heavy grunt from outside the tent. A shadow loomed near the entrance.

"*Nagh!*" the grand lord called. "Enter!"

An ogre officer of Blödian origins edged inside. He sported one broken tusk and his left eye constantly looked as if it were squinting. His skin was a mottled brown.

He glanced at the elf woman. Idaria immediately took up a subservient position behind her master.

"*Aaah,* Khleeg," greeted the grand lord, gesturing to the newcomer with the goblet. "You may speak freely."

The other saluted Golgren. "All warriors gathered," Khleeg rumbled, doing his best not to mangle his Common too badly. "Feed them now?"

Golgren gave him a curt nod. The army did not even eat without his permission.

Saluting again, the other ogre started to leave, then apparently recalled something else he wished to say. Looking anxious, the tusked figure muttered, "Grand Lord, may speak again? About . . . about the Titans?"

"My permission is given."

His brow knitted, Khleeg said, "Grand Lord . . . the Titans . . . cannot trust in them . . . they are—" He struggled for the right phrase. "They are *Jaro Gyun*. Wearers of masks."

The term had nothing to do with the fanciful false faces that Solamnic nobles were rumored to wear at certain private gatherings or even the totemic images ogres themselves employed for rituals on occasion. *Jaro Gyun* meant *deceivers* who acted as blood comrades until the time came to stab the unwary from behind. For one ogre to call another a *Jaro Gyun* was a strong insult. That Khleeg would dare to apply this term to Dauroth and his sorcerers was, to Golgren, a sign of just how great the officer's dislike and distrust of them was. Khleeg knew his master could have him executed for speaking ill of the Titans, for their influence among the ogres was second only to the grand lord's.

But Golgren only nodded understandingly to Khleeg and said, "At first light, we leave. Garantha awaits."

Still visibly uncomfortable, the other ogre grunted. "Yes, Grand Lord."

"Go."

Khleeg bowed again, then, staying bowed, backed out of the tent. Golgren nodded but that time to himself.

"He speaks the truth about the Titans," Idaria murmured, lowering her gaze to avoid the grand lord's eyes.

"And so? You have the opinion to share also?"

The elf kept her eyes to the ground. She could be more easily executed than Khleeg for any hint of disrespect toward ogres. As an elf slave, she was less than nothing in the eyes of ogres.

But still Idaria talked. "The Titans chafe under your rule. They do not serve you willingly. Not even Dauroth."

He chuckled, grinning. The grin revealed a set of teeth that belied the hints of elf blood he might have. His teeth, while in better, cleaner condition than most ogres', were strong, harsh, and sharply edged—in all ways extremely ogrish.

"This is quite a surprise to me," Golgren replied in a tone that indicated otherwise. He gulped some wine. It was sweet and richly colored, typical of the blend traditionally made by her people. "Dauroth and his, they do not adore this one?"

"They will try to kill you sooner or later . . . and soon enough. No matter the hold you have on them, they will do that."

The grand lord's grin reversed into grim, pursed lips. In a voice so cold and dead that it made Idaria flinch, Golgren replied, "Yes, they will."

He put down his goblet then, cupping her chin, he raised her face until it was level with his own. Although Idaria waited—her gaze meeting his—for long seconds, the ogre said nothing. Finally he released her, his attention returning to his wine. The elf resumed her usual position, kneeling in wait, slightly behind him, ready for his next command.

"Garantha awaits me," Golgren uttered without warning. "We must not let her pine for her love." He took another sip then let out a hollow laugh that evinced little humor. "And soon, soon, she and I, we shall be wed!" He glanced at the slave to see if she shared in his bitter jest. "Soon, I will be crowned grand khan of all my people . . . the dream fulfilled."

Idaria said nothing. She had heard the last part before, many times, and always in the same tone.

"The dream fulfilled," the grand lord repeated darkly,

drinking deeply again. His eyes narrowed, glaring from under his brow at the shadows in the tent. "The first dream . . . "

ᦕᦕᦕ᳇ᦕᦕᦕ

In the overcast sky, a winged form alighted onto a high promontory overlooking a chaotic battle site. The shape clung to the dark there, for it had been warned what would become of it if any below noticed its presence. Breathing heavily from exertion, the form folded its leathery wings and climbed to a higher vantage, using its clawed hands and feet with an ease that spoke of its familiarity with such treacherous terrain.

Deep-set eyes surveyed the victorious ogres as they continued to strip the dead and began their preparations to depart. The watcher grunted appreciatively; a bloody victory was respected among his kind as well. He had enjoyed the spectacle, even though the use of magic by the victors had, to his brutish mind, seemed a bit like cheating. What was more pleasurable than personally tearing apart a foe? Still, magic could not be avoided in some instances; even the watcher understood that.

And thinking that over, he reached down to a pouch held by a leather strap looped over his thick neck and shoulder. With a dexterity that was remarkable, considering his pawlike hands, he gently removed from the pouch what looked like an octagonal box made of brass, topped by a rounded knob.

Raising the box to his eye, the watcher pressed the knob.

The metallic artifact shimmered blue. On the side near his eye, a small gap opened.

Peering inside, he observed the interior of a tent, but it was not the tent desired. The watcher focused more toward the right.

There! The tent of the one-handed ogre. The watcher grunted with satisfaction. For a few seconds, he watched intently as the leader of the victors drank his fill; a female elf attended him. Then, using the magical device as his master had dictated, the winged creature shifted his focus to the ogre's chest and what lay beneath his breastplate and garment.

Looking through both barriers as though they were empty air, he immediately spied the larger of the two items he sought to identify. Seeing it disturbed even the grizzled watcher. Then the item shifted slightly and became visible.

A tiny, transparent vial hung from a thin, golden chain that was well hidden by the bulkier one used to keep the first object in place. The vial was no larger than a sewing pin, but through the magic eye, its contents radiated disturbing energies.

The watcher adjusted the artifact. The tendrils of energy faded from his sight, giving him a better view of its actual contents, a red liquid with which his kind was most familiar.

Satisfied, he pressed the knob, and the metallic device reverted to its original state. He spread his wings, already anxious to be away from there. The master awaited his findings.

The ogre had the blood upon him.

III

THE DRAGON WHO IS ZHARANG

Garantha was the city's true name, although those who were not ogres—meaning all other races—called it by the less-glorious appellation of *Kernen*. Kernen was the capital of present-day Kern as well as one of the most ancient cities on all the continent of Ansalon, and even in all of the world of Krynn. Built by the High Ogres, the magnificent ancestors of its current inhabitants, Garantha once had been a jewel among jewels.

When first it had been built, the city had been surrounded by a four-sided, thirty-foot-high marble wall with sets of wide gates forged of—at that time—rare and impervious steel. Towering obelisks carved from the same white marble as the wall stood by each gate, proclaiming, in the flowery language of its founders, the name of the city and welcoming all who visited. The marble wall was covered in fantastic reliefs rising nearly the full height of the protective barrier, highly realistic reliefs beguiling newcomers with the wonders of the capital.

The city within was even more beautiful and

astounding. One could walk through a vast open-air market that filled the southern quarter. Designed to resemble a virgin garden in some lush jungle, it was as much a sight for visitors as it was a destination to purchase or trade foods, crafts, artifacts, and more from every part of Ansalon and the lands beyond the seas.

In the center of Garantha lay the giant domed arena where scholars, politicians, philosophers, and other notables could debate the topics of the day and the issues of the world before audiences numbering well into the thousands. Plays involving full-scale battles and sea journeys were also enacted there.

There had been so much more in the city, long ago. There was the Zoo of Sagrio, home to the rarest of all beasts. The four fabled towers just within the walls, illuminated towers that acted as beacons for the weary pilgrims approaching. The crowns of each of those four towers had been artfully decorated with the city symbol—a majestic, stylized griffon. The towers stood above white cobblestoned streets kept pristine.

Far to the west lay the palace of the grand khan, a sprawling edifice resembling three perfect turtle shells, the smaller two flanking the larger and also huddling up close against it. The outer sections of the palace rose four stories high; the center stood six. The sloping, ridged roof further accented the illusion of giant reptiles in repose. Underneath the roof, arched windows ran along the length of the palace.

Originally, twin towers had also flanked the imposing structure, and the palace itself had been cast in a subtle, greenish pearl luster. Those entering the area of the palace rode under a great arch formed by two battling griffons.

This and much more once was Garantha, though

the present city reflected only a twisted shadow of that ancient glory.

Since the fall and degeneration of the ogre race, the wall had collapsed into a few randomly spaced sections that mocked its function. Over time, feeble and sloppy attempts to rebuild the wall had taken place. They had resulted in worse disarray and damage. The obelisks had also suffered the ravages of the passing of time and the barbarism of the citizens; two were simply no more, their rubble carted away at some point for the efforts to revive the wall. The others were broken at the top and only one still bore the weather-worn name of the city, not that most who entered or even lived there could read the language.

The city had likewise fallen into general disrepair and ruin, with only the grand khan's palace and some of the surrounding ancient villas sporting healthy facades. The two flanking towers of the former remained in pieces, however, and the nearby arena—although still utilized—no longer had any hint of a dome, that having collapsed inward centuries ago. Even the revered symbol of Garantha had suffered, for most of the griffon statues and carvings had long ago toppled and lay in fragments or were worn down so that they had become unrecognizable.

But what had seemed an unstoppable spiral into utter devastation had begun to reverse itself over the past generation. More than half the main wall had been restored, inexpertly patched with gray stone where marble could not be found. The lone identifying obelisk stood at the foremost gate, its crown reshaped to give it some semblance of its original look, with its elaborate script studiously reetched.

THE BLACK TALON

As Golgren's column entered through the gates, he paused from waving to the crowds to admire the work that had been done since his departure. In place of many of the ancient reliefs of High Ogre faces, his own image had begun to take prominence. The craftsmanship and detail involved in those depictions surpassed even the work on a new, intricate griffon statue just being erected on the right side of the gates. The grand lord nodded his approval at the anxious workers who were busy with final work on that statue. The workers knew that their lord had commanded that piece be ready by the time he returned from crushing his rivals, and they hastened to do as expected.

Farther within, other buildings also showed signs of the continuing patchwork and reconstruction. Every portion of Garantha visible to the grand lord as he passed was busy being improved. If Golgren was to be the master of his people, he expected they and their greatest city to be worthy of him.

Idaria rode beside him, ready to hand him a vial of scent or whatever else he desired during the procession. Compared to other slaves, hers was a vaunted position, for most ogres would have insisted that she trail far behind their horses, her feet bare and her back red from whippings. Idaria had only three faint streaks on her back, dating from her one failed escape attempt. There might have been more, only Golgren had not deemed her other minor transgressions worthy of such punishment.

Behind the pair rode Golgren's guards and his senior officers. Khleeg was chief among them. Khleeg had been given the singular and exalted honor of holding aloft at the end of a spear the drying head of the defeated rebel chieftain Trang. The squinty-eyed ogre was very proud of his responsibility and waved the gaping head high above his own to give the trophy maximum visibility to the throngs.

For the coming of the grand lord—an arrival announced in advance by riders from the column some days before—the crowds were tremendous indeed. They were dressed as few outsiders had ever witnessed the race; in robes and other garments mostly refashioned from elven finery, the highest of the caste looked nearly as magnificent as the finely dressed leader whom they greeted with cheers. Many even had crudely brushed and cleaned their hair, and more than a few had filed down their tusks in the manner of the grand lord. To most humans, dwarves, or elves, the scene might have been amusing—brutal beasts playing at civilized behavior— but others would have looked upon the spectacle with wonder, awe . . . and worry.

"Iskar'ai!" the legions of onlookers shouted. *"Iskar'ai!"* The ogre word for *victory* was precious, used only on rare occasions and celebrated for its meaning. Victory was another word for power, and power was the means of domination and rule.

Horns blared from the walls and from the roofs of buildings, where kilted, breastplated sentries announced the approach of the Grand Lord Golgren to the crowds ahead. In the column warriors beat on leather drums in rhythm with the marching of the soldiers. More than four thousand fighters were following Golgren, which was not even his entire army. In the past year, a hundred chieftains and lesser khans had added their oaths of fealty to those already in his service. He had large forces scattered outside the city and all around his realm.

36

In the distance, several high towers loomed. They, too, had been repaired—completely, it appeared—but even then figures dangling from ropes were altering the vast reliefs carved outside the upper levels. Golgren revealed nothing of his inner thoughts, but his eyes flickered at the sight.

Those towers—and much of the initial work on the capital's reconstruction—had been instigated not by Golgren, but rather by the *Titans*. Before he had first set foot in Garantha, before he had taken the *name* Golgren, the city had begun its resurrection under the guidance of the Titans. It was the Titans who initially inspired the people to restore the towers, and they had had their own symbols and images carved on them. Both the grand khan and his counterpart in Blöde had bowed to the Titans. The latter, Donnag, had willingly taken part in their dark rituals, eventually becoming one of the Titans himself.

The entire city had bowed to the Titans. But that time, like the era of the High Ogres, was past, Golgren reflected. He was master. The grand khan was a miserable toady who knew that he survived only at the whim of his former minion. Golgren did not give him much thought. But Donnag, believing in Titan superiority, had challenged the rise of the upstart Golgren—challenged and lost. His fate—his sentence—was an example to all the Titans; no one dared cross the grand lord.

But still Golgren knew that the Titans existed to undermine him. They would do so again and again.

Surrounded by jubilant crowds, the procession moved through the city. Ogres appreciated strength, and Golgren represented a strength that seemed destined to rise and rise. He had brought a pride to the race, and he had done it, for the most part, with cunning and the strength of arms. The people respected and feared him differently than they did the Titans. For all his mixed blood, Golgren knew that they accepted him as one of themselves—unlike his sorcerous rivals, who were regarded as aloof, apart. That did not mean that the ogre masses would not turn on Golgren if at some point he revealed weaknesses. That was life among ogres—harsh choices and mercurial loyalties.

The banner of the severed hand fluttered on buildings throughout Garantha. Golgren's image also appeared here and there—more and more, over time—as reliefs carved into the walls of buildings more recently built and clearly the fine work of artisans who were not ogres. Indeed, as the grand lord neared the palace, he caught a glimpse of two ragged figures at work on a ten-foot-high reproduction of his profile. The image was more refined than the actuality, but Golgren did not mind.

The two hollow-eyed sculptors were toiling as though their lives depended upon it, which they did. Like Idaria, they were elves, and the niceties of their existence depended upon their value to the grand lord. Though they looked worked to death, they lived better than many of their fellows. That was because their talent was useful to Golgren. He wanted his face plastered all over the ogre lands; that pair was one of many helping to spread his reputation and legend among his kind.

The guard standing watch over the sculptors noted Golgren's gaze upon them and immediately began whipping the elves to work harder. Golgren frowned and signaled one of his officers.

"He whips too hard. They must survive in order to do my work."

The other ogre nodded and went off to warn the guard of his overzealousness.

"Thank you," Idaria murmured.

Gazing straight ahead without acknowledging her, Golgren shrugged. He had not done it out of any mercy or sympathy for her people.

Ogres continued to throng the streets, many of them banging clubs and the ends of spears on the stone path. Golgren slowed to give his people one last clear look at their leader before he entered through the gates. Although he was no longer visible to the populace, their cheering and shouting did not diminish, for the grand lord was trailed by impressive ranks of armored warriors, themselves followed by the vanquished, the defeated remnants of the ogre horde bent low from exhaustion, whippings, and their heavy chains. Their fates would make them envy the elf slaves.

After the vanquished would march more of his legions, so many that he would astonish the onlookers with the minimal losses his army had suffered. Golgren had not been hesitant about borrowing fighting methods from both the Uruv Suurt and the Solamnics when it came to training and preparing his warriors. That their training was a rough blend of those two formidable foes was intentional. Too many generations had passed in which the ogres had been slaughtered by superior disciplined and trained forces. He would not let that happen again.

A harsh memory from his early days flashed through his mind, causing the grand lord to jerk on the reins of his horse. Images of bloody ogre corpses, of a burning village, overwhelmed him suddenly. As his mount came to an abrupt halt, he sensed the others' curiosity at his unexpected behavior. But no one uttered any sound; none expected any explanation from him. They merely waited until Golgren prodded the horse with his heels, urging the animal on and pretending nothing had happened. Wise enough to steer clear of their master's ill moods, Khleeg and the other officers had also briefly halted, and they followed suit, resuming the procession, like obedient hounds.

Only Idaria betrayed any hint of interest. Her glittering eyes narrowed briefly as she stared at the grand lord's back, but just as quickly she resumed her downward, subservient gaze.

✥

Zharang had been the grand khan for only a brief time when he had seen the value of the short half-breed who had come into his court offering his services. Since the mantle of rule for an ogre khan rarely exceeded a handful of years, Zharang had been crafty enough to realize that Golgren had obvious ambitions and that they could profit him in the short term. His new grand lord would help to eliminate potential threats and rivals then die when his master saw fit.

But that was not what happened. The assassins Zharang had ultimately recruited to kill Golgren had instead embraced his cause, and when they deserted him, so did many of his other most powerful supporters. As the squat grand khan munched on some scorched goat, his bloodshot eyes observed the nearly one hundred guests seated on the cushions in the chamber. It was very likely that, even right then, more than one of his guests was spying for the half-breed and others were spying on the spies to make certain they remained loyal to Golgren.

Even his own guards could no longer be trusted. As grease dribbled down onto Zharang's already-soiled emerald and gold robes, he awaited the inevitable entrance of the thorn in his side.

A moment later, the thick mastark curtains that separated the feasting room from the entrance chamber swung aside. A hirsute, hefty figure whom the grand khan recognized as the one called Khleeg was the first to barge into the room. The chained musicians, all from Silvanost, ceased playing their silver horns and golden lyres. Several of the guests—all dressed in colorful pillaged elven finery that had been resewn to fit their larger, bulkier—if not corpulent bodies—paused to gaze in expectation at the new arrival. Zharang ignored the lack of respect shown by Khleeg's abrupt entrance as he was forced to ignore so much else. Khleeg wore the emblem of the severed hand on his upper chest. His loyalty was clear.

"Ka i'Urkarun Dracon iZharangi!" growled Khleeg, giving a cursory bow. The other revelers grew silent, some surreptitiously eyeing the grand khan of Kern, who was clearly irritated but struggling to keep a blank, bored expression. *"Ka i'Urkarun Dracon iZharangi!"* The newcomer repeated.

At first Zharang—or The Great Dragon That Is Zharang, as his name-title translated to in the Common that his rebellious lackey so admired—did not acknowledge the ceremonial greeting. Instead, he took up a long clay pipe and inhaled from it more of the scent of the Grmyn flower. The flower was a popular pastime among those of his inner circle, and a thick, purple-tinged cloud already floated over the assembled guests, hindering the efforts of the torches in the walls to keep the chamber properly lit.

The heady smell sent renewed confidence through the grand khan. He finally nodded at Khleeg.

Eyes narrowed, the officer turned toward the curtains at the back and, in a manner most unlike an ogre, snapped to attention, as Zharang had heard human warriors often liked to do. Zharang had hardly ever seen one of his own race look so erect or foolish in military posture, he thought bitterly.

In a wrought-iron cage high off to one side, a fearsome dark-red avian picking at the finger bones of a hand squawked as the curtains flew aside again. The huge bird stretched its wings and snapped with its sharp beak through the bars. At the same time, Zharang found himself unconsciously straightening. Golgren strode into the chamber, his sweeping bow accenting that aspect of his lineage that was rumored to be elf. He grinned widely at the grease- and wine-splattered spectators, some of whom shifted as much as they could to avoid his scrutiny.

"Welcome, Grand Lord," Zharang uttered, showing that he, too, knew enough Common to get along at official occasions. In truth, the heavyset ogre had struggled to learn what little he could speak, but felt obliged, as those who knew the foreign language might be using it to speak ill of him behind his back.

"Your greeting is most gracious," returned Golgren, his words flowing with the ease of a mighty river. Then the grand lord paused without adding the many other titles of the seated figure, as tradition warranted. That was a clear insult to accepted ritual, which Golgren compounded by continuing with words that emphasized his own greatness. "The enemies are broken, their swords and clubs shattered! I bring two for later display and, as a gift to my khan, this wonder!"

He snapped his fingers, and an ogre behind Khleeg brought forth a bagged bundle. Despite himself, Zharang leaned forward in curiosity.

Golgren pointed at the low table upon which square plates full of seasoned goat, amalok, and snake, along with goblets of wine, had been set for the grand khan and his guests. Acting on instinct, many of the latter quickly pushed away from the table.

The armored ogre poured the contents of the bag on the oak table. It bounced once, its vibration spilling several nearby goblets, then rolled along the length of the table toward Zharang. As it did, Golgren's "wonder" rattled wooden dishes and splattered food in all directions—food and still-congealing blood.

The head of the chieftain Trang rolled to a stop with its bulging eyes staring straight up at the grand khan. In its cage, the black-orbed raptor squawked eagerly, hoping for a tidbit.

Zharang took another quick inhalation of the Grmyn flower then nodded his approval to Golgren. "Good. Good," he responded, his skill with Common faltering. *"Corruun i'fhani."*

"A splendid dead he makes, yes." The grand lord snapped his fingers again. "And even more splendid is this."

Two more guards entered; in their grip was a surly figure. The ogre chieftain Guln glared at his hated captors.

"Ja i f'tuuni!" he defiantly rasped at Golgren. *"Ja i f'tuuni!"*

Golgren ignored the insult, instead gesturing for Guln to be brought forward, to Zharang. Having dreamed of that moment, the grand khan grinned wickedly and rose. He extended his hand behind him and was presented with a long, sharp sword cast of steel that Golgren himself had gifted to him after a previous victory over the black-armored humans called Nerakans.

Ogre tradition demanded that a triumphant chieftain bring a powerful foe back home as a present to his lord. The grand khan would acknowledge the chieftain's victory and loyalty with a ceremonial execution of the prisoner as celebrants watched.

Despite his jaded, rotund appearance, Zharang swung the sword back and forth experimentally in a manner that showed his skill as a warrior had not faded entirely. Indeed, he had enjoyed practicing with his sword since that defeat of the Nerakans. His display of prowess earned grunts of approval and banging of fists on tables from his guests, and even Golgren nodded appreciatively.

Guln was shoved to his knees. Even though he was well aware of his doom, the chieftain did not reveal despair or fear. To do so would leave his spirit wandering in shame and also mark his clan for a generation.

Gripping the sword firmly, the grand khan took up a position to the side of the prisoner and near Golgren. The guards stepped away, but they kept their weapons ready should Guln attempt something reckless at the very last moment.

Golgren, his own sword sheathed, watched the events unfold. A hint of amused anticipation touched his countenance.

Zharang, his face twisting into an expression of dark

pleasure, raised the once-Nerakan blade high. With a grunt, he brought the sword down heavily—and at the last moment shifted its angle so as to aim its sharp edge toward *Golgren*.

Thus Zharang had dreamed and plotted for weeks, certain of his opportunity. Golgren's triumphs would prove his own undoing.

But the shorter ogre's throat was no longer where it had been, where it was supposed to be, in the grand khan's scheme. Zharang encountered only empty air. Momentum sent him whirling in a circle, so hard had he thrown himself into the attack.

And when he next caught sight of the grand lord, it was to see the one-handed figure with his own weapon at the ready and grinning as only an ogre could. All hints of elf lineage had vanished from his bestial face, utterly.

Rattled but now committed, Zharang attacked again with ferocity. Still holding the sword with both hands, he beat repeatedly at Golgren's defenses. The grand lord was pushed back.

No one interfered, not even Golgren's guards. Everyone edged away, some gaping. The day had been long in coming, and all were well aware that the loser would die and the winner would own their loyalty—or they, too, would die. There were not even any wagers, as was usual when fights broke out. Not one square copper coin was tossed in the room, for to bet on the outcome of that spectacle was to take chances with one's own future.

The two ogres were zigzagging around the great chamber, others scattering from their path. Zharang had an advantage that few other ogres could claim against Golgren; for a long time, he had been observing the grand lord, carefully studying his fighting moves and noting those that the upstart favored. Zharang believed he knew and could parry the best of them.

Despite being momentarily harried, Golgren continued to smile as though amused and unconcerned. That served only to infuriate Zharang, who advanced and swung his sword all the harder.

Twice, Golgren nearly lost his grip. Zharang continued to pursue him around the chamber, even forcing his smaller opponent against the cage inhabited by the savage, red-crested bird. The vicious avian creature snapped at Golgren's cheek, drawing blood. A favored pet of the grand khan, much of its diet came from the severed fingers of those who had lost favor with Zharang.

Its master grinned devilishly, showing that, while his tusks had been filed down, Zharang had teeth sharpened to points. He was able and eager to bite through bone.

Suddenly, Golgren reached around and grabbed the iron-wrought cage and threw it down to the ground. Crashing on the marble floor, the cage broke open and the angry bird escaped. The added pandemonium briefly distracted Zharang, enabling Golgren to rush under his guard. The grand lord's weapon swept across his khan's chest, cutting a minor but bloody swathe, the initial red ribbon spreading over much of Zharang's ruined robe.

His little wound only energized Zharang, who countered with several bone-shaking strikes. One at last managed to do what seemed inevitable. Golgren's sword went flying out of his sole hand.

No sooner had the grand khan started to crow at his inevitable triumph than Golgren hurled himself at the other ogre, sending both of them crashing atop a small table. Something sharp raked across Zharang's wrists, causing them to momentarily spasm. The grand khan's fingers twitched open, and his sword hilt slipped away. He reached for it, but a heavy force slammed into his windpipe. Belatedly, Zharang realized that it was his adversary's arm, the one lacking a hand.

"F'han, iZharangi," mocked Golgren quietly in his ear. *"F'han."* The shorter ogre held something before Zharang's eyes: a small dagger drenched in blood—the grand khan's blood.

The wounded Zharang spit forcefully in Golgren's face then pushed away from his foe. However, it was too easy; the grand khan realized that his enemy had willingly separated himself.

When the grand khan tried to rise, a heavy foot kicked him back down among the spoiled meats and table shards. Try as he might, Zharang could not seem to struggle up again. His hands and wrists felt numb, and the numbness was quickly spreading along his arms. His breathing became labored.

He heard something metal scrape on the marble floor, and a moment later there it was: his own magnificent sword, clutched in Golgren's hand. Despite the weight of the blade, the other ogre handled it with ease and with obvious relish.

"This sword," Golgren uttered in the Common tongue that Zharang so loathed. "This sword I once told you was yours, oh Great Khan! You did misunderstand what I meant! It was always meant to be for your finish." The grand lord chuckled.

"Ja i f'tuuni!" the wounded ogre rasped. *"Ja i f'tuuni, Guyvir!"*

Golgren's grin turned dark. "Yes, once there was an *unborn,* my Grand Khan. Marked by a name cursed. Guyvir, he was called. But he is no more." The triumphant

Golgren raised the heavy sword high then slowly turned the blade so its point was poised over Zharang's throat. "There is only Golgren now."

With that, he thrust the blade straight down as hard as he could. Zharang let out an enraged cry, one quickly cut off as the sword point not only savaged his throat, but plunged on until it had buried itself deep in the shattered wooden table beneath.

❦

The body of The Great Dragon That Is Zharang, the Grand Khan of all Kern, twitched madly for several seconds, as if he were still furious at the unfortunate turn of events. Then, the spasms ceased and Zharang simply stared sightlessly at the ceiling. Blood spilled from his throat onto the food scattered over the table.

The grand khan's avian pet, attracted by the delicious scent, immediately leaped atop the khan's bleeding carcass. With utter disregard for the one who had fed it most of its life, the bird eagerly began to tear at what remained of Zharang's throat.

Golgren pulled free the sword but did nothing to stop the bird's grisly feasting. He held the dripping weapon for all to see. The other ogres fell to their knees and began chanting his name.

The grand lord grinned.

IV

REBIRTH AND DEATH

The valley lay nestled only two dozen miles from the ogre city of Blöten—capital of Kern's sister and once-rival, Blöde—yet even the most wily of ogre hunters would have had an all but impossible time finding it. That would have assumed that they even knew that it existed, for powers had been at work for decades to strip all of knowledge of its existence—the powers of those who dwelled within.

The Titans.

What had once been, for the ogre realms, an idyllic, forested valley surrounded by imposing mountains was now a fog-enshrouded domain where no sounds of animal life could be detected. Those unfortunate enough to stumble into the deep valley found it impossible to quickly depart, for even the path by which they had entered seemed to change. Instead of heading out, it would lead deeper and deeper into the misty land.

And once trapped into following that direction, there was no escape from the Titans, the guardians of Blöten.

The terrifying fate of such poor lost souls was of little

concern to the giant spellcasters, especially their master, Dauroth. All that interested them was their ambition and their arts. With the latter they hoped to achieve the former, that being the revival of the Golden Age of their forebears.

A revival currently being tarnished and twisted by what some referred to as "the mongrel" to whom they had to bow.

Some questioned why Dauroth let Golgren live, much less command their magic for his own gains, but none brought up the matter to the elder Titan's face. If Golgren somehow held Dauroth in his sway—for surely there could be no other reason for the spell master's tolerance of the half-breed—it was also certainly true that Dauroth held the rest of the Titans just as tightly in his formidable grip. After all, only he knew the secret of the process by which they sustained their power.

And that night, as the fog grew to its thickest, blanketing the entire valley, the blue-skinned sorcerers were busy preparing the ritual of admitting one into their exalted ranks.

There were many chambers in the citadel of Dauroth, many more than even his followers could tally. Oftentimes, those chambers would change their size and location at Dauroth's whim. Those who wandered his citadel soon learned that no one even walked around there without the spell master's permission.

Crystals the color of Nuitari's moon illuminated many of the corridors, but in some, fiery balls the size of apples lit the way. Only Dauroth knew why or how. Most of the halls were built of stone, but a select few boasted walls of iron and were decorated with images of tall, magnificent Titans staring back at their living brethren. Again, it was only the master who knew why the walls varied so, although there was certainly reflection and discussion about the subject among his followers.

In general, there were always two or three of the sorcerers walking the halls to some destination, yet such was not the case at that moment. That night all the Titans were gathered in the circular chamber where most group spells were cast and most general experiments performed. Under the domed roof of the main chamber, the spellcasters—more than five dozen strong—stood in a circle within a circle. At the center of the pattern had been set a platform upon which lay something that to an outsider might chillingly resemble a long, metallic coffin, whose lid could be raised or lowered by use of chains. Yet to the sorcerers, it was not a symbol of death; instead it was *rebirth*. For it was where all Titans began.

Dauroth was positioned nearest the sarcophagus, an array of vials and small objects at his side. Next to him stood two others—his chief apprentices, Hundjal and Safrag. His senior assistant, Hundjal, striking and athletic, even compared to most of his brethren, was just then handing a golden bowl to his master. Safrag, almost a shadow in size compared to the other two, silently mixed herbs together.

Dauroth held up the bowl. The words he spoke were not those of his race's bastardized language nor were they even, in truth, those in the revered tongue of the ancient High Ogres. They came from the language of the latter only as the elder giant dreamed that language to have existed, just as so much about the Titans of late was the product of his dreaming.

It was a dream he was determined would soon become reality for all.

"Aarias asana atilio," Dauroth sang, for *his* High Ogre

language was pure music. *"Afreesia ausias aairias."*

The other Titans repeated his words with the same fervor as their leader. The beauty of their voices would have touched even the souls of an elf court, though the ritual that musical language accompanied might have shocked the cultured race. Even before they finished their chant, a crimson aura had formed over the top of the golden bowl, an aura radiating from its contents.

Dauroth lifted the bowl, displaying it for his followers to admire. The crimson glow illuminated the chamber better than the crystal globes, which hovered at equidistant points along the walls. The red tint turned the Titans' blue-skinned faces into lurid parodies or, perhaps, better revealed their true essences.

At the top of the sarcophagus was a system of tubes and a long, narrow vent. Into the vent, Dauroth poured the crimson liquid from the bowl. As it seeped inside, from within the strange sarcophagus there came a sound like sighing.

"Asiriosio anthrayan isul," Dauroth announced, holding high the empty bowl.

"Asiriosio anthrayan isul," repeated his flock.

Safrag handed his steaming mixture to Hundjal, who handed it to Dauroth. The lead Titan immediately poured the potion into the same vent. Again there came the sighing sound, one that might have been a mixture of pleasure and pain.

Dauroth's apprentices retreated into the shadows. Dauroth himself bent over the coffin, the palms of his hands running across its tremendous length. Black energy crackled at his fingertips, an energy that remained there several seconds after he withdrew his hands.

Gazing up, Dauroth examined the array of tubes.

They ran from various points in the darkness above into the center of the sarcophagus. For three nights upon three, he had imbued what would flow through them with his magic. For three nights upon three, he had added the necessary alchemical ingredients to what the magic had created.

For three nights upon three prior to taking those necessary steps, the screams of elves had echoed throughout the citadel.

Nodding his satisfaction, Dauroth turned his gaze back to the sarcophagus. With one taloned finger, he drew several blazing black runes on the edge of the coffin. That, in turn, caused others already etched in the metal to stir to life.

Stepping back, the senior Titan raised his hands to gesture to his followers. As they in unison repeated his latest movement, the same black energy Dauroth had summoned moments before flared up and erupted around the Titans as a whole.

Dauroth began chanting, with the rest repeating his words moments afterward, a choral echoing. The dark aura grew stronger, spreading from around them to embrace the metal coffin.

And at last, when it had fully enveloped the sinister sarcophagus, Dauroth gestured to the shadows above. There was a brief flash of red, followed by a rushing sound, as if water or some other liquid had suddenly begun to flow with tremendous force.

The tubes shook. The sound of running liquid echoed from inside of them. Then, from inside the sarcophagus, came the first distinct trickle of drops against metal.

Dauroth's hand came whizzing down.

The sarcophagus blazed a startling blue. A shriek

escaped from within. Hard, desperate banging arose against the coffin walls, and as quickly the sound faltered and faded away.

The Titans renewed their chanting, feeding their power into the process of which Dauroth alone was master. The tubes continued to shake as their contents flowed into the fiery coffin.

For more than an hour, the assembled sorcerers repeated their calls without hesitating for breath. By the end of that time, the container flared as hot and as bright as an azure sun.

Then Dauroth cut off the chanting with an abrupt wave of his hand. The other Titans took a step back from their original positions, leaving in front only their leader and his two apprentices.

A snap of the fingers drew two new figures through the ranks toward the red-glowing sarcophagus. Ogres those muscular beasts were—at least according to vague definitions of the race. However, those specimens had heads too small and brains smaller yet. Their eyes were wide and dark like creatures accustomed to only the blackest night. It clearly pained them to approach the hot, blinding sarcophagus, yet they did so without hesitation. Although shorter by far than the Titans, the brutish figures were well muscled. At Dauroth's indication, one began unlatching the steel hooks that kept the metal coffin locked. With that accomplished, both seized the chains used for lifting the lid and began tugging it open.

Even with their strength multiplied by Dauroth's experiments, it took some effort at first for the pair to pull the top free. Finally, with a fierce, sucking sound, the lid came open. A gush of thick, red liquid poured over the sides of the coffin but, oddly, evaporated before reaching the floor.

In utter silence, the servants slowly pulled the lid higher for all to see what lay within. Expressions of growing anticipation spread among the Titans until at last it was revealed: a bubbling, congealing, red mass. Steam rose from the ugly, red bubble and a scent like that of burned flesh wafted past the nostrils of the watching sorcerers. They did not skitter back in disgust, however; rather, they openly welcomed the smell.

As his servants secured the chains so the lid would not drop down again, Dauroth approached the sarcophagus. Hundjal and Safrag followed softly in his wake. The apprentices took up positions on each side of the wider part of the coffin and waited expectantly for their master. Dauroth stretched a hand over the bubbling contents and uttered a single word.

And from within the red mass a howling figure who looked as if he bled profusely all over sat up. The howling went on unabated for several seconds; then the half-seen form shivered. Slowly the red slime dripped and fell away, and for the first time, the brilliant blue skin of the figure became apparent.

The hand that he had held over the sarcophagus Dauroth offered to the shivering figure. Blinking away tears of blood, golden eyes seized eagerly on the hand. The blue-skinned, blood-drenched figure reached for that hand, but his own slipped.

Dauroth smiled like a patient father. Stepping back, he gestured for the figure to rise. When the other faltered, Hundjal and Safrag immediately grabbed him—for it was clear by that point that the striking figure was male—by the arms, assisted their master in guiding the dripping being out of the coffin, helped him to a standing position next to it.

"Issura assalias," murmured Dauroth. The rest of the solidifying red slime burst from the figure's body, but rather than splatter those watching, it immediately dissipated in the air.

Before the assembled spellcasters, the new Titan stood blinking and, to all appearances, looking around. He was perfect in the eyes of the others, just as each thought himself so. Handsome, lean, and muscled, he was the newest and latest created as gods over their kind—over *all* races—an ogre who could crush other ogres as easily as ogres crushed bugs.

Once he had been a subchieftain by the name of Ulgrod. He had bowed to Golgren but with a reluctance not unnoticed by Dauroth. Ulgrod's ambitions and his passion for Dauroth's dream had enabled him to rise up despite many enemies, and in the past he had eagerly performed certain "tasks" for the lead Titan.

What had occurred had been Ulgrod's reward for showing that his loyalty was to Dauroth, not to the half-breed pretender.

The apprentices waited only long enough to make certain Ulgrod could stand on his own then retreated into the shadows again. The new Titan eyed Dauroth, awaiting his command.

But Dauroth did not speak yet. Instead, he pointed at Ulgrod, and suddenly from the darkened recesses of the chamber, cloth and metal converged on the former subchieftain. In the space of a single breath, garments akin to those worn by the others had materialized to clothe the naked form.

Ulgrod stared in wonder at himself then looked again

to Dauroth. Ulgrod's expression twisted awkwardly as he clearly tried to form words that were as yet beyond him.

"We shall speak in Common for the duration of this joyous occasion," Dauroth declared to the transformed ogre. "The barbaric tongue you were once used to is fit only for commanding the unblessed." He put a welcoming hand on Ulgrod's shoulder. "By the morning, the glorious language of our forebears will be known to you as if you had spoken it from your first birth on."

"My head—" Ulgrod murmured, his eyes darting around from one sorcerer to the next in the surrounding circle. "So much fills it! My thoughts are sharper than they've ever been."

"It is only the beginning, my brother . . . only the beginning."

Staring at his right hand—taloned—Ulgrod summoned a ball of fire the size of an apple. Dauroth watched with stoicism, well used to such activity by new converts. The first day was always one of adjustment and amazement; a freshly reborn Titan was like a child given a new toy. They had to test the limits of what they had become, learn what they could do.

"Such power!" the former subchieftain gasped. He stared at the flames at his fingertips; the fiery ball had swollen in size yet did not in the least singe his skin. "I can do *anything!*"

Dauroth frowned, shaking his head. "No, not yet. That will come with time, as I have indicated, my friend."

As if not quite believing this, Ulgrod glared at the fiery ball, furrowing his brow. That time, though, nothing happened.

Ulgrod dismissed the flames. An evil grin spread

across his handsome features. There was still enough in those features to enable anyone to recognize his former identity. All of the Titans retained faint glimmers of their old visages.

"Power enough," the new Titan proclaimed lustily. "Enough to drag that half-breed from the throne he covets and feed him kicking and screaming to the meredrakes!"

"No!" Dauroth's vehemence made Ulgrod step back in surprise and fear. The other Titans wisely kept silent, although among them there were one or two nods of agreement with the newcomer's impulsive sentiment.

"No," the lead Titan repeated more calmly and yet also more threateningly. "Golgren is not to be touched."

"Great Dauroth! I meant no disrespect—"

Dauroth cut him off. The elder giant smiled, his sharp teeth very much in evidence suddenly. "You are new and, therefore, Ulgrod, you are forgiven."

Underlying the sympathetic statement was the threat —quite evident to all who listened—that any further suggestion from Ulgrod of removing the grand lord would not be allowed to pass. Ulgrod swallowed and immediately bowed his head.

"Hundjal. Our brother Ulgrod will need to orient himself to his ascension. Guide him to the meditation room, where he may understand and learn better what he has become."

The apprentice took the new Titan by the arm and led him out of the room. As the pair vanished, Dauroth turned to face the rest of his followers, who knelt before his glory. He acknowledged their gesture then silently strode from the chamber.

Safrag followed at his heels. Not as athletic in build

or fair in face as Hundjal, Safrag was still typical of the Titans in his dark beauty. Yet where his counterpart usually walked at Dauroth's side, Safrag always kept a respectable step behind.

The apprentice did not dare speak until they were far away from the ears of others. When Safrag finally gave voice to his thoughts, the Titan did so in the Common that his master had used in addressing Ulgrod. Safrag did not feel that his concerns were worthy of the wondrous high language Dauroth had introduced to him and the others, which they used in the ceremony.

"They do not suspect how risky that was this evening, my master."

"But you do, of course," returned Dauroth without looking back at his apprentice. "You understand very well, Safrag."

"The mongrel *must* either give us more fresh subjects or stand out of our way while we take them!" The Titan grew more strident as he walked and talked. "And he *must* be taught that he is less than the dirt beneath your glorious feet! The way that he spoke to you earlier, at the very site of battle, a battle that would have proven far more costly to him and his side had you not agreed to lend our talents to his dubious cause!"

Still neither breaking stride nor glancing at his lackey, Dauroth calmly said, "In his own manner, Golgren serves the ultimate cause, Safrag. He does not realize that yet, but he will eventually. We *shall* reclaim the Golden Age of our ancestors—nay! We shall surpass it, and then there will be no more need of the grand lord. Until then, he serves his purpose, and until then, he is to be tolerated in all things."

Although his master could not see Safrag, the

apprentice bowed his head in acknowledgment of Dauroth's wise words.

However, before Safrag could complete that bow, the grand figure striding ahead of him added in an equally calm voice, "And remember, any who seek to touch so much as a hair of the grand lord's before I grant that right will suffer the fate of Falstoch."

Safrag let loose with a hiss at mention of the despised name. Falstoch was a lesson learned to all the Titans; he suffered worse in his punishment than one who had no more elixir with which to rejuvenate himself. The latter would suffer only the horrors of degenerating slowly, becoming less than they had been before becoming the powerful, blue-skinned sorcerers.

Even *that* was better than to become like Falstoch. Even degeneration was better than becoming one of the Abominations.

⚬⚬◯⚬⚬

The knights were not supposed to be there. Their presence was a clear act of war. However, Stefan did not care. He and the seven men with him had come on a scouting mission based on a report passed onto their superior by a free elf. Stefan himself would have discounted any word given by one of the ancients—for their kind had always had a history of looking down on humans—but the mere mention of the Grand Lord Golgren had been enough to set Stefan riding off into that dread ogre land.

The elf's directions had been clear, his warning more so. A vast force of ogres with a military precision worthy of the Knighthood—the *elf's* comparison, the young

60

Knight of the Sword thought with a snort of derision—
had been heading toward that region, possibly to meet
with a large contingent of local warriors. If they were
joining together, then it stood to reason that the grand
lord might be preparing to cross the vaguely defined
border of Kern into the western lands—an incursion that
the Knights of Solamnia could not tolerate.

"We must be on the right track," Willum, a broad-
shouldered knight to his right, exclaimed, pointing
ahead. "That ridge over there, the one with the two
horns, he called it Kinthalas's Helmet or something like
that. Anyway, it's in the missive."

"Who's 'Kinthalas'?" asked another rider. Like
Willum, he sported one of the thick, long mustaches
for which members of the Knighthood were known.
Only Stefan and Hector did not wear such traditional
mustaches—Hector because he seemed not to be able to
grow any facial hair yet and Stefan because he preferred
the close-cut beard his father—bravely slain in battle ten
years earlier—had worn. Stefan's beard ran along his
jaw on both sides and up to the ears. The area above and
around the upper lip was as clean. It was a style worn
more by one of the seafaring nations and some thought
that suggested that Stefan's father acknowledged ancestry
other than Solamnic.

They did not make that suggestion within Stefan's
hearing.

"Kinthalas is Argon, who is also Sargonnas," Stefan
informed the questioner. " 'The Horned One,' as he is
also called."

"A perfect kingdom for him, then, this place," Willum
jovially commented. "Only a god like him could favor
ogres and minotaurs."

Stefan was not entirely certain that Sargonnas favored the ogres, not considering reports of a deep rift between the two races in the past few years. It was widely believed that the current minotaur emperor had put a price on the head of the charismatic leader, once his ally, who was rising up to unite the ogres. Whether or not the rumor was true, there was much evidence of growing bad blood between the races. Stefan doubted Sargonnas would divide his followers and wish them to slaughter themselves. Better that they band together against outsiders, such as those he and his companions represented.

Shaking off that uncomfortable thought, Stefan took a sip from his water sack. Even though it was near dusk, Kern was still hot and dry. Wearing armor hardly helped, but protocol was protocol.

Besides, the armor was a small burden in the face of the exciting prospect ahead: learning more about the strange and mysterious Golgren. That mission had become Stefan's passion over the past few years. He had become convinced early on that the activities of the half-breed signified a monumental shift in the east and had entreated his superiors again and again until they had agreed to let him proceed with his surveillance of the grand lord.

And even Stefan had been astounded by what he had learned and documented about the ogre's ambitions.

The party skirted around Kinthalas's Helmet. The sun had just slipped below the higher peaks, causing large shadows to be cast over the open region ahead.

But those shadows were not yet deep enough to obscure the carnage laid out in front of them for as far as the eye could see.

"Kiri-Jolith protect us!" muttered one knight.

Indeed, to Stefan it seemed that perhaps the bison-headed god of just cause *had* protected his party, for the dead that lay scattered and torn were all ogres. Hundreds, perhaps thousands of ogres lay about, all chopped up, ripped apart, or half eaten. Stefan fought back his disgust; he had seen the losses of battle before, but what lay before him had clearly been a massacre of some sort. One hand slipped to a pouch at his belt, where he took comfort in the warmth of the item within.

Leaning forward, Willum gasped, "The ground looks all torn up! It's as if there was an eruption or earthquake."

"Is that—is that what killed 'em?" Hector asked with just a hint of a tremor in his voice. Out of respect for the youngest knight's relative inexperience, the others gave no indication that they had noticed any fear.

Stefan shook his head, explaining, "No. Most of them were slain in combat, that is clear. You can see the handiwork in the nearest corpses."

Hector swallowed and asked nothing more. The scouting party urged their mounts ahead, wading into the monstrous scene, guiding the animals as best as possible around the many decaying bodies. Black flies and carrion crows flew to the sky as they passed then settled down afterward to renew their gory feasting.

A gigantic animal corpse caught Stefan's attention. "A mastark," he said, nodding to Willum. "The victors had no concern for time. The bodies have been methodically stripped. Most of the dead animals, too, have been stripped of anything useful."

Indeed, there was not a serviceable weapon or decent utensil to be found anywhere.

"Who did this?" asked Hector. "Minotaurs?"

Stefan actually wished it *had* been the horned creatures. That would be less peculiar. "No, the bull-men do not stray this deep into Kern. Not yet, at least." He stiffened, then glanced at Willum. The broad-shouldered knight wore the same brooding expression as Stefan. "Willum, we assumed that the grand lord was putting together a larger force with the intention of heading west, but—"

"Aye! But instead it seems that they were hunting one another!" The mustachioed soldier grinned. "So it's good news we'll be bringing back! Let the beasts kill one another."

But as Stefan surveyed the darkening stretches of grisly remains before him, he could not help but reflect on how ogres had a distinct advantage over humans, in size and strength. And how dangerous might they become if their master managed to whip them into line and actually *teach* them discipline?

He pushed his mount in among the dead. Everyone *knew* that ogres were simple-minded monsters, incapable of organized warfare. That was the way it had been in his father's time, his grandfather's, and for as long as the Knighthood had recorded history.

But Golgren appeared to be writing a new, modern history.

His mount stumbled over the ravaged bones of a particularly large ogre. A stench arose, one that caused the horse to shy. As Stefan fought to regain control of his steed, that stench suddenly made the hairs on the nape of his neck stiffen. It did not come from the dead, but rather from something that had been gnawing on the bones.

Raising a hand, Stefan silently signaled for the party to turn around. No one questioned his decision. As the

Solamnics guided their mounts, Hector—who had been in the rear—momentarily took his place at the head.

All of a sudden, a sleek shadow that at first Stefan mistook for a runner darted at Hector. There was a hiss, and two arms shot forth. The young knight was dragged off his horse. The animal shrieked and tried to run, but another tall, narrow form rose up and slashed through the horse's belly with curved talons as long as human fingers.

And suddenly, seemingly rising from the ground beneath, a dozen reptilian fiends surrounded the scouting party. Their hisses sent chills through Stefan even as he reached for his sword. Those unnerving hisses were punctuated a moment later by Hector's screaming.

"Get that devil off of him!" Willum shouted, charging toward the fallen knight.

Stefan tried to join the rescue, but a long, narrow head out of nightmare thrust itself up at his face. Claws snatched at him, only to scrape against his breastplate.

The creatures were like giant baraki, the bipedal fighting lizards said to be exploited as entertainment by the ogres' upper castes. Researching ogres and Golgren in particular, Stefan had learned how the ogre race enjoyed watching baraki fight one another; he himself had witnessed such bouts and been repulsed by their viciousness. However, those creatures were no more than waist-high even as adults. The creatures before him were as big as men.

Finally freeing his sword, Stefan slashed at the two-legged reptile. He expected to sever its head, but the monster dodged away with a nimbleness that astonished him. A moment later, his own mount cried out and shuddered.

Stefan barely had time to get his feet out of the stirrups

before the horse collapsed on the ground. As he leaped away, another lizard snapped at his hand. The knight managed to avoid getting his limb bitten off, but just barely.

A shrill sound raised his hopes. Someone—likely Willum—had dealt at least one of the creatures a mortal blow. However, it was all Stefan could do to keep from being torn to ribbons as the two lizards pursuing him renewed their onslaught. He slashed again at the nearest and was pleased to see that his sword cut a veritable river through the creature's chest. Hissing angrily, the badly injured beast withdrew.

"There's another one!" a voice called. Stefan tried to locate his companions, but between the deepening shadows and the reptiles harrying him, he caught only glimpses of the fight elsewhere. There seemed to be only one figure still astride a horse, which did not bode well for the situation.

His view filled with the toothy maw of another attacking lizard. Stefan reacted instinctively, thrusting under the creature's jaw. He ran the lizard through the top of its throat, the sword's momentum shoving it through the other side.

Rid of that foe, Stefan once more looked around for his companions. His gaze at first alighted onto the lone horse, but no longer was there any rider. Worse, he saw only two other knights standing; one of them was Willum. The other knight's armor was drenched in blood; he hoped it was that of the reptiles. Although he breathed heavily, Willum still was swinging his sword with impressive strength.

Encouraged, Stefan started toward him. Unfortunately, he got no more than a few steps before another lizard popped up in front of him. For the first time, Stefan understood how the knights could have missed seeing the creatures. Their backs were sleek and dark, blending into the shadows of night. Despite their large back legs, they could also bend down almost flat against the uneven ground, crouching while running.

The lizard's claws raked his breastplate. Growling, Stefan lunged at the beast. It dodged his attack and went for his arm.

Strong teeth clamped down on his elbow. The human screamed as some of those teeth managed to slip in between the pieces of his metal armor. Stefan felt warm blood seeping out of his wound.

Somehow, though, he found the strength to react, bringing the sword down hard along the side of the lizard's head. The blade easily cut through the creature's scaly hide. The monster began to convulse but did not release Stefan's limb.

In desperation, the knight turned the hilt of his sword around and smashed it against the beast's head. The lizard's jaws finally opened. Stefan pounded away until at last the lizard balked, its long, sinewy tail nearly bowling over the human as the creature whipped around and fled away.

But as that monster retreated, Stefan saw Willum go down under the onslaught of two more of the vicious reptiles. The other knight struggled to rise up off the ground, but he was swarmed by claws and teeth and could do little to defend himself.

With a roar, Stefan leaped toward his comrade. He slashed the nearest lizard through the back. As it struggled to turn and face him, the bearded fighter ran it through the chest.

Letting the first monster fall, Stefan kicked at the second, who was still bent over Willum, ravaging him. Slavering, the two-legged reptile spun and snapped at him, catching Stefan's blade in his mouth. There ensued another tug of war, made the worse by the aching in the human's wounded arm.

Stefan reached for the dagger in his belt. Forcing himself to wield the sword with his damaged limb, he drew the smaller weapon and immediately stabbed at the creature's eye.

The tip of the blade sank in with a squishing sound, which was quickly followed by an enraged hiss from the reptile. When the lizard released his sword, Stefan finished it off.

"Willum!" he called, leaning over his comrade. "Give me your hand!"

But Willum could not reach up to him, for one hand was bent underneath him and the other . . . the other was gone. So was his throat and much of his face; the elaborate, jovial smile Willum wore was in fact the curve of jaw bones laid bare by his wounds.

It was all Stefan could do to keep from losing the contents of his stomach. Quickly looking around, he realized that he was alone save for at least seven of the lizards. They slowly encircled him, each one looking poised to leap upon him at any moment.

"As you wish, then," snarled the knight. Stefan had no hope of escape. The lizards were excellent stalkers. Stefan did not fear death, though he would have preferred to die in battle sword against sword, not perish as food for some ravenous beast.

But that was apparently the fate the gods had in mind for him. He gripped both of his weapons tightly, determined to take at least one more creature with him before he breathed his last.

Two of the savage reptiles lunged forward.

An echoing hiss from far to the north caused all of Stefan's monstrous adversaries to suddenly freeze, listening. Another urgent hiss quickly followed the first.

One of the beasts surrounding him hissed a reply. The rest—even the pair that had been moving in on him—immediately retreated from the knight. Stefan remained perfectly still. One false action could return their attention to him.

Moving like graceful runners, the lizards suddenly turned and raced off to the hills in the northwest. Stefan did not move until the last of the creatures was several yards off, moving away from him. Then he cautiously backed away, at the same time looking to see if any of the knights' mounts had survived.

Suddenly, he sensed something. Again, the hair on his neck stood on end. Stefan prayed to the god Kiri-Jolith as he spun around to confront the new, unknown horror.

Something heavy struck him hard on the side of the head; his helmet offered little protection to such a blow. The knight twisted and bent as he lost his balance and, in that brief moment, he caught the outline of a hulking, shaggy-maned figure looming next to him. In one hand the brute held a huge club.

As he collapsed, Stefan's last coherent thought was to wonder if the lizards would be coming back to eat him.

V

TYRANOS

The corpse of the Grand Khan Zharang was unceremoniously burned, and the ashes were brought to Golgren as he sat on the throne of Kern before an assembly of representatives of the highest castes. Elite guards flanked the gathering, with the warriors, wielding keenly honed swords and axes, clad in newly polished breastplates. Golgren's banner hung by the scores from the rafters.

Before the properly respectful throng, the grand lord hefted the round bronze container brought to him by Khleeg then dumped its contents on the steps and the floor before him.

The crowd anxiously stepped back as he stood and, without ceremony, trod harshly over the remains of his former sponsor. Then, with Khleeg's warriors cleaving a path through the onlookers, Golgren strode the length of the long, columned chamber, leaving in his wake a trail of ash gray footprints. Reaching the opposite end of the room, he inspected his handiwork then marched back to the throne, in the process spreading the remnants of Zharang over much of the chamber.

He sat down on the throne, grinning broadly.

By thus treading upon Zharang, literally, Golgren had marked his predecessor as a shamed figure. Any who would associate themselves with the former grand khan's memory would risk the same fate that had befallen the deceased. Zharang's legacy and spirit would be officially shunned from that moment on.

As Golgren sat on the throne, Idaria—silently rushing from the shadows—immediately bent and brushed clean the soles of his sandals. At the same time, the elegantly clad ogres in attendance knelt and placed their faces to the floor. They tried to avoid touching or inhaling the former grand khan.

A gesture from Golgren signaled one warrior to blow a horn. The harsh blare gave permission for the assembled ogres to rise and depart, which they did at a slow, respectful pace.

When the audience had departed, two other slaves entered and began sweeping away the dust and ashes. No more would the name of Zharang be spoken aloud there, and within days every memory of him would be eradicated. His household would be sent into exile. Zharang had no offspring and, therefore, no one else the grand lord needed to execute with dispatch. His key followers were already in custody. The ceremony that day was thus short, although its meaning had been well understood by those in attendance. Golgren leaned back idly as the sweepers worked, ruminating as he waited for Idaria to finish her task.

Then Khleeg returned. "Great One," he rasped, kneeling and respectfully averting his eyes. "There is warrior who begs audience. He claims blood of loyal servant, Nagroch."

Golgren's brow arched. "Yes? Very well. Give him permission."

Idaria herself had started slightly at mention of the name, one that even she recognized. The elf glanced up at her lord, but Golgren only gestured for her to continue with her chore.

The guards stood at wary attention as Khleeg brought the newcomer inside. The warrior was slightly shorter and broader of build than most around him. He was clearly Blödian by birth and his grotesque, toadlike visage bore a striking likeness to not one, but *two* ogres who had served the grand lord early on.

Both of whom were dead.

The Blödian wore a tarnished breastplate obviously inferior to those supplied to Golgren's warriors. His helmet was ill fitting. The Blödian carried no weapons, for they had been confiscated. Golgren didn't pretend to think that all his race adored him.

"Great Grand Lord Golgren," the ogre croaked in surprisingly good Common after he had sank down on one knee. "I am Wargroch, brother to Nagroch and also Belgroch, who served you well."

"Their names are known to this one, yes," replied Golgren smoothly. "And the name of Wargroch was mentioned by them, especially by Nagroch." He gestured for Idaria to stop. The slave retreated to a kneeling position beside the throne. "And Wargroch is honored by this one in memory of his brothers' deeds and loyalty."

The other ogre beamed. "Great Grand Lord Golgren, I would serve as my brothers did. I would serve the true lord of Blöde and Kern, my weapons and life yours in blood oath."

"Yes? So good a wish cannot be denied, but first, Wargroch must prove himself worthy, as his brothers before him did."

Wargroch leaped to his feet, causing Khleeg and the guards to tense and shift nervously. Golgren waved them still.

"Hasag i iWargrochi un f'han!" Wargroch growled, pounding on his breastplate with his heavy fist. "I swear I will do whatever you wish, even to my death, if it must be!"

Golgren nodded his appreciation of the fighter's ardor. "But such a waste that would be, to die so. Your chance, it will come. Khleeg, Wargroch is yours until his loyalty can be tested."

"Ke," replied the officer sharply, his eyes narrowed suspiciously on Wargroch. "Yes, Great One."

Wargroch bowed with eagerness. "My axe will reap many heads! My sword will cut out many hearts!"

The grand lord granted Nagroch's younger brother a benevolent smile as the latter was led out of the room. As Khleeg and his charge vanished through the entrance, Idaria brought a goblet of wine for her master. Golgren did not hesitate to sip from it, aware that from that elf he needed fear no poison.

Suddenly, however, the grand lord stiffened; only Idaria noticed. Handing her the goblet, Golgren rose and, without a word, strode toward the entrance. Encumbered by her chains, Idaria scurried to keep up. The guards stood at attention as both of them passed through the portal.

Like the chamber from which he had just departed,

73

the hall through which Golgren strode was a sad reminder of past glories. There were cracks in all the walls and also in the fluted columns. Many of the cracks had been sealed over, but several were in need of fresh attention. Zharang had grown lax in his duty to upgrade the palace in keeping with his position, perhaps because he had sensed it would not be his responsibility much longer.

Golgren had his own plans for the palace's improvement, but at the moment such mundane matters were far from his thoughts. His pace increased as he neared what had been his predecessor's private sanctum. Once disposing of Zharang, Golgren had wasted no time in ordering all that had belonged to the grand khan removed—including the spoils given to the khan by those commanders who had served him best—and his own possessions installed.

Tattered tapestries hung along the walls, many of them scavenged from other races, especially the admired craftwork of the elves. None of the tapestries displayed ogre figures. Instead, the grand khans had chosen depictions that were more enduring: castles atop mountains, great creatures, such as dragons or griffons, even images of the coats-of-arms of human knights. Swords, shields, banners were exhibited too.

One tapestry caught Idaria's attention as she hurried to keep up with Golgren. Once it had been a beautiful landscape of high green trees and mythic dancing beasts. A vast oak stood in the center and in a hollow in its trunk glowed a bright star.

The tapestry was one of the more recent prizes, she knew, taken in the fall of elven Silvanost. It had been taken, by sheer coincidence, from the house of Idaria's family. Even Golgren did not know that fact, nor did he know how it marked her lineage—*Oakborn*. It was said that her first ancestor had been born in the hollow of such a tree and, thus, her family name. Since the Age of Dreams, the Oakborn had stood at the forefront of the elf culture, often as architects or as counselors to its leaders.

But no more.

Her expression set as if in stone, the slave moved on. Golgren had the faster stride, but her kind were swift of foot, even shackled. She caught up with him just as he reached the guarded doorway. The ogre giants on duty crisply saluted the grand lord as if *he* towered over them, not the other way around.

"Azaln!" Golgren snapped, momentarily slipping back into his native tongue. "Leave!"

The guards did not query or hesitate, rushing off as if a swarm of meredrakes were snapping at their heels. The dictates of the grand lord were not to be questioned.

Golgren entered without further ado, Idaria slipping in next and shutting the door after herself. Inside, shadows of the lost day filled the chamber. Some cast odd and disconcerting silhouettes.

Idaria went to light an oil lamp, but Golgren barked, "No!"

The elf quickly drew her hands close to her side and bowed her head as she waited for his next command.

However, Golgren said nothing else directly, at least not to her. Instead, the grand lord peered intently at the shadows, choosing the deepest of them upon which to focus. "Face me." He commanded with a strong hint of annoyance. "Face me."

Idaria kept still, watching carefully. Some of the

shadows came together, coalescing into a figure not quite as tall as Golgren, but far broader in its shoulders. The shape further defined, becoming a hooded figure with a thick mane that gave him a considerable leonine aspect. That was all that either Golgren or even Idaria, whose eyesight was far sharper in the darkness than her master's, could make out of the newcomer.

In a voice that rumbled like a bull's, the shadowed figure said almost casually, "As you wish, oh Grand Lord."

One hand emerged from the figure's voluminous sleeve. As it turned palm down, a staff sprouted whose bottom tip just touched the floor. The top of the staff rose as far as the mysterious visitor's chest, at which point a five-sided crystal the size of a fist abruptly flared into a silvery illumination.

In the macabre glow of the crystal, the stranger was better revealed. Human his countenance was, though his resemblance to a lion was even more evident. His hair was golden brown and thick, and his nose and jaw were broad. To any onlooker, he appeared more akin to a fighter than the mage he certainly was.

Yet his robes and cloak were not obviously a mage's, for they were not white, red, or black, no color of any of the known orders. Rather they were colored a deep, rich brown.

"Play no games with this one, Tyranos," murmured Golgren in an equally diffident tone. "Play no games."

"But all aspects of existence are part of one grand game, Grand Lord, and our part in that game could be considered quite amusing, wouldn't you say?"

The grand lord put his lone hand to his chest, clutching the larger object hidden beneath his garments.

His grin was unnervingly humorless. "Oh, yes . . . very amusing."

Tyranos's expression tightened. He suddenly strode past Golgren, peering at the other shadows but not at all seeming to notice Idaria. The elf remained perfectly still, yet there was a hint in her eyes that she trusted the strange mage even less than the ogre who had tyrannized and enslaved her kind.

"A very theatrical performance earlier," the mage commented dryly. "You were born to the stage. A born actor. A shame that in most plays you would only be cast as a monster."

"Or conqueror," returned Golgren, surprisingly not offended. He turned not to Tyranos, but rather his slave. He reached out to Idaria, who stretched her chained hands to his one and allowed him to guide her to his side in what almost appeared to be a protective gesture. "A glimpse there was of you in the chamber, caster of spells. Your own act of theater, which must mean there is news that needs to be passed on to me, yes?"

Tyranos abruptly glanced over his shoulder, teeth bared. "News, yes. The empire has managed to send a second legion to Ambeon this week. Your own spies will not know of this until at least a few days more." The mage tapped the floor once with his staff. "That makes *seven* legions now, if you've bothered counting."

That news was indeed important. After his ascension to the imperial throne, the former slave Faros had been forced to remove all but three legions from the mainland colony—formerly the location of Silvanost—to quell disorder among the eastern islands. Even after the death of the infamous Lady Nephera—widow of an emperor she had likely used her dark arts to murder, the mother of another who had been more beast than ruler—remnants of her once-powerful sect, the Forerunners, had tried to reorganize. There were even said to be a few Protectors left, those fanatical Forerunners willing to surrender their lives to wreak whatever carnage they could against the ones responsible for their mistress's demise.

But from what Tyranos had just said, Golgren knew that problem was contained for the moment. Faros had shifted his attention to the mainland. The grand lord grinned wider as he said admiringly, "He is very capable, the emperor of the Uruv Suurt."

"Very handy, indeed," said Tyranos, emphasizing the "hand" as a taunting joke.

Idaria uttered a barely audible gasp, but Golgren merely cocked his head noncommittally in reaction to the robed figure's cutting remark, responding, "Good one. 'Handy.' Very, yes."

"And the Solamnics, they are growing more bold on your borders too."

"Yes, so close entwined are the efforts of the humans and the Uruv Suurt. Fascinating, do you not think?"

Tyranos briefly eyed the grand lord as if he were mad. "So you still will persist in your plans?"

The grand lord nodded firmly. "And dear Tyranos will assist my plans because it is what he must do."

That brought a dark chuckle from the spellcaster. He tapped the staff on the floor again, and abruptly both the stick and the crystal atop shriveled into his palm. As the silver light faded out, its last glimmers revealed a smile equally as broad and deadly as that worn by Golgren. "Oh, there's no fear there, oh Grand Lord! There's no fear there."

And with that, the hooded form once more slunk into the shadows, gradually disappearing among them.

❦

"The lamp!" commanded Golgren.

Idaria quickly scurried to the thick, round lamp, using a nearby tinderbox to light the wick. The rising flame illuminated the silhouette of a human knight on horseback etched into the brass. As with nearly all else the ogres owned, even that was the result of plunder, not skilled crafting on their part.

The shadows melted away into the farther corners. Though Golgren stared, he did not expect to see any further sign of his ally, if Tyranos could be called such. They had mutual goals; that was all. As with the late Hotak and his sinister bride—Nephera—their agreement would last only as long as those goals were mutually beneficial. There were, naturally, times when Golgren was tempted to dispense with the arrogant human, but magic was a weapon lacking in his personal arsenal. He had to be wary of the Titans, always chafing at having him, a vermin in their eyes, in control of them and leader of the race. If not for Dauroth, Golgren well recognized, the Titans would act upon their hatred of the grand lord.

Still, there would come a day when no advantage would be worth the mage's insults and presumed superiority.

Golgren clutched his chest again, seeking not the larger object hanging there, but the smaller. It felt warm and alive next to his skin, not like the shriveled appendage that hung next to it, the mummified right hand he had lost to Faros.

Yes, there would come a day—soon enough, he vowed —when he would no longer need *anyone* else's magic . . . Not even where *Dauroth* was concerned.

❦❦❦

There will come a day, the leader of the Titans swore to himself. *There will come a day . . .*

And that day would soon be dawning, the day when the ogre race would once more take its preeminence among the peoples of Krynn. No longer would the ogres be derided as degenerate shadows of their once-glorious ancestors. Ogres would be revered and feared, as was their birthright.

On that day, Dauroth, too, would be revered and feared by all. It would be his reward for all his hard work, his long diligence, his unrelenting faith.

Dauroth sat with legs folded in his private meditation chamber. Before him floated a pure, golden teardrop in which his own hallowed reflection peered back at him. Had one of the other Titans dared at that moment to enter, Dauroth would not even have noticed him, so focused was he on the hovering artifact.

Of course, had *anyone* been foolish enough to intrude upon him when he was away from the mortal world, they would have died quickly and horribly. Dauroth never left himself unguarded.

His chest rose slightly then stilled again. In his current state, Dauroth breathed but once every quarter hour. It was yet another sign of his advanced state that he could perform so miraculous a feat while retaining consciousness. Even Hundjal, who had been with him longest, had to breathe at least eight times every hour—

80

and that, with luck and effort.

Learning to slow his breathing was part of why Dauroth spent so much time in his private meditation chamber. More important, there the lead Titan communed with his memories, drawing upon them to reexperience the glorious visions that kept his hopes alive and encouraged him to greater efforts.

It had all begun with the first vision, or dream—whatever it had truly been—the first time the ancient ogre spirit had visited him. Dauroth had been a weary mage in a world with little magic still remaining, back then. That was during the time of the single moon, when sorcerers were ascendant.

He had been wandering, seeking clues to the past secrets of his people, hoping to find some way to restore magic and his race's glory. Ogres had once been so powerful, so commanding. Dauroth yearned for that age, wishing that he could have lived as one of the legendary spellcasters back in the time when ogres ruled Ansalon.

And one day, that wish of his had been answered. It had come about while he was scouring a historic site of the High Ogres deep in the wilderness. The ancient structure, long ago half buried by an avalanche, was little more than a shell. Dauroth's search for relics was coming up empty and, in a fit of frustration, the normally stoic mage had let out a cry of absolute fury while banging his fist against a crumbling wall.

"Dauroth . . . " a voice had called to him then, a voice that sang sweeter than a songbird. "Dauroth . . . there is no need for your despair and rage. Your pleas have reached us."

Spinning around, Dauroth had beheld a magnificent

image, the wondrous spirit of a handsome, perfect figure with blue skin and shimmering robes—a Titan. The ogre had no doubt as to the nature of his vision. He knelt before the robed form.

"Dauroth . . . " the Titan said in a voice at once female and male. "We have waited your coming. We have waited for the one who shall restore to this world our rightful glory."

He could scarcely believe it. "I?"

"There can be no other. We have watched long. You are worthy. In you lies our greatest hope."

"But . . . what can I do? I am but one being of limited skills in magic—"

The spirit glowed brighter. A complicit smile graced its lips. "That will change, Dauroth. You will inherit all the knowledge you need, all the power you need. We will teach you everything we know . . . everything you must know."

As grateful as the ogre mage was, he wondered in his mind if he was truly worthy. How long would his education in magic take? The great knowledge of the High Ogres surely took decades of study and learning, possibly more years than he had left in life.

But as if reading his thoughts, the robed shade said reassuringly, "Fear not, dear Dauroth . . . the gifts we give to you will not take so long to collect and understand."

Then the shade pointed a long, tapering finger ending in a black talon at him.

Dauroth let out a gasp as his head filled with incredible visions. The visions flashed one after another through his mind, sinking deep into his consciousness. Each lasted scarcely a second, yet the aggregate left a profound impact upon Dauroth. With each vision, his view of the world, of his place in the scheme of things, grew. He saw and understood, faster than he would have deemed possible, what needed to be done to achieve the resurrection of the ogre race. In a quick blur of time, he learned all the powerful spells that would need to be cast.

And most important of all, he saw how he himself could become as perfect as his ancestors had been. He saw how he could become the first of a new age of Ogre Titans.

The moment the visions dimmed and retreated, Dauroth cried out from gratitude. Tears flowed down his cheeks. He questioned nothing that the spirit had granted him, for never in a hundred lifetimes could he have learned all that he knew. The ogre knew the spells, the history . . . he knew it all.

"You are the beginning," the shade proclaimed, slowly dissipating. "You shall be the end. You shall bring to Krynn the Golden Age again, and all will sing your name."

Then Dauroth had found himself alone again, but no longer did he feel alone. Indeed, the ogre mage felt surrounded by others, for the ghosts of all the High Ogres stood with him.

Thinking back, he had been so eager to begin. He had grabbed his paltry findings and possessions and, in only minutes after that grand encounter, had headed in search of what he knew he would need to accomplish his goal, including one of the most important and rare ingredients—the blood of elves.

So much had happened since that time, so much that continued to propel him closer to his goal. Yet there had been setbacks along the way too. At times Dauroth wondered if he was still on the right path, whether things were happening too slowly.

Dauroth had prayed for some sort of sign, some hint that he was still the chosen one. For the longest time, his prayers had gone unanswered, and he'd feared the worst. Then, just when he was growing desperate, the golden teardrop had fallen into his hands.

Dauroth stared deeper and deeper into the artifact, staring at his own face looking back at him until—it was like a transition to dreaming—he suddenly stood within the teardrop, staring out at his colossal form. Then the huge Dauroth faded and the one within the teardrop turned and slowly began to drift in an ecstasy through a golden land.

He knew that place, for, despite its brilliant hue, it was the very valley in which his sanctum lay. Dauroth's astral form came upon a blinding, sun-drenched tree with a crown that swept across the sky. Pausing, he knelt at its base, paying homage. Yes, there at those roots he had spotted the tiny, glistening object. It should have been easy for anyone to find, but it had lain there waiting for him. The moment that he had plucked it up, he had known it for what it was and how it had been meant to stir anew his determination to succeed.

Dauroth's spirit form drifted on eagerly. In the sky distant creatures that might have been birds or something much larger soared by. The land below was lush with vegetation, all of it bathed in the same wondrous gold. Even Dauroth's flesh—or the facsimile of it—had taken on that warm hue.

Hovering a few inches above the ground, the Titan easily rose over one hill after another. His speed multiplied. In barely the time it took to blink, Dauroth crossed the edge of the hidden valley—

And froze there, completely in awe despite the fact

that he had witnessed that sight in his mind several times before.

It was a gleaming city cast in mirrorlike gold and sparkling diamond colors. Banners fluttered from its proud, turreted towers, and mingled within, Dauroth could see the sweeping, arched roofs of other great structures. Unfortunately, there was little more to see, for a vast, metal wall surrounded the city, a wall several times the height of the Titan. Above the roofs, sleek avian creatures soared in great numbers.

With an almost shy, childlike expression, Dauroth darted forward again. Perhaps he would be permitted . . .

But a huge ball of light suddenly burst before him. As he shielded his eyes, Dauroth made out something in the midst of the light. He did not need to see it coalesce to know what it was, for each time he sought the golden city, the guardian materialized.

For a brief moment, it evinced the shape and color of a Titan, but then it turned into something else equally astonishing. It was a being forged of magnificent gold. Dauroth sometimes termed the being a male, although there was nothing of either gender apparent in its appearance.

The golden guardian raised a hand toward him. Although it had no mouth, the Titan heard in his head words of a musical tongue; that which he himself spoke was but a pale imitation. As it had been since his first time there, Dauroth understood each word clearly as if he'd been born to the language.

It is not yet earned . . . not yet . . . soon perhaps.

In the mortal world, Dauroth's body nearly jerked awake. Within the teardrop, his spirit form briefly lost cohesion. Only his strict discipline enabled the Titan leader to recover.

Each time he had confronted the guardian in the past, it had uttered those same words. More times than Dauroth cared to recall, he had been sent back with those words echoing through his mind like a condemnation. *It is not yet earned ... not yet ...*

But *never* before had the guardian added the last two words.

Both the body and spirit of Dauroth smiled. He was close to achieving his ultimate goal. The city was in reach.

The city held the final secrets that he needed to restore the glory of the ogre race and transform all of Krynn.

Its hand still raised against Dauroth, the guardian repeated one last time, *It is not yet earned ... not yet ...*

The last two words—those words of tremendous hope—were not repeated, and Dauroth feared that perhaps he had imagined them the first time. The city, the landscape, and their golden guardian began to fade. Dauroth felt the tug of his mortal shell, demanding that he return to the earthly plane. Yet the blue-skinned sorcerer fought to linger in the vision, silently demanding to hear the encouragement he had heard earlier.

And as the last of the guardian faded, those words came again.

But soon perhaps ... it said in its toneless voice. *Soon perhaps ...* it echoed, much to his delight.

With that, Dauroth ceased his struggle to remain free of his corporeal form. The tension built up by his resistance caused him to snap awake in the meditation chamber, his body wracked with pain and his head pounding so harshly that it felt as if it were about to explode. Yet those sensations quickly passed, urged away by his utter exuberance. Dauroth leaped to his feet, stretching one hand out to catch the teardrop, which suddenly no longer had the power to hover and was about to fall.

With utmost reverence, the robed spellcaster placed the artifact in a small ivory chest atop a shelf in the wall. Dauroth uttered a single syllable and a faint red glow surrounded the chest. A moment later, the container itself faded away, as though it were smoke blown on the wind.

He was so close . . . so very close.

He started as he sensed an approaching presence. Identifying the newcomer, Dauroth nodded. In the next second, the door to the chamber swung open.

Safrag bowed low as he entered. In the tongue that Dauroth had created, he said, "Venerable One, may this humble apprentice approach you with words of possible import?"

To the lead Titan's ears—which had just heard what he was certain was the pure language of the High Ogres— Safrag might as well have been speaking in the debased tongue used in Kern and Blöde. Nothing else—absolutely nothing—was more than a befouled bastardization of the perfect music with which the golden guardian had assured him of his future.

Still, Dauroth forced himself to reply in the same debased tongue, reminding himself that someday soon all would change.

"You may speak, Safrag."

The other Titan's expression grew anxious, an unbecoming look for one of Dauroth's proud chosen. If Safrag did not have a good reason for his uncertainty, Dauroth would have to reconsider his value as an apprentice.

"Master, I would not speak out of turn, naturally, and this is so delicate a matter—"

Dauroth's stare cut him short. "Proceed, Safrag."

The apprentice bowed his head low. His words sounded more strident than musical, evidence of his mounting distress. "Master, it concerns one who should be above reproach, one for whom my respect is second only to that which I have for you . . . I speak of none other than Hundjal."

For Safrag to even suggest something amiss with Dauroth's most promising convert worried the elder Titan. Dauroth had been grooming Hundjal to eventually take over all dealings with the others, so the lead Titan could delve completely into his research and further hasten the return of the Golden Age.

The Titan leader ushered his apprentice inside and sealed the door with a simple gesture of his hand. Eyes blazing as golden as the world in the teardrop, Dauroth demanded, "And what potential offense is it that good Hundjal has committed?"

Safrag winced, for even his angry master no longer sounded as if he sang his words. "Master—Master, I fear that Hundjal seeks the forbidden. I fear that Hundjal has delved into the legend of the Fire Rose."

Dauroth couldn't help it; he flinched. His expression must have been terrifying, for Safrag nearly flattened himself against the door. The lead Titan immediately took a calming breath, which, at least outwardly, appeared to work.

"It has been forbidden by those who know of it to even speak the name," he reminded Safrag coldly.

The studious Safrag kept his head low. "And if I must be punished, Master, for speaking it, so be it."

Dauroth stared past his second apprentice. "Yet the crime that is most heinous is to dare disturb even the memory of that foul artifact. Worse even is to hope to make the legend into truth."

"Perhaps Hundjal does not understand the implications."

That defense sounded weak, especially to Dauroth. Of all of them, Hundjal likely understood best—nearly as well as his mentor—the danger of resurrecting the dream of the Fire Rose. If Safrag was right . . . Well, there was no choice but to investigate.

"From this point on, Safrag, you will neither speak nor even think of the Fire Rose. I will study Hundjal and determine his innocence or guilt."

"Yes, great Dauroth." The door behind the younger Titan swung open without warning. Safrag needed no other hint to understand that he had been dismissed. He slipped into the hall and scurried away.

"Hundjal . . ." Dauroth muttered. "Hundjal, if you have disobeyed me in this—you of all who should know better—you will *envy* Falstoch. Yes, you will."

Baring his teeth, the sorcerer suddenly whirled from the doorway and rushed deeper into the recesses of his sanctum. A change came over Dauroth, one that would have set even the most powerful Titans—including the select few who were a part of the Black Talon—on fearful edge. They would have seen a Dauroth unfamiliar to them, a Dauroth in a cold sweat.

To those who observed the master spellcaster's chamber from outside, it would have appeared a normal-sized room. But as with the rest of the edifice in which he dwelled, Dauroth's domain did not follow physical laws, and in fact, there were rooms within rooms within rooms, all shifting according to his desires.

And one of those hidden rooms took form before the Titan, who flung open the iron door protecting it and stepped into an even larger and certainly more arcane place.

The vast room was covered in ice and filled with a coldness that even Dauroth felt with a shiver. Great mounds resembling snow-shrouded stalagmites dotted the bizarre inner chamber. More than twenty of those stood at intervals in the path between Dauroth and the other side of the room.

And there, half buried in ice, stood a black, metal chest chained with long, silver tendrils.

Dauroth took a step toward the chest, and the first of the mounds immediately shattered. A grotesque form shook free the last remnants of its prison and stepped forward to confront the sorcerer. It had the size and shape of an ogre, but one with only vestiges of skin and armor over its yellowed bones. Black, hollow eye sockets somehow glared murderously as the undead creature menaced the Titan leader with a huge, worn axe.

"Asymnopti isidiu," sang Dauroth.

The grotesque guardian stumbled to a halt, then retreated to his original position. As if time were reversing itself, the skeleton's icy shell swiftly reformed around it.

As Dauroth moved on, the rest of the mounds remained quiescent. His command to the first undead to return to his sleep also had affected all the others. However, the way to avoid his monstrous guardians was not merely a case of knowing the right magical phrases. The warriors—chosen from strong, living ogres whom Dauroth poisoned, then stripped of their flesh—were enchanted to obey only his voice, no other.

There were other, more subtle safeguards, but the Titan leader silently nullified those as he moved deeper inside. He had no patience for anything standing in his way.

As Dauroth approached the chest, the silver tendrils became fanged serpents that stretched for his wrist. He let the first one bite him, at which point it collapsed into a simple strand of rope. The other serpents likewise transformed harmlessly.

But with nothing between himself and the chest, Dauroth hesitated. A part of him wanted to rush from that dread magical place, while another longed to examine the chest's contents. At last, a combination of both fear and desire forced him to open the sinister box.

Instantly, a fiery white light burst from the chest. Dauroth turned away for a moment then forced himself to look again.

And in the center of the chest, floating in a clear liquid that was not water, was a tiny, pointed fragment—no larger than a pea—that looked as if it were made of iridescent pearl. Within the fragment, a fiery force that occasionally tinted the piece bright orange-red shifted about like a caged animal. Dauroth was uncertain whether that force lived or not but preferred to err on the side of caution, so he didn't intend to disturb it.

Yet the Titan already sensed the growing heat and, indeed, the first trickle of melting ice reached his ears a breath later. More important, he found his fingers reaching toward the fragment in spite of his efforts to resist.

Exerting tremendous willpower, Dauroth grasped the lid and shut the chest tightly. Only then did he exhale. Around him, the chamber quickly cooled.

Although the strain of the moment was still upon

him, Dauroth felt some relief. Neither Hundjal nor anyone else had found their way into the chamber. The secret was safe, for the moment.

But as he retreated to the doorway, the Titan felt a growing heat within him that tempted him to return to the chest. Dauroth fought the temptation and finally managed to exit into the main chamber. Once there, he made a gesture, sending the icy chamber back into hiding from the mortal plane.

The desire to go back and hold the fragment in his hands lingered, to use the powerful artifact as he had only once before.

That single incident had proven to be costly.

Dauroth suddenly felt unsteady on his feet. A chair quickly summoned by magic gave him respite just before he would have collapsed. His weakness shocked him but also served as a grim reminder of just how dangerous his unholy prize was.

He held out his hand. A shadow briefly crossed it, leaving in its wake a goblet filled with a clear liquid of Dauroth's concoction. The Titan quickly sipped from the goblet, feeling his composure and strength returning. Yet even after he had downed the entire drink, he remained apprehensive, as if, somehow by checking on the fragment's security, Dauroth had actually set into motion something he would not be able to stop.

But that was absurd, the sorcerer thought. Surely, that was absurd . . .

Dauroth rose, banishing the goblet at the same time. Hundjal's innocence or guilt had to be determined. It had to be done quickly and quietly. The secret of the Fire Rose had to remain a secret. That tiny fragment was the most important discovery of his researches.

That fragment was so potent that even Dauroth shuddered to think what would happen if the complete artifact ever again saw light.

VI

THE JAKA HWUNAR

Ogre life was brutal, and it was twice as brutal for a warrior defeated or shamed. An ogre was measured by his victories, and only one loss could completely alter his standing.

When any chieftain, khan, or lord of the race had a fresh victory to crow long about, an elaborate party was in order.

The minotaur empire had its Great Circus, a huge, oval stadium in which tens of thousands could sit and watch huge spectacles and duels between skilled gladiators. Stories of the battles that took place in the Great Circus were known as far away as the island of Northern Ergoth, off the western edge of Ansalon.

The ogres had a similar arena, which, when first constructed, had been considered one of the wonders of the ancient world. Even with its dome long gone, it was still an imposing structure rivaling in size that of the cursed horned ones. However, like all else in Kern or Blöde, it had suffered the ravages of time and neglect

94

and uncivilized behavior. Its dome was gone. Its surrounding walls—once covered with elegant reliefs of griffons and athletes—had either been scoured flat by the elements or battered into ruins during the many vicious power struggles that had decimated the once-proud capital over the centuries. The statues that had stood atop the gates had long been reduced to merely the sandaled feet of some forgotten ruler or the paws of the city's guardian.

Within the arena—called the Jaka Hwunar by ogres, which roughly translated to the Place of Glorious Blooding in the Common tongue—the signs of decline and decay were also prevalent. The rows of marble benches, which long ago had lost their woven, padded backings, were cracked and mottled. Some parts were broken or missing, due to generations of enthusiastic onlookers bashing at the marble with their clubs. Large rocks and fragments from the wall had been scavenged to fill gaps, but if anything, that added to the ugliness of the setting.

Reaching one of the benches was a precarious job, for the steps and walkways had also suffered over the years. Those areas not worn away by multitudes of heavy feet constantly treading the surface were likely cracked from the same clubs, dropped or pounded, that had brutalized the once-pristine marble seats.

Yet despite such destruction, the Jaka Hwunar had never fallen into disuse in all its long history. Every ruler had shed blood there to prove his power and delight his subjects, who generally reveled in such entertainment. It was a place where warriors vied against other warriors for status, where ogres engaged in competitions with savage beasts, and it was also a place for the public shaming and execution of rivals.

Thus, Golgren took the next step in cementing his mystique by parading out into the arena an array of sorry-looking captives led by the defeated chieftains Wulfgarn and Guln. Wulfgarn wore a look of exhausted resignation, while Guln constantly swung his head back and forth and snarled like a mountain cat at any among the crowd he thought was jeering him. They were followed by a ragtag line of warriors from the beaten horde then a number of figures clad in ruined robes that marked their wearers as formerly among the elite castes. Those last were those Golgren had deemed too close to Zharang to be allowed to go unharmed. Each new ruler of the ogres did the exact same thing, eliminating all family and associates of his predecessor.

Khleeg and a newly armored Wargroch had the honor of standing guard over their master, who sat upon the pillowed couch that had once been reserved for Zharang. Idaria knelt nearby at Golgren's right, a flask of wine sitting on a small tray before her. The elf showed no more discomfort with what was unfolding before her eyes than anyone else in the audience.

Next to Golgren, there stood a tall, high-backed seat carved from rare black oak, which was found in the mountains toward the northeast. Upon it had been carved various symbols in the ancient writing of the High Ogres. Its dimensions made it look far too large to accommodate any of the ogres assembled thus far. Golgren eyed it briefly with a slight, humorless smile. Dauroth did not think that he could read the ancient symbols, but he could. They honored whoever sat there as lord of the land, and while the script referred originally to some forgotten ruler of the ancients, the grand lord had no doubt that Dauroth saw himself as the heir to those words.

The Titan was not there, though Golgren had commanded his presence. That slight would be addressed at some future point.

The warriors in charge of the prisoners arranged them into groups according to the grand lord's prior instructions. Khleeg signaled to a trumpeter, who raised his goat horn and let loose a long, baleful note.

The first group, which included only captured common warriors from the horde, was ushered forward into a wide, open area of the arena. As they took their places, the seated throngs began to bark and beat their clubs against the stone.

From the other end of the arena marched a long line of armored guards with clubs and other heavy weapons. They formed twin ranks before the warriors, creating a menacing gauntlet.

The first of the prisoners was shoved forward. Chained, he stumbled at first then began to run awkwardly through the gauntlet.

The second fighter he passed swung brutally at him. The club struck the prisoner's shoulder so hard, the crack of bone echoed throughout the arena. The crowd lustily barked its approval and battered the seating area into further ruin.

Somehow the chained ogre managed to keep his footing and throw himself forward. However, that merely set him up as victim for a savage series of blows that rained all over his back. Blood splattered the victim, the guards standing in line, and indeed into the front rows of spectators. The prisoner finally let out a howl and slumped to the ground. That, though, brought him no mercy. Instead, the nearest warriors began beating on him in true earnest until finally what lay between them was nearly unrecognizable as a once-living creature.

With long braided whips, two guards forced a couple of the remaining prisoners to advance and drag away the bloody remains. As they did, another captive was picked to be next for the gauntlet.

The prize for any prisoner who managed to make it all the way through the deadly gauntlet was freedom and a place of pride once again among his own kind. The odds were great against such a hope, however, and no one remembered any prisoner ever doing so.

The moment the second prisoner was prodded to move, he tried to run with all the swiftness his exhausted body and the chains allowed. He ducked and dodged as the first guards swung at him, landing only glancing blows. His early success brought momentary cheers of encouragement from the stands.

But no prisoner could withstand such repeated, vicious attacks. That one made it partway but then was caught by a volley from both sides that sent him crashing into the line. One grinning warrior picked him up and shoved him back into the center then cracked him across the jaw with his thick club.

The prisoner fell on his back. Another guard brought down his weapon, and again it was time to drag the corpse out of the way.

Over and over the gruesome scene repeated itself. The sturdiest of the captives managed to get almost halfway. At one point, the captain of the guard had his warriors switch positions, placing those at the end of the gauntlet closer to the front, so they could have their fun too. Not one prisoner gained his freedom, pleasing the Grand Lord Golgren. Despite that, and despite the fact that the carnage went on for more than two hours, the packed crowd was not in the least put off or bored. They had come for blood, and blood was what they got.

And they wanted more.

When the last of the bodies had been unceremoniously dragged away, the captain looked up at Golgren. The grand lord gave an almost congenial nod then looked to Idaria for more wine.

"You are pleased at so many ogres dead?" he murmured to her, his tone possibly mocking, possibly merely inquisitive.

"I have no thoughts on the matter," Idaria replied calmly with her gaze lowered. "I exist only to serve."

She was expected to say that. He didn't pay her any further attention. Golgren accepted the wine, refocusing on the events below.

The warriors who had formed the gauntlet had departed. The robed ogres who had been Zharang's most ardent supporters were prodded forward at spear point to stand before the grand lord.

At that point they surprised everyone by suddenly whirling about as a group and punching and attacking their guards.

One warrior reacted too slowly, and for his failure he died with his throat crushed in by a set of chains tightly wrapped around it. Another of the prisoners quickly seized his spear and whirled toward Golgren.

But Wargroch reacted quicker, grabbing a nearby guard's spear and positioning himself in front of the grand lord's seat. With expert aim, he hurled the spear at the would-be assassin.

The force of his throw shoved the sharp missile right through the robed ogre, who dropped his weapon and grasped at his chest where Wargroch had struck him. However, the spear had sunk in so deep that the prisoner could not pull it free.

The ogre dropped abjectly. Soon his companions lost heart and were subdued.

Khleeg grinned at his lord. "Wargroch prove himself, *ke?*"

Golgren nodded then beckoned Nagroch's brother over closer to him. Falling down on one knee, Wargroch awaited his reward.

"You have my favor," the grand lord decreed. "Let the honor of the executions be by your hand, for that favor."

The Blödian ogre was gleeful. "Great is the grand lord! Great is Golgren!"

With one eye on the breathless crowd, Golgren rose. He drew the sword at his side—the very blade with which the grand lord had dispatched his former khan—and presented it to Wargroch. The Blödian's eyes bulged, an even wider grin crossing his toadlike features. The honor that Golgren had bestowed on him with his gesture was not lost on any present.

"Agrani ahwuni i ihwuni! Their blood is your blood!" Wargroch roared, raising the blade up in front of his face in salute to his lord.

Golgren indicated with a thrust of his chin that the fighter had his permission to begin. With incredible agility for one of his massive girth, Wargroch turned and leaped down into the arena, an act that would have left a lesser ogre with a shattered ankle or injured leg. Khleeg let out a grunt of respect at the other warrior's manifest abilities.

"Golgren is indeed fortunate to have such a one

THE BLACK TALON

watching his back," Idaria murmured near the grand lord's ear.

"But I do not need him, do I?" he replied, his eyes still on the tableau before him. "I have you to watch my back, do I not, my Idaria?"

There was a slight hesitation before she said, "Oh, yes, my master."

Below, the guard captain had organized the robed prisoners into a tight line and forced them to kneel. Wargroch strode around them, hefting the sword in a manner that enabled him to better get the feel of its weight. Drums beat a steady rhythm, heightening anticipation among the crowd. Satisfied with his grip finally, Wargroch took up a position near the first figure in line and looked up to the grand lord for a signal.

Golgren made a slight cutting motion with his hand.

Teeth bared and with spittle on his lip, Wargroch raised the sword with both hands and slashed downward.

A collective grunt escaped the assembled ogres as the cleanly severed head fell and rolled over toward the wall below Golgren. The grunt of exclamation was immediately followed by the ritual beating of clubs and barking and cheering.

Pleased at the results of his handiwork, Wargroch took up a position behind the next victim. Blood from the previous execution dripped onto the neck of the kneeling robed ogre, who, despite the intense pressure, did not so much as breathe hard.

The drums beat again. Nagroch's brother steadied himself before he slashed viciously down. Again, the victim's head rolled cleanly away as the torso flopped forward onto the rocky ground.

One by one, Wargroch solidified his status and

reputation by eliminating the rest of Zharang's inner circle. Khleeg nodded his approval as the others died. Golgren shifted position, looking distracted and once more eyeing Dauroth's empty seat.

The only two left alive were Wulfgarn and Guln. They had been given a prominent spot to view the proceedings, knowing that their own executions would be the climax and highlight of the day's events. The older chieftain grew restive, and Guln struggled with his guards, who nonetheless kept their grip on him.

A horn blared, and from the side where the bodies of the dead lay piled like refuse, herders brought forth four huge mastarks. Raised for blood and battle, the beasts were not at all unnerved to find themselves surrounded by the smells of death.

Briefly Guln managed to break free. He made a dash for the nearest exit, but his guards quickly tackled him.

Wargroch, meanwhile, had returned to Golgren and the others. Kneeling before the grand lord, he presented the blade.

Indifferent to the blood staining Wargroch's garments, Golgren stood and accepted the sword with an approving nod. As Wargroch stepped away, Golgren raised the sword high for all to see.

The crowd roared. Golgren brandished the sword three times then, to the surprise of many in the arena, beckoned Wargroch and handed it back to the Blödian.

Wargroch took the sword and, holding it across his outspread hands, kissed the crimson-tinged blade. He then stepped back, grinning like a child, as the guards prepared the next and final act in the sordid drama.

The giant mastarks stood two abreast with one pair facing the other. The mastarks wore the harnesses designed for toting wagons and such behind them. However, they also wore two chains ending in empty manacles, dangling at the back end of those harnesses.

Using the chains from one animal, the guards snapped a manacle to Wulfgarn's left wrist. As he desperately tried to resist, they attached the manacle from the other chain to his left ankle.

For Guln, a different torture was to be utilized. Instead of a wrist and ankle, he had both of his wrists manacled to one mastark and both of his ankles manacled to another.

Despite their attempts to struggle free of the guards, both defeated chieftains were quickly chained in place. The crowd shouted its eagerness, the swelling noise causing the mastarks to grow nervous. One of those to whom Wulfgarn was attached took a step forward, tightening the chain and tearing from the ogre an unearthly shriek as bone and muscle threatened to give way.

"A very dramatic display," a voice next to Golgren quietly proclaimed in perfect Common.

Khleeg, Wargroch, and the other guards gave a start. Only Golgren and Idaria looked unsurprised at the sudden arrival of Dauroth, who sat in the tall seat looking very much at home, as if he had been there the entire time. The Titan was sipping from a goblet of his own, an elegant gold-and-silver chalice with a row of blood-red rubies lining the middle.

"A very dramatic display," repeated the gigantic spellcaster. He took another sip of the clear liquid in his elegant goblet then glanced at Golgren and added, "One would hardly think you'd need to stage a coronation, however. Your exalted position is certainly secure among the race, isn't it?"

"I will be named grand khan and lord chieftain," Golgren returned just as confidently. "It will be so."

"Then you are determined to follow through with all of it?"

The grand lord's eyes narrowed slightly. *"All* of it . . . "

The mastarks began swaying back and forth impatiently. The guard captain stood waiting for some sign from the grand lord.

At last Golgren nodded. The handlers urged the great beasts, and they began to lumber forward.

The chains tightened. The two prisoners fought furiously to free themselves, but their efforts were doomed.

The mastarks continued unhindered. The chains grew taut.

Guln's shrieks lasted nearly twice as long as Wulfgarn's. Even the cheers of the audience could not drown out their suffering. All in all, it took only two or three minutes for the beasts to finish their awful task. The arena floor was awash with blood and other bodily fluids, not to mention gobbets of flesh.

Golgren stood once more. A silence fell upon the Jaka Hwunar. All present, even the late-arrived Dauroth, rose to their feet.

The grand lord thrust out his hands toward his people, and they, in turn, began to shout a single word— or rather, a *name*.

"Golgren," they cried, their voices growing louder, more emphatic, with each repetition. "Golgren . . . Golgren . . . "

And as they continued to shout, the grand lord glanced over his shoulder at Dauroth, expressionless, as though unfazed by all the acclaim.

"It will be so," the grand lord murmured.

Dauroth took another sip from his drink, his golden eyes revealing nothing of his thoughts. He bowed slightly to Golgren, then raised his goblet in a toast.

The smaller ogre lowered his arms, but the crowd continued shouting. Golgren looked to Khleeg, who, with a gesture to the arena, indicated the grand lord's imminent departure. Horns blared and drums beat as Golgren and his retinue—Dauroth assuming a place on his left side—left the Jaka Hwunar.

Once Golgren was gone, the calls eventually died down. Stirred by the event, the ogres shambled out of the ancient arena. They grunted and growled among themselves, arguing over which part of the bloodbath had been the most entertaining.

When the Jaka Hwunar was empty of its audience, the handlers and guards began the cleanup. Slaves, both ogres and otherwise, began the messy task of loading up the rickety, two-wheeled carts with ruined corpses, tossing what remained of Wulfgarn and Guln among the others without thought or ceremony.

The tainted bodies would receive neither burial nor burning. The ogre race had many hungry pets such as the meredrakes and the baraki to feed. That day, the voracious reptiles would feast well.

And when all were gone, brownish red stains remained, spreading over the floor and marking a day when the Place of Glorious Blooding had more than lived up to its name.

⚬⚬✦⚬⚬

A crowd as large as that inside the arena awaited the grand lord outside. Golgren raised his arms to acknowledge the crowd's approbation as his name was roared over and over.

Dauroth suddenly edged toward Golgren and, with a quick bow, whispered, "With your august permission, oh Grand Lord, I shall take my leave. There are matters of great import—"

Without even glancing at the sorcerer, Golgren casually muttered, "No."

The Titan's handsome features twisted irritably but only for a moment. Only Idaria was close enough to notice. The elf involuntarily moved nearer to her master.

The Titan cleared his throat. "I beg your pardon?"

"No. Dauroth will come to the palace, yes?"

Dauroth bowed again. "Of course, oh Grand Lord. I am as ever at your beck and call."

Golgren grinned toward the crowd pressing from all directions, but his smile was not for them. "Yes."

The journey was a short one; the grand lord was in a hurry and did not pause to take the usual accolades from his people. Khleeg, Wargroch, and the guards matched Golgren's determined pace as the entire party, including Dauroth, arrived at the former abode of the Great Dragon That Is—Was—Zharang.

Golgren did not proceed to his quarters, instead entering a vast balcony situated beyond the throne room. Patchwork had returned the balcony to close to its original glory but also made it safe and secure. The legs of the banisters had once been carved to resemble griffons and, under the reign of Zharang's predecessor, some had been repaired. The floor, originally a marble mosaic forming the silhouette of the fabled beast, was in fair condition, save that the griffon was missing a leg and most of one wing. Its hide was also perforated with white squares, the outcome of inept restoration work.

Khleeg angrily ushered out the elf slaves who were engaged in repair work. Dauroth watched the chained figures scurry past, as if sizing up each one of them. It was ironic, he reflected, that the slaves toiled so hard to restore Garantha's icon to its greatness. The royal family of Silvanost honored the same beast as their symbol; the elves believed it was their tradition from the beginning of time. Yet ogres believed the elves had stolen the legacy of the griffons from ogres. It was Golgren's intention to restore the griffon as an emblem of *his* people's might and a symbol of the elves' downfall.

The grand lord paused at the rail of the balcony. The sight was breathtaking, for the city looked beautiful from that distance, and beyond Garantha the local mountain range offered an equally picturesque vista. But in reality Golgren cared little about the view. He had other things on his mind.

"Khleeg!" he abruptly declared, reverting to the Ogre tongue. *"Falan du hach!"*

"Falan du hach?"

"Ke!"

Puzzled, the officer began commanding the others to join them on the balcony. However, Golgren shook his head. *"Bin iDaurothi!"*

The warrior and the sorcerer exchanged a look; then Khleeg reluctantly nodded, following the others as they left. Only Idaria remained behind with Dauroth and the grand lord.

"You have a sudden fondness for the mongrel tongue with which most of our people bark?" the Titan asked in Common when the others were safely out of hearing.

"As much a sudden fondness as you have for my company, spellcaster." When Dauroth chose not to remark on his peculiar comment, Golgren turned and glared at the giant. "We do not pretend here, yes?"

"We have never pretended, Grand Lord."

Golgren's hand grazed his chest. "No, good Dauroth, this one believes you have not." The grand lord bared his teeth. "Our goals, they are both the same and completely different."

"An astute way in which to state it."

"But one thing must be agreed. The future of the ogre is for the ogre to decide."

The Titan nodded. "There can be no other way, no thought of intrusion by another race."

"Yes." Golgren continued to bare his teeth. "Thus, the Titans first must see to the Uruv Suurt. They test the borders. They must be taught the borders are ours to define, ours to cross."

"This is surely a task for your commanders, Grand Lord—"

The smaller half-breed shook his head. "That would be war. This would be . . . " Golgren searched for the right phrase. "This would be *'Kyethna Uulusaar.'* "

" 'The Gods' Laughter,' " Dauroth repeated. "The word or phrase in Common you seek, oh Grand Lord, might be *happenstance* or better *pure coincidence.*"

"Yes . . . what befalls the Uruv Suurt will be coincidence, will it not, good Dauroth?"

"As you say," the blue-skinned spellcaster replied, his tone even. "As you say."

Without warning, Golgren turned away from Dauroth, suddenly seeming more interested in the view. He did not see the momentary gleam in the Titan's eyes, but Idaria did. She almost let out a cry of warning, but Dauroth's gaze shifted to the elf, stifling her.

Then the Titan vanished in a swirl of black tendrils of smoke.

As if sensing the departure, Golgren immediately turned back toward the elf woman. Triumph shone in his own eyes.

His triumph was tempered by the knowledge that his victory was only temporary.

"Now the Titans will be kept busy for a time, do you not think, my Idaria?"

"I . . . I suppose so, master."

Golgren chuckled softly. He took her chin in his hand and guided her face so she was forced to look up intimately into his eyes. "Fear not, my Idaria. Golgren will not let him have you." His expression hardened as his gaze returned to where the sorcerer had stood before he departed. "No . . . I have only one gift in mind for Dauroth and his Titans."

VII

HADA KY F'HAN

Stefan trudged along the barren land, watched carefully by his captors even though his arms were bound. The ogres holding him belonged to a small nomadic band that had come upon the battle site at the same time as he and his party of knights. There were about forty in all, led by a young chieftain named Atolgus. Although Kern was led by a grand khan, and lesser khans governed vast stretches of the realm in his name, chieftains were the backbone of ogre rule in Kern as they were in Blöde. Atolgus ruled with the iron fist and heavy club necessary for survival there. Stefan knew that, not the least after having witnessed the shaggy, black-mopped giant beat into submission at least one surly warrior who resisted his commands.

Stefan himself had been struck only once in the nearly six days since his capture. Atolgus had no sympathy for the human. He was keeping the knight alive for only one reason. The chieftain was a minor figure among leaders in his realm; that was obvious from the small size of the party, which roamed around without belonging to an actual village. However, Atolgus would elevate his status by presenting his captive to one of the khans, who in turn could use the knight to increase his own standing.

All that would happen, assuming that Stefan survived the long, arduous trek to wherever Atolgus intended to take him.

Stefan observed his guards warily, especially a scarred, vicious beast named Thraas. Nearly bald and with a nose obviously broken more than once, Thraas was ugly, even for an ogre, and more ill-tempered than the typical member of the race. Atolgus wielded the ultimate authority, but Thraas clearly boasted some unique status of his own among the clan, for more than once he balked slyly at orders given him by the chieftain, sidestepping actual disagreement. Yet Thraas did not directly defy his leader, nor did Atolgus call his underling to task.

Atolgus was the only male who could speak Common at all. However, his mate, the only slightly less fearsome Torma, proved to be something of a sophisticate. She was well versed enough to translate most of the chieftain's garbled words and phrases.

"Atolgus learn from shelled ones," Torma explained with a grunt. "Shiny, like you." Although younger than Stefan, her face was sadly worn by life in the rough wild and her breasts—barely covered by the ragged animal skin she wore—hung very low. Most ogres failed to live past forty years.

"While fighting the Nerakans . . . uh, the black shells?"

The ogress nodded affirmatively. It was Torma who had the duty of feeding the prisoner. Normally, such a task would have fallen on a lesser female, but Atolgus did not trust any of the others and, in truth, Torma seemed to enjoy the opportunity to practice her Common.

"They taught you, did they?" Stefan asked, honestly curious.

Torma stuffed a piece of meat tougher than jerky into his mouth. Her eyes burned fiercely. "Females not taught, but Torma listened much . . . learn some."

Female ogres usually joined in the fighting and even on a rare occasion took up the mantle of chieftain, but the conventional wisdom was that most of them existed simply to breed more male ogres. The women's inferior position obliged them to deal with most of the camp work whenever the clan settled down for the night. It was often the women who pitched the rounded frame tents that were covered in long-abused animal skins; the females did the main cooking, and they saw that order was kept among the young, especially the hot-headed males.

Torma finished feeding the captive. "Sleep now," she said sternly in Common. "Long journey Garantha is."

Sleep Stefan did, for he had no other choice and in fact he was bone weary. The ground was as crude and inhospitable as his taskmasters, but the march had truly exhausted him. He drifted off almost immediately into a very deep slumber.

That was why he did not wake until the shadowy figure in the dark hovering over him had nearly freed his limbs.

It was actually the shush of breathing that woke the Solamnic, breathing that sounded as if some savage animal loomed very close to him. Stefan jerked awake then heard a low, bestial grunt. As he started to rise—realizing at that moment that he was no longer bound—there came a sound like the fluttering of wings. Taloned hands clutched his shoulders.

Stefan tried to punch his attacker, aiming for where he assumed the head of the creature must be, and was rewarded with a *thwack* on the side of his enemy's jaw. The shadowy form snarled but did not release its hold. Stefan kicked up, but the winged form's chest proved to be better protected than its jaw, and the knight ended up only ramming his leg into something very solid.

Stefan's foe was nearly as tall as he and about half again as broad. Its strength seemed on par with that of an ogre.

Stefan was about to cry out when from nearby came someone else's shout of alarm. Suddenly, Stefan's attacker lost all interest in him.

"Fool," grunted a voice that was neither human nor ogre. The shape retreated, melting into the darkness. Leaping to his feet, Stefan tried to grab him or it, but once more there sounded a rapid flapping of wings and suddenly the human was alone.

Although that did not last for long. A hissing filled the air. Stefan gasped as something sinewy enfolded him, cutting off his breath. He fought for air, only to be pulled off his feet without warning.

He landed on the ground with such force that he nearly blacked out. A heavy foot slammed into him hard in the side. Through tearing eyes, the Solamnic beheld Thraas looming over him, a torch in one hand and the handle of a whip—the source of the knight's breathing difficulties—in the other.

"Magaros ul i f'han, Shok G'Ran," snarled the ogre. *Shok G'Ran* was the phrase used by the monstrous race for the

Solamnics. It literally meant *the shelled ones who bite like lions* and was a reflection of the ogres' grudging respect for the Knighthood's skills. *Shok* meant a powerful beast.

Thraas had his foot planted on the human's chest and was busy squeezing the air out of Stefan's windpipe. At the same time, he thrust his torch dangerously close to the knight's face.

"Vardok! Da i vardok!" Atolgus had arrived, shoving Thraas to the side just before the ogre would have succeeded in killing Stefan. As the knight gasped for air, the two ogres began arguing. Thraas pointed insistently into the dark landscape and, as other ogres gathered around, rushed out of the camp in that direction. Another warrior followed close at his heels.

Moments later, they returned with a grisly burden between them. It was another ogre, likely one of the guards, dead. The back of his neck had been ripped open, and for good measure his head had been twisted around and nearly off. Someone had then gone to the extra trouble of cleanly removing *both* his hands by means of a blade. Of the severed appendages, there was no sign.

With an odd gentleness, Thraas and the other male ogre set the corpse down in front of Stefan. Thraas barked something at his chieftain, and his furious gaze fixed on the human.

Atolgus, too, glared at Stefan, who was dumbfounded. The chieftain reluctantly nodded then rounded on his prisoner.

"D'ihra tu Shok G'Ran!" Atolgus growled ferociously. "Shelled one is to blame! How? What! Blood of Thraas slain coward! Kill like ji-baraki and take the warrior from him!"

Stefan did his best to comprehend. The guard was

kin to Thraas, and the knight was accused of being his murderer, that much was clear. But that in itself was not the trouble; rather that Thraas was claiming Stefan had slain the ogre in a fashion considered base and cowardly even by the bestial race. Ji-baraki—which essentially meant larger baraki—were considered foul creatures by ogres. To be called a ji-baraki was a high insult and didn't bode well for Stefan's fate.

The chieftain turned to his mate, who had rushed up belatedly to join the others. He jammed an accusing finger at the captive then repeated, *"D'ihra tu Shok G'Ran!"*

As Atolgus and Thraas fell into another heated discussion, Torma and two guards took charge of the prisoner. The ogress avoided Stefan's eyes, looking as though she were embarrassed by the human's transgression and no longer wished to be associated with him.

"I did not kill the ogre," Stefan tried to tell her, "but if I had, why would that be cowardly? I am a prisoner. Surely it is brave to try and escape and kill one's captors."

The ogress thrust up both hands in front of Stefan. "Hunter with no hands! Warrior with no hands! Craal's spirit not to be hunter, not to be warrior! Must beg always!"

The human's brow furrowed thoughtfully. "You are saying that because of this—because Craal's—hands were cut off and taken away, his spirit will also have no hands and—"

"No hunt! No fight! No honor!" She spit at Stefan. "No honor, *Shok G'Ran!* Craal was cousin to Thraas. Personal insult to Thraas too. Very evil thing to do, even for human!"

"I did *not* slay him, and I would certainly not have

taken his hands! When could I have done it? Where did
I put them?"

She only shook her head. "Only *Hada ky F'han*
answer! *Shok G'Ran* and Thraas must do *Hada ky F'han!*
Death battle."

"*Hada ky F'han?* A battle to the death? With Thraas?"

"*Ke!* Thraas! *Shok G'Ran! Hada ky F'han!*"

Despite himself, Stefan felt a deep fear. He wore
no armor. Thraas was likely twice as big and heavy as
he, and most of the ogre was muscle. The knight was
tired and dazed; he had been walking without much
nourishment for days, whereas Thraas was one of the
few ogres who owned a horse and had been riding it on
the journey. The odds were greatly against the human.

"How soon?" he asked Torma as she turned from
him. "When the Burning comes?" Ogres called the
daytime *iSirriti Siroth*—or Sirrion's Burning—in their
tongue. The phrase harkened to the god of fire whom
they believed lived in the sun and daily tried to set the
land on fire merely for his entertainment.

The ogress grunted. "*Ne iSirriti Siroth! Byyn!*"

He was suddenly grabbed by the guards and shoved
back in the same direction where Atolgus and Thraas
had gone. The ogres had no intention of waiting until
daybreak. Whatever his condition, Stefan would have to
fight Thraas *right then* ... and likely die.

The entire clan had gathered in the center of camp.
Even before Stefan reached the area, all the mature males
other than his guards, including Atolgus and Thraas,
had formed a crude circle several yards in diameter. All
of those in the circle hefted thick, wooden clubs. Outside
of the circle, torches held high by females lit up the area
almost as bright as noon.

Memories of the stories a senior knight—one Tempion—had related came back to Stefan in a rush. Tempion had been among the Nerakans sent to help the ogres learn tactics in the early days of their fractious alliance. The older knight—a trainer of novices after having suffered a savage wound in one battle—once described a curious ogre ritual he and his comrades had been forced to watch.

When an ogre was accused of disgracing the honor of another ogre, the accused and the accuser were obliged to settle their differences within a circle of armed warriors. They each were given weapons and, at a signal, were expected to fight to the death.

But that was only one aspect of the ritual. There was a harsh penalty for stepping over or even too near the boundaries of the circle. The nearest ogre on the perimeter had the pleasure of taking a swing with his club at the trespasser and imparting whatever damage he could to the one who had made a misstep.

Thraas was already building himself up into an ecstasy of bloodlust. He whirled his club eagerly. Atolgus suddenly thrust a much smaller weapon into the human's hand. Glancing down, Stefan stared in shock at the rusty dagger—Nerakan, by its markings—with which he was somehow expected to defend himself.

"Where is my sword?" the Solamnic demanded, almost sputtering. "I demand by right the weapon of my choice!"

Thraas let out a coughing sound that passed for ogre laughter. With a grunt, Atolgus said, "No right. Thraas choice."

The Solamnic grimaced. "If I win," he asked of the chieftain, "do I go free?"

Atolgus snorted, emitting more ogre laughter. "You live."

With that, the lead ogre stepped back. Thraas struck the ground hard with his club then grinned at the puny human.

"Jeka!" shouted Atolgus, departing to stand outside the circle.

Thraas lunged forward, swinging as he charged. Stefan drew back then twisted to Thraas's right just as something grazed the back of his leg. He had come too close to the circle of warriors. Another inch or two, and his leg would have been shattered.

Thraas grinned lewdly. Showing incredible dexterity for one so huge, the ogre reached quickly and managed to snag the human's wrist, the hand with his weapon. The ogre's grip tightened so much that Stefan nearly fumbled his rusty blade.

As the bestial warrior dragged Stefan closer, the knight did drop his blade and twisted and picked it up with his left hand. Before Thraas could react, the knight jabbed.

The human's dagger penetrated the ogre's thick hide but just barely. Worse, the blade snapped in half, the upper portion of it sticking out of the shallow wound.

Thraas laughed and grabbed for the Solamnic, but Stefan kicked up hard at the piece of metal sticking out of his adversary's side. The dagger blade was forced in deeper.

At last Thraas felt pain, even if it was only minor, annoying pain. However, the surprise made his grip loosen, enabling Stefan to pull free and dodge around the ogre.

Eager, tusked faces eyed the knight and more than

one ogre in the circle looked tempted to break ranks and strike out at him. Two or three steps in any direction would be enough to unleash them, but he kept his footing and stayed away.

Stefan spun around as Thraas came toward him again. Eagerly, the ogre raised his club—just as Stefan threw himself shoulder-first as hard as he could into his giant foe.

Thraas was heavy, but Stefan had the propulsive edge. The impact of their collision sent the ogre stumbling back.

A club slammed into Thraas's shoulder as one of the ogres in the circle took advantage of his clumsy maneuvering. He howled, dropping his weapon. Stefan attempted to seize the fallen club, but its weight was such that the best he could do was drag it away. The Solamnic shoved it behind him, where it rolled to a halt at the feet of some of the warriors of the circle.

Thraas recovered and started to lumber toward him again, then appeared to think twice about his strategy, for he suddenly hesitated and circled the knight with a fresh wariness.

"Kya i f'han, Shok G'Ran!" snarled Thraas.

"We shall see who death claims," the knight retorted. His gaze darted around the circle at the bloodthirsty warriors, eager to bash either one of them if they drew too close.

Thraas lunged again. Stefan's attempt to leap over the diving ogre fell short. The tusked giant managed to grab him. Rolling around on the ground, Thraas wrapped his huge arms around Stefan's midsection and squeezed.

With both fists, the knight pummeled Thraas's injured shoulder. The ogre let out a howl and let go. With some effort, Stefan pushed himself to the side.

He saw that Thraas's side was dripping blood. Gritting his teeth, Stefan jumped on the ogre, who was slowly getting to his feet, thrusting his fingers into the wound and doing his best to push the piece of broken blade deeper inside.

His initial reward was a backhanded slap that sent him hurtling across the circle. As Stefan landed on his back, he looked up at a toothy warrior preparing to swing down at him. Reacting instinctively, the Solamnic pushed himself away just as the club came crashing down where his skull had been.

Another form loomed above him. Thraas grabbed for the twisting human, but the knight avoided his meaty hands and rose.

Breathing heavily, the ogre stomped toward him. Again, Stefan avoided the reaching, clutching hands. Then, all of a sudden, Thraas staggered, momentarily seeming to lose his bearings.

The ogre's wounds were taking their toll. Stefan barreled into his adversary. Caught off guard, the injured giant was knocked back.

Thraas collided with several ogres in the line of the circle. They shoved him forward then began swinging.

The first blow fell squarely on Thraas's already damaged shoulder. The second slammed into his legs. Under the onslaught, he buckled, first to one knee then to all fours.

Despite being their favorite, Thraas was clubbed eagerly, over and over, until he crawled away from his tormentors. Without his monstrous strength and tough hide, he wouldn't have survived.

But survive he did, and somehow the ogre got away from the onslaught. Bruised and bloodied, Thraas finally straightened and again moved toward Stefan. Arms spread wide, the ogre herded his smaller opponent to one corner of the circle. Thraas looked battered and weary but still capable of great harm.

Taking a deep breath and making a short, silent prayer to the patron gods of the knighthood—Habbakuk, Kiri-Jolith, even lost Paladine—Stefan again surprised the ogre by charging straight at him.

The tusked behemoth waited, grinning. His thick arms embraced his victim just as Stefan smashed into him. Despite his injuries, Thraas absorbed the collision and held on.

But Stefan, his arm bent wildly, jammed his elbow hard into Thraas's throat. The ogre let out a harsh rasp and couldn't breathe again. He bobbled his grip on the human. Stefan elbowed him hard again, that time in one eye, and Thraas turned away, gasping frantically for breath and stumbling.

He almost stumbled within range of some of the guards—their jaws agape at the sudden turn of events—but fell down on one knee and tried to crawl away.

Stefan, himself panting, stepped up behind the struggling ogre. He grabbed Thraas by the head and twisted with all his might. There was a sickening crack, and Thraas struggled no more.

As he let the ogre's body fall forward, the circle suddenly gave a roar and began to batter the ground with their clubs.

The battering rose in volume as Atolgus stepped into the circle, his own club in his hand. Although the Solamnic was too exhausted to defend himself anew, he nevertheless straightened, refusing to beg or die without honor.

Atolgus raised his club then turned to the other ogres and shouted something unintelligible in his own tongue. Immediately, the cries from those in the circle—from *all* the ogres present—increased tenfold. Grunting barks filled the air.

They were *cheering* Stefan's victory.

"Ahgarad, Shok G'Ran," rumbled the young chieftain, using his free hand to slap Stefan on the shoulder so hard that the human nearly collapsed. "Good fight!"

"I—I am honored by you—and your people, Chieftain Atolgus. Thraas fought well; I w-will remember his name."

Atolgus slowly digested his words, making sure of their meaning. Then the tusked giant nodded. However, bearing something of a grin, he then added, *"Shok G'Ran* still prisoner."

Maintaining a proud stance, the knight was marched away with Torma and his guards. As a mark of his victory, the guards did not tie him up until he was far from the circle. Torma then brought him a water sack and, using her own hands to guide the flow, let Stefan drink to his heart's content. The clear liquid was a valuable commodity in that harsh land, and was the surest sign that Stefan had risen in the ogre's eyes.

Torma left him, and the guard took up a position farther away. Bones aching as he stretched out, the captive human pondered the mercurial nature of his captors. He had no idea who killed the ogre guard or why. And it was as if the others had utterly forgotten his supposed earlier transgression.

There is no understanding ogres, Stefan thought. But understand them he would have to if he hoped to have any chance of escape.

And that brought his mind back to the shadowy creature who, he now understood, was seeking to unbind him in the dark, and he wondered just what that unseen creature wanted of the Solamnic.

❦

The village was burning. Most of the males were dead, including his father, for whom he had never had much love. His mother, though, his mother was cleverer, far more clever. She would still be alive . . . if only he could find her in time.

It was ironic that his shorter, slimmer frame for once was of great advantage to him. Unlike his brutish brethren, he could hide better, run faster, and thus, avoid the killing blades. A horse snorted. Out of the smoke rising from another fiery hut, a black-armored figure emerged, mounted on a sleek, brown steed, and nearly ran him down. Although the face was hidden by the visored helmet, it was clearly one of the humans his mother called "Nerakans." The word sent a chill through him, for he could never have imagined humans—only about as tall as he was, as a youth—so easily slaughtering muscular warriors who towered over them by several feet in height.

And yet it was happening to his village.

The rider swung at him with a sword far sharper than the rusty, pillaged one his father had wielded. Only swift reflexes saved the youth, and even then the tip of the blade left a burning cut in his left shoulder.

With nowhere else to go, he leaped into the burning hut. Flames licked at his body, and his kilt smoldered. He expected the human to charge in after him; then in an instant understood why he didn't.

The roof of the hut came crashing down. It was only by a

miracle that he was not buried under the burning wood and furs. In the background, the sound of hoofbeats receded. The Nerakan assumed he was dead, which would be the case if he did not hurry.

Beating at the burning wall at the back, the youth managed to create an opening big enough to leap through without getting singed too badly. The moment that he was out, he continued along his path toward his family's hut. He had been out beyond the borders of the village when the attack occurred, staring—as he often did, despite the beatings his father gave him for doing so—in the direction from which she said her people came. Only when he had heard the first scream had he rushed back, fearful for her safety alone. The rest of the village could have been slaughtered for all he cared. His only concern was his mother.

There was the family hut. His heart leaped, for as far as he could see, the structure was still intact. He ran faster, ignored by the other riders who were in pursuit of more threatening targets.

But as he neared the entrance, he saw that the opposite side of the hut had been crushed in. Choking, the youth shoved through the wreckage of the fur-covered entrance and peered inside.

She lay sprawled on the ground, her torso awash in blood. He knelt down beside her, determined to carry her slight body away and give it a decent burial rather than let it rot with the others. She wasn't heavy to lift. Had she been like his father, big and bulky, the task would have been impossible, for ogres were among the heaviest of races.

Whereas elves such as his mother were different.

She had silver hair that hung down to her shoulders, which had been to him, as a child, fascinating in its delicacy. It had once hung much longer, so she had said, but *that had been when she still lived among her own kind.*

As he touched her, her eyes fluttered open.

Those emerald green orbs, which he had inherited, reminded him of the rare blossoming of mountain flowers during the early spring. Her narrow face had many age lines but was still the most beautiful face in all the village. He leaned close and smelled the faint scent, almost like that of the aforementioned mountain flowers.

"Guy . . . Guyvir . . . "

He hated his name, for it was a curse imposed upon him by his father. Guyvir, the unborn, he was called that by even his mother, who more than once had said she wished, for his sake, that he had not been born of his captive mother and her obsessed enslaver. Yet when she said the name, he could always sense the love that she had had for the half-breed who bore her heritage.

And she was dying.

"Mother," he mouthed, despite his tusks, preferring the Common word to the ogre Lagruu ul, *which did not truly mean* mother *but rather something akin to* breeder.

"Guyvir . . . Braag . . . your father . . . "

His father, the chieftain, was dead already. Guyvir had witnessed his slaying. He had felt only a slight pang of emotion when the three knights had cut the chieftain down, not like the sea of turmoil overwhelming him at that moment.

She saw his expression, and he, in turn, read not only the satisfaction in hers, but also some deep-seated regret.

The moment passed. Clearly summoning her last strength, his mother said, "To the north! Braag's cousin . . . his village is safe from this incursion! Go to him . . . he . . . he is softer and has no heir . . . "

Guyvir had met his cousin twice and had respect for

the one-eyed warrior. The chieftain had looked at the puny child and nodded at the slim body while making a swift arc with his hand. He knew that there was more than what met the eyes to the young one whose appearance lacked size and muscle.

"I'll take you with," Guyvir replied in Common. His mother had taught him the language in secret.

She put her trembling hand to his cheek. "I will always be with—"

Her hand fell; her eyes grew slack. At the same time, Guyvir sensed someone enter the hut. He freed the dagger hidden by his kilt and faced a slim ogre clad in elegant, unblemished robes, an ogre whose tusks were shaved down and who had only one hand.

It was himself.

At that moment, Golgren awoke with a start. Cold sweat bathed him. He shivered and stared at the darkness, his gaze finally fixing on Idaria.

With a hiss of anger, the grand lord lay back again. He had many dreams, most of them of conquest and triumph, but only one that played itself over and over, ending in damnation. There were some memories that could never be forgotten, could never be buried.

At the same time, those memories also drove Golgren as nothing else. As he shut his eyes, the grand lord imagined a land that he had only briefly and surreptitiously explored, but that always beckoned—a land that was his waking dream to conquer.

"I will come, Silvanost," he murmured. "I will come . . . "

VIII

The Price Of Betrayal

As he was their leader in all matters, minor or significant, the Black Talon convened at Dauroth's pleasure. In a central chamber on the main floor of the Titans' sweeping edifice, the robed sorcerers gathered. For each of the eleven, there awaited a massive, stone chair whose arched back rose high over its occupant. The chairs were set behind a curved, wooden platform that gave the seated giants the appearance of condemnatory judges. Once, when first that place had been built, a massive chandelier had lit the chamber, but it had been replaced with a ball of white-blue energy that hovered over the oval of chairs.

It was there, in that central chamber, that the Black Talon discussed daily events and how the lives of ogres could be manipulated for the Titans' ultimate goal. The Grand Lord Golgren was often a part of those discussions, and many sharp, disapproving comments were made about the half-breed, although such comments were always moderated in tone so Dauroth would not take offense and punish the speaker.

The platform was arched like a crescent moon so all the Titans had some glimpse of the others and any who stood before them. At the center of the platform, seated slightly higher than the rest, was Dauroth. Hundjal and Safrag flanked him. The others were divided evenly on each side, with those farthest away of least importance; all had an equal vote in decisions, although even their unanimity could be overturned by their leader should Dauroth deem such a step necessary.

"He treats us like collared mastarks!" growled Hundjal, his handsome face twisted into an ugly sneer by his fury. In his anger, he had slipped into Common, a tongue very useful and even more eloquent than the Titans' musical language when it came to complaining about the grand lord's dictates. "Go out and crush his enemies then return to our stalls until needed again!"

Dauroth's expression remained consistently neutral. Among the others, Safrag and the lesser Titans watched, most wise enough to keep their opinions to themselves for the moment.

"His concern about the borders with Ambeon are not without merit," the lead Titan finally answered, choosing Common because his apprentice had also spoken in that language. "And although the views of some among the Black Talon may differ on that issue, I, as its head, have decided that we will abide by his request."

"*Request?*" Hundjal nearly spit before recalling his place. "He *ordered* it, master! Ordered *you.*"

"This particular discussion is ended." Dauroth switched back to the more superior Titan tongue. His words were a beautiful song to the ears of the others, but in Common they would have translated as, "Let us now turn to another matter. There is one among our number who wishes to speak to the Talon."

The others grew animated. Few among the ranks of the Titans would care to bring unnecessary notice to themselves by requesting an audience with the inner circle. Such an act of daring could just as easily diminish their standing among their kind.

Narrowed, golden eyes turned to the empty area before the Talon. On the stone floor was etched the symbol of the gathering, a set of avian claws, utterly dark in color and seeming poised as if to grasp whomever stood above them.

Dauroth stretched a hand toward that spot, and as he did, sinister black flames erupted from the stones there. They burst into high flame, leaping toward the illuminating sphere.

But no sooner had the black flames erupted than the magical fire died again, and where they had been stood a figure that caused everyone to gasp—everyone, that was, except Dauroth.

She was as beautiful as an elf maid, though as shadowy in cast as the Titans were like the sun. Her unbound raven tresses nearly flowed down to her waist. That she was garbed much like a member of the Talon—though hers was more form fitting in preferred places—was no coincidence.

"Asahna inaris oMorgada," Dauroth sang. "Welcome to you, our sister Morgada."

Long lashes half veiled the golden eyes of the Titaness. The full, artfully black lips parted, and if Morgada's teeth were not as large as those of the males in the room, they were, without a doubt, cleaner and sharper.

"Great to me is the gift of this audience," she sang back

in the Titan tongue, "even if it is not I for whom I speak."

"You come for another?"

Smiling, the ogress surveyed the darkened figures. She knew well the effect she had on the powerful males; they were keenly aware of her unusual beauty. The spell that had transformed her was intended to give her just that advantage.

"I come for a brother known to you all, who, by the curse of the mongrel playing at khan, has now suffered as none of us would wish." The Titaness shuddered sincerely, for she, especially, appreciated what such a fate would mean.

Dauroth straightened, understanding. "Ah! It is *Donnag* of whom you speak."

"Donnag . . . yes, great Dauroth . . . poor, pitiful Donnag." And as Morgada sang those words, she stepped to the side, revealing a misshapen *thing* her magical arts had hidden until that moment.

The living thing crudely resembled an ogre if some giant hand had managed, only half successfully, to conjure one of the race from a short, muttered description. The creature had bones that did not seem to align with those with which they were joined. One thick club of an arm dragged on the stone floor, while the other seemed to have atrophied. The thing was hunched and bent to the right, and it was clear to all that when the figure moved, he did so using three of his stronger limbs.

A worn, brown cloak covered much of the pathetic creature's body, fortunately, as much of its visible skin was mottled and covered in boils or warts. There was not much hair on its body, which was contrary to the norm for ogres, and what little there was were wisps that had turned a sickly gray.

A general nervousness spread throughout the Black Talon, with even Dauroth frowning at the sight. The lead Titan's nose twitched; a rancid smell permeated the august chamber and clearly that stink was emanating from the foul, misshapen Donnag.

The twisted mouth with four angled tusks opened, and a voice that would have made even a toad's sound beautiful croaked in Common, "G-great D-Dauroth . . . why . . . " The thing paused, its watery, round eyes that were too big for its head squeezing tightly shut in an attempt to formulate its thoughts. "Why . . . " the cloaked form tried again, "you forsaken D-Donnag?"

Once, there had been a powerful chieftain called Donnag, who had, through his savage might, fought his way up to become ruler of Blöde, and he had exerted a great influence over the court of Kern as well. That Donnag had been a fierce warrior with a trail of blood honored in legend, even before his ascension to the throne. Once, ogres had believed that if the race ever were to unite, it would unite under the iron club of Donnag.

And for a long while, there had been nothing to make anyone believe otherwise. Indeed, at one point, the ruler of Blöde had been approached by the Black Talon as a candidate deemed possibly worthy of rising to even greater glory; perhaps he might even join the Titan ranks. That Donnag had been no fool; he knew the magic of the Titans would be a valuable weapon to add to his arsenal.

Donnag's future had appeared glorious and inevitable until the emergence in Kern of the slight—to Donnag, almost childlike—half-breed calling himself Golgren.

How it was that Golgren had ingratiated himself with

the grand khan was not difficult to understand. Zharang had become little more than a self-indulgent wastrel. Golgren had thus easily manipulated events so the servant became the master. But Donnag was no Zharang. He had intended Golgren to serve him until the half-breed was drained of any use; then would he be executed.

But Donnag had erred even more stupidly than the grand khan. Golgren cleverly built alliances, and one of those had been a partnership with the foul Uruv Suurt priestess, Nephera. The Titans blamed Nephera for much of their troubles, for her malevolent deity had enabled the witch to steal the secrets of the spellcasters and pass some of those secrets on to Golgren. That put them into the hands—*hand*—of the dog from Kern.

Dauroth alone did not seem to regard Golgren suspiciously, and, in fact, the leader of the Titans appeared to welcome Golgren as a potentially useful tool in re-creating the High Ogre race. Action was in Donnag's blood; he had moved to squash the half-breed, rashly convinced that, together, his magic and his might would be sufficient to destroy the spindly half-breed.

But he had underestimated Golgren. Donnag had failed, and for his failure, Golgren had commanded—*commanded*—that no Titan provide the elixir and spell work that the chieftain of Blöde so badly required to resuscitate and maintain himself.

Within two months of his defeat, Donnag had lost all of his magical ability. His understanding of the Titan tongue had melted away, and even Common and Ogre required tremendous effort. Worse, as his mind went, his body degenerated at an even swifter pace. His once-glorious form had suddenly bent and twisted, and none of his limbs moved as they should. The festering boils and strange warts popped up with grim abandon.

By the end of three months, Donnag had become the barely sentient blight that *tried* to stand before the Talon.

"W-why?" he asked Dauroth again. "Why?"

"Donnag knows the reason why," returned the lead Titan as succinctly as possible in Common. "Donnag did not listen. Donnag was told his course was wrong, but he failed to listen."

The once-glorious Titan shambled past Morgada, who, although she had acted as his sponsor, seemed eager to edge away from his stench. "Know this!" growled the macabre form. "Know this! But—but look!" Donnag held up a hand that was more a paw. Two of his fingers had fused together, and the others had grown stunted. "G-grows worse! No—never s-stops!"

That was what frightened *any* Titan, even those of the inner circle, the most. The degeneration did, indeed, appear to be endless. Always there was something changing, something mutating. There was no one there who did not recognize how Donnag had grown worse since last they had glimpsed him. Then he had been petitioning for some relief, some assistance, from the Black Talon or, more to the point, from Dauroth.

But Dauroth was unmoved, just as on those past occasions. "Donnag brought this sorry circumstance upon himself. He knows that there is nothing we can do for him—"

"Coward! Bec-cause Dauroth—Dauroth is coward!"

Even Hundjal gave an involuntary shiver as the rest of the Black Talon froze, waiting for the punishment that would surely befall the chieftain for his blasphemous words. Yet Dauroth did not burn Donnag to ash or have his insides become his outsides. Rather, Dauroth looked calm and even solicitous, gazing upon the monstrous figure with a mask of pity.

"Donnag will be excused for his words, for all here know his mind is slowing, his understanding of his actions is regressing." Then the spellcaster stood, a giant towering even among the other giants in the room. "There is a balance currently necessary to the goals and ideals of the Titans that goes far beyond the needs of one. Donnag will and must accept this."

The fallen Titan's grotesque features shifted back and forth luridly as he fought with all his mental faculties to comprehend Dauroth's reply. Morgada, meanwhile, had moved away, so far away from the repellant creature that the Titaness had become lost in the shadows at the edge of the chamber.

Dauroth's burning gaze touched every Titan present. "Donnag will not come here again unless I have summoned him."

The dark flames erupted again. At first, Donnag did not seem to recognize their presence, but when he finally noticed the flames, beckoning him, he reached instead toward his former mentor and shouted, "No! Not—not send me b-back—"

The flames swelled to engulf Donnag . . . and he vanished.

"Morgada."

At Dauroth's summons, the lone Titaness swept back into the center of the chamber, her eyes meeting the leader's. Her blank expression covered any resentment, much less fear she might be hiding.

Dispensing with Common as he switched to his own beloved tongue, Dauroth sang out his challenge,

"Morgada, how is it that you, of all of us, dare to press Donnag's cause despite the past?"

Also reverting to the Titan language, she replied without guilt, "Donnag was blood, and called blood in order to plead my aid."

"You are one of us, and that is the only call you will answer. All past ties are gone and have never been, my Morgada."

The dark temptress bowed her head. "You are correct as always, master."

"Raise your eyes," Dauroth commanded, looking kindly on her. "The fault is Donnag's more than yours, I know. You will remember this incident well and, I suspect, repeat it not."

"No, master." Under the thick lashes, the golden eyes stared at the lead Titan as if no one else existed in the chamber.

"We will speak no more of this, yes?"

Morgada nodded, a slight smile crossing her perfect features. Then, at Dauroth's gesture, the flames engulfed her too and, like Donnag, she vanished from the Talon's sight.

"This will not end it for Donnag," Hundjal murmured as his master sat back down in his tall chair.

"No." Dauroth's tone, which seemed more understanding when he was speaking with Morgada, suddenly grew cold, dangerous. That coldness frosted the words he sang. "No . . . as with so many things, I will likely have to act."

Uncertain what the leader meant and not really wanting to know the details, Hundjal nodded vaguely. If he noticed that Dauroth turned his back slightly to him, the younger Titan gave no sign.

"And so," began the Black Talon's master, "we must now discuss just *how* the grand lord's goals and ambitions for the border with Ambeon shall be fulfilled."

❧❦❀❦❧

Another night came and Golgren slept without experiencing the dream. It was a rare dreamless night for him, and he slept well. Sleep was rare enough for him since seizing power. The grand lord often went for two or three days without so much as a nap, during which he always contrived to appear to have one eye still open. That was one hazard of ruling; even in the safest of places, it was never safe enough to sleep truly.

Golgren lay sprawled on the array of elven pillows, his closed eyes toward the ceiling. That night his dutiful servant watched over him, and if there were anyone the ogre trusted to keep him alive and protected, it was Idaria.

Elves themselves had peculiar sleeping habits. Rarely did anyone see Idaria looking as if she needed rest; she was almost always present or nearby just when her master ordered some task.

And the elf slave did not look in the least weary ever, certainly not at that moment. Neither, it must be said, did she appear to be overly concerned with Golgren's safety, for the silver-haired maiden stood expectantly at a high, arched window that overlooked a drop of several stories. She had stood there for more than half an hour, her sharp ears listening not only for noises outside the room, but alert to the ogre's breathing. She counted on the steady breathing of sleep with no alteration.

Finally, there came a slight fluttering of wings, so light only the elf could hear it approach. A moment later, a small brown bird alighted on the sill.

Idaria cooed quietly as the bird flew to her hand. She petted the bird gently then glanced over her shoulder for reassurance. The grand lord remained lying on his back with his hand cupping the object that rested atop his chest.

Satisfied, the elf sought the bird's left leg. There, she located a tiny leather pouch bound to its limb. From the pouch, Idaria pulled forth a piece of parchment. Unfolding it, she read the brief missive with eyes well accustomed to the dark.

The reading took but a few seconds. Whatever the contents of the message, Idaria's expression betrayed nothing. Placing the note in a fold of her garment, she then withdrew from another fold a similar parchment and thrust it in the pouch.

Making certain that the missive was secure, Idaria brought the bird's gaze to meet her own. The communication that passed between them was thought to be a folk tale by most other races, and such ability was rare even among her own kind. But the bird knew where it had to go and when it needed to return.

"Fly carefully," Idaria whispered, a warning she always gave. The bird endangered itself for her out of love, and the elf regretted each time she had to exploit the creature.

Raising high the hand upon which the bird rested, the slave waved her messenger up and away. As quietly as it had arrived, with its light fluttering, the bird departed through the window.

Even as it vanished from her sight, from the pillows behind her Idaria heard a shifting. Her footfalls quieter than the shadows, the slave returned to her proper place near her master—without disturbing him—despite the chains she always wore.

Even then, Idaria had barely stretched out near Golgren before the ogre's eyes flickered open. His hand closed, as if he sought to reassure himself that he still clutched what hung around his neck. That done, the grand lord's eyes sought out Idaria.

"Master," she murmured, lowering her gaze.

The ogre brushed her cheek. "My Idaria . . . always watching, always faithful, yes?"

"Yes, my master."

"It pleases—" The grand lord tensed. Idaria likewise froze.

"Such a touching scene, a king and his concubine."

Abruptly, from the shadows, materialized Tyranos. The towering mage tapped the floor once with his staff. The crystal's silver light softly filtered through the darkness. "Perhaps you can find another elf slave to paint it."

"You are concerned all of a sudden with the elves?" returned Golgren. "Perhaps Tyranos now hopes to plead their freedom?"

"What you do with them is of no concern to me, unless it happens to interest the Titans." Glancing at Idaria, Tyranos performed a mock bow. "Oh dear, my words have made you shudder. Do forgive me."

As a slave, Idaria did not—dared not—respond. Golgren rose from the pillows to face the wizard on equal footing.

"Tyranos must have something he wishes urgently to speak of to come to a place he has never been permitted to enter." Golgren stared past the intruder to the doorway through which guards should have already been bursting. "And to spend precious magic to shield what goes on in here from all outside."

"Indeed. I've brought something very interesting for you to see." The leonine face cracked into a grim smile as the mage turned the crystal toward the floor. "Careful . . . he bites."

And under the staff's magical light, a winged form took shape. At first it was no larger than a songbird. From Idaria there came a gasp she could not stifle, but fortunately the thing that Tyranos had summoned proved to be—not her pet—but such a creature that both the spellcaster and Golgren could have taken her exclamation for fright, not concern of discovery.

Within a single breath, the creature had grown to the size of a hound. In two breaths, it was already nearly the length of a human. Its wings were long, wide, and leathery—and at the moment bound tight by invisible bonds gripping its scaly body. Under a ridge of thick brows, red eyes both animal and intelligent glared ferociously at the three of them, and from the toothy, almost beaklike maw erupted a vicious snarl. Its body was as broad as that of an ogre and well muscled. The gray beast attempted to slash out at Tyranos with taloned hands but encountered an unseen barrier just inches beyond its body that sparked hotly where the tips of its talons touched.

The tall human grandly gestured at his prize. "I've been told that Garantha is the city of the griffon. Look what I found. Have you chosen to take the symbol of the gargoyle instead?"

Golgren, his hand resting on his chest, strode toward the creature. The gargoyle, in turn, tried to lunge at the grand lord but again ran afoul of Tyranos's magical barrier.

"I've told the beast he's just going to hurt himself, battering away like that, but you know how thick headed they are, especially the mountain varieties."

"This was found in Garantha?"

"Found atop your palace," the wizard replied with a chuckle. "Perched like a statue . . . a statue with long, acute ears, though."

Gargoyles were not unknown in the ogre lands, especially the mountainous regions. Ogres sometimes hunted them for sport or simple extermination, for gargoyle meat was foul by even an ogre's low standards of edibility. Of course, the winged creatures were not adverse to doing a little hunting of their own, and no ogre excursion ever returned without having suffered a few victims. They were legendarily ferocious creatures.

But gargoyles were not simple-minded animals. Their intelligence was said to be nearly as great as ogres, and there were rumors that some could even speak a crude form of Common.

That thought ran through Golgren's mind. "You have questioned this beast?"

In response, Tyranos uttered a single, odd word. *"Tivak!"*

The crystal flared. The barrier around the gargoyle revealed itself in a savage crackle of silver energy. Within, the winged captive let out a mournful shriek. It dropped to the floor, writhing. Idaria's eyes widened, evincing some sympathy for the gargoyle's plight despite its ominous presence in the capital.

"Tivak!" The fearsome crackling died down. As the gargoyle lay there panting, the brown-robed mage nonchalantly replied, "As you can see, if he had anything to

tell, he'd have told it gladly. I merely brought him along with me to ensure that you'd not think I was making it up when I told you live gargoyles are skulking around your palace."

Golgren nodded, his interest darting from the creature to the wizard and back again. "This watched over the palace this very night?"

"I trust I have made that clear."

"And good Tyranos *happened* to be nearby and noticed."

The broad-shouldered human let out a gruff laugh. "I've a vested interest in your welfare, oh Grand Lord."

"Yes, you do." Golgren turned his back on both spell-caster and gargoyle. He stared pointedly at Idaria then, still facing the elf, commanded, "Release the winged one."

"I beg your pardon?" asked Tyranos.

"I would have you release the *voru tzyn,*" the grand lord repeated, using the old ogre term for gargoyles. Golgren still faced Idaria. "Here. Now."

Tyranos grunted with amusement. "As you like."

From the direction of the gargoyle there came a flash. Golgren, though, didn't turn around; he watched Idaria's eyes, which opened wide.

The gargoyle screeched.

Golgren whirled around. In his hand there was a long, slim dagger. He hurled it at the gargoyle just as the creature was about to leap at the ogre with its three-inch-long talons.

The blade buried itself in one eye. With a howl, the gargoyle collapsed on the floor again. It twisted in agony for a moment and finally lay still.

With satisfaction, the grand lord retrieved the elegant

dagger from his victim. He wiped the gargoyle's life fluids off on its leathery wings.

"A very pretty and effective blade," remarked Tyranos. "Another elven spoil for you to enjoy, I see." Glancing down disinterestedly at the gargoyle's corpse, the mage added, "Of course I could have done that for you with a lot less bother."

Golgren returned the dagger to its hiding place. "Yes. You could have." He gestured at the gargoyle. "You may still take that thing with you. Its blood may still be good."

"I am not a Titan. I've no need for this filth." The crystal flashed once more and the silver light enveloped the dead creature. A moment later, the corpse and all other traces of it vanished. "As to its reasons for having come here, I'll investigate further . . . and inform you of my findings, naturally."

The grand lord nodded his appreciation, but Tyranos did not depart. "You have some other reason for visiting, spellcaster?"

"Yes, there was one more thing. A minor thing. You're to have a visitor in—oh, I'd say two days. Providing he does not die in the meantime."

He had Golgren's attention. "A visitor? Yes?"

The crystal dulled. At the same time, Tyranos's voice grew less distinct. "A Solamnic . . . a sorry Solamnic, but still a Solamnic."

That brought a sudden, wide grin from the wizard's host. "Ah! One of the shelled ones? A true Solamnic? That would be a rare pleasure."

The hooded figure grinned back. "I thought you'd be pleased."

And with that, Tyranos faded into the shadows.

IX

HUNDJAL THE HUNTER

The minotaur patrol stalked through the rising landscape, each soldier growing more wary as the forest gave way to the drier, hotter landscape north of Ambeon. Yet the seven-foot-tall, breastplated figures moved with a confidence borne of recent triumph, thanks to a leader whose command they respected.

High hills spread before the patrol, which consisted of five squads of ten soldiers, each led by an officer called a dekarian. Some distance to the east, another fifty—similarly divided into five squads—also marched north, deeper into what was the territory of their former allies, the ogres. That fifty were led by the overall commander of their expedition, a hekturion named Kulanthos, who once had served the emperor himself when the latter was an outcast from his native realm.

The hundred legionaries and their officers had been ordered by their general to probe the region for any evidence of ogre incursions. The minotaurs were not technically at war with their neighbors, but neither side would have shunned a fight.

Perhaps Boar Legion did not boast the reputation of Warhorse or Wyvern Legion, but neither was it without some storied accomplishments. The soldiers of Boar Legion considered themselves exemplary fighters loyal to whoever by right held the imperial throne, which was currently the former slave Faros Es-Kalin. The emperor's recent ascension to power was a tale that stirred the blood of all minotaurs. His family had been slaughtered by enemies, he himself was thrown into captivity—first among fellow minotaurs and, later, exiled to ogre lands—but Faros had escaped his slavery and fought back, gaining followers and becoming a champion of all minotaurs in a time of upheaval.

Many believed he was the emperor of destiny, the one that legend said the god Sargonnas—known to older minotaurs as Sargas—had promised to deliver to his chosen people in their time of need. Certainly Faros had begun to unite the realm as it had not been since the earliest days of the reign of his late, unlamented uncle, Chot the Terrible. One policy of the past that Faros honored, pursuing it as zealously as his predecessors, was solidifying the minotaurs' hold on the mainland.

One of the dekarians paused. His brow wrinkling, he lifted his muzzle as he sniffed the air. Minotaurs bore more than a passing resemblance to cattle—if cattle walked and spoke like men and fought with more skill than most humans—but there was nothing otherwise cowlike in their demeanors. The eyes of a minotaur sparkled with an intelligence nearly human, and those of that particular officer suddenly radiated suspicion.

He tapped the blade of his shining broadsword on the ground, the dull, low thumping quickly gaining the attention of his men. The dekarian silently gestured for three of his warriors to sidle off toward a huge rock only a few yards ahead. As the three hurried away, he indicated to three others that they should slip free the bows they carried. It took but a few seconds for the archers to ready a protective fire for their comrades.

The first of the scouts reached the huge rock formation. With the other two watching his back, he slipped around the rock, briefly vanishing from the dekarian's sight.

Almost immediately the legionary returned to view, however. He waved his sword in the air and shook his head.

The dekarian let out a snort of annoyance. Under his breath, he muttered to his chief lieutenant, "I swear I sensed something there, and to my nostrils, it *stank* like an ogre."

"Perhaps they fled rapidly, Thados," the other replied softly. "Perhaps they were smart and ran before our swords."

"Ogres aren't smart enough to run away. Still . . . "

With no threat apparent, the legionaries pushed on. They were already a half hour beyond the boundaries that had been agreed upon and set in place by the late Emperor Hotak and the ogres' Grand Lord Golgren, not that either side had ever planned on accepting those borders for very long. Ogres had been moving south for the past few months, which, in the eyes of the Imperium, made it absolutely essential for the minotaurs to penetrate the north. Minotaur military logic held that the best way to reduce the odds of an enemy invading was to invade first.

As yet there were no formal invasion plans, but

the empress—Hotak's daughter Maritia and a former legion commander herself—exerted influence on her mate . . . not that he needed any encouragement to harry or kill his former slave masters.

Some trees still managed to thrive there despite the harsh landscape. Thados had not risen to third dekarian of his legion by ignoring such possible hiding places. Two of his men quickly climbed up the nearest tree, disappearing in the foliage.

A brief glance to his left revealed to Thados that the other squads were also making steady progress. Despite all the recent rumors, they had come across scant signs of ogres; that race did not seem ready for a full-scale raid into Ambeon. The empire would have a distinct advantage if it moved first.

Still, again the scent of ogre—or something akin to ogre—momentarily wafted past his nostrils. "There, do you smell that, Vul?" he asked his second. "You must smell that!"

The other legionary thrust his muzzle into the air. "I think perhaps . . . I really can't say, Thados, maybe a trace . . . "

Thados removed his helmet, which was skillfully cast to allow for not only the protrusion of his horns, but also for the extension of his long ears. He pricked his ears without success. He let some of the heat dissipate then shoved the helmet back on.

"Get those two out of the tree and let's move on. The other squads are pulling ahead." War was a competition among the individual minotaur squads. The quickest way to rise up in the ranks was to bloody one's weapon before one's comrades could.

Vul trotted over to the tree. He tapped his sword

against the side several times then irritably stared up among the branches.

Growing more impatient by the minute, Thados finally joined him, staring up. "What by the Lady Nephera's lists is going on? Get them down right—"

But as he joined Vul, the lead minotaur saw what his comrade was staring at . . . or rather, what his comrade was *not* staring at.

There was no one in the tree.

Thados circled the trunk. That enabled him to see all sides of the branches and deep into the foliage. Nothing as large as a cat could have escaped his view, much less two full-grown, armored minotaur fighters. No, the tree top was empty.

Leaving Vul still gaping up at the branches, the dekarian backed away warily, looking around. Three of his subordinates were continuing their slow but steady advance, yet he could not spot *any* of those who had been standing near the rocks.

"Vul! Where did—"

But when the minotaur officer turned back to his comrade, he realized Vul was also among the missing.

Thados searched around the tree then, after a hesitation, glanced up again. Once more he saw branches but no minotaurs.

The fur on the back of his neck stiffening, Thados immediately returned his attention to his remaining soldiers. A tremendous exhalation of relief escaped him when he saw the trio was still there. The dekarian gave a shout, and they came running back.

"Any of you see the others?" he demanded. When they shook their heads, he let out a furious snort. "Something's playing nasty tricks on us. Maybe it's magic!

We must stick close together! No one loses sight of the others!"

Minotaurs were a stolid race, but anything that smelled of magic made them anxious. Magic did not—at least in general—offer a foe that one could fight with a sturdy weapon.

Thados tried to think. On the one hand, the logical thing would have been to retreat. On the other, such a retreat—with no explanation as to how he had lost Vul and the others—was sure to disgrace him in the eyes of his superiors and comrades.

Disgrace was worse than death. Third Dekarian Thados thus chose instead to push on and hope for the best. His hekturion had given each squad specific instructions as to how deep they were to penetrate the territory, and Thados's soldiers still had some distance to cover. The dekarian was determined to take his squad at least as far as the tops of the first rocky hills.

It's only a little farther, Thados pointed out to himself. If we stick together, whatever took the others won't be able to touch us.

A whistling sound cut through the air, followed by a pair of harsh *thunks*.

Two legionaries crumpled, silver bolts through the backs of their necks where their helmets and armor left just bare openings. To pinpoint such a target required exceptional marksmanship.

Thados and his surviving soldier whirled in the direction from which the arrows had come—and a third missile suddenly blossomed in the throat of the dekarian's companion.

Frustration mixed with rage as the last minotaur under his command fell. "Where are you, you damned elf?" He bellowed, waving his sword about wildly. "Show yourself!"

Again he smelled that slight stink, that smell that was and was not ogre. It was so near as to be almost right behind him.

Spinning around, Thados swung his blade at just the level he would guess might behead an elf. However, instead his sword struck some surface so resilient that the weapon snapped in half. The top portion of the blade went flying away.

And as that dire turn of events registered on him, so too did the fact that what stood before the minotaur was much, much taller and even more startling than any elf he could imagine.

"What are you?" Thados blurted, gazing up in awe at the blue-tinged countenance of a creature that suggested elf lineage but also more, so much more.

"The hunter," the handsome giant responded with a display of sharp teeth. "Though I must say you Uruv Suurt have not offered much sport today. Too easy, the lot of you."

Uruv Suurt—in the legionary's mind, those ancient words left no doubt that the curious-looking giant was somehow tied to the ogre race. Very much aware of the odds against him, Thados nonetheless bent forward and, with a roar, charged headfirst at the towering spellcaster. Although rarely used in that manner, a minotaur's horns could be very lethal.

But before he got at all close to the giant's stomach, Thados heard a swishing sound; that was the last thing he heard. His head dropped from his neck, the cut so clean, his body continued forward two steps before it realized it was dead.

Hundjal dismissed the gleaming silver blade he had summoned, just as moments before he had banished the bow he used to slay the three other minotaurs. It had not been much of a hunt, true, but still a better passing of the time than the previous day.

Another Titan materialized next to him. Unlike Hundjal, there was no evident pleasure in the second Titan's face. In fact, the other spellcaster wore a rare, worried expression.

"This is not as Dauroth commanded," the other declared in the singsong language of their kind. "The Uruv Suurt, if they were to die, were supposed to do so as if by accident."

Dauroth's senior apprentice held out his hand, and the bolts he had used to slay the three minotaurs momentarily appeared in his palm before vanishing elsewhere. "And so they were."

With a wave of his hand, the legionaries' corpses also disappeared. Hundjal eyed the high rocks toward which the squad had been marching. A brief rumbling like thunder arose, and the upper third of the formation collapsed.

"They'll find them all there underneath the rocks, that is, if they really feel like digging. A rockslide, very accidental."

His companion was not easily convinced. "Hundjal, you may be Dauroth's favored, but still the leader may find such recklessness—"

However, a sharp glance from Hundjal not only silenced the other Titan, but made him decide the prudent course was to himself vanish.

Dauroth's favored—Hundjal did not see himself that way anymore. He should not have been out there in the borderlands, spending his might harassing and hunting Uruv Suurt. There was some fleeting enjoyment in that, true, but overall such a task was for the likes of lesser beings and conscripts, such as the Titans' latest addition, Ulgrod. That was a good proving ground for young Titans, not for veterans such as Hundjal, who assumed— as did many others—he would someday inherit the mantle of leadership over the Black Talon and the Titans in general.

Yet Dauroth had insisted that Hundjal supervise the mission, as though it were of any consequence. Hundjal knew as well as his master that Golgren had only insisted on the Titans' involvement there because he wanted to keep them occupied. The grand lord was a mongrel . . . but a mongrel with cunning.

Hundjal sensed more soldiers in the distance. His blood boiling from reflecting on his exile, the Titan found himself suddenly looking forward to a little more slaughter. Still, the pleasure would be as momentary as his last experience. A thousand slain Uruv Suurt could not make up for the slight to his pride.

It was a slight the Titan would never forgive his master.

Summoning power, Hundjal vanished immediately and just as rapidly reappeared within striking distance of the new soldiers. They, naturally, could not see him any better than the ones who had come before them. He detected the presence of two other Titans, who wisely acknowledged his superiority then retreated. All knew that the senior apprentice liked to hunt on his own.

He was acting recklessly; even Hundjal understood

that. The deaths would look like accidents but only barely, and surely the Uruv Suurt would question how so many accidents could occur.

But Hundjal did not care. He knew only that he could not stand their treatment for much longer. Something would have to be done.

A change would have to be made . . . and soon.

❧☙

The high walls ahead did not bode well for Stefan, who stared at them hopelessly. He was in Kernen, a place no living Solamnic—probably very few humans in general—had visited and lived to talk about. Its ancient splendor was obvious and the active rebuilding going on surprised him. It was not the dying, decaying city that the Command constantly spoke about.

A guard shoved him forward. Stefan had been so overawed by his first sight of Kernen that he had stopped walking. The knight quickly picked up his pace, straightening as he went. Even as a prisoner facing doom, a Solamnic entered the stronghold of his enemies with courage and honor.

Atolgus was not escorting him to a lesser khan after all, but intended to present the Solamnic to one of those in the august circle of the Grand Lord Golgren himself. The notion that Stefan might actually lay eyes on the grand lord stirred his blood. He had an opportunity to learn firsthand about the subject of his mission.

Atolgus grunted something to the guards at the gate, a pair of ugly beasts who eyed Stefan as if he were a rat that needed exterminating. A slight argument ensued, but before the ogres could come to blows, Atolgus slipped something into the meaty paws of one of the guards. The language of bribery was as universal as those of love and war.

They shuffled him past the sentries, who were already debating what sort of payment they could squeeze out of the next in line. Stefan glanced up at the gateway as he passed underneath the legendary portal; he knew he would never escape, but at least he would learn more than he had ever hoped about ogre civilization.

Inner Kernen was even more astounding than he imagined; beyond the walls the old city was filled with more ogres than any human could have dreamed existed in all the realm. The capital was in every way a bustling city, more vibrant than some vast human settlements to the west. There was a definite energy in the air, a sense of excitement and expectation. The ogres saw a future filled with promise. That could not be good for the rest of Ansalon.

Stefan beheld an unsettling sight as he entered the capital: ogres clad in finery. True, compared to the rulers of Solamnia, the well-dressed ogres looked rather gaudy and even ridiculous, but the very fact that such creatures existed was another sign of the ogres' attempt to rise above their ignominious past.

They passed through the market area, crude by the standards of Solamnia but still bursting with more variety than any outsider could have anticipated. Many of the fashioned items clearly had been scavenged from other races, with most of them coming, of course, from the elves. There were many weapons stalls. In fact, there were more than seemed possible or necessary. Swords, spears, clubs, daggers . . . the list went on.

There were beasts aplenty too. They consisted of

not only the stolid ogre steeds, but also baraki fighting lizards favored for sport; savage, red-crested raptors; and fearsome, wild goats that appeared half-wolf with their vicious, long snouts and glaring eyes. There were also several variations of an animal that Stefan heard his captors refer to as amaloks, most of them long-necked, yellow-and-gray-striped terrors kept in small groups in high-walled pens. Their bodies were sleek and obviously designed for swiftness. While they bore lupine features, they also resembled horses, albeit horses with a long, nasty pair of horns—clearly capable of being wielded as weapons—and sharp teeth.

While familiar with the traditional patron of the city, Stefan beheld another symbol vying for predominance that bespoke something more recent and ominous. The icon appeared mostly on banners flying over the roofs of many of the buildings, but several of those of high castes even wore the emblem on their person. It was a severed hand clutching a bloody dagger.

Even in Solamnia, reports had filtered in that the Grand Lord Golgren had turned his lost hand into a symbol of defiance.

A horn blared up ahead. Atolgus's people clustered together, surrounding the human. Much shorter than they, Stefan could see nothing but the backs of heads and furry spines. Then a shifting among the bodies gave him a glimpse of armored forms that for a split second evoked the Knighthood.

Yet they were not Solamnic warriors; rather, to his astonishment, they were ogres who wore gleaming breastplates and helmets. They vanished from his view within moments, but by then the knight had witnessed enough to know that all the rumors were true. The new ogre leader had begun to whip together a fighting force on par with other races. Those ogres had order and discipline, the foundation for any successful army.

Atolgus again started forward with his band, only to be halted by a broad, armored figure whose origins clearly did not lie in Kern. Stefan had already seen several Blödian ogres, but that was the first who flaunted any position of authority.

"Isaga i ny Shok G'Ran?"

The Solamnic tensed at the pejorative words describing his kind.

The chieftain stepped aside. *"Ny Shok G'Ran. Hodig i caru i Gestan uth Knophros . . . Gestan uth Knophros iGolgreni!"*

The armored ogre loomed over Stefan. He was rotund and ugly even when compared with his comrades, sporting a broken tusk and one eye that stayed half hidden behind its lid. The knight had grown more or less accustomed to the odors of his captors, but the Blödian stank in an especially repulsive manner. At the same time, with each exhalation of breath, a second but equally nauseating stench assailed the human.

To his surprise, the armored ogre addressed him in Common. "You are Solamnic, yes?" he rumbled.

The question did not really need answering, but Stefan nevertheless nodded. Satisfied, the officer snarled something to Atolgus that the knight could not understand. The chieftain beamed. He made a dismissive gesture to the rest of his band—even his mate—then seized the bound knight by the arm.

Other ogres gave way before the armored ogre as he led Atolgus and Stefan away from the others. A half dozen or so steps away, the three were suddenly joined by six guards who took up positions on all sides of the small party.

They left the market area. Ahead lay a carriage pulled by a team of amaloks. The carriage itself was of obvious human design but had been redecorated in a rather gaudy manner with gold leaf and precious stones inlaid around the door frame.

The mark of the severed hand had been painted on the door, and the skill of the artist was such that the famous lost appendage looked monstrously real.

The armored ogre thrust a heavy, muscled arm in front of both Stefan and the suddenly trepidant Atolgus. The pair waited nervously while their companion trotted over to the carriage.

Stefan had not quite known what to expect, but certainly it was not the face, the vision, that peered out at him. It was no ogre. Rather, the female's slim form and ethereal beauty marked her as naught but an elf . . . and one born of high station.

She peered almost ruefully at him then spoke in whispered tones with the officer. What they said, Stefan could not discern, but after they were finished, the elf woman surprised him further by extending a hand—a manacled hand—to the human.

"Please enter. As a guest."

Blinking, the Solamnic merely stood there. Taking that as, at best, reluctance, or at worst, defiance, the ogre near the carriage reached for the heavy sword sheathed at his side.

"No, Khleeg," murmured the elf, concerned eyes on Stefan. "Please," she repeated. "As a guest of the grand lord."

The knight rediscovered the mobility of his limbs. Atolgus did not wish to release him, but the ogre had no choice. As Stefan neared the carriage, the ogre named Khleeg reached for a dagger near his sword. He came around to the human's back.

As the elf silently reassured Stefan with her pitying eyes, Khleeg sliced away his bonds. The knight tensed, ready for whatever injustice was next, but a look from the elf stilled him.

"Inside," ordered Khleeg. The Blödian looked past the human knight to where Atolgus still stood, agape. "Follow."

The chieftain did so obediently and without protest. Stefan, meanwhile, had climbed inside the carriage, where the elf indicated he should sit across from her. Despite her chains and weathered clothing, she sat like a regal lady of the court.

The pretty image of her was abruptly ruined by the intrusion of Khleeg, who sat at his side. The ogre took up more than half the seat, and his helmed head nearly poked the ceiling.

A strange spitting sound was heard from without; then the carriage started moving. Flexing stiff arms, Stefan asked, "Uh, the grand lord . . . how did he find out so fast that I am here?"

His question had been directed at the elf woman, but it was Khleeg who initially responded. "He is Golgren."

Stefan understood such an answer coming from one of the grand lord's minions but hoped for more enlightenment from his attractive companion. Instead, though, the elf merely nodded solemnly and repeated what the ogre had said. "He is Golgren."

And for some reason, those same words, echoed in a drone from the elf woman, left the Solamnic most disturbed.

X

BEFORE THE GRAND LORD

The meredrake hissed, the first hint that something was happening. The guards, stationed at evenly spaced intervals around the ancient chamber, were already standing at attention; they attempted to look even more wary. Golgren, seated upon the stone throne used by countless grand khans of the past, stirred from his dark reveries. Images of a burning village and a dead elf woman retreated but did not entirely vanish.

Nostrils flaring, the meredrake tried to move in the direction of the fresh scent, but the chain attached to its leather collar yanked the beast back toward the wall on Golgren's right. Frustrated, the giant lizard continued to hiss until the grand lord signaled one of the guards to throw it a piece of fly-covered mastark meat from a clay pot near the great reptile. With savage gusto, the meredrake happily tore into the rank tidbit, the approaching intruder momentarily forgotten.

The doors swung open and four figures entered the audience of the grand lord. Two immediately went down on one knee, while the third—Idaria—silently strode over to her master, taking her place on his left. Behind her, the fourth visitor stood defiant.

Golgren hid his bemusement. Having met that kind of human before, he had expected nothing less from him. Solamnic Knights were nothing if not stubborn and proud. It was a trait—or fault—of theirs that he had exploited more than once in the past.

Khleeg had just noticed the human's disrespect for the grand lord. With a growl, the other ogre rose. The meredrake, sensing a clash, grew alert and hopeful. It dropped the piece of mastark, for something fresher and bloodier might be imminent.

Though unarmed, the Solamnic stepped back into a fighting stance. Khleeg swiftly drew his sword.

Golgren deigned to interfere. "Such a fight this would be," he said with a loud sigh, "but the human is guest, Khleeg."

"Shows no respect!" Yet the armored ogre, obeying his lord, backed away, sheathing his sword as he glared at the knight.

That settled, Golgren gestured not to the knight, but rather at the chieftain who had brought him this prize. *"Tahun ur?"*

The young ogre slapped a meaty fist to his broad chest. *"¡Atolgusi! Ur nahm i fallo hucht!"*

"Gefyn ol oKomeni?"

Atolgus beamed. "Yes, talk good Common!" He pointed at the knight. "Talk him!"

"So good." Golgren leaned inquisitively toward the human. "I am the Grand Lord Golgren," he said in a matter-of-fact tone that belied his vaunted prestige. "What name have you?"

Abandoning his fighting stance—although as a Solamnic Knight, he intended to stay vigilant—the bearded figure responded stoutly, "I am Sir Stefan Rennert, Knight of the Sword!"

Then the human clamped his mouth tight. There were a thousand ways by which Golgren could have wrenched more information out of him, but that was not what the ogre desired—at least not at the moment. His gaze shifted back to the chieftain. "His armor and weapon? They are not here?"

Atolgus, likely fearing some extravagant punishment for his unforeseeable mistake, looked suddenly worried at the drift in the conversation. "We have! We have! Can get!"

"Do so."

With a frantic bow, the younger ogre fled the chamber. Golgren dismissed any further thought of him. If Atolgus brought all of the Solamnic's items back quickly and in good order, he would receive ample reward for the knight's presence. If not, then there were also a thousand ways by which Golgren could punish the fool. The Solamnic's trust would be hard to gain, but gain it the grand lord was *determined* to do at all cost.

Golgren studied the knight. "My Idaria. Our guest has come a long way. He needs food and wine."

Without a word, the elf scurried to find sustenance for the human. Despite his deliberately impassive expression, the very mention of food and wine must have momentarily made the knight's spirits soar. Though he was a prisoner of the "savage" ogres, at least they were not going to starve him. And he was, Golgren was sure, famished.

The meredrake grew restive. Possibly disappointed

in the lack of violence and blood, the beast again began tugging at his chain.

Stefan, alarmed by the creature, reached instinctively for the sword that no longer hung at his side. Golgren extended his arms in an apologetic gesture, which in part served, as he planned, to bring his missing hand to the attention of the human.

"You see this? The emperor of the Uruv Suurt—the minotaurs—he once took offense at it," the grand lord quipped, his mouth twisted to approximate, as best he could, a human grin. "As he takes offense at humans who tread upon his Ambeon."

The knight, thinking he was being provoked, made no comment, but at that moment, after so much deprivation, his strength began to give out and his body swayed noticeably.

Golgren frowned. "Khleeg! My guest will sit!"

To his credit, the massive ogre moved quickly enough to catch the wobbling Stefan before he could collapse on the ground. Almost as if guiding a child, Khleeg led the man toward his master while another ogre rushed forward with a small wooden bench.

The Solamnic accepted the seat with a grateful nod. "I thank the Grand Lord for his courtesy, but if he wishes any facts from me, he will not get them either by pleasantries or torture."

The latter was debatable, Golgren thought, but "facts" were not exactly what the grand lord desired, not entirely. And the knight's defiance amused him. Before Golgren had a chance to say another word, however, Idaria returned with the food and drink.

"So!" Golgren merrily exclaimed. "No talk of torture! No talk at all! First, Sir Stefan Rennert, Knight of the

Sword, you will dine! The food will be excellent"—he gave Idaria a warning glance—"for it is cooked by fine elves!"

After an appraising look at the meal, which consisted of seasoned goat meat, black mushrooms from small caverns located underneath the capital, and some rare, pale-yellow tzena melons—one of the few fruits hardy enough to exist in the northern climes of Kern—Golgren allowed Idaria to serve the knight.

The Solamnic immediately dug into the appetizing meal. Perhaps because he had expected poison and, thus, fully intended to die earlier or maybe because he wondered if the food would be taken away at any moment, Stefan ate with a frantic speed that caused even Golgren to stare incredulously at the knight.

"Please! Better to slow down!" said the grand lord.

Idaria served the knight just as she always did her lord, but her unusual attentiveness caught Golgren's gaze and caused him to frown, despite his desire to keep an air of amiability about him. As she leaned close to pour the human more wine, the grand lord irritably snapped his fingers, recalling the elf slave to his side. Once she joined him, he reached with his hand to take one of hers. Her beautiful countenance gave no hint that he deliberately squeezed much harder than he knew was comfortable.

"You serve me well," he murmured, finally loosening his grip on the elf. "You serve me always."

He released her. Idaria retreated behind him.

The knight ate more slowly then, with his eyes darting around the chamber. Golgren noted that those eyes lingered on each of his guards for more than several seconds. Even in the very heart of the ogre realm, the human was on alert, constantly analyzing his surroundings. He was clearly more than a mere scout.

"You did not come to our realm alone," Golgren interjected with another smile. The grand lord tried not to sound accusing, even though there was no good reason for any Solamnic to cross the border into lands inhabited principally by minotaurs and ogres.

Stefan finished a swallow of goat meat and said, "No, I didn't. Giant . . . giant baraki caught us by surprise."

"Ah, the ji-baraki, they are treacherous." Atolgus would have to be questioned later about the veracity of his information, but it was clear to Golgren that the knights had been probing deep inside his lands; Khleeg had informed him the Solamnics were caught near the site of his victory over the rebellious chieftains. "Your comrades, they are mourned."

Under the circumstances, the human had to acknowledge the grand lord's apparent sympathy. Stefan nodded, still chewing.

The rest of the story Golgren could figure out. So Atolgus had come upon the knight and captured him, understanding his value to a higher lord. Still, it was a credit to the human to have made the rough trek all the way to the capital. Stefan Rennert was a fighter strong of will and body, just the type of person who might prove to be some real use to Golgren.

"The home of the Solamnics, it is very beautiful, it is said," the ogre suddenly commented, shifting topics.

Stefan swallowed another bite of goat. His expression was one of undisguised pride. "The finest of all lands."

"And protected by good warriors like yourself. Much I hear of Solamnia. Tell me, Sir Stefan Rennert, what do you think of my warriors?"

The knight's expression grew wary as he more openly regarded the guards in the room. "They seem strong and brave."

"And better armored, more disciplined than expected perhaps?"

Stefan hesitated. It was as though Golgren had read his thoughts. Finally, the human nodded. "Certainly not what I expected."

Khleeg, who was close by standing watch, grunted in amusement. To his lord, he muttered, *"Junach i falgos tuum."*

The human eyed the armored ogre distrustfully. He thought he heard some insults aimed at him. Golgren, shaking a finger at his subordinate as if the latter were a small child, moved quickly to defuse the situation. "Ah, good Khleeg! For our guest, only Common must be spoken . . . and with politeness, yes?"

As Stefan waited, Khleeg, eyes narrowed in concentration, said to the knight, "Warriors must . . . always . . . expect . . . all."

It was not what Khleeg actually had said, but the Solamnic appeared to accept that as the translation. Had the ogre's statement been accurately translated— Khleeg had commented on how naive and stupid warriors die the quickest—the Solamnic would have had to take umbrage. Golgren didn't want that to happen, and neither, for the moment, did Stefan.

The grand lord did not wish to take any more chances at provoking a confrontation. "Khleeg, you may go now."

The officer slapped his fist against his breastplate and marched out.

Stefan finished his food. Sliding the remnants to the

side, he stood before Golgren, his jaw set. "If I am a guest, then am I permitted to leave Kernen now?"

"Soon . . . and sooner than you might think, Sir Stefan Rennert." Golgren also rose. He rubbed his chin. "But we must speak first, yes? Of a—a partnership—between our peoples."

As he had expected, the knight looked utterly amazed. There had not been any contact between the ogre and human races for many years, not since Solamnia had stopped sending men to train ogres to fight against the Nerakans. Even that had been done "unofficially" on both sides, and the grand khan knew little about it.

"A partnership?" Stefan blurted, brow furrowing.

The grand lord shook his head, pretending he was rummaging for the proper word. "Nay!" His face lit up and he grinned. Extending his good hand toward the human, Golgren declared, "Not partnership, but *alliance,* an alliance between the humans and ogres."

❦

It was fortunate that Golgren stood with his back to Idaria and that the Solamnic's attention was focused on the ogre. Neither of them noticed the fleeting expression of dismay and disbelief that crossed the elf slave's usually placid features.

Stefan also looked incredulous, and at first he couldn't imagine that ogres and knights shared any common interests . . . that was, until he thought about Neraka and Silvanost.

It was true they might find common ground on those two subjects.

"An alliance?" the human repeated, involuntarily

shaking his head, as though to clear it of musty ideas of the past.

"Yes." Golgren stepped down to approach the knight, trying to put them on even ground, eye-to-eye level, as much as possible. Idaria had watched the grand lord brilliantly manipulate many who had come before him with their hopes and entreaties, including many who thought they were manipulating the grand lord. But if Golgren desired some sort of pact with Solamnia, he had his work cut out for him, she thought.

That was not the urgent thought in her mind, however. She had to warn her own partners, her confederates. But that would require some maneuvering of her own; another message dispatched so soon after the last one was risky; Idaria feared discovery.

Yet she would risk all for the freeing of her homeland from the minotaurs; she would do anything to save her people from not only the pitiable slavery to which they were subjected, but from the foul arts of the Titans. Compared to the Titans, Golgren was almost a benevolent despot. Certainly because of him, scores of elves had been saved from the terrible fate that had been prepared for them in the hidden sanctum of Dauroth.

Of course, Golgren had kept the slaves from the Titans' grasp largely to satisfy his own ambitions; Idaria's influence on him was subtle, and what little she had accomplished had cost her heavily. There was a part of her that buried the painful experience of the months of her captivity, and what she herself had elected to do: become a slave—then the concubine—of the ogre half-breed. She had strived hard to sneak to his notice, and she had succeeded. Idaria had willingly done what few other elf women could imagine.

She, who had been safely ferried out of the ancient home of her people at the expense of her parents' lives, had returned with the aid of her friends and comrades in order to contrive her capture by the personal guard of the grand lord himself. If Idaria somehow helped her people regain their freedom, the cost of all that would be worth her life . . . and her tainted honor.

"The two races have many concerns in common," Golgren was saying smoothly to the human. "The black-shelled ones are a bane on both Solamnics and ogres. They have long been so. Yet they are not what troubles us most now, yes? There is also Ambeon, from where the minotaurs eye more lands west and north."

Stefan nodded agreement, even as he reflected that it had been Golgren and his followers who had aided the horned warriors in gaining a foothold on the continent in the first instance.

"But come!" continued Golgren companionably, all but throwing his arm around the human's shoulder. "You have eaten; you are tired now. Of course, tired. All talk of grand things we do will come after Sir Stefan Rennert has slept, yes?"

The Solamnic indeed felt near to exhaustion, but it was not entirely natural. At Golgren's earlier bidding, Idaria had put a sleeping herb in the human's food. Stefan would slumber peacefully for hours, giving the grand lord ample time to set in motion his scheme to win over the man.

Golgren himself helped the Solamnic in walking, but when Idaria also came to assist—as was her duty—the ogre bared his teeth. Startled, the slave retreated. The grand lord led the sleepy human out of the chamber and toward the large rooms once inhabited by Zharang's favored concubines.

Idaria followed at a safe distance, her eyes on her master's back. Had he trusted her less, Golgren would have been granting the elf slave an easy target. He knew that she would not strike him down for any reason, though. She dared not, and not merely for her own sake. If Golgren perished, whoever succeeded him would revenge his death on her enslaved brethren.

"Idaria," Golgren abruptly hissed.

The elf scurried forward. Her chains, as much a part of her now as a second skin, made as little noise as she did.

She shoved the ancient wooden door open for her "master" and his burden, revealing a room filled with red, yellow, and green tapestries and a massive pile of colorful pillows. Although once they had been breathtaking, the dark, dull crimson stains spotting many of the tapestries and pillows remained as sober reminders as to their recent history. Idaria passed tapestries with symbols marking elf families that she had formerly known, some of them related to her by blood. Once, the mere sight of those precious relics of the glorious elf past would have nearly caused her to break down in tears but no more.

"I'm very . . . grateful . . . my lord," Stefan mumbled as he lurched along. "The journey . . . was a long one."

"Yes, very long, I have made it on foot also," the grand lord replied evenly as he lowered the human onto pillows.

Idaria waited patiently as the ogre assisted Stefan. Golgren did everything himself with the same care that any of the knight's comrades would have taken with him. Only when her master called for water did she hasten to oblige, bringing a goblet and a dented metal decanter to the nearly unconscious human.

The human stared up at her, his round eyes so young and innocent compared to her own. Both ogres and humans lived scant moments in time compared to the long-lived elves, but whenever Idaria looked into Golgren's eyes, by comparison, she saw an old, wily intelligence beyond the ogre's actual age. In Stefan's case, the vibrancy of youth was still fresh and appealing.

The slave poured him a drink. He fumbled with the cup, so much so that, despite Golgren's evident displeasure, the elf held Stefan's hand as she guided the goblet to his lips.

After he had taken a sip, the knight managed a courteous nod. "My lady." Almost as an afterthought, he looked again at his host. "My lord." Then he drifted off.

Immediately, Golgren straightened. Idaria, all too familiar with the ogre's body language, quickly but smoothly retreated to the ledge from which she had taken the cup and decanter.

The grand lord peered at her for a moment then asked, "You will tend to him, yes?"

Surprised, Idaria managed a nod.

Golgren scowled at the sleeping figure. "Be there when he wakes. Let his eyes first cast upon you."

"Yes, my master."

The ogre leader surveyed the chamber. Walls built from stone blocks larger than his own body hid behind the tapestries. Should the knight think to seek escape, he would discover that his room also passed as an excellent cell. The only ways out were through the door—which would be guarded for the human's *safety*—and the small, arched window at the opposite end.

Even unarmored, the human could just barely fit through that window, and his descent would be ill advised. Below the window was a drop of several stories and, assuming he survived that long fall, Sir Stefan would land in a pen where the palace's meredrakes were let loose for exercise.

Golgren did not want his "guest" departing before the grand lord had the opportunity to cement his proposed alliance.

"You will wait by his side, my Idaria," Golgren murmured as he started to the doorway. As he passed her, however, the ogre paused to meet her gaze with his own. "As you ever wait by mine."

He looked ready to say more but then stalked out. Idaria froze briefly, wondering if she should follow him for some reason. Then Stefan mumbled in his sleep, and the elf recalled her orders.

However, it was not to the knight's side that she went immediately, but rather to the window. Peering out as best she could, she saw that there were no guards to be seen on the grounds below. The elf leaned forward and, pursing her lips, whistled quietly.

What emerged from her lips was no sound that humans, dwarves, or—certainly—ogres could re-create. It was as if an actual bird had vocalized. Only an elf was capable of such sounds that could fool even the wisest avian creature into coming to her.

But the bird she sought knew her and would come because she had called it. It was one of the many messengers she utilized to contact the others, and of all times, Idaria needed to contact her comrades quickly after learning what she had. They would not like talk of alliances, however far-fetched it might seem to them.

They would need to know about the events, and they would advise her what to do.

As she waited for the bird to come, the elf slave looked over her shoulder at the Solamnic. He had witnessed terrible things, including the savage deaths of those close to him, something with which she could identify. He was a captive of Golgren, and it remained to be seen for him how much suffering was in store. She, too, had witnessed the deaths of friends and family; she, too, suffered as a captive slave.

Yes, Idaria Oakborn could well sympathize with the Knight of Solamnia, but that did not mean she would not kill him without regret if it proved necessary for the sake of her own goals.

❦

Golgren knew exactly who Stefan Rennert was, and he richly savored the irony of that particular knight's having been handed over to the grand lord. Indeed, Golgren mused that many things in his life seemed predestined, and perhaps the Solamnic had been sent there deliberately as some kind of spy.

But Solamnics did not sacrifice their fellows in such a clever manner, so Golgren felt fairly certain that things had merely gone awry for the human. Fate, it appeared, was simply on the grand lord's side again, silently aiding his plans.

Reaching the throne room, Golgren summoned Khleeg. The ever-resourceful Blödian returned scant minutes later, by which time Golgren had thought it over and knew better what he wanted of him.

When he gave his orders to the other ogre, Khleeg

looked at him in dismay. "Grand Lord, not a wise thing!"

"But you will obey!"

The officer banged his fist on his breastplate. "Aye."

"Then see it is done."

Looking not at all pleased, the Blödian rushed off again.

Golgren nodded to himself then departed for his private quarters. The guards saluted him then shut the doors behind him after he passed through, relaxing slightly out of his view.

Alone, the grand lord surveyed the lush chamber, elven in its design, ogrish in its decadence. He strode to a side wall and shoved aside one of the elegant but weathered tapestries with his maimed limb. Then, with his hand, he pressed the blank wall at a point that was generally level with his broad chest.

An area roughly a foot square shimmered red and slid forward.

Golgren had divined the secret of the hidden drawer from his studies of the High Ogres. It had taken him very little time to discover the one in the grand khan's very chamber. Certainly, neither Zharang nor his immediate predecessors had ever suspected the existence of the magical drawer, for inside the compartment Golgren had found a crumbling parchment in the written language of his ancestors. Regrettably, the parchment had turned to dust when he touched it, but the drawer had remained useful for storing a few other precious items.

From within, Golgren removed a single object: a small, almost delicate, dagger. Its intricate craftsmanship hinted of ancient derivation, and he had found it far from that place as an exhausted, bleeding youth, still carrying his mother's drying corpse over his shoulder. Golgren had been on his last legs then, desperately trying to throw off two ji-baraki that were following his scent. Yet that had not worried him so much as what they would do to the body of his beloved mother, which he had struggled so hard to save and carry away.

The crevasse through which he had slipped into the hill cave had truly been little more than a slight tear barely wide enough to allow him inside and, he hoped, would keep the huge lizards outside. Inside it was blissfully cool. He had set down his mother's body then paused to take stock of his surroundings.

That was when the gleam had caught his eye, the gleam of orange-red stone. Instantly mesmerized, Golgren—he was still Guyvir then—had been drawn closer to that gleam.

There he had happened upon the crumbling temple. The stone had been part of a shattered relief, the eye of one of two fighting mastarks. The rest of the imagery was no longer visible, erosion having done its job in ruining the art.

Even the most backwater village knew the tales of the great High Ogres, although most of those tales grew distorted with time. Thinking of those tales of the High Ogres' supposed miracles, Golgren had scavenged through the cracked stone walls and small alcoves, hoping to find something precious, something magical with which to restore his mother to him.

But there had been nothing. There were ruins only. Defeated, the youth had slumped back against one cracked wall and nearly died when he broke through its weakened structure, falling. Golgren had dropped

RICHARD A. KNAAK

down several feet and landed upon what could best be described as junk and refuse.

However, he also found trickling water. From a crack in the rock, a few drops at a time were slipping down to the ground, where the water seeped into the soil. There was evidence that the forgotten priests of yore had crafted some fine watering system, but to the young ogre's mind, all that mattered was he could drink his fill. That in itself was a miracle.

Climbing out was another, more troublesome matter, and at first he wondered if he would die there, where he had fallen, sated with water. Indeed, on his first attempt to climb back up, Golgren had made it only halfway before falling back onto the stone and garbage. At that point, his hand had closed around that very dagger; why it had been discarded, he couldn't fathom.

Oddly, once armed, his confidence rose enough that on his next try, Golgren made it back up and into the cave. Feeling proud, he returned to where he had left his mother's body . . .

Only to discover a male ji-baraki was busy ripping apart the still-tender torso.

Golgren screamed, a sound that echoed in the small, natural chamber, making it seem as though a hundred warriors had surrounded the reptile. Mouth stained, the ji-baraki spun around, confused and alarmed.

Not caring what happened to himself, Golgren had leaped upon the beast. He felt its talons slash at his arms, but all he cared about was avenging his mother's ravaging. He had intended to punish her true killers, but the ji-baraki became their surrogate. Golgren slashed again and again and again, not even stopping when he and the beast lay on the ground, the latter dead.

Scarred, bleeding freshly, the young half-breed finally halted. He stood and kicked aside the reptile and went over to the elf remains. Even his mother's face had not been left unmarred, but Golgren nonetheless clutched the ruined body tight.

Then, growing cold of mind, he carried her to what had once been a platform below the fighting mastarks. Golgren arranged her corpse then returned to the dead beast. With deliberate ferocity, he cut deep into the ji-baraki and removed a hunk of its flesh. Then, seating himself, the ogre devoured his fill. As she had always done, his mother had provided him with a meal.

He covered her with stones from around the temple's centerpiece, guaranteeing that no scavenger would have an easy time with what remained. Golgren had removed what other meat he could from the ji-baraki before he dropped it down to where the ancient refuse lay in a scattered pile. Finally, clutching his dagger, the youth leaned against the inner wall and dared to sleep.

Four days later, he reached the village of his father's cousin.

As the memories faded, Golgren turned the dagger over and inspected it in his room. It had become stained with the blood of many enemies over the years, but since he had taken his present name, it had waited for only one more use. With the Solamnic's arrival, that use seemed almost imminent.

"Do not sleep deep, my little one," the grand lord murmured. "Your time is coming."

He touched the drawer, which slid away, vanishing into the wall again. Then, with a humorless grin, he secreted the dagger within his garments where the lone hand could easily reach it.

His thoughts drifted back to that crevasse long ago. Golgren's eyes narrowed. "No, do not sleep deep."

∞∞⬥∞∞

Ji-baraki were determined feeders, seeking morsels long past when other predators or scavengers gave up. They had an acute sense of smell that few beasts in all of Krynn could match.

Some of those that had attacked the knights still foraged among the vast array of bones at the battle site, on occasion finding something worth squabbling over. A few tiny lizards and insects that had made temporary homes among the carnage fled as the larger, more predatory ji-baraki neared their locations.

Then something in the moonless night sky caused the ferocious reptiles to look up. Several of the ji-baraki hissed. One of the smaller ones suddenly turned and fled from the scene. That caused a mass exodus by the rest. The ji-baraki kicked up bones and dust as they rushed away, and one even accidentally uncovered a choice bit of bone and gristle, but the morsel was ignored, so frantic were the reptiles to abandon the scene.

And as the last of the ji-baraki vanished from the battle site, countless winged forms descended among the dead. Landing, they took up positions all around the area, waiting.

A flicker of silver light materialized in their center . . .

XI

THE FESTIVAL OF THE GRIFFON

Safrag smelled Morgada's presence long before the Titaness materialized. Dauroth's apprentice tightly rolled together the scroll through which he had been searching. Morgada had a scent that both enticed and disturbed, for it always carried blood, fresh blood. None of the males bore such a scent.

"Dear Safrag," she sang. "Is there something that you do not wish me to see?"

"The secrets of the master are not for you, Morgada," he returned coolly.

"Perhaps not now . . . " the raven-haired temptress cooed.

Her words were fair warning. She should have never existed, but Dauroth had not only forgiven that error, but showed some fascination in the possibilities presented by her existence. Whether or not those possibilities held any interest to Morgada was another question, but she used the potential of them to keep herself in the master's excellent favor.

Safrag sat in one of Dauroth's private libraries, a round chamber whose walls were lined with silver bookshelves set into the stone. There was no artistic reason for the ornate shelves; the fact that they were silver had more to do with their ability to keep the inherent magic within many of the scrolls and tomes sealed inside. Magic, no matter what its origins, had a tendency to leak out and cause havoc. As it was, the library was already saturated with ancient power, and thus, even admittance to the library was reserved for those who had proven their ability to walk carefully without disturbing the shelves.

Morgada had never been seen at the library as far as Safrag knew.

"You have permission to be here?" he asked, rising from the wide, rectangular table—also silver, due to the same concerns. Silver, in fact, lined the walls themselves.

Silver was also the color of the light currently illuminating the chamber too, although that was by Safrag's choice. The glowing sphere always hung two feet above his head and thus, as he stood, it rose higher to keep the same distance.

"Do I need permission? I am so sorry, Safrag. I wasn't aware that I did."

A lie but one it would do no good for the apprentice to report. Dauroth was curious about the level of the Titaness's magical skills and would probably encourage her presence there if the matter were brought to him; that was not what Safrag desired.

He replaced the scroll on the shelf then turned back to Morgada. "I am leaving. You will, therefore, leave too . . . unless there is something else you wish here?"

Her eyes studied the contents of the shelves with clear interest—no, Safrag thought, avarice. "There is so much here I wish, dear Safrag, so very much." She strode closer. "Is there anything you might suggest of special interest to me?"

His eyes met hers. "One thing, perhaps," he murmured, suddenly guiding her along with him. "You have only heard of it, but I think Dauroth would want you to know more about it now."

Her voice grew throaty with excitement. "What is it? What?"

The apprentice led her to one particular shelf. Safrag passed one hand over a single red stone inlaid in the center of the middle shelf.

The gem flared and the entire shelf rippled as if suddenly turned to water.

"Falstoch," whispered Safrag. "Come out, Falstoch. In Dauroth's name, I so command you."

And from within the liquefying shelf there arose a deep, monstrous moan, as if something in the throes of horrible agony had just been stirred to life. For once, Morgada balked, losing some of her confidence, noticeable to Safrag by the way she pressed back against his arm, an arm supposedly protective but also keeping the Titaness from retreating any farther.

"Coooommmmmmeeee . . . " a voice managed to croak, sounding as though it came from someone drowning in mud. The sound was made worse by the fact that the word was spoken in the Titan tongue, albeit in such a crude manner that both spellcasters flinched. A stench like that of rotting flesh permeated the chamber. Morgada covered her nose, but Safrag merely steeled himself.

A sloshing sound touched their ears. It grew louder, closer, seeming to presage something huge and terrible.

"Safrag . . . this is Falstoch approaching?" asked Morgada. "From where?"

"From a place created by the master, to house each of the Abominations." Safrag said no more, waiting for the one he had invited to show himself, to make himself known.

Through the rippling, a murky outline began to emerge. At times, the shape appeared to have some form akin to an ogre or Titan, but it constantly seemed to melt and reconfigure differently.

Then . . . then through the bookcase thrust a hand or rather, a mockery of one. Five fingers—more than could be counted on either one of Donnag's hands—grasped for anything within reach. They were thick, and the skin bubbled. The flesh dripped on the floor, where it sizzled. Two of the fingers shrank into the hand, just as two others sprouted elsewhere.

Safrag was reminded of a thing made out of hot wax. It was the best description he could come up with in his own mind. Yet he knew it was too simple a comparison and much too kind a one.

"Ssssaaafffrrraaaggg . . . Daaauurrrroth fffff -forgivessss?"

"You should know better than that, Falstoch."

The thing let loose with another baleful moan. Morgada gasped as the hulking shadow—still going through a constant and unsettling metamorphosis— prepared to emerge into the light. The prospect proved to be too much for the apprentice's companion.

"Send it back, Safrag! Send it back! I don't wish to see the rest!"

Stretching his hand forth, Safrag sang the words of dismissal. Immediately, the bookcase began to solidify again. The dripping, gray-white appendage pulled back at the last moment, just before the shelves completely solidified.

Morgada couldn't stop shivering. Releasing her from his grasp, Safrag stepped closer to the shelves and adjusted a pair of tomes that had tipped over during the transformation.

"Is there anything else you wish to see?" he asked placidly. When there came no reply, Safrag turned. He expected to find the Titaness gone, but Morgada still stood there. Her skin, however, had turned a paler shade of blue.

"It *is* worse than Donnag," she breathed. "Though I saw but little, it is far more terrible! How did it happen? What went awry?"

"What went awry?" The apprentice was honestly puzzled for a moment by her question; then understanding dawned. "Ah! Nothing went awry, Morgada, as you should have been informed! These creatures are just as Dauroth *condemned* them! This is his punishment for those Titans who seek to betray his dreams . . . and him."

The other Titan shook her head in horror and disbelief, perhaps reflecting on some of her own past actions, not to mention future plans. She stepped farther away from the shelves, and her retreat continued until she stood safely at the entrance.

Then, still speechless, Morgada fled down the halls.

Safrag narrowly eyed the doorway then glanced back at the wall area from where he had summoned Falstoch. The apprentice rubbed his chin thoughtfully and quickly departed.

Although Golgren was master of his people, he still had not been technically designated as their grand khan. He could have simply declared that he had taken the title, but he was well aware that his enemies would whisper against him; the deficiencies of his appearance, the suggestion of half-breeding, would always haunt him. Thus Golgren looked to ogre rituals and tradition to strengthen the bond between himself and his people.

Already he was planning a coronation ritual to coincide with the changing of the season from summer to fall. Ogres traditionally gave thanks for fall, when the heat abated—somewhat, anyway—and life became a little more tolerable.

But the changing of the season was still a month away, and Golgren had to cement his authority in the meantime. Fortunately, another important tradition that presaged the changing of summer to fall was the annual Festival of the Griffon.

Ogres believed in the power of their totems, and for Garantha there was no more powerful spirit than their patron animal. The Festival of the Griffon ran for three days, during which time warriors vied for honors representing the griffon spirit's attributes: ferocity, might, and endurance. Victors were acclaimed, and the toll of blood was often higher during the festival than any other time. Such was the proper manner by which to celebrate the great griffon; for many centuries, before the downfall of Silvanost, the pampered elf royalty had also honored the griffon, but with a festival of flowers and offerings of fruit. Ogres sneered at such genteel foolishness.

The ruling khan traditionally presided over the

Festival of the Griffon, and all would see Golgren in that role.

The conclusion to the festival was the offering of sacrifice at the *Garan i Seraith*—the Nest of the Griffon. The temple, an oval structure with a barred roof in its center, sat near the palace, so the spirit's favor would not be far from the grand khan. That the spirit's favor had not saved his predecessor was a moot point; even Golgren respected the code of the spirit, and, more important, his subjects' faith in it.

The upcoming festival would serve another useful purpose: to further impress Sir Stefan Rennert with the power wielded by Golgren and the many changes his rule was destined to bring to a people other races considered uncivilized beasts.

For the competitions, which took place in the Jaka Hwunar, the Solamnic was given a seat of honor next to the grand lord, a vantage from which he could view every aspect of the games. Khleeg, Wargroch, and other trusted warriors were keeping guard around the immediate area, as much to protect the human from any overzealous ogres as to keep him from trying to slip away. To lessen any sense of confinement that Stefan must be feeling, Idaria stood attentively near his side while another slave, a dour male elf, temporarily served the grand lord.

The banner of the severed hand fluttered everywhere, but for the occasion was accompanied by a white banner with the black silhouette of the patron beast. It was the last of the three-day event, so all competitions involved the champions of previous days. Golgren was watching the Solamnic's reactions as much as he watched the games, surreptitiously noting what Stefan did or did not approve of.

"You have such public festivals in Solamnia?" Golgren asked, gesturing for Idaria to fill the human's goblet.

"We have events honoring various patrons and our special gods, yes."

"Perhaps, I someday see them."

Stefan cautiously nodded. Save for his helmet, which rested in his lap, he was clad in his armor. Even his sword hung at his side, a suggestion made by Golgren that had surprised not only the human, but Khleeg and the others.

"A guest trusts his host and is trusted by his host," the grand lord had stated.

The Solamnic remained unconvinced of the merits of any kind of alliance with Golgren and the ogre race, but at the very least the ogre's flattery and courting had him off guard. Indeed, Stefan did not know exactly what to think about Golgren, which was just as the grand lord preferred from all under his sway.

An appreciative grunt escaped another ogre seated just one level down from Stefan. Atolgus, rewarded with a special place at the events for his part in bringing the knight to Garantha, was smiling up at them, almost like a child. His genuinely optimistic loyalty to Golgren had already caused the grand lord to consider what future use the young chieftain might serve.

In the arena, two unarmed ogres were facing off against each other. The left hand of one was bound to the left of the other, so their arms crossed. With their free hands, the combatants sought to bring down each other. Their struggles were brutal and, despite lacking weapons, both were bloodied.

A grim cast spread over Stefan's face, and Golgren noticed his discomfiture. The more bloody the fighting, the more unsettled the knight became. Golgren brooded on that curious fact, recalling those Solamnics he had encountered in the past. They had something of the elf race in them—their politeness and stuffy manners. He did not want the festival to offend the knight.

Matters were not improved when, at the end of the match, the victor—a hirsute giant with tusks nearly reaching his eyes—smashed his adversary's face into the ground with such force that the spray of blood flew all over the field, flecking the spectators too, then repeated the process twice more before a horn sounded, ordering him to cease and accept his prize.

Before Golgren could comment on the unseemly outcome, another spoke up, diplomatically explaining things to the knight.

"The grand lord struggles against centuries," Idaria murmured to Stefan, handing him a full cup of the finest elven wine in Golgren's possession. "Before his coming, the festival was awash in blood such as makes this pale. He is bringing civilization back to his people, but it cannot change at once. Change is sometimes fast, but great change can be slow."

The Solamnic glanced from the elf slave to Golgren. "Yes, I've noticed your chains, always inhibiting your movements. They must be part of the slow changes you mention."

Golgren grinned, the nubs of his tusks in evidence. "To have a knight walk around free is one thing; to have an elf do so is another. I am no god, Sir Stefan Rennert. All things must come slow, but Idaria understands this, of course."

"My chains are exceedingly light," added the elf, turning away without meeting the knight's eyes. She busied herself with replacing the wine flask, returning it to a silver tray near the human.

The Solamnic eyed her thoughtfully then returned his attention to the arena, where the winner had departed in triumph and the loser had been dragged off unceremoniously and left for dead. Once the area was cleared, the two huge wooden doorways at the opposing ends of the Jaka Hwunar swung open. Barking echoed through the arena, but it did not originate from raucous members of the audience. A long-necked beast peered out from one side of the double doorway.

For the first time in more than an hour, the human seemed pleased, his eyes alight with curiosity. Stefan leaned forward to see the beasts better. "I've seen those. What are they?"

"Amaloks," the grand lord offered, fully aware that the knight had not forgotten the name. Stefan Rennert played his own game. Golgren hid his pleasure at sensing the knight's tactics. "Amaloks."

But the four creatures being herded with strenuous effort by half a dozen handlers toward the center of the arena were not typical of the variety seen in most pens around the capital. These amaloks—all males—were giants of their species, their lupine and equine heads looming a foot taller than their handlers. Their lofty horns added to their height. The specimens were also more thickly muscled, with shoulders powerful and broad. They had been bred for that very moment.

The ogres managed to prod and herd three into the center, but the fourth—a male with an eye socket gouged out from some long-ago mishap—was proving a rebellious demon. The amalok snarled and snapped at its handlers, catching one with a bite on the arm. Despite any outward resemblance to a horse, the amalok had sharp, wide teeth that curved inward slightly; the result was that the handler suffered a deep gash.

The fresh scent of blood stirred the other beasts. Surrendering to the fact that the largest male would not cooperate, the handlers released it, and also the others. The hardy ogres raced from the vicinity as quickly as they could.

And not a moment too soon, for the male amaloks—already aroused by the presence of each other and the thousands of ogres pressed together—began to paw at the ground with their sharp hooves while whirling about viciously. Two dropped their heads and briefly sparred with their spearlike horns.

The clatter of that first clash among the beasts echoed throughout the Jaka Hwunar, and the gathered throng was sent into a barking frenzy. Stefan surveyed the onlookers and asked, "Are they imitating the amaloks? They sound similar."

"We honor them, yes, because of their prowess. The amaloks are swifter than the ji-baraki, who respect their horns that are so sharp and deadly. The amaloks, too, they thrive where no other beast can, in places with no water and little shrub."

"How's that possible?"

Golgren shrugged, the answer obvious to all ogres. "They are amaloks." He grinned teasingly. "Not nice animals."

One of the smaller males dared lower its head toward the largest, barking at the other. The second amalok pawed the ground, scraping a small ditch, and answered with a savage bark.

Both males dived into each other, dueling almost like

skilled swordsmen with their horns. Their crash caused several ogres to leap to their feet and brought Stefan to his as well. He'd hesitate to admit it, but the beasts' fight was thrilling.

One of the two remaining males joined the fray, siding with the smaller animal by lunging at the larger amalok from off to the side. However, its would-be target managed to dodge away out of reach just in time before turning and slashing at both foes.

As the three mixed it up, the fourth seemed content to watch from the sidelines. The knight, already on the edge of his seat, asked, "Do they fight in a natural-born fashion, or are these trained?"

"The males, they are solitary. They fight when together . . . for food and mates. Like all males, yes?"

The human's eyes darted toward Idaria, who was deliberately busying herself with some minor task, avoiding his glance. Then his attention returned to the fighting beasts. Golgren saw all.

"Those horns! They look as strong as steel!"

Golgren nodded, but his interest in the struggle had momentarily faded. He studied the elf; then his gaze shifted to the human. Something bothered him. His hand went to his chest, cupping the hidden objects hanging from his neck.

"Look there!" cried the Solamnic, leaping up. At the same time, the throng roared, many in the crowd also jumped up, barking louder than ever. The largest male was out-dueling both smaller ones. Its head twisted right, then left, then right again as it countered their horns. It even slipped under the defense of one, jabbing the amalok harshly in the shoulder.

The injured animal rose onto its hind legs and kicked

out powerfully. The sharp edges of its hooves tore pieces of fur from the huge male's chest. The second attacker thrust.

The larger beast could not defend itself. One horn slashed across its chest. The huge amalok barked defiantly but backed off.

Suddenly, at that point, the fourth creature, previously uninvolved, leaped forward, charging the biggest amalok's open flank. Its horns pierced deeply before its target could react.

Once again, the knight could not but enjoy the fight and maneuvering. He glanced over at Golgren, astonishment filling his expression. "They've joined forces! They're using strategy!"

Indeed, the fourth amalok's effort put the dominant animal on the desperate defensive. Blood dribbled on the ground as the beast warily adjusted its stance to face three instead of two enemies. The last wound was a telling one. The lone amalok's short, whiplike tail swung back and forth as if on fire.

The middle of its three adversaries refused to allow a lull in the struggle. The eager male bore down on the injured one.

But the large male caught the other's horns on its own, forcing the attacker's head nearly to the ground. A heavy hoof came down. The ends of the tough horns cracked like dried twigs.

The smaller amalok barked furiously. The large beast dipped its head and ran its horns through the other's long neck, so far that they briefly jutted out of the other side.

Yet as the one creature fell limp, its two companions renewed their attack from both sides, charging the big amalok. One set of horns was deflected, but the other bore deep in the dominant male's rib cage.

A pained moan escaped the animal. He teetered to one side. The amalok who had struck true pulled free, its horns coming out with a horrific, moist sound that echoed around the arena.

Sensing another imminent death, the ogres battered their clubs against the stones of the arena. They barked loudly, sounding at that moment almost like legions of furious amaloks.

The badly wounded male made two sharp, defensive swings at its adversaries, but the pair easily kept out of reach. The large amalok staggered, its forelegs finally folding at the knees.

The two smaller beasts moved in for the kill. The one that had inflicted the mortal blow feinted, drawing the larger male's attention.

The other, its head low, impaled their stubborn foe in the chest. Blood poured over the besieged amalok's long horns.

It was over quickly after that. The impaled amalok slumped to one side, panting. The remaining beasts lunged to bite at its body, in the process colliding with and snapping at one another.

Finally, the large amalok stilled. The pair sniffed the corpse then, with a snort, one took up a defensive posture. The other reacted by turning away. A moment later, the second one trotted to a spot some distance from the place of the struggle.

The lone amalok still near the corpses let loose with a series of harsh barks. It pawed the ground and twisted its head almost completely around to survey its audience.

Stefan sat back in his chair, exhaling. "Is he the winner?"

"Yes, the other has chosen to delay their fight, but fight they will another day."

"But for a while they worked together as allies . . . "

The grand lord beamed as though a lesson had been learned. "With amaloks and many creatures, the ally of before can be the enemy of later, and the enemy of before might, therefore, become an ally, yes?"

"It . . . has happened . . . " Stefan admitted. He leaned forward again to better survey the scene. The ogre handlers were just then daring to approach the restless surviving creatures. "I've never seen such an animal fight! Do you ride them also?"

"Those who try are likely to die."

The Solamnic's expression did not change, but Golgren knew that the human had briefly considered that his escape might be aided by an amalok. What the ogre said was true; an amalok would have a tendency to either bite, kill, or spear anyone thinking to turn it into a horse, but it *had* been done once. That risky accomplishment had been the only thing that had kept Golgren alive once, long ago, when the black knights had turned his trap into one of their own. They had slain half his warriors that day, the worst defeat that he had suffered after taking the place of his father's cousin as chieftain of the village.

And shortly after that, he had met the wizard, Tyranos.

Thinking of the mage, Golgren looked around the arena, but there was no evidence of the attendance of the mysterious wizard. Yet the grand lord's hand suddenly gripped his armrest tautly.

No, Tyranos was nowhere to be seen, which did not necessarily preclude his presence, but something else caught his attention, something that stared back almost mockingly at Golgren from the very top wall of the Jaka Hwunar. It met his gaze for a moment before fluttering off without anyone else seeming to notice it.

Another gargoyle . . .

❦

Dipping his finger in the silver bowl, Dauroth bent down to draw the symbols. The dark, thick liquid with which the Titan created the spellwork flared bright red and settled into a deep black.

The rest of the Black Talon—absent Hundjal—sang the words of power that would keep their spell going. They had no intention of faltering, for that would require another hour's spellcasting and they might miss the propitious moment.

"It is strengthened again," Dauroth sang. "We may continue."

He repositioned himself in the circle that the giant spellcasters had formed, a circle surrounding a vast rip in the air. Within that rip, the Talon surveyed the Jaka Hwunar and its activities, each of its members experiencing the same viewpoint no matter to which side of the tear they stood.

Unlike the crowds or even those nearest Golgren, the Titans did not miss the momentary glimpse of the winged creature.

"That is not the same vermin seen a few days prior," sang one of the Titans. "This is larger and more arrogant."

"Certainly less cunning," replied another, "to come out in the open so conspicuously."

"Less cunning?" questioned Dauroth. "Nay, much,

much more, I think." The senior Titan drew a five-sided symbol in the air, and the image of the gargoyle's departure was replayed. The Talon watched as the beast dwindled in the sky then winked out of existence. It had not simply flown so far away as to be no longer visible. It had vanished by what was surely magic. "Someone plays games with the grand lord."

"Then of what interest is this to us?" sang the first Titan. "Unless the vermin so disrupts the mongrel's plans as to allow us to finally be rid of his insipid presence!"

Dauroth stared down his nose at the speaker. "It is of interest, Kallel, because we do not know who it is the gargoyle serves. It is of interest to us because I have interest in the grand lord. It is too early for us to usurp him; we tried that once and failed. We overextended our resources. The result was that he was strengthened. Now we need him to remain in place for a time, drawing together the necessary elements for our future success." He bared his teeth. "I trust I do not need to repeat myself over and over again in this regard!"

Chastened, Kallel bowed to Dauroth's wisdom.

"Safrag, we will speak of this situation in private," the lead Titan announced. After his second apprentice nodded, Dauroth looked to the rest of the Talon. "I will change the image. We have more important matters to review than the festival."

The Talon collectively shifted its singing. Dauroth used the dark liquid to draw a second vision before the rip.

Like a blinking eye turned sideways, the gap shut and opened wide again. The scene within revealed a different land, a place of chilling, ice-topped peaks and turbulent skies. Dauroth gestured, and the scene refocused upon a small cavelike opening in one of the mountains, an opening marked by much-weathered symbols of a language recognizable to any Titan.

"I have found one," Dauroth stated without obvious emotion. "I have found a burial chamber of the High Ogres."

Among the rest of the Talon, there radiated excitement, but no one yet spoke, out of deference to their master.

"Yes," replied their leader to the silent question. At last a hint of similar excitement illuminated his golden eyes. "The seal has not been breached. The chamber should be intact."

"Intact!" breathed another Titan.

"The sacred works said to be buried with the dead," murmured Kallel. "The scrolls and the signets . . . " He grinned almost lasciviously. "The signets . . . "

Among the Black Talon, that last remark struck home. The signets of the High Ogres were vital to the secrets of their vast power, power that even the Titans did not possess yet.

Power, they hoped, with which they might be able to achieve, in one fell swoop, their ideals and grandiose plans.

Twenty years Dauroth had searched for even a fragment of the legendary signets, all to no avail. He had begun to doubt, wondering why the ancestral spirit had left him knowledge of the signets if they were to be forever lost beyond his grasp. The High Ogres had appeared to have taken those particular secrets with them to the very grave.

But he had discovered one of those graves.

"There is hope, yes, that we have located some of the signets, and, if so, then the gods and our ancestors truly bless our great task," the lead Titan intoned solemnly. "Our perseverance will have been rewarded a thousand times over."

"Far more than that!" insisted Kallel.

"Far more than that, yes, *if* there are signets within." Dauroth immediately silenced the protests rising at his caveat. "And if there are no signets, we must be grateful for an even more significant treasure that surely lies within, one that may make the holy signets pale by comparison." He gestured at the mouth of the remote tomb. "At last, my brethren, we have the *bones*."

XII

THE NEST

Stefan peered out of the tiny window in his room. It was obviously too dangerous for him to climb through and down. He did not want to escape anymore anyway, at least not yet. The information he had gathered thus far was invaluable, and the grand lord's vague suggestion of alliance had the knight intrigued.

There was another factor explaining his reluctance to try to escape, and her name was Idaria. Stefan had never personally known an elf, and, in fact, had seen only a couple from a distance. Those had been males, seeking assistance from knightly councils—fairly unsuccessfully— for their dispossessed people. In fact, the various factions sprouting up among the long-lived race seemed to have spread throughout Ansalon, with many refugees seeking aid from nearly every bastion of power.

Stefan stepped back from the window. He remained armored out of habit more than necessity. The knight tested one of the joints of his armor, which squeaked, then searched among the leftover food on the small table by his bed. In the absence of oil, many other things could be used to lubricate his armor.

"Do I disturb you?"

Stefan turned to the doorway, visibly fighting to keep from showing that she had startled him with her sudden appearance. For someone chained both hand and feet, Idaria moved like a ghost, rattling her links only when she cared to, it seemed.

"No. What is it?"

"The festival which honors Garantha's patron beast ends shortly at the ancient temple. The grand lord hopes that you will wish to attend and observe the closing ceremony."

"I would. I am bored in my room." The knight seized his helmet and sword, which lay on his bed, then followed her out.

As with so much of the palace, the walls were lined with worn and obviously ancient reliefs of beings that Idaria explained to Stefan were depictions of the builders of the capital. Their quality and detail amazed him. Shown in positions of repose, of study, and of creative endeavor, the figures hinted at a society once richer in beauty and culture than he possibly could have imagined. He had to look quickly and closely, for the reliefs were shadowed by dim light cast by the insufficient windows and torches illuminating the corridors.

"Such a tremendous contrast these ancient figures are to our present captors," Stefan commented, his gaze shifting from one to the next. The guards they passed indeed seemed the opposite, for they were ugly monsters who eyed the Solamnic with malice. However, none dared give in to their baser instincts and harm him. Every one of the armored behemoths clearly feared and respected their master, Stefan knew, ironically, as he was slighter and surely weaker than the least of them.

As they passed another guard, Stefan finally asked a question burning in his mind. "My Lady Idaria, how is it you can so calmly walk the halls of your enslaver? And why do you not have any attending guards when you are alone on this errand?"

"The Grand Lord Golgren is your host, Sir Stefan," she calmly reproached him. "Everything is according to his dictate." Her blue, crystalline eyes remained on the hall ahead.

"My host and my jailer . . . and yours too." His expression grew grim. "He is the lord of a people who've slaughtered hundreds of your kind and keeps hundreds more in chains." He seized the chains between her wrists. "Although you wear yours almost as if they were bracelets of gold from your paramour—"

He stopped dead in his tracks as Idaria whirled on him. Her eyes betrayed a deep disdain for Stefan. "Perceptions are always colored by beliefs, and there are worse evils that could and have befallen the Silvanesti than the grand lord."

Idaria strode on brusquely. Stefan started after her and nearly collided with her as the elf halted suddenly again.

Her eyes widening, Idaria quickly stepped to the side. The human, taking his cue from her, just as quickly followed suit.

At first there seemed no reason for her apprehension, but then a shadow swept across the floor ahead of them, where the corridor intersected another. The shadow grew to incredible length before at last a gigantic form hove into sight.

It was all the Solamnic could do to restrain himself from uttering an oath of exclamation. A blue-skinned figure, who made the towering guards seem dwarves by comparison, appeared, gliding down the hall in the very direction the elf slave had been leading him. Although Stefan was a fairly tall man, the gowned behemoth stood more than twice his height. Even with the palace's high ceilings, there was scarcely any space between it and the top of the strange being's head. The momentary glimpse he had of the immense figure's features left an impression of perfection marred by something dark festering inside. The giant was clad in elegant garments that made the grand lord's appear shabby.

The enormous figure vanished down the corridor, but Idaria remained where she was, breathing fearfully, for more than a minute after he was gone. Finally, the elf, her expression composed again, resumed walking ahead without a word to Stefan.

"Who—what was *that?*" the knight felt compelled to ask.

"It is one of the Titans," she answered reluctantly, gaze ahead.

" 'Titans'? I've heard the name, I think, yes, but . . . I've never seen such a creature! What's it doing here? What is it exactly?"

A sigh of exasperation escaped Idaria. She turned on the human, her eyes blazing again. "You recall but a moment ago, Sir Stefan Rennert, when I said that there are worse evils that could and have befallen the Silvanesti than that of your host?"

"Yes."

"Pray to your patron gods, then, that this is the closest you will ever come to the company of any of the Titans, and then pray to those gods for the well-being of my lord Golgren, the only one who stands between them and rule of the ogres, the only one, I dare say, of whom the Titans themselves are afraid."

And with that uncharacteristically lengthy speech, the elf slave started off again. Stefan hesitated, still reeling from the vision of the giant, then hurried to catch up.

∞∞✞∞∞

Golgren had ordered the Titans to stay away from the Festival of the Griffon despite its significance to the populace. He had informed Dauroth of his wishes, and the lead Titan, through his lowly apprentice Safrag, had acquiesced.

Thus, Golgren was surprised and displeased when, before the final ceremony, Safrag came bowing and scraping through the halls of the palace to relay a message from his master.

"Great and glorious Grand Lord Golgren," the Titan intoned in Common, bending so low that he came to eye level with the smaller ogre. Golgren was unimpressed; of all the Titans, Golgren found Safrag the least impressive. He hadn't known him before Safrag was chosen to join the spellcasters' ranks and could not understand what it was about the ogre that appealed to Dauroth—why he was chosen not only to be a Titan, but as Dauroth's second apprentice. "My master begs your leave that he sends me with what he feels is news of import to you."

Golgren, already clad in his sandals and elegant green and brown robes, bared his sharp teeth and filed-down tusks to show he was irritated at the interruption. He waved his hand impatiently at the Titan. "Speak what it is you must say and begone!"

Safrag somehow managed to bow even lower. "My master wishes to warn the grand lord of a winged sentinel noticed around the palace more than once. There may be a connection to this human. We are naturally seeking the answers—"

"This one knows of the creature. The Titans, they are commended for doing their duty, but there is no need for concern. You may leave me if that is all Dauroth wishes you to say—"

"There is more. My master would wish you to reconsider our absence at the honoring of the griffon, especially with this human attending unchained and, most worriedly, armed."

The grand lord shrugged off the warning. "The human is a guest and will be of no threat. This audience is done."

Straightening, the Titan nodded to Golgren then, without further ado, turned and started to leave the chamber.

"No!" At Golgren's cry, Safrag froze. "Since you are a Titan," the smaller ogre growled, "I would prefer that you leave from here by your magic, not simply wander the halls as you did earlier, showing your presence to any and all, yes?"

The apprentice did not protest. "As you wish."

Black smoke curled around Safrag's feet, winding quickly around the Titan until he was obscured. The smoke thickened, then dissipated, leaving in its wake no trace of the azure giant.

Snapping his fingers, Golgren beckoned his other slaves, who had been sent out of the room upon Safrag's arrival. They went back to work finishing his appearance. As some dressed him, one brushed his thick, dark hair; the grand lord's scowl gradually relaxed. Golgren could not fault Dauroth for wanting to warn him about the winged creature, but had it merely been an excuse for Safrag to skulk around and spy on the human?

Khleeg and Wargroch entered, their armor resplendent. Both warriors slapped their fists on their breastplates.

"All ready," declared Khleeg.

"Good." The slaves were dismissed again. Golgren stood before his underlings. "Then it is time for the feeding."

∞•∞

The temple to honor the gods had been built, so it was said, at the zenith of the High Ogres' civilization. However, the temple had fallen into disuse long before the race had degenerated, when the High Ogres came to worship themselves more than any one deity. Then somewhere along the way, the ancient rites honoring Garantha's patron spirit had been revived, and the grand khans had begun acting as priests of the festival, all the better to mark themselves as favored ones of the spirit.

Not only had time taken its toll on the temple, but much of the maintenance and rebuilding before Golgren's time had been of a vastly inferior quality compared to the original work. There were cracks that were barely covered by weak mortar, and one column was composed of two different styles cobbled together. However, under Golgren's not-so-delicate persuasion, his elf artisans had managed in time for that year's ritual to restore the stylized silhouette of the winged beast set above the entrance, and they also finished two intricate statues of the creature, each standing on one of the thick rails lining the wide steps.

Drumbeats proclaimed the grand lord's arrival, the steady pounding setting the correct atmosphere. Temple guards—marked by the crude griffon insignias on the apple-sized disks hanging over their breastplates—raised goat horns to announce the entrance of the ogre leader. The banner of the severed hand rose in all directions, in sync with the blaring horns.

The crowds filled every avenue, every veranda, every rooftop. Here and there, individual ogres broke out into fights as they competed for the best view. To be part of the events—and part of Golgren's moment of glory—was their opportunity to snatch some vestige of glory for themselves.

On horseback, Golgren—resplendent in his brown and green elven robes and with his flattened features accented by subtle makeup to evoke the High Ogres—entered the square surrounding the temple, dismounting just before reaching the ancient structure's grounds. A large armed escort flanked him and the small party—including Sir Stefan and Idaria—who had accompanied the grand lord. Khleeg directed the warriors along the path to the steps, where the temple guards took over. One of the latter blew a horn, and a hush fell over the sea of onlookers.

The knight was ushered to one side, where Wargroch took over supervision of the "guest." Golgren stretched his hand toward Idaria. The elf slave unwrapped a two-foot-long bundle of furs that she had been carrying, revealing within a steel mace whose head had been molded to resemble that of a shrieking griffon. The eyes were red rubies, while the beak of the avian creature had been shaped to effect maximum damage. Symbolic the weapon might have been, but as was the way of ogres, it also had a use.

Gripping the mace and resting the head of it across his other arm, Golgren strode up the steps. Idaria, her head low, retreated near the human. Khleeg accompanied his lord, both as honor guard and as one honored. Only the most favored were so fortunate.

At the top of the steps, with temple warriors standing at rigid attention, Golgren turned to face the masses. Thrusting the mace high, he shouted, *"Ishari i iGarantha tu Huun!"*

Idaria leaned close to Stefan, "Listen People of the City of the Griffon . . . "

"Tulan kylochna i oGolgreni, jekar un Gaya ng!"

"Your servant, Golgren, calls upon the great spirit . . . "

The grand lord shifted so as to let others view his rapt expression. *"Vaka Huun i Baresh, Korphus, nu Iskar'ai!"*

The ogres roared wildly, forcing Idaria to nearly shout the last translation. "Bless the People with strength, cunning, and victory!"

A grinning Khleeg signaled for the horns to sound. Golgren continued to smile and wave the mace until, at last, the horns brought the crowds under control again.

When silence ruled once more, the grand lord turned to the temple doorway. Two guards flung open the iron doors.

From within erupted an extraordinary sound that sent a shock wave through everyone present and made Stefan finger his sword. Idaria quickly placed her hand upon his, keeping the weapon sheathed before a wary Wargroch could take offense. The knight looked at the slave for some explanation.

"This is *Garan i Seraith,* the Nest of the Griffon," she explained.

A second call arose from within, and although it was slightly higher in tone and pitch, it surely came from the same source. Each of the two cries had sounded as if both a hawk and a lion had sought to speak at the same time from the same mouth.

The stench that emerged from the temple interior caused even some of the ogres to briefly turn their heads aside. Even Golgren couldn't help but wrinkle his nose, while Stefan and Idaria had to cover theirs to keep from gagging.

Golgren turned to his followers once more, calling out commands in the degenerate tongue. When Idaria did not bother to translate, the Solamnic asked, "Why does he speak in this language when I've come to believe he prefers Common?"

"For the Festival of the Griffon, there are far too many who do not know even a word of Common. He speaks now the praises of the people, which are long and full of winding phrases which even I cannot follow well enough to translate, Sir Stefan."

Golgren finally finished speaking. He then turned toward the elf and human. With a smile, the ogre leader gestured for them to come forward.

"Go," Khleeg breathed in Stefan's ear.

Stefan looked to Idaria, whose face was almost expressionless. The elf slave went up the steps, walking as though she were a high priestess. Her chains made no sound.

When Stefan and Khleeg had joined Golgren, the grand lord, holding the mace ahead of him, led the procession inside.

And with a rattle of heavy chains, two huge forms leaped forward.

"Kiri-Jolith's beard!" Stefan exclaimed, again reaching for his sword. Khleeg, too, reacted but to block the human.

"Hold!" snapped Golgren, eyes never parting from the massive shapes before them. The shadowy, four-legged forms suddenly jerked to a halt a few yards ahead of the newcomers.

Two temple warriors set torches in the walls. The torches and a series of narrow window vents along the edge of the ceiling revealed two winged behemoths as tall as horses.

They were griffons, of course. They had been fed well throughout their lives, enabling them to reach proportions rare in the wilderness. Their bodies were those of muscular cats; but their paws ended in fearsome talons. Their heads were avian and much like a raptor's. One griffon clacked its beak hard as it stretched to bite at the puny figures. Its beak was capable of cutting through flesh and bone; the proof of that was the ruined remains of amaloks scattered around the chamber.

The second griffon attempted another leap at them, its wingspread almost as wide as the chamber. Even had there been no iron collar and chain to restrain the beast, the griffon could not have flown far; its wings had been clipped.

Brown eyes with a definite feline cast darted from ogre to human to elf. Both creatures squawked loudly, the noise so piercing that all within the temple but Golgren flinched.

From behind the party came handlers leading a blindfolded young amalok whose horns had been severed and whose neck had three ritual cuts that were bleeding freshly. Nostrils flaring, the bleeding creature barked madly, which only served to stir the griffons more.

The ogres brought the amalok before Golgren, who raised the mace and uttered, *"Garan i fatuuth un if'hani amolaki."*

With that, he swung hard. The mace struck the beast on the side of the skull. The amalok let loose with an abbreviated bark, then dropped to its knees. Despite the force with which the grand lord had struck it, the amalok was only stunned.

But that was enough for the handlers to hoist and shove the dazed animal toward the griffons—

With tremendous eagerness, the winged beasts went to work tearing the frantic amalok to bloody shreds. Their talons they used like lions on the hunt, holding the prey down, and with their beaks, they stabbed and ripped at the amalok's long throat.

As the griffons fought over the grisly scraps, a temple warrior stepped outside. A moment later a horn sounded and the roar of the crowd briefly drowned out the griffons' squabbling.

Golgren signaled for the next amalok. As it was brought forward, the winged predators lost interest in what remained of their first victim. They strained at their chains, eager for fresher blood.

There was suddenly a screech of distressed metal, and in the next breath, the griffon in front of them managed to break its chain. Fortunately, it was so startled by its own success that it hesitated, disbelieving that it might be free. That enabled Golgren, directly in its path, to leap out of the way.

Another warrior jumped in to help Golgren. He

pulled the grand lord up and away, but just as Golgren regained his footing, his would-be rescuer vanished in a flurry of monstrous talons. Blood and gobbets of flesh rained down on the ogre leader.

Seizing up the mace, Golgren staunchly swatted at the winged beast. The head of his weapon struck the side of the griffon's skull but had less effect than it had on the amalok. Screeching, the griffon pressed its attack, slashing at Golgren, forcing the half-breed to retreat.

But as Golgren backed away, he heard a rattling sound coming from deeper inside, followed by the clatter of heavy chains. The other griffon had also somehow broken free, multiplying his danger and persuading the grand lord that it was no mere accident. The chains were constantly tested, especially before something so momentous as that ceremony.

Someone had taken the opportunity to prepare the trap, intending that the powerful predators—driven to a frenzy by so much nearby fresh meat and blood—would run riot. That *both* griffons had done so at the same time was a stroke of luck for the evildoer and a stroke of misfortune for Golgren.

The griffon dived for him again, snapping at him with a beak huge enough to rip the ogre's head off. Golgren deflected one such lunge, but the beast's talons came close enough to tear his robe and leave a line of gashes across his stomach. The grand lord gave thanks to his patron spirit, aware of the irony that said patron was a griffon, as he twisted and dodged to keep alive.

Then to each side of him appeared a temple guard. With their long spears, they were better able to parry the griffon as another figure—Khleeg—forcibly drew his lord toward the entrance.

But Golgren was caught between survival and reputation. His retreat couldn't be perceived as cowardly. The grand lord could not be seen as being rescued by helpmates, as an infant or a female.

So he broke free of Khleeg, startling the ogre. Before the officer could protest, Golgren seized a sword left by the slaughtered guard. "All out!" he commanded. The grand lord pointed at Stefan Rennert, who was frozen in place, but also had his weapon out and ready. "Khleeg! Remove the knight!"

Knowing better than to argue, Khleeg slapped his breastplate and followed orders. With a meaty hand, he dragged the knight away. The guards shifted toward the entrance.

Then, from behind the griffons, a figure appeared that turned Golgren's plan upside down. Idaria pressed against the far wall, her face calm despite being painfully aware of the terrible risk surrounding her. The griffons, intent on the busy prey in front of them, had somehow failed to notice the easier target.

There was no reason for Golgren to do anything but leave the female slave to her fate. One elf more or less meant nothing to the ogre realms or the continent of Ansalon itself.

But then . . .

Golgren charged toward where Idaria stood. Both his followers and the beasts were caught by surprise by his audacious action. Khleeg let out a grunt of dismay. The nearest griffon took a swat at Golgren, but the grand lord evaded the blow. Dropping from a run, he slid under the second monster just shy of its beak. As he passed, he let the keen edge of his blade cut a gash across the griffon's underside.

As the winged predator shrieked and bucked from the pain, Golgren rolled to a halt and stood before the elf.

"Come!" he barked, stretching out his maimed limb. Her expression still steady, Idaria grabbed hold. The grand lord guided them both to where Khleeg and several warriors desperately maneuvered to keep open a narrow escape route for the two.

One griffon, though, suddenly recalled its wings, and even though those wings were clipped, they were strong enough to assist the freed beast in leaping through the air. The creature soared over the heads of the guards, escaping to the outside.

With a curse at having lost the one griffon, Golgren battled against the other. The escaping griffon would no doubt wreak catastrophe outside. Eventually it would be brought down, but any deaths or destruction it caused would undermine his power. Many would read in that episode not only a distinct lack of favor from the patron spirit, but worse omens ahead.

Grand khans had been deposed for far less.

The griffon's beak came at Golgren again, snapping within inches of his face. He swung his sword, which clattered against the griffon's maw, only serving to annoy the beast.

Suddenly, the lone monster was surrounded by Khleeg and the guards. Golgren almost swore at the officer for failing to heed his order to retreat—especially with the second griffon on the loose—but he knew that Khleeg was single-mindedly devoted to his lord's welfare. The escaped beast was a secondary concern, no matter how much carnage it might unleash.

Golgren swept past his warriors, not even sparing a glance at Khleeg. Idaria held tight to his arm as they left the temple. Outside, however, they were still not safe.

There, the grand lord beheld Sir Stefan Rennert and a pair of guards attempting to keep the second beast at bay. The human's countenance was twisted into so fierce an expression that he almost resembled an ogre. Along the creature's path, three guards lay mauled and a fourth hung back, his arm in tatters.

The throng had edged away to a safe perimeter. Golgren's impressionable and superstitious people were not quite certain how to read the chaos. The grand lord would have preferred that they had all simply fled in case he further disgraced himself.

Golgren glanced at Idaria, commanding, "To the palace! Return to the palace!"

Confident in her obedience, the ogre leader paid her no further mind; he rushed to aid the knight, who might still be of value should they actually live to discuss Golgren's proposed "alliance." But as he neared man and beast, a shadow loomed over him. Golgren heard the familiar cry and knew that the other griffon had slipped past Khleeg and the others.

The ogre barely had time to whirl about and defend himself. He struggled to bring his sword up to meet his foe.

Razor-sharp talons and a monstrous beak bore down on Golgren . . .

XIII

WINGED TERROR

If the griffon had just leaped a little more to his left, the ogre would have stood a chance, but—

Then the winged beast let out a harsh cry and twisted in midflight. Its shift in trajectory brought it exactly where Golgren desired.

Aware he was still in great danger of being crushed, the grand lord nevertheless used all his strength to force the blade up.

The sword drove into the griffon's underside, digging deep just below the rib cage and cutting down into the belly. A shower of steaming blood and other fluids drenched Golgren, nearly gagging him. The griffon let out an ear-splitting shriek.

Several tons of flesh collapsed toward him, threatening to crush the ogre. Using the sword roughly as a pole, Golgren steered the heavy body away from him as much as possible as he tried to jump away.

It was not enough. The badly wounded beast fell awkwardly on his right side, one huge leg draped across

Golgren's head and face. Fighting for air, he squirmed under the flailing giant. His lungs felt crushed and burned from a lack of air.

As the griffon's struggles grew more chaotic, the leg blanketing Golgren rose and convulsed. The grand lord thrust his arm up, protecting his face from another blow from the leg. The grand lord took in as much air as he could then used his other arm to drag himself out and away from the huge animal.

Someone grabbed hold of his shoulders and pulled the ogre leader free. Golgren caught a glimpse of Idaria's solemn face.

The thrashing griffon suddenly noticed them. Crawling, it made for the pair, its sharp beak snapping at Golgren's ankle.

The elf thrust a shorter sword into the half-breed ogre's hand. Golgren lunged as best he could.

He jammed the blade into the griffon's maw with such force that the hilt and his hand sank deep into the monster's gullet. All the griffon had to do to relieve the grand lord of his sole good hand was to clamp its beak shut and chop it off.

But the ogre's strength and desperation were such that the sword not only penetrated the back of the griffon's throat, but tore through sinew and flesh until the point burst out the back side. Instead of biting down, the griffon opened its beak wide in a failed attempt to dislodge the blade. Twisting its head back and forth, it pulled weapon and wielder up in the air.

As he flew off the ground, Golgren dropped the second sword. No matter, for the griffon, overcome by injuries and loss of blood, finally stumbled and fell, flopping onto its back. With the short blade still lodged in its throat, the behemoth shook once and at last died.

Golgren managed to roll and land on his feet, although the impact shook his bones. He exhaled in relief and victory. However, another animal shriek reminded Golgren that the nightmare was far from over. As he fought to keep his wits, the grand lord saw that Stefan was keeping the second griffon occupied, but his situation was desperate. The two guards still stood with the knight, but their skills were clumsy compared with the human's, and if anything, the ogres impeded the knight.

But the griffon had had enough. Flapping its wings, the creature sprang to fly away and escape for good. Because of its special breeding and size, however, the creature rose no higher than two yards into the sky before plummeting back down like a rock . . . on top of a guard who had been gaping up at it.

The frustrated griffon tore into the hapless ogre with abandon, scattering pieces of flesh everywhere. Some of those in the crowd abandoned the area without care for anything but saving their own hides. Golgren swore; it was more humiliation for the grand lord, and the fleeing witnesses would spread the news of his fall from Garantha's patron spirit's favor.

The Solamnic bravely pressed the attack, trying to force the animal back. That only served to infuriate the griffon. Scattering aside the gruesome remains of the ogre, it lunged for the human.

The beak clamped down on Sir Stefan's arm. If not for his armor, much of his limb would have been ripped away. As it was, Stefan did lose his grip on the sword. It was all he could do just to keep his footing as the griffon stomped about.

Finding that it could not bite through the knight's

armor, the winged creature angrily shook its head, tossing the Solamnic back and forth like a doll.

As Stefan struggled, other guards produced a massive net to toss over the griffon. They tossed the net over the animal's head but overshot their mark, entangling the griffon's wings.

The net briefly distracted the griffon, who did not notice that Golgren had sneaked up behind it. With a spear seized from one of the strewn corpses, the grand lord maneuvered stealthily toward the beast. If he hoped to salvage the situation, it was a matter of utmost importance that he, and he alone, slay the beast and win back the day.

At a gesture from Golgren, those guards nearest the knight withdrew cautiously. Stefan, preoccupied with fending off the griffon, noticed neither their withdrawal nor Golgren's advance.

Then the grand lord tried a trick, imitating the barking of a young amalok, a plaintive cry as though one were separated from its mother. Sure enough, instinct made the griffon turn swiftly in his direction, momentarily dropping its defenses.

Golgren thrust.

The spear penetrated the eye nearest to him. The griffon let out an enraged scream and caught the weapon's staff in its beak. With a single bite, it snapped the spear. Then, shaking its head wildly, it managed to dislodge the dripping tip of the weapon from its damaged orb.

The winged behemoth, shrieking with anger and fury, saw only Golgren. It swung completely around to face the grand lord, incidentally swatting away with its tail and killing instantly an ogre guard who had strayed too close.

Golgren did not have much of a weapon left, only the splintered end of the spear. Regardless, he grasped the piece and used it cleverly to parry his monstrous foe's talons. Yet one sharp nail drew a red line over his forearm.

Staggering, Golgren sought the griffon's throat. He could not hope to impale the beast, but perhaps he could do some damage.

The griffon leaped at him. The move was so sudden, the grand lord almost lost his head as the beak snapped at where his own throat might have been if the giant predator hadn't misjudged its leap—likely owing to the loss of one eye. Instead, the beak slammed the ogre leader in the chest, striking him like a blow from a battering ram. He was thrown back.

As the griffon readied another leap, a sound drew Golgren's attention. A length of chain dangling from its metal collar dragged beneath the beast. The grand lord thought for a moment then lunged down to grab the loose links. Seizing up the chain, he grabbed hold of the griffon's shoulder and pulled himself up.

His stunt would have failed immediately if he hadn't deliberately picked the beast's blind side. As it was, Golgren barely got hold before the creature's beak came whipping around, trying to bite off the ogre's leg.

Golgren took the chain and quickly looped it around the griffon's thick neck. The moment that was done, he wrapped the remainder around his waist then leaned back as much as he could and pulled with all his might, tightening the noose.

The griffon let out a complaining rasp as Golgren threw his weight and strength into it. The grand lord struggled to keep his grip as the winged giant writhed and staggered. Because of its wings, the griffon was not likely to roll onto its back, although all bets were off in its dire situation.

As Golgren strained and pulled, the griffon's head arched upward. The griffon's rasping grew harsher, more rapid. The beast stumbled about as though drunk. It flailed its talons in an effort to remove the obstacle around its throat but only succeeded in scarring its own feathered and furred hide.

The knuckles of Golgren's hand went white with strain. He felt his heart pounding, his own breathing fast and hard.

Rising to its hind legs, the griffon clawed at the air then tumbled over on its side.

Golgren jumped off the creature just before being partially crushed by its heavy body. He landed hard on the stone walkway.

Immediately, Khleeg and a host of guards surged toward the scene. Khleeg signaled for several ogres with spears to dispatch the griffon, which was momentarily quiet, perhaps unconscious.

"No!" snapped Golgren, biting back the pain coursing through his body. "No!" he repeated. *"Gya ku f'han!"*

"Gya ku f'han?" Khleeg asked, grimacing in disagreement. "Great one," the officer rumbled in Common. "Not to kill?"

"It is helpless now," replied the grand lord coolly. "Would Khleeg offend the spirit by killing it so?"

From his expression, Khleeg thought slaying the vulnerable beast was the sensible thing to do, but he knew better than to argue with his master. Slapping his fist on his breastplate, the warrior shouted to his subordinates, *"Baroos ni igarani ko fothos!"*

The guards quickly retrieved the net lost earlier and

began draping it over the griffon's prone body. Others rushed up with rope, securing the creature's limbs so it would barely be able to walk. Someone wisely ordered that its beak be bound tight.

As those things were being accomplished, Golgren, after catching his breath, said, "Khleeg! There must be a ceremony! The dead one must be honored in the name of the patron!"

"It shall be done!"

But before Khleeg could act, Golgren added, "Its chain. Its collar. They shall be brought to me, yes? You guard my back, Khleeg?"

Khleeg's weak eye seemed to sink deeper beneath its lid, for he had failed his master. "Lord? Khleeg swears *Ophri N'mim!*"

No greater oath could be sworn by the officer. To fail such a vow would mean casting a perpetual curse on the ogre's parents and all his descendants. Not to mention Khleeg himself.

"Jakul i nur Ophri N'mim iKhleegi," replied Golgren. "There is no need for oaths, but you have already sworn it, yes?"

"Ke!"

As Khleeg rushed away, Golgren, eyes narrowed, looked around, wondering, if not Khleeg, who? Someone had tried to humiliate or kill him, and something had to be done about it. He moved past Stefan, who was still catching his breath, striding up the steps of the temple with renewed vigor.

Once at the top, Golgren seized a horn abandoned by one of the trumpeters during the chaos. Whirling, the grand lord turned back toward the crowd and blew on the horn three times.

By the third blast, he had the attention of everyone within sight. Raising his arms to the heavens, the ogre leader proclaimed, *"Bendaka uth iGaranaki! Inom uth iGaranaki!"*

He received immediate cheers from his more ardent followers among the throng. Those cheers encouraged others, more timid, until finally there were repeated roars of approval from all present.

Nodding, the grand lord folded his arms and stood triumphant before his people. He had just told the ogres that it had been a test of the griffon spirit, and that he had passed the test; the spirit approved of his rule. The people were willing to believe that, for Golgren had given them quite a show, fighting well and turning the tide in his favor. None were willing to openly question his version of events.

But even though he had saved face, Golgren knew that his enemies were still hiding out there, somewhere, plotting new ways to attack and undermine him. There would still be rumors that his rivals would surreptitiously spread. The question of his worth and lineage—owing to his stature, his maimed hand, and the suspicious circumstances of his birth—would not easily go away.

Golgren glanced over at the human, still dazed by all that had transpired. A pact with the Solamnics would be very useful indeed.

⚬⚬✦⚬⚬

Dauroth furiously dismissed the scrying sphere, sending it back to oblivion. Safrag, sensing his anger, wisely kept to the shadows. His master would speak to him if Dauroth thought it necessary.

But the first words sung by the lead Titan were meant for himself, not his apprentice. "His recklessness should have destroyed him by now, yet he lives and enjoys the masses' idolization more than ever."

Safrag bowed low as Dauroth turned to him. Only then did the apprentice dare speak. "But surely he was ever safe," Safrag sang. "Surely great Dauroth was ever there to see that he did not perish!"

"Are you suggesting that I am some nursemaid for the grand lord, Safrag? The mongrel is useful, but I can hardly spare my valuable time to keep him safe all the time. He is becoming more of an annoyance than a useful tool."

"Nay! I said nothing about you being a nursemaid! I understand why you let the cur live, despite what the others say! Besides, surely this was a strange occurrence! Surely, great one, you believe this only an accident, nothing—absolutely nothing—more."

The senior Titan's golden eyes narrowed. "Until you spoke now, I did. You have filled me with a suspicion, Safrag, and for that alone I should condemn you to existence as an Abomination!"

"My comment was not meant to alarm you, great one!" Safrag insisted, making himself as small as a fourteen-foot giant could. "You would surely know if anything was not as it seemed, and since you do not even suspect—"

Dauroth angrily gestured. "Be silent!"

A gray haze formed over the apprentice's mouth. His words were immediately cut off. Safrag stood as still as a statue as his mentor turned his own thoughts inward.

That not one, but both, griffons had broken their chains was, in hindsight, too great a coincidence. Dauroth berated himself for being so preoccupied with his other musings that he had missed the obvious. Safrag had actually done him a favor, bringing up the possibility of some outside involvement, some conspiracy.

There were many still who wished the mongrel dead; Dauroth counted himself among them, despite his outward show of indifference for the benefit of the other members of the Talon. There were times—especially just after he was done dealing with the half-breed—that Dauroth imagined shrinking the grand lord to the size of a piece of fruit and squeezing him to a pulp in the palm of his hand. While such a spell was beyond any Titan—at least thus far—there were other spells at his beckoning that would have served just as well.

But he would use them only when it became clear that Golgren's usefulness was truly at an end.

What was crucial—and seeming more likely by the moment—was that, if Safrag's suggestion had any merit, someone else had sought Golgren's end, using the spectacle as a shield.

"Safrag," Dauroth sang the other's name as if summoning a beloved child. "Safrag, if you were to see this as not an accident, but rather as a deliberate ruse, a foul play by someone . . . who would it be that you would investigate . . . ?"

Despite realizing that his voice had been returned to him, the apprentice looked hesitant to revive that treacherous conversation. Yet in the end, Safrag felt obliged to reply.

"Great master, if I had to choose one, it would be from among our own . . . or one who used to be."

" 'Used to be' " Dauroth's brow furrowed. The apprentice was affirming his own notions. Dauroth raised his left palm up, and in its center formed the vision of a grotesque, misshapen countenance. He showed it to Safrag. "You mean *Donnag.*"

"In truth, I can see no other with such daring or desperation or such understandable need for vengeance, oh master."

"Indeed." They both stared at the former ruler's repulsive face, the image formed in Dauroth's hand. Yes, the accusation made sense to Dauroth. Donnag sought vengeance, and perhaps he was ambitious too; perhaps he thought to return to the Titans as their chief. Ambitious Donnag always had been . . . foolish.

"Donnag . . . I believe you are correct, Safrag. I believe the chieftain has again acted injudiciously. He must not do so anymore. His actions interfere with my desires."

"The Black Talon must deal with him?"

Dauroth shook his head. "No, we shall have the mongrel taken care of in a special way, like one beast set upon another. After all, we do not want to serve the grand lord's interests, for he wishes to know who it is who has sought his assassination."

The apprentice bowed his head in acknowledgment of Dauroth's wisdom. The lead Titan smiled, but the smile faded abruptly.

"And then . . . and then, at least, I think that something must have to be done about the Grand Lord Golgren." Dauroth grinned fiercely, his teeth clamped tightly together. "Yes, I think that we are nearing that time, after all."

Safrag bowed his head gratefully. "There may be danger, great one! The mongrel has his hidden tricks! I feel certain there is magic that serves him and not us! Recall Donnag's utter defeat! 'Twas magic that tripped him in the end, powerful magic!"

"Of that I am keenly aware, but fortunately, the key to understanding the situation has been near us all along. We can thank dear Hundjal for awakening me to the possibility."

"Hundjal? Nay, Master Dauroth! You cannot mean what I think you mean. To do such a thing, to wield such a thing!"

The elder sorcerer shook off his apprentice's apprehensive tone. "Don't worry, I will use only the barest fragment, and I will not be the one to wield it, at least not physically."

"But there is still the tomb, not yet opened by your command! If there are signets within, as we hope—and surely there are bones of the dead—then would not those suffice—and with far less threat to yourself—to deal with this matter?"

Yet the Black Talon had not deciphered how to undo the ancient protections of the tomb without causing them to destroy what lay within. The High Ogres had arranged everything using a delicate balance of powerful energies. Remove one in the wrong manner, and the years of Dauroth's research would be for naught.

Besides, Dauroth did not know if anything within the tomb would work as hoped. The fragment . . . the fragment was another story.

"It will be as I say. For Hundjal, this will be a most important assignment . . . a most appropriate choice."

Safrag again bowed his head in acceptance of his master's wisdom.

His gaze suddenly shifting to the right, Dauroth dismissed that subject as another flitted into his mind. "Ahh . . . Captain Moak and his warriors are with us at last. Come, Safrag."

With a sweep of his hand, Dauroth sent the two of them from his chamber to the massive courtyard at the front gate of the citadel. The stone entrance area was large enough to hold a small army and, indeed, part of it did. Nearly twenty surly-looking and impatient ogre warriors waited there with their prize. Captain Moak—a beefy Blödian with one tusk that curled to the side and four ritual scars across his forehead—was their commander. He had led them on their journey—without the knowledge of Golgren's toady, Khleeg—through the dread valley surrounding Dauroth's domain to fulfill a pact that he had long ago made with the master Titan.

Moak did not look pleased, not that Dauroth cared. Each time the ogre captain made the treacherous journey, he usually sacrificed two or three careless underlings to the hidden sentinels beyond the high, spiked walls and the massive, iron-grate gateway. The trip had been ordered; it was no whim.

"Great one," snarled the heavy but muscular officer in Common, for he had learned long ago that, like Golgren, Dauroth preferred not to hear the bastardized tongue spoken widely in the ogre realms. Moak performed a cursory slap on his breastplate that almost made Safrag snort in disdain. "Brought as many as could be taken! Good stock! See here?"

His warriors parted to reveal eleven haggard elves. They stared at the Titans with eyes almost dead, for they knew the legends concerning the giant sorcerers. None brought to the secret sanctum ever returned, it was said.

"This paltry few?" muttered Safrag. "Great Dauroth expected several times that amount!"

The lead Titan raised a gently admonishing hand. "Hush, Safrag. I am certain Moak has an explanation

224

for using the valuable spellstone to bring fewer than the warriors who guard them."

Moak glanced back at the vine-covered walls and the thick treetops just visible above. The only successful path to and from the citadel was the one that Dauroth's spellstone illuminated for the captain. The ogre clearly did not savor the thought of being punished for his failure, and he knew there were few safe ways to return home.

"Golgren is fault," Moak finally grunted. "Golgren! That ji-baraki—Khleeg!—he sends order to Blöde! Says, all elves be gathered, taken to Garantha! Already they begin!"

Dauroth looked to Safrag, who shared his master's frown. "*All* elves, you say?"

"All! Moak work hard to gather these! Strong! See?" The captain gestured, and a warrior shoved a male elf forward. The slave, wearing soiled rags that barely covered him, stumbled to one knee. Moak moved in and slapped the elf, forcing him to stand. "Strong! Only these, but all strong! Good blood!"

The other elves huddled together. Moak's followers bobbed their heads up and down in eager agreement with their commander.

Dauroth came to a decision. "And when can you next procure more?" Moak's method of procurement was, of course, by kidnapping any slave he came across or by bribing guards of other elf captives willing to betray their masters. "By the next full white moon?"

Moak made a face at that. "Might be longer, might be! Maybe need more to pay. Must go farther . . . must take more chances."

"No. Too much notice. This will be the last from you.

There will come other methods . . . if they are needed even."
As he spoke, Dauroth concentrated. He felt the Black Talon
heed his silent command. Those in the sanctum prepared.
"But your usefulness to me will not end; have no fear of
that, Captain Moak."

Moak, who had started to look uneasy, brightened.
Greed shone in his eyes. "Will serve you well, great one!
Serve you well!"

"Yes, you shall. Safrag?"

Bowing his head, the apprentice thrust out a single
finger toward the elves. Above them, a gray haze suddenly
formed. The slaves suddenly showed signs of life, some
of them struggling to flee despite the heavy chains their
captors had clamped on them.

But the moment that the haze drifted down onto their
heads, the elves froze. Their arms dropped to their sides.
Eyes dulled, unblinking, they slowly staggered away
from Moak's warriors, heading toward a doorway Safrag
pointed out to them.

Watching the slaves leave in that docile fashion, Moak
grew anxious again. "We serve you well again, great one!
Give orders and we leave now!"

"The orders are simple, and it is this: only into the
woods should you go."

Moak started to ask a question, but his mouth hung
open without a sound as six Titans materialized around
the band of slave traders.

As one, Dauroth and his followers raised their left
hands and gestured toward Moak's warriors. Some of the
ogres tried to react, even to attack the Titans, but their
limbs would not work. Moak let out a furious growl, but
that was all he could do.

Dauroth sang the words then drew a six-sided symbol

in the air. The red rune flared bright, then shot toward Moak.

It struck the captain in the skull then split in two. Moak let out a groan as the rune burned into his flesh while the split ones flew toward the next closest warriors. Those ogres were also struck in their skulls, and again, each of their runes split into two more that coursed toward the next victims.

Within a single blink, all the slave traders had been so targeted. Their groans filled the air. The Black Talon sang, stirring up the fearsome energies Dauroth required for his task. He had always intended that to be the outcome when Moak proved no longer useful, for the ogre knew too much. Moak had always said he was willing to serve Dauroth for the rest of his life.

However, Dauroth demanded that the captain and his warriors serve the Titans longer than that.

"Asyriana Idariosia u alleas!" Dauroth sang.

Moak screamed. His scream was joined by all his followers'. The savage ogre fighters howled as their runes burned deeper.

And as the runes burned, the ogres' flesh and sinew began to melt away like butter in the Kernian sun. It dribbled off Moak, spilling onto the stone walkway and dripping into the cracks. A hand that the captain had raised toward Dauroth just before the spell was stripped clean within moments. The ogre's face was no longer recognizable.

But the Titans were not done. Each raised his left hand high above his head. Dauroth drew another rune, a three-sided one that, had Moak been able to read, he might have recognized as the Voice of Sirrion.

The other sorcerers repeated the same symbol. Dauroth

dropped his hand, and the rest followed suit.

The runes that they had drawn shot toward one another, colliding just over the heads of the victims.

A gush of white fire enveloped Moak's entire band, utterly engulfing the warriors and obscuring them from sight.

When Dauroth deemed the deed done, he sang, *"Ysirria assyros ios!"*

The fire dwindled.

Some twenty armed figures stood before him, twenty ogres stripped to their skeletons. The hollow-eyed monstrosities stood as still as statues.

Dauroth was pleased. Generally, the spell was done with more precaution and using other tools in the very same chamber where new Titans were born.

He pointed at the gate, which opened. The skeletons suddenly moved, turning as one toward the entrance to the woods. Without a word, they silently marched out of the citadel yard, heading off to join the rest of Dauroth's magical servants.

As the gate lowered again, the other Titans left him to his seclusion. Such tremendous use of power would, in the end, demand that even he would have to rejuvenate himself. And until things changed, that still meant a substantial need for elf blood.

For reasons known only to the grand lord, that was going to become more difficult than ever.

You have become more detriment than worth, Guyvir, much more, Dauroth thought.

That brought to mind Hundjal's transgression. Yes, it was time to follow through with all of his plans.

Two birds with one stone . . .

XIV

TOMB RAIDER

The High Ogres had left a great legacy, although that legacy was scattered and buried throughout much of Ansalon. Partly for that reason, few could claim to be knowledgeable about the High Ogres. Tyranos was one of the august few, a master of the history of a race long dead that still affected the living.

It was a legacy that extended far beyond the borders of Kern and Blöde.

The hill where Tyranos worked lay in the northern reaches of what once had been Silvanost and was at that moment part of the imperial minotaur colony of Ambeon. In truth, Tyranos was not that far from the Titans sent by Dauroth to harass the empire, but the wards he had cast would keep his presence a secret from the gigantic spellcasters for the time being . . . or so he hoped. Tyranos knew he had been expending too much power lately, that the staff and artifacts he utilized were at their limit. His own magic ability was impressive, but the wizard knew better than to think that he could face down two or more Titans, especially those, the most powerful, in the inner circle.

But the thought of what might lie deep within that particular hill had obliged him to take chances.

Indeed, it was not really a hill, despite the many oaks and firs topping it and giving it the appearance of roundness and size. Once, in fact, it had been a burial mound, and although it was on formerly elf soil, the burial mound had been there for a long, long time, possibly predating the elven realm.

It had been there as long, perhaps, as the earliest days of the High Ogres' supremacy.

After mentally double-checking his defensive wards for the tenth time, the imposing wizard pointed his staff toward a slight depression on the upward slope. Elves had taken little notice of the small, nondescript hill, so thoroughly had those who had created it worked to hide it from enemies. That hinted at a potential treasure trove of potent arcane magic.

Or it might be another fool's quest.

"Sarath!"

At his command, a silver beam of light erupted from the crystal head of his staff, the shining beam burrowing its way into the hillside. With the silence Tyranos desired, tons of earth divided to each side, creating a corridor into the hillside that ended before a stone doorway. Upon the door was carved the profile of a woman so beautiful that, despite the haste with which he worked, the wizard paused to admire her.

But his admiration was only momentary, for he had much to do. The Titans, too, were constantly seeking such mounds—said to be scattered across not only Ansalon, but the rest of the world as well—and from his spying, the wizard believed that the Black Talon was on the trail of something significant. He could only hope that his find would be more significant, as time was growing short; he knew that better than anyone, even the Titans.

Dismissing the light, Tyranos approached the door. He could sense the latent forces that cemented its seal and marveled at their strength after so many centuries. With one hand, the wizard traced the runes carved around the image. He recognized a handful of them and could hazard a guess at about half a dozen more. Nodding, Tyranos began whispering—speaking the runes as he could best interpret them—his voice taking on a singing quality that lacked something in its skill, yet sounded so much more beautiful simply because of the rune language. The Titans thought that they spoke something akin to the old language, Tyranos reflected, but they did not understand how wrong they were. Even the elegant elves spoke with the squeals of pigs in comparison to the language of the High Ogres.

As Tyranos finished the last rune, the door sank inward with a low, scraping sound. A hiss of air escaped the tomb, emitting a scent that Tyranos identified as rosemary.

A shadow crept over the doorway. The day was nearly spent, and soon the entire hillside would be drenched in darkness. Aware that he might be inside for hours, Tyranos quickly stepped through the door. He was anxious for his long-planned exploration, anxious to collect the artifacts he believed were at his fingertips.

The scent of rosemary grew stronger. There was a headiness to the scent that had nothing to do with the rosemary, though, and Tyranos hesitated, cursing his impatience. He leaned against a rocky wall as fresh air from outside mixed with the stale atmosphere of the tomb. Another precious minute had passed before Tyranos dared to continue.

Illuminating the crystal atop his staff, the leonine wizard surveyed his surroundings. The walls were no longer raw stone; they were smooth and polished with intricate images of High Ogre life etched into them every five paces. The visions were so lifelike that Tyranos paused before one to study it better.

In it, a woman stood at the center of a group of other robed figures. In her hands she offered something to one of the group, but the object was too tiny for the wizard to identify. He leaned closer, at the same time cautiously putting two fingertips against the image to aid his balance—

And suddenly Tyranos himself stood among the small group of honored guests awaiting the woman's favor for their accomplishments. A light breeze tousled his long—*red*—hair. He stood in the green and blue ornamented robe of his house.

No, not his house, but rather that of the one in whose place he stood. An awestruck Tyranos felt his body, the body he wore, step forward. The woman filled his gaze, her beauty beyond anything he could have dreamed. It did not matter if they were not of the same race; no goblin, elf, or kyrie could have failed to note her wondrous being. Her hair might have been gold, silver, or some other gleaming color, but that did not matter, nor did the fact that her features, although perfect, could be described a hundred ways and more without ever coming close.

His awe of her beauty was secondary to his amazement at what she was doing. The contents of her hands were revealed to him, and with one of his own, he reached for something lying in the very center of her right palm.

It was a signet.

Tyranos strained to identify the design on it, but his host's fingers wrapped around the prize, drawing it into his fist.

The High Ogre female smiled at him then—and suddenly the wizard once more stood before the inert image on the wall.

"By the Kraken's tentacles!" Tyranos angrily snapped. He started to reach toward the scene but hesitated. There was no point in seeking entrance back into that vision; the casters had created the scene to mark that moment and that moment only. If he reentered, Tyranos would only relive the exact same frustrating instant. He could look nowhere else, do nothing else.

But that brief glimpse into the past had done more than give him an extraordinary view of the High Ogres. It had told him clearly that whoever was interred in the tomb was probably buried with the very same signet he had beheld in the vision.

Despite the allure of the other images on the walls, Tyranos moved swiftly ahead, concerned only with his goal. A signet would aid him tremendously or, at the very least, equalize any advantage the Talon might gain should they locate a similar burial chamber, as he believed they might already have done.

Unseen but felt, energies swirled around the tomb, many of them utilized for shielding the place from mortal sight. Tyranos frowned. He sniffed the air but sensed nothing malicious.

The crystal continued to light the way, but its illumination had grown muted. The wizard could see barely a foot or two beyond the staff's head. Worse, with each step, it was as if someone loaded heavy and still heavier iron weights on his shoulders. His mind started to cloud, the spells he had labored so long to memorize beginning to fade.

He knew that it was the tomb's protective spells surreptitiously working on him. He had underestimated the High Ogres' skills, blundering into their traps like a bull.

Then the wizard sensed that he was no longer alone.

Swinging the staff from one side to the next, Tyranos caught glimpses of golden-skinned warriors clad in flexible, blue-silver armor. But those glimpses were no more than fleeting looks, the figures vanishing whenever the light approached them. He swung the crystal toward where he had seen one, and very briefly the figure appeared again before vanishing once more. However, the wizard had seen just enough to know that they were converging on him with trouble in mind.

Another sweep of his staff revealed at least four guardians and in the right hand of each was grasped what Tyranos took to be short, squat maces, less than a foot in length. More details than that the wizard could not make out, save that each guardian bore a different rune across its armored hide.

Tyranos stood waiting, but the guardians had melted away and failed to materialize again. Then a terrible cold touched his shoulder, and the wizard screamed. Barely had he registered the cold than suddenly his lungs felt as though filled with water.

Choking, Tyranos dropped to his knees. In the process, his staff swung about wildly, revealing one of the armored figures raising his short mace in preparation for a strike.

The wizard threw himself forward, but if he expected to bowl over his foe, he was disappointed. Instead, Tyranos rolled unimpeded through the place where the guardian had stood—and vanished. The spellcaster grasped desperately for his staff, the most powerful magical item he had, the only one that might keep him alive.

"Fight like warriors!" he snarled at the unseen guardians as he shifted to a crouching position. "Show yourselves at least!"

They did not heed his demand, of course. Swearing an oath, Tyranos seized the staff like a club and shouted out another spell.

As the crystal slashed through the air, one of the guardians momentarily flickered into view. Tyranos uttered a different spell. The crystal's light shifted from silver to utter white.

With a low moan, the guardian vanished in midswing.

Baring his teeth in satisfaction, the wizard steadied himself. The spell he had summoned should have been far stronger, but at least it had done some apparent damage.

His satisfaction was short-lived, though, as something touched him on his left arm, which sent him flying against one of the walls. The spellcaster dropped to the floor like a wet sack.

Fighting to keep his wits, Tyranos pushed himself up into a sitting position. The remaining three guardians were very near, he sensed, but his staff was out of reach, so he could only guess at their whereabouts. He understood that they were not ghosts, but rather elemental forces bound by the ancients into the semblances of mortals. However, that knowledge would do Tyranos little good if he failed to regain the staff.

The spellcaster lunged toward the lost weapon. He managed to cover half the distance when the cold hit him like a wall, stronger than before. Tyranos's limbs stiffened as if numbed. He dropped forward, landing face first on the harsh stone.

Yet he was far from finished. With a roar of anger, Tyranos forced himself up on his frozen elbows and dragged himself toward his goal. His legs were so cold that they burned; then they really did begin to burn, hotter and hotter. As Tyranos neared the staff, the horrific heat coursed through his body, sending him into a new agony.

Eyes tearing, he stretched for his goal. A shaking hand grasped the artifact.

Tyranos spit out the words he needed then swung wildly.

A second guardian materialized in the brief blaze of white light he had summoned. Seen up close at last, its face was a parody of the beauty of the High Ogres, a mask of gold intricately shaped into facial features lacking a soul.

As the first had done, this one also emitted a chilling moan then faded away to nothing. Tyranos, ignoring the pain wracking his body, swerved around to where he judged one of his other attackers to be lurking.

Sure enough, the guardian was there but slightly farther away than Tyranos had anticipated. His magic light flashed, but not with the strength and reach necessary to eliminate that one.

"Yaaa!" A new wave of burning engulfed him. Still clutching the staff, the spellcaster rolled onto his back, writhing. He all but gasped out the required spell.

The crystal flared, eradicating a third guardian.

Instantly, the burning ceased. His breathing ragged, Tyranos used the staff to prop himself up to his feet.

There was another touch on his forearm.

A fear filled the wizard. He felt the walls closing in on him. No, not just the walls, but the entire mound, the entire hill. He realized he was being buried alive and that his bones would rot forever beside those of the tomb's inhabitant.

A primal sound escaped Tyranos. Shivering, with tears running from his eyes, the wizard made a desperate stab with the staff, at the same time calling out the trusted spell.

He caught the last guardian square in the chest, his crystal light streaming toward and seemingly piercing the rune. The white light swallowed the inhuman figure—

And suddenly the walls felt as if they were receding. Tyranos still shivered but from exhaustion, not fear. He leaned on the staff, trying to catch his breath.

But the tomb's builders did not intend for him to have any respite. From the darkness ahead slithered a murky form that vanished into and out of any patch of darkness available. Tyranos turned the staff's light toward it, but it dived into a shadow and vanished without any further trace.

The wizard thrust into his pocket in search of a small vial. As he pulled it out, he heard a hiss close by his ear.

Something sought his throat, but he managed to twist out of the way of its grasp. Popping open the vial, Tyranos thrust it ahead of him, where he believed his attacker lurked.

There was a second, more virulent hiss, followed by a sucking sound from within the vial. The tiny container shook with such violence that the weary wizard could barely hold onto it.

The sucking sound grew louder, deafening. But the hiss did the opposite, shrinking, not only becoming fainter, but seeming to change its place of origin. It sounded as though it came from the same place as the other noise—from within the vial.

At last, the hiss ceased utterly. Daring to release his staff, Tyranos searched the floor until he located the stopper then quickly shoved it into the neck of the container.

Silence reigned in the tomb.

Retrieving his staff, the spellcaster used its silver light to closely inspect the vial. Shaking the vial, Tyranos noticed a tiny black blot within that swirled around almost angrily.

"You might be of some use in the future," he murmured at the contents.

Replacing the vial in his pocket, Tyranos readied himself for whatever threat or guardian the tomb next hurled at him. Yet more than a minute passed and nothing happened; no further trap was sprung. Cautiously, the wizard decided to resume his journey.

And barely a moment later, he entered the burial chamber.

The swiftness with which he reached the center of the tomb made Tyranos frown, however. There should have been some long, byzantine trek through myriad passages—some of them false, some real—occasionally broken by the discovery of auxiliary rooms filled with unusual artifacts. To reach his destination so quickly did not speak highly of the tomb's occupant.

Yet the buried one had been granted a signet, a rare and powerful gift among the High Ogres.

The chamber itself was perfectly round, with niches at waist level that hinted at possible treasures. However, it was the middle of the room that riveted Tyranos's attention, for there, set upon a round platform of what looked like alabaster—a platform upon which were etched more depictions of High Ogre history—was a sarcophagus made of diamond. In the light of the staff, it glittered like a rainbow, its facets creating a startling light show with each movement of the hooded wizard.

Within, a stately form dressed in robes of silver and black—the ancient race's colors of mourning during the epoch indicated in the vision—lay in repose. As Tyranos stepped up to the remarkable diamond coffin, he saw that the corpse was entirely intact and preserved, as though it had been buried only yesterday. The brilliant blue skin; the perfect, chiseled features; the finely woven garments . . . none were worn by time.

"Incredible," he whispered. Tyranos circled the sarcophagus, inspecting every detail of the body. Unlike modern ogres, who were nine feet tall and muscular in the manner of a wrestler, the ancient one was only about as tall as the wizard himself. He was slimmer than Tyranos, with a build more like that of an acrobat. The body appeared to be that of someone who died when he was only in the middle of his third decade, but with the ancients, the look of youthfulness could be deceiving. It was very possible that the ogre had been far, far older at the time of his passing. It was said that the legendary forebears of the savages living in Kern and Blöde had been granted life spans longer than those of elves.

The corpse's expression was calm, serene. One hand lay at his side, the other rested over his heart.

And that hand was decorated with a ring.

The ring drew Tyranos closer and not only because of its eerie beauty. High Ogres had worn their signets in many ways, but the most obvious way was just as common today, in a ring. He could not see what was set into the deceased one's piece—the ring had been turned inward toward the chest—but where else would the mourners have placed the most valuable of gifts?

That was assuming, of course, that someone else had not stolen the prize upon the deceased's death.

The muscular wizard searched frantically for a way to open the coffin. He tried to shove at the top half then searched both ends for a gap that might have been sealed after the body was slid inside. His desperate hunt revealed nothing. It was as if the diamond shell were a living thing that had been planted and grown up around the body, but such a thing was not possible—

Tyranos blinked. Or *was* it?

He performed another, even more thorough examination with the same lack of results. The body lay like a pupa in a glistening chrysalis. There was no manner by which to open it.

No manner but one.

With all his might and with all the magic he could muster, the leonine mage struck the top of the sarcophagus with his staff. Raw energy crackled like lightning around both him and it. A sharp, keening sound echoed throughout the chamber.

Cracks shot across the diamond coffin. Huge pieces

suddenly exploded into the air. Some of the shards flew at Tyranos, who managed to shield himself with his cloak.

He stumbled back as the keening sounds amplified. The wizard's eyes bulged as the figure within the coffin reached up toward the sky with both hands and promptly disintegrated. The beautiful blue skin wrinkled and cracked before falling away. The long, dark hair turned gray, then white. The perfect face sank into itself, the ashy remnants spilling into the suddenly empty eye sockets, the gaping jaws, and the deep nostrils.

The transformation into skeleton was swiftly followed by the decay of the bones themselves. With no ligaments or anything else to hold them together, the bones collapsed, yellowed, then broke into pieces. The pieces dissolved into dust.

Even the garments were not left untouched. They, too, faded, then shriveled. Unlike the body, the robes did not completely vanish, but what little was left could scarcely be identified as the same wondrous clothing Tyranos had first seen.

Undeterred by the destruction he had wrought, Tyranos thrust one hand into the dust, groping around and seeking the ring. It, of all things, should have survived intact.

His fingers closed on a small, circular object. Shaking off bits of the dead ogre, the wizard raised the object up and in the light.

"By the Kraken," he murmured.

Tyranos had found a signet.

"Yes . . . yes."

He held it up to inspect it, focusing the full illumination of his staff upon the ring. The signet in its center was circular with a rune that looked like a double-bladed sword turned upside down at the center. Half a circle arced over the sword, and underneath both lay a symbol the spellcaster recognized from his studies as representing heat or fire.

Wanting to look closer still, Tyranos brought the staff's head nearer.

The rune shimmered bright orange. What felt like an invisible hand briefly caressed the wizard's countenance.

Then the rune lost its glow. Tyranos held the signet as close to the crystal as he dared, but there was no repeat of that shimmering, that strange sensation of an invisible hand.

Recalling some of his researches, the wizard uttered some runes he knew. None, however, caused any reaction in the ring.

Rather than frown in frustration, he suddenly chuckled. The High Ogres had, for most of their existence, been meticulous recorders of their magical craft. His brief glance at the wall niches had taken in scrolls, tomes, and other forms of documentation. Somewhere among them would be the key to using the signet. Tyranos had only to look hard.

But when he turned his gaze to the niches, there remained in each only a few rusty boxes and thick piles of dust that had moments before contained the secrets he desired more than anything.

Secrets that his impatience to reach the signet had evidently condemned to the dustbin of history. When the mortal remains of the dead ogre had been awoken and returned to their basic elements, so, too, had the protected works of his life.

Tyranos more than chuckled at that; he bellowed

with laughter, bellowed at the foul jest played upon him by the ghosts of the past and his own greed. The High Ogres had planned for his ilk; so long as the tomb served its venerated purpose, the dead would forever have his life, his power, surrounding him. By shattering the sarcophagus—as any base robber would have done, thinking only of riches—Tyranos had dispersed the spell holding the coffin, the dead body, and the ancient magic together.

And so he had been rewarded for all his strenuous effort . . . with nothing.

The wizard ruefully raised the staff toward one of the nearest niches, shoving aside the piles of dust and over-turning one ruined box. The rusting container clattered to the floor, revealing that it contained only more dust. Dust here, dust there.

Tyranos let out a snort and went through a few more niches. There was not one item of value to him . . .

Not one item save the signet he grasped in his hand.

He studied it closely again. It once held immense power. The spellcaster could sense that. Even after so many centuries, it must hold that power undiminished. Somehow, Tyranos would find out the key to unlocking that power. Somehow he would yet wield it.

There was only the small matter of time running out.

His thoughts abruptly turned to the ogre, the Grand Lord Golgren. The two of them were playing a dangerous game with Dauroth and his Black Talon. Tyranos's blundering made it essential that he either steal the secrets of the Titans' find from them or see to it that they ended up, like him, with nothing. Golgren need not know about his failure, of course.

He eyed the signet. It would take some risks, but it would be worth it.

His decision made, the tall wizard abandoned the burial chamber. There was nothing remaining for him there. Even the beautiful runes and depictions had fallen to ruin, the images little more than vague outlines; the magic that had enabled Tyranos to relive one glorious moment in the dead ogre's life was gone. He grunted to think of that loss; the lost history of the High Ogres was precious, all but a mystery to the modern world. In the end, however, all that mattered was the plan. And Tyranos would endeavor to give the grand lord what he needed to gain the upper hand over Dauroth and the Black Talon.

The crystal barely lit his way, his overuse having drained it of some power. Soon it would revitalize itself, but for the time being, the spellcaster would have to rely upon his own talents only.

He stepped out onto the hillside, the shadows deep with scant light coming from above. Raising the staff, Tyranos resigned himself to using it one last time for the day.

But as he aimed its illumination, from somewhere among the trees he heard the flutter of heavy wings. Tyranos quickly turned to face the sound, the words of a spell forming on his lips.

A gray shape swooped down. It landed before him, a huge brute of a gargoyle more than half again the size of the one the wizard had presented to Golgren. The creature's wingspan stretched nearly twice Tyranos's height. Red eyes glared at him from under its thick brow, and the thing's heavy jaw moved back and forth, its sharp teeth scraping together.

The gargoyle, a male, moved closer to Tyranos, moving as much on its knuckles as on its feet.

The lion-maned spellcaster lowered his staff. "Ah, it's you."

XV

DONNAG

The prisoner screamed. Golgren made a *tsk* sound. No one outside of that place could hear the screams, so he was not concerned about alerting Sir Stefan Rennert, but thus far the screams were all his torturers had gotten out of the temple guard.

The imprisoned ogre was stretched tight across a huge oak table worn from decades of torture work. Much of the wood was no longer brown but had turned a dull red. Red-green ropes made from the dread mavau plant had been bound around the captive's wrists and ankles. The curled thorns dug into his flesh, sending blood dripping to the floor. Struggling only made the bleeding worse and had little effect on the bonds; hardened mavau vines were nearly as strong as steel.

The Solamnic would never have believed it, but the grand lord did not act unreasonably or viciously by the standards of his people. He had not selected the guard at random, as Zharang might have done, torturing him until agony made his victim confess to anything, however implausible. Golgren had first conducted an investigation to determine that that sentry was the one most likely responsible, at least in part, for the disastrous ceremony. Only then did he have the unfortunate dragged to the chamber deep beneath the palace.

The hexagonal room, with its thick, mossy stone walls and wide slate floor, was perfect for such torture and had been so utilized for centuries. However, Golgren knew that once it had been a different place where magic spells had been tested and cast. Tyranos had informed him of that history once, when the mage was visiting. In fact, Tyranos had seemed unusually uncomfortable in the chamber, evidently having to do with the residual magic still permeating the walls. At least, that was the impression the wizard had given Golgren.

What mattered at that moment, though, was determining just who claimed the guard's loyalty, so much so that he would suffer on their behalf. Golgren had his suspicions but needed to know with certainty. His hand moved to the hidden dagger as the grand lord reflected on how a careless move could hurt him; he could lose all.

Other races did not think ogres capable of subtlety, but they were wrong. The device keeping the prisoner's eyes open was a fine example of subtle craftsmanship. The needles that prevented the lids from shutting even a little had come from the *tuscru j'in,* a thick, barrel-shaped plant that thrived in the hottest and driest parts of Kern and was believed to be part of an amalok's diet. Thousands of needles covered the *tuscru j'in,* but only those of a certain length and diameter, which did not break or pierce the eye, were used in the tool. It took a skilled hunter to pick those out and, with even more skill, to fashion from other needles the frame that held the first in place.

The eyes needed to be open, for the torturer worked in their reflection. There were a variety of methods that ogres used for torture, but the eyes were a favorite part of the body for the best results. Ogres might boast tough hides and stubborn wills, but their eyes were soft and sensitive.

The torturer silently reached into a clay jar and removed, with the aid of brass tongs, a scorpionlike arachnid with a heavily bloated thorax and only a vestigial tail. The creature, perhaps the length of Golgren's tiniest finger, hardly looked sinister enough to affect a muscular ogre, but the sight of it caused the captive to renew his struggles, albeit in vain.

With another set of tongs, the torturer took hold of the thorax. There were scars all over the arms and hands of the ogre entrusted to handle the grand lord's work, far more than even the most veteran warrior would have garnered. None of them were ceremonial, either, but rather the results of occupational hazards, such as the tiny vermin with which he now dealt.

The torturer turned an equally scarred visage toward Golgren. The grand lord nodded approvingly.

"Kifu i harag ne! Kifu i harag ne!" shouted the intended torture victim, but his claims of ignorance about any plot fell, as they had for the past half day, on stone-deaf ears.

With deft precision, Golgren's servant positioned the arachnid over the suspected traitor's left eye. The bloated thorax hung less than two inches above the pupil.

The tongs holding the thorax squeezed ever so slightly. A single yellow drop of liquid slipped from the tip of the tiny tail. It landed without a sound on the eye.

The ogre strapped to the table shrieked. He tore at his bonds with such vehemence that the thorns in the rope tore bits of flesh away. A guard stationed at the doorway moved to reinforce the prisoner's bonds, but Golgren waved him back.

"Venemok," the grand lord murmured just loud enough for his captive to hear. *"Venemok."*

The eye was blood red and badly damaged. Even had the tortured ogre been allowed to shut it, he would have found the simple act impossible. The eye was swollen and growing more so.

"Kifu i harag ne!" the prisoner blurted. *"Kifu i harag ne!"*

The torturer, bald from age, had only one tusk, one that was almost completely broken off. He grunted at the defiance and looked to Golgren for his orders once more.

Baring his filed-down tusks, Golgren indicated the torturer should get on with his work.

A second delicate squeeze of the thorax sent another miniscule drop squirting onto the ogre's eye, landing almost exactly where the other had fallen.

And just as happened with the first drop, that one sent the traitorous guard into shrieks and spasms of agony.

"If you would have commanded it," said a voice in Common. "I could have given you his answers long ago, oh Grand Lord."

The guard on duty flinched, belatedly readying his heavy sword for action. The torturer, who had seen so much in his job, only gave Golgren's visitor a surreptitious glance before resuming his study of the effects of the arachnid's poison.

"Dauroth." Golgren's tone indicated he had expected the Titan, even though there had been no request by the ogre leader for the spellcaster's presence. "Your studies have gone well?"

"Well enough," the Titan replied vaguely.

Golgren returned his attention to the prisoner. At his nod, the torturer prepared the arachnid for another application.

"The ghlideesh is an effective torture for most prisoners, but this guard appears especially resistant, oh Grand Lord." The Titan glided forward. Out of deference, the torturer quickly pulled back. "Please to allow me."

Golgren said nothing. The giant spellcaster leaned over the prisoner, who reacted to him the same way he had reacted to the ghlideesh, writhing and shrieking.

"Hush," whispered Dauroth, slowly moving his palm above the captive's face. "Calm."

"Kifu i harag ne," murmured the bound figure. *"Kifu i harag—"*

"Hush . . . silence."

The prisoner suddenly became motionless. Dauroth brought his other palm over the victim's face. A faint, purple glow emanated between the spellcaster's two hands.

The torturer watched closely because he was always interested in variations of his craft, even magical ones.

"Zin isala, zin isol . . . " The Titan repeated the words several times. Although they sounded like words in the ogre tongue, for Golgren and the rest they had no obvious meaning.

But the captive guard reacted to them as though he understood. His body jerked, his eyes focusing on the purple glow.

"Venemok . . . venemok," Dauroth said slowly.

The figure on the table gasped. His eyes—even the reddened one—glazed over.

"Venemok," continued Dauroth. "The name . . . "

But the first sounds out of the prisoner's mouth were far from a name. "D—d—d—"

The Titan's hands drew nearer to the face, the tips of the ebony talons actually digging into the flesh. The captive did not even flinch, so utterly did Dauroth control his will.

"Venemok . . . "

"D—d—Donnnnaggg . . . Donnag. Donnag. Donnag. Donnag."

It seemed likely the temple guard would have gone on repeating the disgraced chieftain's name forever if Dauroth had not jerked away from him as if he'd been slapped in the face. The lead Titan spun toward Golgren.

"Grand Lord! We have nothing to do with this treachery! Donnag is not even one of us anymore! You cannot believe—"

"Donnag is guilty, yes, this and only this I believe," Golgren, his face set grimly, replied.

"Naturally, it is we who should deal with this monstrous traitor."

"No. Donnag shall present his head to me. As you said, the chieftain is not a Titan any longer. They and you should not be concerned, yes?"

Dauroth bowed his head in agreement.

Emerald eyes narrowed, Golgren strode past the spellcaster to inspect the abject prisoner. The former guard was only just coming out of the trance that had been cast over him by Dauroth. His frantic eyes met the grand lord's.

"F'han," the ogre leader whispered to him.

Golgren's lone hand shot out, striking the prisoner directly across the throat with incredible force. The prisoner gagged for a moment; then his head slumped to the side, the needle framework keeping the dead orbs staring sightlessly.

The grand lord turned to give his attention to the giant spellcaster, but Dauroth was already gone.

A grin that held no mirth spread across Golgren's half-elf face.

❦

The riders and messenger birds departed within the hour to alert all khans and chieftains in both ogre lands that Donnag was guilty of high treason against the grand lord and that any, even clan, who offered the former ruler sanctuary would share his fate. The word of the Grand Lord Golgren was absolute.

But even Golgren knew that there would be those who would aid Donnag despite the danger to themselves.

❦

Donnag's transformation continued unabated. Even his most loyal kin and guards—many of whom had served him since before the days when *he,* not the mongrel, had seemed destined to unite the ogre race—sought to avoid contact with him as much as possible. He would have turned for aid to his son, who was a mage, but Maldred was as despised by Donnag as he was by Golgren, and besides, Maldred had mysteriously vanished some months back. The once-great chieftain had fallen so low he would have been willing to scrape before his dubious offspring.

Donnag was well aware of the Abominations,

Dauroth's punishment for those he felt had betrayed him. At least his fate was better than theirs . . . for the time being. Though, as his degeneration continued, Donnag wondered if a point would come when there would be little difference between him and the accursed ones.

A terrible thirst overcame him. He was always thirsty. No matter how much water, wine, or other liquid he swallowed, the once-mighty chieftain always felt parched. Thick stubs that were all that remained of the fingers on his one hand clumsily fought to grip the handle of a curved, clay jug. After a struggle, Donnag managed to maneuver the vessel close to the lips of his misshapen mouth and pour most of the contents—yellow-tinted *tuscru j'in* ale—down his gullet. As usual, the rest of the quickly-souring drink spilled over his chin and down his robe, which was already badly stained and soiled.

In a sudden burst of frustration at his inability to perform even that simple task, the mockery that had once been a powerful warlord hurled the jug to the side. It bounced harmlessly against the interior of the goatskin tent then struck the rocky ground hard enough to break, cracking open. The *tuscru j'in* ale spilled over the ground inside the tent.

Donnag rose to his feet, although he was far from the height he had once commanded. When younger, he had stood nearly ten feet tall; as a Titan, he had actually been taller than the others by a hand. That time seemed a long-ago dream, not any past reality; a period so short he could barely recall it.

A young female entered through the goatskin flaps of the tent to check on the disturbance she had heard. Her curved hips and smaller tusks enticed Donnag, but he made no move to grab lustily at her as he once would have done. The obvious revulsion and fear in her eyes were only part of the reason; Donnag was beyond the pleasures of the flesh, and his own shame at what he had become made him simply wish for her to leave.

That the female did the moment she had retrieved the pieces of the shattered pot. With one last, fleeting glance at the former ruler—likely from fear that he *would* after all try to clutch her—the other ogre vanished through the tent flaps.

Donnag let out a growl, which out of his twisted throat emerged more like a rasping cough. Spittle dripped over the thick growth that passed for his lower lip. With tremendous effort, he shoved himself up off the soiled animal skin upon which he had been resting and tried to straighten up. Unfortunately, his back was more malformed than ever, so he stood bent and looked as though he were contemplating his feet.

His first step nearly sent him tripping over the hem of the ragged brown robe he wore. The robe made him feel like an elderly female. He, who used to go into battle with his chest unprotected, covered himself from head to toe. His most ardent supporters could not bear to see his disgusting flesh, and even he was revolted by the sight of so many thick boils, the rampant scaly patches of skin, and worse sores.

How much longer any of his followers, even his kin, would continue to give him any support was a question he pondered every day. They knew of his connections to the Titans and, because of those connections, believed his assurances that one day he would be restored to beauty and power. They did not yet suspect the truth, that Morgada's failure to convince the spellcasters to give him another chance spelled his certain doom . . . unless something no one expected befell the half-breed.

Yes, for Donnag to live, Golgren *had* to die.

"My poor, poor Donnag," came the voice that he secretly hated as much as the grand lord's. "I did all that I could for you, and this is the gratitude with which you remember me."

"D-Dauroth!" The lead Titan loomed before him so suddenly and so tall that Donnag gave a start. He could not even see his face until the blue-skinned giant had backed up a few paces.

"You may save your breath, my old friend. I know how troublesome it is for you to speak."

With a guttural roar, Donnag flung himself at the Titan only to be sent hurtling back in the opposite direction.

"That would have once been beneath you," Dauroth reproached him calmly. "As is so much you have done of late. Did I not promise you once that there would come a day when you *would* be brought back into the fold if only you could be patient?"

"H-have! Patient, have been!" Donnag gazed past the other, wondering why no one had come running at his shouts. Once, a mere whisper by the chieftain would have brought a dozen able guards to his side. Apparently, they had turned deaf to his plight.

The Titan sighed. "Oh, I have blocked all sound from those without. That is why no one is coming to your aid. Really, Donnag! Have you forgotten so much?"

The grotesque figure spit. The ugly missile did not come even close to Dauroth, but the spellcaster nevertheless shook his head disapprovingly.

"You were and are ungrateful. Despite that, I have done what I could for you even in the face of Golgren's wrath. He has condemned you now for attempting to slay him and all in the two lands are now to hunt you and bring you to his feet."

"But I . . . d-did . . . *nothing!*" Donnag managed.

"I dare not rescind his command," Dauroth replied, seeming not to hear or care about the other's protest of innocence. "But out of a last gesture for our former friendship, I have done you a blessing." The spellcaster held out his hand, and a well-worn, twin-edged battle axe that sat to the side of Donnag flew up into the Titan's hand. Dauroth easily wielded it, testing its weight. "You will have need of this."

The axe flew at Donnag, who, despite his twisted form, managed to catch it.

"Through other channels, I have let your kin know the news of your condemnation." Ignoring Donnag's grunt of outrage, the Titan added, "They know what aiding you would mean for them now."

"But . . . I . . . did not—"

"What you did or did not do does not matter anymore." Dauroth cocked an ear toward the tent flap. "Ready yourself, my old friend. I think they come even now."

Reacting instinctively, the fallen chieftain swung at the giant.

His axe met only air. Dauroth was gone.

But another figure materialized through the entrance barely a breath afterward. Donnag recognized him as one of his cousins, a young and capable warrior whom he had once intended to command his personal guard.

The one who had been intended to protect Donnag's life sought to take it instead. Wielding an axe nearly as great as that gripped by his adversary, the cousin—a lean, eager fighter in his prime—leaped at Donnag.

Yet although the latter was not the warrior he had once been, there remained residual skills and training that even the monstrous transformation could not yet eradicate. Donnag blocked one blow then a second then, using his shorter stature to his advantage, jammed the pointed axe head into his kinsman's stomach.

The younger warrior let out a gasp. Eyes bulging, he dropped his weapon.

Donnag finished him off with a swift slash across the chest. It was the first pleasure that he had felt in a long time.

But as the one intruder fell, two more charged into the tent. One was distant kin, the other a warrior sworn to the clan.

"Du daka f'han iDonnagi!" shouted his blood relation.

"Jaro Gyun!" the elder ogre managed to rasp back, adding his spit to the insult. They dared demand that *he* had to die for their sake, he who had given them so much?

It was odd that, even as his fate was sealed, Donnag found his thoughts clear. He had been thinking clearly for the past hour or so. Perhaps the gods had played a final trick on him, letting him understand and be aware of his downfall. Indeed, that sounded like Sirrion; for was that god not the bane of all ogres, setting the sun so hot over the land?

His accursed blood and the other warrior came at him from opposite sides. The guard wielded a sword, which, thanks to the good deeds of the Grand Lord Golgren, was sharply honed and polished. Donnag had little hope of quickly smashing the blade apart, as used to happen often when he fought in the old days.

He met the blade dead on then blocked the other axe. Twice more, Donnag managed to deflect the pair's blows. He began to feel like a real fighter again, aware that only his monstrous body kept him from easily dispatching the pair.

Indeed, Donnag succeeded in slicing his relation across the forearm, which caused the latter to momentarily retreat. Unfortunately, another pair of foes rushed into the tent, including one close cousin whose father had been Donnag's father's brother. Among ogres, such a male-linked relationship was akin to a brotherly bond.

"*iKarnagi.*" The former chieftain swung back and forth, clearing the path to his greatest of betrayers. If he could at least take his cousin to the grave with him . . .

The guard with the sword thrust. Unable to move as nimbly as in the past, Donnag could not entirely evade the attack. The blade sank into his side. Blood and pus spilled forth. The bleeding was heavy; his reflexes would be further slowed.

His cousin Karnag stood before him, an axe in one hand, a sword in the other. Donnag had taught his cousin many of his tricks, and even then Karnag executed a move that the older warrior well recognized. Donnag countered it with one he had not shown his cousin and then, while Karnag was caught off guard, followed through with a lunge of his own.

But the warped body he was trapped inside began to betray Donnag. His swing went awry, and he stumbled to his knees. His usable fingers lost their grip on the axe.

Then Karnag's axe swung true, burying itself in his shoulder. Ironically, Donnag's transformation kept the weapon from sinking as deeply as it should have, for the blade found instead of soft flesh a hardened mass almost like stone.

But more was coming. First a sword pierced his other shoulder, then another axe all but severed his right arm. Crying out, his blood gushing, Donnag sprawled onto the ground.

"*F'han, iDonnagi . . . dukara f'han,*" his cousin pronounced.

Donnag forced his face up, meeting, as best he could, the eyes of his executioner.

Karnag's axe cut through his neck. Donnag's head fell past the cousin, almost but not quite rolling out of the tent.

⊷⊶❦⊷⊶

Idaria waited for more than an hour after Golgren had drifted off before daring to sneak away and write her latest missive. There was far more to tell than the tiny parchment allowed, so she kept to the key details. The grand lord had nearly been slain, and his authority had been undermined. A culprit had been named, and his arrest and execution would have repercussions. Whether or not that would play well into the hands of those for whom she spied, only they could answer.

The moment she was finished writing, Idaria rushed to the window. By then, there were birds who expected her summons, be it day or night, and one came quickly in response to her quiet call.

"Thank you, little one," the slave murmured as she kissed the bird lightly on the beak. "You are so brave."

She attached the message by a string. That one

especially could be trusted to carry her messages far and beyond the ogre lands, if need be. The bird loved her that much.

"Fly safely now," she ordered.

The bird fluttered from her hand and out through the window. Idaria watched as it vanished into the night then turned back toward the bed of her master, who lay sleeping.

She was startled by a tall shape that materialized between the bed and her, nearly causing the elf to gasp. Only a long-honed sense of survival kept the gasp smothered in her throat.

Within the shadows of his hood, Tyranos smiled. In an overly innocent tone, he whispered, "I see you admire the night fliers too."

The dagger appeared in her hand as if by magic. She lunged for the wizard's chest, but he moved quicker than any human should have been able, even a spellcaster. Tyranos evaded her attack and seized her wrist, twisting it upward. The dagger fell free, but before it could clatter on the floor, the wizard grabbed it in his other hand, which for once did not hold his precious staff.

"Careful," he murmured. "Mustn't wake the master."

Her eyes darted to Golgren, who remained still. "You do not plan to alert—to tell him?"

"Are you certain he doesn't already know?" Tyranos pulled her nearer. "You're a puzzle, Lady Idaria. On the one hand, you volunteer for slavery after escaping Silvanost in order to spy for those whom you should loathe nearly as much as the ogres. On the other, you had the perfect opportunity to let events take their course and see the grand lord die, yet you went out of the way to divert the griffon so Golgren could survive."

She lowered her eyes. "I did it to save myself. Without him, I would be taken away by the Titans. You know the fate awaiting me—awaiting all elves—in their lair."

"Huh. You know very well you could escape at almost any time."

He released her hand, then, unexpectedly, returned her dagger to her. The wizard turned his gaze back to the slumbering form.

"Fascinating," Tyranos rumbled, eyes flickering back to the elf. "Very fascinating." He reached out to hand something else to Idaria. "When he wakes, give this to him. He should know what it means, but tell him that he ought to show it to the leader of the Titans—show it but not surrender it."

The slave eyed the dark object in her palm: a ring, a very old ring.

Idaria, from a race nearly as ancient as the High Ogres, had little trouble recognizing its origins or its potential. Her eyes widened. She looked to the human for explanation.

But Tyranos was already vanishing. The mage said but one last thing as he turned into shadow then empty air. "Oh. I meant to tell you also; I don't think your message is going to make it through this time. There are more gargoyles about, you see."

And with that, he left Idaria holding the signet and staring narrow-eyed at the still sleeping form in the bed.

XVI

GOLGREN'S PLEDGE

Donnag's death at the hands of his own kin did not sit well with Golgren, although on the surface he pretended to be satisfied with the news. The grand lord would have preferred to broadcast Donnag's disgrace to all before he was executed. After the execution his corpse would be of no use, for the heat of the ogre lands would turn any dead body into something vile within a day or two. Much of Donnag's transformation could be blamed on decay.

Golgren could not even punish the kin, for they had acted according to a tradition that dated back to the old days. There were traditions that he could and would change and traditions that he dared not. Worse, Donnag's clan had bought its way into his good graces, whether he really endorsed their actions or not.

All that told him that he had to act as soon as possible with regard to the human. Golgren summoned Khleeg and Wargroch, giving them orders. He then had the Solamnic brought to him.

"We must talk," Golgren bluntly informed Stefan. "But not here, not now. You have seen little of Garantha and all its surroundings! I would have you see its changes."

"I'd be very interested, indeed," Stefan admitted. "You are too kind—"

The grand lord waved off his gratitude. "It is my duty as host! Come."

The mounts he ordered were ready within minutes, three instead of the two the Solamnic expected. In addition, some fifteen warriors also stood ready as the riders' escort around the city.

Khleeg gave commands to the guards, but then, to the human's surprise, the officer saluted them and departed.

"I am here," Idaria's voice softly called from behind the pair.

Stefan frowned. "She rides with us?"

"There is objection?"

"No, no."

The elf solemnly mounted her horse as best as her shackles enabled her. Of necessity, the silver-tressed female rode sidesaddle.

Golgren grinned. "Like the females of a Solamnic court, is she not?"

"Only they are not chained, Grand Lord."

The ogre shrugged. "Are they not?"

At his command, the sizable party entered the streets. Golgren set the pace, leisurely enough that the escort could keep up, but not so much that they grew lax.

Stefan had seen a good deal of Garantha from the gate to the palace, but Golgren led him toward the northeastern sector.

There the stone streets were cracked and worn

from generations of neglect, but they were cleaner than under any previous grand khan. With the knowledge that he would eventually take the human on just such an excursion, Golgren had issued orders that that part of Garantha would be made as presentable as possible. At an intersection far ahead, he noted some of Khleeg's officers urging a cadre of ogres to swifter and better cleaning. Using wooden brooms with bristles made from the stiff hair of sturdy Kernian horses, the workers attacked the street as though it were an enemy. The grand lord began to slow his pace and introduced the topic that most interested him.

"I have spoken of alliance but left you wondering about more, yes?"

"I've been curious, definitely," the Solamnic cautiously replied. "I still find it hard to fathom what you might be suggesting."

Golgren sensed that the human fathomed far more than he cared to let on. But he didn't know as much about the ogres as Golgren knew about the knighthood and its goals. "It is simple," he said, his hand retrieving a vial of scent from his belt pouch. "Solamnics and ogres, they have a common problem: the Uruv Suurt. They must be watched."

"Uruv Suurt?"

Raising the vial to his nostrils, the grand lord bent open the stopper and inhaled. Memories of his childhood briefly drifted through his thoughts, although he gave no sign of his distraction to the human. "I think you understand a few of our simple phrases. I mean the minotaurs of course," Golgren said. "The invaders of Ansalon . . . that is how Solamnia sees them, yes?"

Stefan Rennert nodded. If the knighthood had been

blind to the empire's slow but steady advance through Silvanost, then they could boast themselves greater fools than gully dwarves.

"As I said, a common problem. We, too, inhabit the mainland, and so the minotaurs also crowd our nation." Golgren returned the stoppered vial to the pouch before adding, "But would not Solamnia enjoy to know that ogres will not march west? Ogres would certainly be pleased if *Shok G'Ran* did not try to seize ogre lands."

"You speak of a nonaggression pact," the bearded knight declared. "Peace between your kind and ours because of the minotaurs. But we have no designs on ogre lands!"

"And I can assure you we have no desire for knightly lands. But if the Uruv Suurt attack either, the other comes to the aid."

Despite what Sir Stefan said, Golgren knew that the Solamnics would willingly enter the ogre lands if it suited their purpose. They might even establish a "permanent" presence. That didn't really worry him, although a pact would definitely forestall such a possibility. Buying time was part of his plan.

Stefan brooded over Golgren's words, tantalized by the idea of—what did he call it?—a nonaggression pact. The grand lord's emerald eyes hid his pleasure at having read the knight so well.

"Such a pact might indeed be of interest to my superiors," Stefan finally admitted. Yet, like the ogre, he didn't want to say too much. "I need to consider this proposal longer, though."

"This is understood."

The knight met the ogre leader's gaze. "I must tell you truthfully, as you have treated me so graciously as your guest, that I fear an acceptance is hardly likely. The knights have too long regarded ogres as, uh, dire enemies."

Golgren grinned like a human. "Of course, we will have to overcome the past and prejudices. But we must try, yes? Think of it! Ogres and knights, they have been allies before, in times of necessity; they can be so again. Even more so. Solamnia and Golthuu can be brothers in all things."

The knight's hands tightened on the reins. "Golthuu?"

"The ogres of Kern and those of Blöde, they are the same under the skin. Each has khans and chieftains, both make two lands. I intend to remake the two lands into one, as it was in the beginning."

From beside the human, Idaria quietly explained, *"Golthuu* means *the dream of Golgren."*

"My loyal followers, they will insist on such a name." The grand lord tried to look modest. "I could not deny them."

Stefan nodded but stayed silent. The human suddenly found his surroundings of great interest. They were passing ogres on the city streets; many of those citizens glowered at him, though their hostility always vanished quickly under Golgren's scrutiny. Younger ogres stared more wide eyed, more openly curious, never likely having seen one of Stefan's kind—at least not alive—in their city and in the company of the grand lord at that.

Most of the males were clad in brown, cloth kilts and sandals of newer make than those available beyond the capital. Various crude symbols sewn into the kilts marked the clan of each onlooker. Females wore simple cloth dresses that covered everything from the neck down to the knees, a style that the grand lord thought was more civilized than the ragged skins that often did not hide their breasts. Golgren was proud to point out to the Solamnic that all the garments were of ogre make.

"I've seen other ogres dressed in finery like those of elves," Stefan pointed out with a quick glance at Idaria. "Ogres dressed even more grandly than yourself."

"All will someday be dressed so, as we learn the skills. Perhaps Solamnia can help teach us these? That, too, can be part of our alliance. I have seen such good clothes on humans."

"Aren't your slaves proficient enough?"

The question—its accusing tone—might have caused a crude ruler such as Zharang to order the knight flayed alive over a pit of hungry meredrakes, but Golgren did not blink. "Ogres must learn to rely on themselves alone, as humans most of the time do, yes?"

He did not care to remind Stefan that there were many areas of so-called human civilization where other races were enslaved, even fellow men. The Knighthood, Golgren knew, was choosy about what races it befriended and what slaves it freed. Therefore, Stefan could say anything he wanted, and Golgren found it amusing. After all, he sought a pact with these choosy knights.

The grand lord signaled the escort to turn further east, which caused Idaria, at least, to glance up briefly in surprise. The Solamnic did not appear to have noticed her reaction.

Then, ahead of them, came a sight that forced the party to grind to a halt. Stefan stood in the saddle to get a better look, staring at the huge, lumbering beasts. Under the guidance of several handlers, the three mastarks—collars around their thick throats and massive chains attached to the backs of those collars—strained together as they headed to the north. Their chains rose several stories in the air behind them and looped over a series of wheels, creating pulleys.

The object of their labor was a gigantic piece of newly cut marble on which had been carved a relief of Garantha's powerful patron spirit. The griffon image was shown leaping into the air, its tremendous wings so detailed in their craftsmanship that one could note the individual feathers. The work was very skilled, Stefan had to admit. At the moment, the block was being lifted up to enable several ogres high above to maneuver it into place on a new tower being constructed.

The half-built tower appeared to be another marvel. Oval in shape, its newness alone made it stand out among the many ancient, often decrepit structures in the vicinity. Immediately striking were the several massive, almond-shaped openings on one side of the tower—openings resembling nothing less than the grand lord's eyes. The other side of the tower had been left utterly blank with no windows and not even a door in sight.

"The House of Night," answered Golgren to the Solamnic's silent question. "To mark the passing of the *iSirriti Siroth,* Sirrion's Burning. The wall with no opening, it faces the morning, when the Burning comes. The other side, with many windows, counts the final fall of the sun. Twelve intervals of growing shadow, twelve windows. It is a ritual of many ages ago, after the High Ones fell and Kern and Blöde suffered more and more heat. It is a ritual with special meaning to this humble servant."

Stefan continued to watch the mastarks toil at their herculean task. The shoulder muscles of the great beasts strained as they pulled tons of stone higher and higher.

The pulley framework creaked and shook as the block rose, but somehow it held. Already, the block was some five stories up, with maybe two yet to go.

"How tall will it be when the tower is finished?"

"Five levels upon five, as the first was. Two windows at the bottom, two at top. The old tower, it was destroyed many generations ago from the earthquakes." Kern, especially, was a land prone to tremors and quakes, some of them exceedingly violent. "This one," the grand lord went on proudly. "This one will stand stronger. It is built . . . it is built more *clever.*"

Indeed, within the half-open structure, thick oaken beams—as valuable as gold in Kern—could be seen crisscrossing the length of the temple. The crossbeams would give Golgren's new project more solidity and stability during tremors.

"Garantha cannot live only on the old," the ogre leader went on. "To grow, Garantha must also have the new." To stir his people to the glory of old, so they would be worthy of him, Golgren needed to remake his chosen city into a jewel.

"Impressive." Stefan admitted. "It will be a great accomplishment when it is done."

"Perhaps you will return to see it then."

The knight said nothing. The handlers urged on the mastarks. Only a few more feet remained before the block would rise to a level even with the workers. For the last steps, the beasts had to be led cautiously; if they did not work precisely, the framework might lean to one side, leading to catastrophe and, worse, the grand lord's displeasure.

The huge stone rocked back and forth. From it dangled several thick ropes, which the workers above used hooked staffs to snag and hold. One by one, the ogres caught the ropes with the unusual tool, then seized those ropes in powerful grips.

Elves, although strong, could never have been trusted with such a formidable task. The Uruv Suurt— the minotaurs—would have been perfect, in muscle and size, but the ogres only pretended a friendship with the bull-men, for the moment. His own people, Golgren had decided, worked best. Besides, the grand lord had found that when his warriors were kept busy with building, they did not have the tendency to fall into brawling.

"Come," commanded the grand lord, deciding that the building demonstration had served its purpose for the moment. He brushed back his dark, leonine mane, which had fallen over his upturned face while watching the work. "We ride on."

Stefan continued to eye the impressive construction as they moved past it, which pleased Golgren. As they passed the site, it was the Solamnic who again broached the subject of an alliance.

"I've been thinking . . . "

Golgren merely cocked his head and waited. He kept his lips pursed, the better to accent his nonogre traits. The grand lord wished the human to feel as comfortable as possible.

"If . . . it was at all possible to consider an agreement of peace and cooperation between our two lands, my superiors would expect much more proof of the ogres' desires and plans."

"So many things to discuss, yes, but first there must actually be discussion set in motion. Would not it show Solamnia's great influence in all of Ansalon if peace would be agreed between knights and ogres? Would not all say, 'Look! The lords of Solamnia, they have tamed even the ogres! Such power! We, too, must seek alliance with the civilizing knights!' "

That brought a chuckle from Stefan. "My superiors would love all to say that, although I doubt I'll live to see such a miraculous day."

"Perhaps not . . . perhaps though . . . " Ahead rose a high wall formed by layers of mud-packed stone. At its center stood a single vast iron door with the crude image of a griffon, guarded by half a dozen armored warriors. Golgren looked to Idaria, whose eyes momentarily revealed the confusion her face usually hid. She fully expected the half-breed ruler to turn about and head in the opposite direction, yet he did not.

"Sir Stefan Rennert," the grand lord began carefully. "The lords of Solamnia, if they were to be given proof that ogres seek this peaceful alliance—so that Ansalon can be spared any further conquest by the minotaurs, let us say—good proof, then they would discuss this, yes?"

"I must be honest. They would expect very much from you. They would probably expect more than you could offer."

"Yes?" The high wooden wall waited only a short distance ahead of them. Warriors on the walkway above and at the tall gate toward which they rode did their best to come to smart attention. Golgren grinned, pleased by their effort. "There is perhaps one thing that might make them listen . . . "

He gestured dramatically at the gate. After a momentary pause to enjoy the curious look on the Solamnic's face, the husky, heavy-browed officer grunted a command.

Inside, they could hear a large bolt being slid aside.

Then, with a loud creak, the gate swung open. Golgren led the party forward.

"My lord—" Idaria started, but Golgren paid her no mind. With Stefan riding next to him and the elf on her horse lagging behind, he entered.

"By Kiri-Jolith's beard!" exclaimed the knight, seeing at last what the walls had kept veiled.

Before them stood elves, more elves than Solamnia likely ever suspected were held in all of Kern and Blöde combined. There were hundreds of elves. Most wore ragged clothes that had once been counted as finery. The slaves themselves could be described as ragged, worked hard by their masters. There were adults and young, far more of the former than the latter. Many bore tattooed marks on their cheeks, the parts of their bodies where ogre overlords often placed their signs of ownership.

Yet if one studied the elves closer, they could see that, despite such long servitude, they were mostly fairly healthy. They were thin, perhaps, but not starved. Golgren had insisted that Khleeg make certain that they were fed well for the past several days before the knight saw them.

They tried to carry on some semblance of a civilized life there. They shared food, they attempted to keep clean despite the surrounding filth, and more. However, whatever they had been doing before the party entered, all actions jarred to a stop as the slaves recognized who it was who had just entered.

"Barbaric!" Stefan blurted, all his previous congeniality swept away by the spectacle. The Knighthood had not always been on the best of terms with the elves, but only the most hardened fighter could not have been disturbed by the degradation of slavery.

"Barbaric?" Golgren gestured beyond the throng. "There is shelter," he pointed out, indicating row upon row of thatched, roofed long houses, all of recent make. They were simple—and made of the same stone as the surrounding walls—but sturdy, far better housing than in some lands, Golgren reckoned. "There is food," the grand lord continued, pointing at a younger elf munching on a piece of coarse bread. "Perhaps," he added, "it is not the wondrous, lavish fare said to have been served in Silvanost, but the elves are not starving and the food is by no means inedible."

"Such slavery is still barbaric!" the human insisted. "And it would make any hope of peace, let alone alliance, impossible between us!"

Golgren nodded. "So, too, I thought."

"What?"

"Sir Stefan Rennert, all of these you see, are they as you would expect? Truly?"

"A slave is still a slave," the Solamnic insisted, "but no, I expected worse, I must admit."

"And it has been." The grand lord swept his arm across the scene. "But it shall be no more."

"I don't follow you."

"It is very simple, Sir Stefan Rennert. I sincerely wish this pact of no aggression, this alliance against the wave of Uruv Suurt, so very much that I will do this! When I am crowned grand khan, if Solamnia will merely agree to *meet* for peace—merely that—all these that you see here—all elves elsewhere in my domain—they will be set *free.*"

His declaration left not only Stefan speechless, but Idaria also open mouthed. The grand lord grinned at the knight, then turned a much more thoughtful expression to his slave.

"*All* elves will be set free," he repeated for her. "All of them."

⌘

It was not the time of year for the river to overflow its banks, but overflow it had, sweeping the three legionaries off to their dooms. Most minotaurs were exceptional swimmers, but those three could not fight the treacherous current, especially weighed down as they were by their armor.

And so the series of misfortunes and mishaps striking the northernmost legions continued. Some of the generals suspected that the "accidents" were more than that, but there was no proof.

For the Titans, especially those in the Black Talon, were meticulous about covering their tracks.

Hundjal watched the last trace of the legionaries vanish beneath the waves. The bodies would not be found for some time and distance, if at all. Once again, he had pleased his master and the grand lord.

The Titan spit, the ground sizzling where the liquid hit.

A waste of energy and effort, he thought not for the first time. *The mongrel ever holds the rein on Dauroth! It cannot continue!*

Hundjal did not fear the half-breed. But Dauroth's wrath was something to be feared, especially by the one who knew him best. Over the past few days, Hundjal had come up with some ideas about what to do about Dauroth, but he would have to tread lightly.

Of course, none of that mattered until he was able to return to the sanctum. He could hardly accomplish anything while still essentially exiled to that foul wilderness.

Hundjal spun about, a gleaming dagger of gold suddenly in his hand. The point of the magical blade paused at the very flesh of the one who had materialized behind him.

"Safrag," the senior apprentice greeted the newcomer, sharp teeth bared in a smile. "You come to visit me?"

"I come bearing word," replied the other, eyes poised on the weapon at his throat, "and surely I am not mistaken for the Uruv Suurt."

Hundjal laughed harshly. "One of them might someday think to take up the arts, crude as the effort would be." He dismissed the weapon to oblivion. "And what word do you bring me, menial one? Does the mongrel command that Dauroth now send us to Nethosak itself to deal with the Uruv Suurt's emperor?"

"Nay, and your tone should be more grateful. The master desires you back at his side, for there is work that must be done to safely open the magical seals of a tomb of the ancients."

"Is that so?" Indeed Hundjal's new tone sung his gratitude at Dauroth's decision. "It is all intact, then?"

"It is and it shall stay so until the Talon can find the manner in which to not destroy what we seek."

"And thus I am needed. Praise Dauroth for his wisdom! If he had only summoned me back earlier, we could already be enjoying the fruits of success!"

The junior apprentice grimaced. "Promise not too much to the master; he may expect everything from you."

"He shall have it!" Hundjal spit again at his surroundings with the same sizzling results. "But come, Safrag! I would already be gone from this wretched place!"

The second Titan concurred. As the two prepared to combine their efforts to ease the teleport to the sanctum, Safrag murmured, "Between us, Hundjal, the master is so insistent that this tomb be breached quickly that he will certainly grant you—and only you, I say with some envy—access to his innermost secrets and research!"

That happy revelation nearly made Hundjal forfeit his concentration. "I am truly his favored again!" The air around the Titans shimmered. "Make no mistake about it, Safrag, I'll delve deep into everything, leave nothing untouched."

As was his way, Hundjal took guidance of the spell they were casting. Safrag lent his power but otherwise was passive. As the pair vanished from the borderlands, he murmured to his companion, "And that is what the master hopes, good Hundjal. That is exactly what the master hopes you will do."

XVII

ASSASSINS WITHIN

Golgren's promise had thrown Stefan off guard. Up to that point, Stefan's true interest had been in analyzing the ogre's character and his stronghold, then, if at all possible, escaping to report everything he had learned to his superiors.

Yet the half-breed had again proven himself a surprising leader, much different from what the Solamnic had assumed. His vow to release the elf slaves was significant, and it was true that the Knighthood *was* very anxious about the minotaurs' spread west.

Although he dined with Golgren that same evening, the grand lord said nothing more about the elves. His conversation concerned only the knight's impressions of the capital, which were as favorable as the ogre had hoped. All the while stern guards kept watch over the dinner. Idaria joined them while two other elves took care of serving the meal, the centerpiece of which was a wonderfully seasoned, roasted side of amalok. For such an ill-tempered beast, the amalok proved quite tender and savory on the palate, one of the finest meats upon which the Solamnic had ever dined. Turmeric and rosemary added to the unique flavor.

"This is superb, Grand Lord," Stefan remarked as he swallowed another bite. "I think that any of the great houses of Solamnia would serve it with pride to their most illustrious guests. Perhaps you might offer a small herd as a token during negotiations—"

"The amalok is good eating, yes," interjected Golgren casually. "I have raised them myself in the past." The ogre then went into some detail concerning the care of the creatures, including how sometimes they had to be tethered during feeding time so the handlers would not be injured by a frenzied bite or kick.

The slaves tending to the meal acted like ghosts, silent and almost invisible with their tasks. With ample opportunity for the slaves—or the cooks, for that matter, for they also were elves—to poison the fare, Golgren had insisted that all the food be tasted before he and the human ate. The casual manner in which Idaria had tasted not only her master's meal, but the knight's as well, left Sir Stefan frowning.

"They will not poison her, who they so love," the grand lord remarked upon noticing the knight's tense expression. "And thus, she and we are all in no danger, but it is better to always make certain they know she will do some tasting first."

Near the end of their repast, Khleeg marched into the chamber. Slapping his breastplate, he muttered in the grand lord's ear. Golgren's face revealed nothing of his reaction, but he did rise immediately from the table.

"Please to forgive my need for departure, Sir Stefan Rennert! My Idaria will certainly be much better company, yes?"

Stefan, who had risen politely at the same time as his host, bowed deeply. "I hope to speak with you tomorrow."

"We shall, we shall . . . "

As the ogre leader—Khleeg at his side and several guards surrounding both of them—stalked out, Idaria's hand reached to gently touch the Solamnic's arm. Again, she had walked up so silently behind the veteran warrior that he hadn't noticed. "Your meal is unfinished, Sir Stefan. Please, be seated."

He obeyed her request, but he was frowning again, that time at her. "I don't understand you. I don't understand this entire affair." He surveyed the chamber. Every guard had left with the grand lord. They were alone. "You seem like more than a slave, Lady Idaria. You seem almost . . . at home."

"Your food is getting cold, Sir Stefan. Amalok is delicious when freshly cooked, but its taste will sour if left untouched too long."

He shoved the plate forward. "Well, I'm full."

The elf gave a slight nod. Another hand suddenly materialized next to the Solamnic, one of the other slaves sneaking up on him to remove his plate. Again the knight started, not having noticed when the other had entered.

"There is more wine, if you like," Idaria said when they were alone again. She poured him another glass.

He swirled the aromatic, rose-colored liquid in his goblet. "The wine is excellent, better than I've ever tasted. Elven, too, like the meal, am I right?"

"The grand lord procured a heavy stock of wine and other items during the invasion." She made the statement blandly, as if speaking of the weather.

He leaped to his feet suddenly, his eyes challenging

her. "Lady Idaria! You knew nothing about the ogre's offer of freeing your people before I did, isn't that true?"

Something flickered in her eyes. "I knew nothing of it."

"Yet you're hardly filled with relief, exuberance, gratefulness, as far as I can tell!" He pounded his fist on the table, an artfully crafted mahogany piece of elven craftsmanship. Oddly, it was blood-red in color. The table shook furiously, and the goblet—which he had just drained—fell over and clattered across its etched surface. "Is there no emotion left inside of you? Has he beaten it all out?" Stefan angrily rubbed his bearded chin. "Or do you suspect that he makes a hollow promise simply to get me to act as his messenger?"

"The grand lord promised you he would free all elves. He will stand by that promise, Sir Stefan."

The certainty in her tone soothed his anger. "Will he?"

Her eyes bored deep into his own. "He will. It means that much to him." Idaria came around the table again, standing close to the knight. "Since you are done, Sir Stefan, might I suggest that, as it is growing dark, we walk to your quarters?"

"Yes, that would probably be best." The Solamnic instinctively sought to take her arm, as any noble would have done to escort a lady departing from a dining hall, but Idaria somehow avoided his reach without seeming to even notice it.

After they stepped out into the dark, silent corridor, he couldn't stop himself from asking, "Do you look forward to becoming free?"

After a moment's silence, she answered, "Everyone yearns to be free."

"Is it because of you that this daring notion has occurred to Golgren? Is he doing this for you then, my lady?"

"I don't know what you are insinuating, but such thoughts are unworthy of a Knight of Solamnia," the elf reproached him, her tone frosty. "And such a topic is unworthy of conversation."

His face flushed. As they turned down another shadowy hallway, he stammered, "My lady, I never meant to insult you in any—"

A guard's abrupt appearance ahead of them saved him from saying anything to worsen the situation. The gargantuan ogre stood almost like a statue, so still that even Idaria did not at first see him. He held a long sword at his shoulder, and only the faint glint of torchlight gave any indication that his eyes watched them. Two more guards stood farther down the hall. As with all of Golgren's palace guards, they wore new breastplates and even helmets that fit snugly over their shaggy heads.

"The guards are back," the knight murmured to his companion. "I guess Golgren only trusts me up to a point."

"If there are guards posted along the way to your rooms, it is because he is concerned for your well-being," Idaria returned. Yet Stefan could tell that the sudden presence of the guards made even her uncomfortable. "There was—" But she stopped, bit her lip, then resumed her pose of indifference.

Stefan gripped the hilt of his sword. He peered closer at the nearby guard. "There is something unusual in his—"

The guard shifted, his blade suddenly moving.

"Watch out!" Stefan roared, shoving the elf to the side. Even as he did that, he drew his weapon with his other hand.

The ogre's blade threw up sparks when its edge scraped the floor, briefly illuminating the guard's monstrous face. Only Stefan's training had saved him from being cut wide open; his armor would not have saved him from such a close blow.

"Beware!" warned Idaria from the side, where the knight had shoved her. "The others come!"

The knight swapped blows with the first guard, discovering quickly that his adversary was better versed in fighting maneuvers than he would have expected. He retreated from a hard swing then saw an opening and cut the ogre across his sword arm. The guard dropped his blade, clutching his wound as he retreated.

No sooner had Stefan fended off the first ogre than the two reinforcements were upon him. He faced a sword and axe, the two ogres swinging their weapons at him nearly simultaneously.

Despite his predicament, the knight worried about Idaria. He shouted, "Run, my lady! Run!"

There was no response from the elf woman, nor was there even the sound of any movement from her direction. Stefan swore an oath then fought to press the two ogres near each other, the better to hamper their movements. If they moved apart and came after him from opposite sides, he would stand less of a chance.

Each time his weapon deflected that of one of his foes, Stefan's entire body shook. Solamnic weapons were well forged, but the guards' brutish strength was astounding. Worse, the ogre guards, like the first one, were better trained than the average ogre.

From behind him, he heard the sound of metal scraping against stone. The first ogre had recovered his sword and was rejoining the attack on the knight. In desperation, Stefan lunged at the close ogre fighting with a sword, catching the giant as the latter drew his arm back for a swing.

The Solamnic impaled his foe between the ribs. The guard let out a growl and stumbled into his nearby comrade.

As the two collided, Stefan spun around to face the first ogre again. That guard, still bleeding from his wound, had his massive sword gripped clumsily in both hands. He slashed wildly at the knight, forcing the human back toward the other ogres.

Out of the corner of his eye, Stefan saw the guard with the axe shove his limp comrade aside. The ogre the knight had stabbed tumbled to the floor and lay there motionless, like a sack of grain. That was one less foe. However, Stefan was caught between the remaining two, who were on either side of him.

He managed to avoid a swing by the axe wielder, but then a jab by the swordfighter pierced his side. Only the armor kept it from doing much harm. Even still, the blow knocked Stefan off balance.

The ogres were oddly silent throughout the struggle, making only small grunts of effort or gasps when wounded. They fought with a strange fanaticism in their eyes, as though they were doomed no matter what the outcome of the fight.

Stefan scored the axe wielder's hand, but the wound was shallow and, for an ogre, of no consequence. Slowly but surely, they were pushing him into a small corner against the wall. Once trapped there, the knight would be vulnerable.

Then shouts arose from down the corridor. The ogre waving a sword glanced warily over his shoulder.

Seizing the opening, the knight buried his own weapon deep in the giant's stomach.

Unfortunately, although the treacherous guard perished instantly, his heavy body crashed toward the human. His hand still clutching his sword, Stefan was buried under the corpse.

As he struggled, his view was blocked by the dead ogre's head. He was doomed. Yet the last assassin did not materialize. Instead, Stefan heard an odd but not unfamiliar sound.

The beating of wings.

That was followed by a violent growl from the last assassin. A hiss arose from elsewhere; then a heavy thud resounded nearby.

A momentary silence reigned; then several ogre voices and a very welcome elf one filled the human's ears.

The dead body shifted and was dragged off. The Solamnic was hauled to his feet, gulping air.

Wargroch steadied him. The ogre wore a puzzled look as his eyes shifted from the knight to the bodies and back again.

"Huh! Well fought, *Shok G'Ran,*" Wargroch rumbled, clearly caught between admiration for any fighter's skill and the fact that a puny human had done so well against his own kind.

Only then did Stefan notice the third ogre's dead body, compliments of a slit throat. The knight started to ask what had happened when Idaria interrupted.

"These warriors . . . they are not familiar to me, Wargroch."

The ogre grunted. "I am new. Khleeg, he knows maybe."

"Then they should be brought to him for identifying. See that it is done promptly."

Wargroch reacted to her words as though she were Golgren himself. He told some of the guards with him to take the bodies away. As the guards obeyed, Wargroch again eyed the Solamnic.

"Well fought," he repeated then followed the other guards hefting their grisly burdens.

Two ogre guards remained behind; they were clearly known and trusted by Idaria. They took up discreet positions flanking the pair.

Meanwhile, the elf inspected Stefan. "These bruises and this cut must be treated." Idaria probed one of his wounds, which caused the knight to flinch. "Once you are safe in your chambers, I will have some herbs and cloths brought to aid your healing."

"You don't have to go to any trouble for me. These wounds are slight."

One brow arched. "It would seem trouble follows you. I feared that even though I was bringing help, I would arrive much too late, and instead here you are, the victor against tremendous odds! Probably your worst wound comes from one of their corpses falling on you. It seems you had little to fear from three formidable attackers. Are all Solamnics so skilled?"

"I didn't kill the third one," Stefan admitted. "While I was trapped under—"

Her eyes cut him off. With a glance toward their escort, Idaria replied, "The blow to your head still bothers you, I see. I will brew a tea that will ease your pain and restore your thoughts. If you can walk, we should go now, Sir Stefan."

"I . . . I can walk."

She pointed in the direction of his rooms and as the party started off, surprised him by taking his arm, and, once again, he thought, it seemed the chains were no impediment to her.

❦

Only minutes later, Golgren burst into Stefan's rooms without preamble. He took in the scene: a concerned Idaria was bending close to the human's face. However, she leaped to her feet as her master entered with Wargroch and four guards at his heels. Golgren hesitated, something about the sight displeasing him. Over the centuries, humans and elves had often intermingled. The scene before him meant nothing, and yet it bothered him. It was more of a struggle than usual to keep his emotions under control, to keep his expression less . . . ogre.

"His head struck hard when one of the assassins fell upon him," the elf slave dutifully informed the grand lord as she stood up and went to rinse out the cloth she had been using. "I have treated the area. His other wounds are superficial."

Still, Golgren said nothing. He told the guards to step outside but kept Wargroch with him. Then, adopting a friendly grin, the ogre leader went up to the knight and exclaimed, "So terrible what has happened, yes? But so glad I am to hear that Sir Stefan Rennert has triumphed and is well! And once again, the tales of the mighty Solamnics prove no legend! Three taken down, even while you were trapped! Ha! You see, Wargroch, how worthwhile a pact between these knights and ogres is?"

"The grand lord is wise."

The knight looked uncomfortable, but Golgren did not press him as to the reason. "I swear to you, this will not go unpunished, Sir Stefan Rennert. Khleeg is like the hound on the hunt; he will seek out our enemies and find the culprits."

"If I can be of any service—"

The grand lord grinned even wider. "I would hear the story. It may be that something occurs to my mind."

"Gladly." The knight gave a short but succinct detailing of the incident. Golgren listened. On the surface, there was nothing he could question, but the ogre did have his suspicions, especially since he had viewed the bodies with Khleeg and Wargroch.

No blade had so savagely torn out the throat of the one guard.

Throughout the telling, Golgren watched Idaria. Her beautiful face was devoid of expression, but that was expected. Golgren had other ways of reading her, and what he saw further fueled his thoughts about the full truth of the attack.

But, of course, the grand lord gave no hint of his suspicions. After all, he had utter trust in only one person—himself. The only other person in whom he had ever confided had been slaughtered by the black-shelled warriors. Slaughtered, in fact, by humans not that dissimilar from Stefan Rennert.

"Such a tale, such a fight," Golgren said admiringly when the knight had finished. "Sir Stefan Rennert, you are a *G'Rath Itar,* a warrior favored by the spirits!"

"Fortune smiled upon me," the human remarked, wincing from one of his small wounds.

"Yes. Oh, but you must rest still! My Idaria, she will see to your needs. Come, Wargroch!"

The grand lord marched out without sparing another glance at the elf. He was determined to investigate the incident further. In the meantime, Idaria knew what he expected of her, no more, no less.

"Donnag has clan," suggested Wargroch as he left with Golgren. "There is the son, a magic one, Maldred."

"Yes, but they are not so foolish, I think. Maldred also has no more love for his father or clan." Golgren's hands stroked his chest where the larger of the two objects hanging around his neck dangled. "Perhaps, though . . . "

They were met in the hallway by Khleeg. Saluting his lord, he grunted in Common, "These assassins, all guards I know. All loyal."

"Huh! Hated humans?" Wargroch asked. "Maybe that?"

Golgren bared his teeth. "How can they be loyal? They would not thus risk my wrath. There is more, Khleeg. You. Wargroch. Find the truth. Maldred, perhaps. Others . . . find them."

They slammed their fists on their chests and hurried off. Golgren sent his remaining guards with them. He did not need bodyguards in his own palace.

In the years prior to his slaying of Zharang, he would have gone in search of the truth himself rather than leave it in the hands of minions. But since his old master was dead—and Donnag too—Golgren was forced to delegate many tasks.

Still, there were avenues of investigation that only he could follow, for none of those even among his inner circle knew of Tyranos's monstrous catch. Golgren suspected that the one assassin's demise was caused by some predator. Yet no meredrake or ji-baraki wandered the halls unfettered. Besides, they would have been just as likely to feast on the human afterward.

The slaying had also been done with too much purpose for a simple beast, and that brought Golgren's thinking around to only one possibility: a gargoyle.

But what did the gargoyle want with Golgren? Why would a gargoyle help Golgren? Why save the human when his death would have upset the grand lord's plans tremendously?

Something suddenly dropped near his feet. Golgren recoiled, but when the object did not move, he cautiously bent to retrieve it.

He pulled back his hand almost immediately, his fingers wet with a familiar crimson moistness. The object lay mangled, but he recognized what covered most of it:

Flesh, gobbets of the flesh of an ogre.

Quickly recovering from his astonishment, Golgren inspected the object. Seizing it up, the grand lord wiped it clean on his own garment in order to see it better. It was a talisman of some sort, shaped into a small golden starburst. From what the ogre could see, it had once been fastened into the very skin in which it lay.

Was it skin from the throat of the third assassin?

Golgren turned it toward the light of the nearest torch, trying to better make out a symbol in the very center of the talisman.

That symbol flared to life, a brief puff of flame rising up from it, a momentary, living representation of the symbol.

Startled again, Golgren dropped the talisman. As it clattered to the floor, all hint of fire vanished.

Cursing himself for his carelessness, the ogre leader bent to find the piece and clutch it in his hand. Already suspicions formed in his mind as to its significance and why it had been worn on the throat of the assassin, a guard considered loyal by Khleeg.

Something swooped down from the dark corners above. It landed on two heavy feet, its wings nearly spreading from one wall to the other. It stood almost as tall as the ogre and certainly as wide as any of his guards, none of whom were around, thanks to Golgren having dismissed them.

It was a gargoyle.

The male gargoyle appeared to dwarf the one Tyranos had captured. It had eyes more aware than the other one too, eyes that stared intently, as if reading far more about the grand lord's true self than the half-breed desired anyone to know.

Golgren poised to defend himself, reaching for the dagger hidden in his garments, always available as a quick and devious weapon.

But the gargoyle did a strange thing. It laughed—a coarse, mocking sound—then uttered in crude Common, "Fool of a ruler."

And with that, it took to the air, flying directly at Golgren. The grand lord grabbed for the dagger, but at the last moment, the gargoyle veered above him. The winged creature soared past the ogre then vanished through a window.

The last thing Golgren heard was another short, mocking laugh.

✺✺◆✺✺

All the Titans required the elixir to regularly rejuvenate themselves, otherwise they would enjoy the fate of Donnag. That eve of elixir-taking was a particularly momentous one, for it was none other than Dauroth himself who would imbibe.

All the Titans were assembled for the occasion, though if it had been other than Dauroth, a mere handful would have sufficed. Their leader stood in the center of the chamber, a small, square, stone pedestal with a flat face before him. Safrag stood behind him, empty hands cupped together. The rest of the Titans stood like pillars, their hands similarly cupped.

At the hour of midnight—as intuited by Dauroth—the Titans abruptly raised their cupped hands to the ceiling.

"The dream is the destiny," Dauroth sang. "The destiny is the dream."

His followers repeated the holy singing words, their chorus both wondrous and frightening to hear. They spread their arms wide as their leader intoned the second line.

"We are the dream; we are the destiny; the race will rise again, and the world will rejoice."

"The world will rejoice," they repeated, their expressions like innocent children. The white-blue globe above them added to the surreal nature of the ceremony.

Dauroth looked to the darkness on his left. "Let the gifts of the ancestors be brought forth."

From the shadows emerged Hundjal. Even in so serious a ceremony, his pleasure at returning to his place as his master's favored was apparent. He cradled the two small objects in his palms as if he himself were the one giving them as gifts.

In his left hand there was nestled a tiny ivory box that faintly glowed. Various runes had been etched upon its rounded lid. Anyone standing too close would have felt a heat radiating from it—not a terrible heat, but a noticeable one.

And in Hundjal's right hand he carried a small onyx flask shaped like a crouching dragon. The curling, snapping head was the stopper. The detail was lifelike, right down to its dragon scales.

Stepping to the master's side, Hundjal presented Dauroth with the flask. Dauroth accepted it, then placed the onyx container on the pedestal.

"Blood is life; blood is rebirth," he called out in song.

"Blood is life; blood is rebirth," the rest repeated.

Dauroth passed a hand over the flask. A faint crimson aura descended from his downturned palm toward the bottle.

The dragon's head let out a hiss, then stilled again.

Ever so gently, Dauroth removed the stopper. He placed the dragon's head to the side, but instead of taking up the flask, he stretched his hand to Hundjal.

The senior apprentice handed him the small ivory box. Dauroth let it sit in one palm while he passed the other over it.

The lid swung open. Dauroth removed the contents for all to see, at the same time returning the box to Hundjal.

The heart still beat. Slim it was, slimmer than the heavy organ inside an ogre or even the smaller but sturdy one within a human. It beat very slowly but not because of the magic that kept it animated. Had it remained within the body from which it had been torn by Dauroth and his apprentices barely an hour before, it would have beaten no faster. Elf hearts worked at a rate more sedate than most races' did, perhaps because they measured years in decades and their lives in centuries.

"From the usurpers, we take back that which was ours." He held the heart over the open flask and squeezed his hand tight. Rather than merely being crushed to a pulp, the heart became glittering red dust that trickled unerringly into the flask's mouth. Dauroth held his hand over the mouth until all the dust had fallen inside. "From them is the heart of all Krynn ours again."

He took up the flask, raising it above his head. The other Titans cupped their hands together once more, hands that began to glow red.

Dauroth downed the flask's contents. He drank and swallowed until it was all gone.

A startling blue aura blossomed around him. He thrust the empty flask at Hundjal as the aura intensified. A smile spread across his face, a smile of ultimate bliss.

With a gasp, Dauroth slumped back into Safrag's waiting arms. Those who could see best closely watched as the lead Titan's face softened. There was a hint of youth in his visage that had been lacking before. When, with Safrag's aid, the leader stood again, all there could have sworn that Dauroth stood an inch or two taller and was more muscular than before.

Returning to the pedestal, Dauroth sang in a voice stronger and louder. "The dream is the destiny; the destiny is the dream; the dream . . . the dream is the future."

"The dream is the future," the others repeated, their expressions still marveling. Although they had witnessed others among them—and they themselves had drunk the restorative elixir—its magic powers never ceased to astound them.

Standing proud and confident, Dauroth bowed his head to his followers. "I thank you for sharing with me as I share with you. The Titans go on. The Titans will go on."

The back ranks began to filter out into the darkness until soon there remained only Dauroth and his two apprentices.

"How much remains?" he asked Safrag.

"Not enough for all among us to rejuvenate ourselves another time."

Dauroth nodded then glanced at Hundjal. "It will be enough for now. Hundjal, we will talk."

The senior apprentice bowed. "I am yours, my master."

They strode off into the darkness, leaving Safrag to remove the few objects left. Last he took the ivory box, which Hundjal had casually set on the pedestal before departing with Dauroth.

Safrag eyed the box, studying its interior. Traces of blood still marked the spot. The heart had not been essential to the ceremony; Dauroth had merely used it for drama. But the drama was important, even Safrag understood.

Safrag imagined Golgren's heart likewise stored for use. On the night the Titans crushed Golgren's heart into the elixir, the ceremony would surely be something to remember.

On that night . . . very soon . . .

XVIII

F'HANOS

Tarkus had served the grand lord nearly as long as Khleeg, and while he had the utmost respect for Golgren, the ogre captain had to wonder if he had done something that merited punishment. Why else had he and the dozen warriors with him been sent out on such a long-range patrol? Who was in those parts for the grand lord to fear? All his enemies were dead.

The band was three days out of Garantha, and Tarkus hoped to complete his task in time to return just prior to Golgren's coronation. There would be much feasting and many competitions of strength and skill. There would also be many young females eager to spend their time with a strong warrior such as he.

With those thoughts in mind, Tarkus pushed his small troop well into the night. They grunted and growled at that but not much, for they were as eager as he to be done with their job and return for the celebrations. Still, there came a point when even the hardy ogre horses demanded a rest. Tarkus chose a location near a toothy outcropping

295

and had his warriors set up camp.

The sky was overcast, something rare during the summer season. The last time the sky had been like that, the ogre recalled, was when his lord had ordered the blue ones to deal with the rebellion. As superstitious as any of his kind, Tarkus ordered the others to stay close to the small fire and made certain that guards were posted at all times. The only reason for any ogre to leave the vicinity was if nature demanded it.

And for Tarkus himself, that demand occurred deep into the night. Stirred from sleep after such an arduous ride, the captain sought out privacy on the other side of the outcropping. The location was not far from and barely out of sight of the nearest guard.

However, without even the light of stars to illuminate his way, Tarkus failed to see the sudden drop just around the bend. His left foot only grazed the ground; then he stumbled. The ogre fell and rolled for some distance. He was so startled by his accident that he let out no more than a grunt all the way down.

Fortunately, the slope was harsh but not deadly. Tarkus wound up in a heap just shy of a pair of spindly plants with long, sharp needles covering their many thin branches. The captain lay there for a while, briefly dazed.

But just as his head cleared, a huge shadow rose up before him. For all its size, the thing moved without a sound. Its vague outline suggested it was a mastark, albeit an exceedingly thin one. The creature was barely more than bones.

There was something with it, something walking on two feet and about the size of an ogre. Tarkus recalled no knowledge of another patrol or other armed force in the region but knew that his information was limited. It was very possible that one of the nomadic clans simply happened to be crossing his party's path.

Whatever the case, it behooved the ogre captain to identify himself and find out who the intruders were. Drawing his sword, Tarkus stepped up to where he could get a better view.

He nearly dropped his weapon. His hands shook, and it amazed him that he did not run away screaming in fear.

The mastark was not barely more than bones; it was *only* bones. What still connected them with the sinew and such all gone, he could not say. Despite its deficiency, the skeleton moved exactly as a living beast would have.

Yet even more terrifying than that was the figure Tarkus had also glimpsed. It was not an ogre, no, but the bones of one.

No, it was not merely the bones of one ogre, for behind that first ghoulish warrior marched another and another and another.

"Garduuk i solum if'hanosi!" someone in the camp shouted. That call was followed by a shriek that was cut off by the unmistakable sound of the clash of weapons.

Tarkus was shaken from his stupor. He and his warriors faced great danger: *f'hanos*—the dead that lived. The tales his mother's mother had told him as a child all came back.

He started for the camp but found his way blocked, suddenly, by a skeleton with a badly battered, twin-edged axe. Instinct made the ogre captain dodge away and deflect the monster's attack. The axe should have shattered, but instead it flashed silver—surely a sign that it carried magic.

Tarkus kicked at the skeleton and was grateful to find that the force of a strong leg was able to knock the ghoul back. He leaped over his grisly foe, hoping to make it to the horses.

But more undead blocked his path. They moved with a silent determination, surrounding him and swiping relentlessly at the captain, even if all they carried were rocks or what might have been the cracked bones of other creatures. Tarkus swung madly, somehow blocking most, if not all, of the hapless blows.

Yet the f'hanos' numbers only grew. They pressed on him. Fleshless fingers grasped his arms, his body. Others seized his blade by the edge because the undead didn't mind cutting themselves.

When at last they tugged his sword free, Tarkus let out a wail. He slammed his fist against the hollow-eyed faces, ignoring the cuts and bleeding that caused him. His frenzied effort enabled the ogre to create a narrow opening in their midst, and through that he blindly plunged.

Stumbling across the landscape, Tarkus sought some means to get away from the monstrous horde, and only then did he realize just who the *f'hanos* must be. It was the eve of the grand lord's crowning. They were his slaughtered foes, streaming in the direction of Garantha.

Despite that realization, Tarkus wasn't thinking much about the capital. All that mattered to him was his own life. The flickering flames of the campfire beckoned him. The horses surely could be not much farther.

In the camp, though, the scene was so terrible that he froze. Body parts from his troops lay scattered all about the vicinity. One warrior lay facedown in the fire, slowly roasting, the stench of his burning flesh filling the captain's nostrils. Another had been almost flayed before dying, but skeletal nails, not blades, had clearly done the terrible task.

Recovering from his shock, the ogre headed to where the horses were kept. All he needed was one . . . just one.

But of their many mounts, there was only one left: a single ruined corpse. The rest had evidently made their escape. Tarkus shook his head, trying to will a different reality.

Something struck him in the back of the head. He fell to his knees but managed to rise again. Glancing over his shoulder, Tarkus saw that a score of *f'hanos* were swarming the campsite.

He started forward, but from the darkness a new line of undead approached. Tarkus spun in a circle, seeing nothing but horror wherever he looked. The ogre reached for his sword then recalled he had lost it. In despair, Tarkus seized the largest object he could find—the cut-off forearm of one of his warriors.

As the *f'hanos* converged upon him, he let out another wail and swung as hard as he could, caring only that he hit something, anything. He landed a blow that shattered one *f'hanos*, but his momentary exhilaration faded when the pieces simply reformed immediately into a fresh skeleton. Worse, his gory club began to come apart. The slickness made it almost impossible to retain a hold on what pulpy flesh remained.

The fingers grasped him everywhere. Tarkus saw nothing but shadowed bones.

Then he saw nothing.

The glittering runes leaped off the parchment, dancing before Hundjal's eyes as he scoured them for anything of importance. One by one, the apprentice dismissed them back to the page, then summoned up fresh ones to read.

As before, he came up empty.

Rolling up the latest parchment, Hundjal sent it flying back to its proper place on the shelves of Dauroth's personal sanctum. He extended his hand, and a thick black-spined book flew to him. His hopes were not high as he opened the book. Hundjal was not usually one to accept defeat, but he was coming close. The Titan had poured over his master's previous attempts to circumvent the tomb's protections without destroying the contents and found no fault with them. He would have even chosen several as his own, had not they already been tested and failed.

It had been an honor when the master had chosen him for the task of opening the tomb, but that honor was becoming a burdensome yoke on his shoulders. Those spells Hundjal had thus far created had fared no better against the ancients' magic than any previously cast by Dauroth. Even in death, the High Ogres proved themselves again the greatest masters of the arts. After his fifth attempt turned out to be as much folly as the prior ones, Dauroth's apprentice secreted himself in his master's sanctum—not the library, which had works useful only to lesser Titans, such as Safrag—and pored over every tome, parchment, and artifact that he could lay his hands on.

That Dauroth left him to his task made Hundjal assume that he was being tested. He had to prove himself as he had back when the lead Titan had first approached him with the offer of apprenticeship. Hundjal swore that he would not fail in his task, just as he had not failed his master then . . . not ever.

His senses sharper than any of his brethren's, Hundjal noticed Morgada's unique presence even before she announced herself. The lone female in their ranks fascinated him as much as she fascinated Dauroth. However, Hundjal was very much aware of Dauroth's intentions concerning a certain experiment in mating, and thus he kept a cautious distance from the Titaness.

"Dear, sweet Hundjal," she purred. "Such a pleasure to have you here among us again."

He did not look up from the ancient tome. "Fair Morgada. Forgive my less-than-appropriate discourtesy, for I am hard at work for the master."

"And if there is anyone who can be trusted to achieve what the master desires, it is surely Hundjal." She draped her arm over his shoulder as she pretended to peer at the book he was reading. "Has the clue been found to open the way?"

"As with all things the master teaches, the clues ever lie before us. We are but blind to their reading."

The Titaness giggled. "Perhaps if I joined your efforts, our two heads together might between them gain the insight needed."

There was no question that she was crafty, and Hundjal was tempted to accept her partnership, but the glory or failure ought to be his alone. Dauroth would expect his lead apprentice to rely upon no other. That surely was part of the test.

He shut the tome but still did not look at her. "The offer is generous but must still be declined, fair Morgada. I must continue this quest on my own."

Her face swung down very close to his. "But surely the

two of us can stoke the fires of inspiration as none of the others could alone or together. You shall see; we will find the answer."

Hundjal was no longer truly listening to her. Something she had said had stirred a notion previously unthinkable, something that *could* work.

He rose, pulling her up with him at the same time. "I think not, fair Morgada."

She gave him a seductive smile as he steered her toward the door. At a later time, Hundjal would endeavor to find out how she had gained entrance to Dauroth's rooms. For the moment, he was busy with more important matters. "As you like . . . a shame."

It was all Hundjal could do to keep himself contained until he was certain that the other Titan was gone. That time, the apprentice made certain that the seal on the door was intact. Only he and Dauroth could open it.

Thinking of his mentor, Hundjal decided to act quickly, just in case the master might be coming to check on his progress.

As the heir apparent to Dauroth's secrets, Hundjal had taken it upon himself to learn and understand all of them, even those his master had not yet officially revealed to either him or Safrag. Both apprentices knew the legend that interested Hundjal; both knew that there must be some fact behind the legend. Both knew, even, that the master hid the only proof within his sanctum. But neither was supposed to know more than that.

That was true, at least, for *Safrag*.

It had taken Hundjal many months to decipher the master's protective spells, but, as with all he hunted, the secrets of those spells had eventually fallen to him. He did not hesitate to summon the pathway to the hidden chamber, a place that he had visited only once before but could never, ever forget.

Once the way was open, it took mere seconds to reach the Chamber of Ice, as Hundjal knew it would. Immediately, he noted the various mounds, recalling what was hidden inside of them. Utterly confident, the apprentice stepped inside the chamber.

Barely had his foot touched the chill floor when the first of the skeletal warriors broke free of its prison. A second and a third followed.

In a voice that was an exact replication of Dauroth's, Hundjal sang the words. *"Asymnopti isidiu."*

He watched with impatience as the guardians stepped back and allowed ice and snow to bury them again. Although the entire encounter had taken but a mere handful of seconds, to Hundjal it felt as if dangerous years had passed.

When the mounds were at last still, the Titan rushed to the ice-encrusted box. Anticipation and apprehension gnawed at him like starving meredrakes. Suddenly he wondered why he had waited so long to once more witness the glory of its contents.

When the silver tendrils came at him, he used a spell of his own crafting to suspend them. The spell would last only for a hundred heartbeats, but by then Hundjal would be long gone.

His breathing rapid, the apprentice opened the chest. He was prepared for the intense light and kept his eyes turned away until he felt able to adjust them accordingly.

Within, floating trapped in the clear liquid that Hundjal knew Dauroth had created, the minute fragment awaited him.

The fragment was out of legend.

Hundjal snorted at the tale Dauroth had once told him, that even that piece called all those who had used it every time it was used again . . . and again . . . and again. After all, since the one time he had been there, months had passed. It had not even been his idea to use the fragment; that inspiration had sprung from Morgada's mouth, when she had spoken of fire.

And once Hundjal was done using the fragment for his vital task, he would never have to touch it again.

Although . . . how fascinating it would be to hunt down the full truth, hunt to see if the rest of the artifact still existed.

The Titan shook his head. *Enough dreaming! Time is of the essence, fool!*

Hundjal thrust his hand into the liquid. A sense of warmth spread up his arm as he seized hold of his quarry. However, the apprentice did not remove the piece, but kept it submerged. That was the key to its use, Hundjal had determined, something he was certain even his illustrious mentor had not realized.

With absolute care, Hundjal began mentally formulating his spell. The fragment would help him bypass and overcome the delicate magics involved in the tomb's protections. All Hundjal had to do was absorb the magic power of the fragment, then hold those forces in reserve using thought control.

Of course, he would have to depart immediately for the mountainside after that, for the fragment's abilities were very powerful and had the potential to burn out his mind.

It was done, done so easily. Hundjal beamed with pride at his own cleverness. It suddenly occurred to him that his prize could be utilized for other complex troubles plaguing the Black Talon, complex troubles such as the problem of the Grand Lord Golgren. The master had said that the mongrel's usefulness was nearing its end, especially with the news discovered that not only did Golgren seek a pact with the humans—*humans!*—but he hoped to do so by freeing *all* the elves held by the ogres.

Yes, it was time to put an end to the grand lord, and with the fragment, the magic that protected him would count for nothing.

Hundjal's golden eyes reflected the fiery light from within the box. One more use of the fragment would be all that he required. But first, he had to prove himself trustworthy to his master by safely opening the tomb. Then . . . then Dauroth would see his genius and agree to the plan of his favored apprentice.

One of the silver tendrils started to move. The Titan reluctantly pulled his hand free then shut the lid. Hundjal held the chest away from him. After a futile grab, the tendrils vanished. Eyes on the icy mounds, the apprentice left the chamber.

Returning to Dauroth's study, Hundjal exulted. He gathered up some random parchments and the two thickest tomes and left the chambers, singing out, "I have it! I have the key."

❧❧❧❧❧

The Talon assembled on the edge of the chill peak within sight of the mountain tomb. Day had given way to night, but through their enhanced senses, they could see the entrance as well as any nocturnal creature might have. The spells disguising the tomb had been easy enough to rip away without danger to the interior, but the band awaited Hundjal's promised efforts.

And no one waited more eagerly than Dauroth.

"You are very certain of the construction of your spell?" he asked his pupil, more than a hint of menace in his tone.

A fierce gust of wind blew through the area, but none of the Titans were affected by something so mundane. Hair bound back and perfectly groomed, Hundjal answered, "I am, my master."

"Yet you have required no fresh blood nor any sacrifice for it."

"Nor did the ancients," the senior apprentice immediately pointed out, as if he had expected that question and had the reply ready. "And that is part of the path to understanding."

Dauroth nodded his appreciation. "I would hear more on this subject at a more convenient time, good Hundjal."

"And I would be so honored to discuss my beliefs with you, my master." He abruptly winced, one hand clutching the side of his head.

"Something ails you, my pupil?"

"Merely the result of much research. With your permission, shall I begin?"

Dauroth eyed the tomb. "Do so. I shall order the others into position."

"There is no need, great one! For this, I do not require the rest of the Talon. I require only my own efforts. It will take but a few moments."

"Indeed? Most impressive. Proceed. I will have the others stand by should any assistance be required after all."

Already anxious to begin, Hundjal scarcely paid any mind to Dauroth's last statement. He stood atop a rocky outcropping overlooking the tomb. Below was the stone entrance with its markings in the tongue of their ancestors over the archway.

Hundjal looked proud, undaunted. He began to sing loudly, wondrously, as energies rose from within him and gathered from without.

Kallel and Safrag were among those who looked to Dauroth for commands, for all had assumed that the Black Talon would act in concert, as one. However, the lead Titan ignored the others, continuing to watch Hundjal expectantly.

The senior apprentice finished his chanting then drew the symbol of the Talon—raptor's claws—in the air.

From the glowing claws emanated a field of black light that swept over both the entrance of the tomb and a good portion of the surrounding rock and earth. It settled onto the area then seeped through the ground, vanishing into the mountainside.

There was a brief crackle of static energy in its wake, then silence.

"That is it?" blurted one of the other Titans, already starting to drift toward the tomb. "All this expectation and nothing but another failure—"

An explosion of magical forces shot out from the mountain without stirring a single pebble or disrupting a flake of snow. The presumptuous Titan was thrown back. He might have fallen down the mountain to his doom, but Dauroth, feeling magnanimous, forgave his arrogance and used a spell to push him back to safety.

"Now it is done," Hundjal proudly remarked. "The forces used by the ancients to both seal the entrance to the tomb and destroy its contents should someone manage to enter have been cast out and will dissipate in the emptiness of this land."

"Well done, my pupil," Dauroth declared heartily. "For your reward, you may be the first to enter."

It also meant that Hundjal would be the first to possibly face any unexpected traps lying within, but the apprentice was more than confident in himself and pleased to take the lead. He bowed to his mentor, then leaped up into the air and let his power allow him to alight just before the stone barrier.

Raising his left arm, Hundjal let his hand sweep across the symbols above the entrance. He sang each of them loudly, the musical tones causing the assembled Titans to listen in fascination.

As Hundjal ceased his singing, the stone slid inward. The apprentice strode forward as if master of all within.

Dauroth descended to the doorway then followed behind. The other Titans, Safrag at their rear, entered one by one.

Inside the chamber, Hundjal and Dauroth paused to gaze at some of the illuminated images lining the stone walls. There were more than a score on both sides of the corridor.

"It is as written," the lead Titan remarked reverently. "The life of the dead is set out for the gods to see so they may know this one was worthy." Dauroth placed his fingers on one illustration. Immediately, his eyes stared off into space.

"A trap!" Kallel hissed, reaching for their master.

Hundjal slapped his hand away. "Do not touch him!"

Barely a breath later, Dauroth blinked. He stepped back, his expression almost childlike. "I was there! I was the one! A female! This was the burial of a personage of much power!"

"There may be signets after all!" someone else murmured.

Dauroth signaled for attention. "And if there are, then we shall find them. Lead on, Hundjal."

The apprentice walked slowly but confidently down the corridor, with Dauroth but a step behind. Near the image of two robed figures—one male and the other female—holding up what seemed to be a crescent moon, Hundjal came to a sudden halt.

"A spell spawned from the magical essence of dragonfear," he informed his master. "Old but still potent." After a pause, he added, "It is dealt with."

As they proceeded, the illumination from the reliefs proved less and less sufficient, even for Titans.

"There is a magic-dampening spell," Dauroth explained. "Not enough to stop us. We shall have to make our own light from now on, though."

Hundjal created a small sphere of blue and white energy, which hovered over his palm. Some of the others followed suit.

Then the corridor simply ended. Ahead lay a darkened chamber. Hundjal glanced at his master, who bade him to enter.

The moment that the apprentice did so, however, the entire chamber blossomed with bright light. Dauroth immediately joined him inside and the two stared at the walls, which were of crystal and silver and reflected the low illumination of Hundjal's sphere a thousand times stronger than the source.

Kallel approached behind them. The chamber light suddenly grew brighter, glaring.

"Kallel!" the lead Titan called. "You will keep your sphere active! Hundjal! The rest of you! Dismiss yours!"

As the others swiftly obeyed, the light diminished to a tolerable level. Dauroth nodded with pleasure as he examined their find.

"Intact! Utterly intact," he declared triumphantly. "It is ours!" His gaze focused on the item most central to the chamber. "There! The sarcophagus! Nothing matters more!"

Even Hundjal and the other members of the inner circle could not help but gape at the score of ivory pedestals encircling the pearl stand upon which a diamond coffin lay. Each of those platforms held artifacts with mysterious and valuable contents. There were scrolls, boxes, talismans, and other objects of arcane use. Each artifact alone was a precious treasure, but all together were nothing compared with the coffin.

More pearls floated above the coffin structure, pearls three times the size of a head. They were just translucent enough to hint at other artifacts, other riches held within. They hovered in a five-sided arrangement and numbered more than two score, an astounding cache of High Ogre relics.

Dauroth gestured Hundjal aside and took the lead. "Touch nothing. First the sarcophagus; then all else."

The Titans flowed as one toward the glorious coffin, cautiously bypassing the pedestals and their prizes. That did not mean that their eyes did not covetously survey the many artifacts as the spellcasters passed. More than one Titan marked items he desired later for himself . . . if Dauroth did not notice.

Within a foot of the sarcophagus, Dauroth suddenly raised his hand. "Stand still!"

The others obeyed instantly. Dauroth alone circled the sarcophagus, studying the figure within. She was beautiful, so very beautiful that against all other females—even Morgada—there were no comparisons. Clad in shimmering silver-and-black robes, the High Ogre lay in perfect repose. Her blue skin wore a sheen that his own lacked, and her long tresses draped a face that seemed shaped by the gods. Her lips and eyelids had been painted gold, and to gaze at her was to think she was no more than twenty summers old and dead only that very day. Yet Dauroth knew that she had likely lived three to four times longer than he and had gained far more wisdom in the arts.

That she was much shorter and lacking the talons and barbed elbows of a Titan did not in the least disturb Dauroth or the others. Through the knowledge originally granted him by the ancestral spirit, Dauroth understood that only the most skilled among the High Ogres actually achieved the mighty likenesses worn by him and his followers. That they had been given that gift reflected the hopes their forebears had invested in them.

Dauroth glanced down to where the female's hands lay, studying her long, slim fingers, naked of any adornment.

Frowning, Dauroth eyed the glittering case in which she lay then glanced at Hundjal. "You are certain that the spell of decay on the tomb's other contents has been removed, my pupil?"

"I stake my life on it."

Dauroth raised his hands and sang a single word.

Thunder boomed so loud that the other Titans had to clutch their ears.

The sarcophagus exploded, shards flying everywhere.

Dauroth sang another word, however, and the shards abruptly slowed as if whirling through honey. They then stopped completely and fell with a harsh clatter to the floor.

And as they did, the beautiful figure they had once shielded shriveled and aged. The unmarred skin wrinkled, dried, and peeled off. The perfect face became that of a horrific ghoul, with the aged flesh continuing to rapidly turn to dust until there remained nothing but the white skull beneath.

Immediately, Dauroth gestured. A blue haze fell over the skeleton and its shredded finery.

The decay ceased with the bones still intact.

"Safrag! Kallel! I leave it to you to remove the bones cautiously. The spell will keep them from turning to dust, but I wish them unmarred."

"Yes, great one," Safrag quickly replied.

"Hundjal, attend me."

The senior apprentice stepped next to Dauroth, observing with him, for the moment, the fastidious efforts of the other two Titans in following the leader's orders. "These are perfect, my master. Bones untouched, the magic in them still fresh."

"Yes, a pity about the lack of signets upon her, but the remains will prove invaluable once they are prepared." Dauroth gazed around at the other treasures. "And there may yet be a signet among the other relics. I want to know that before we leave the chamber."

"You distrust some of the rest of the Talon?"

Dauroth pursed his lips. "I trust no one but myself . . . and you, naturally, my favored pupil."

Hundjal bowed his head ever so slightly at that great compliment. "There may be a few individual traps among these riches. I did not dare perform a sweeping spell for fear that I would damage the casket's power and let time reduce the body to complete dust. I knew the value of the bones, after all."

"The brethren will just have to be extra cautious." Dauroth turned to the rest. "The signets are the prime objective now. However, if you find anything so unidentifiable that you deem it may be of interest to me, summon me."

The seven other Titans moved to various pedestals to begin their cautious inspections. Dauroth watched Safrag and Kallel at work then, satisfied by their meticulous labors, indicated that Hundjal and he should begin their own searches.

It did not take long to verify that the female buried there had indeed been a personage of high esteem. There were intricately created talismans among the artifacts, whose purpose promised years of intriguing research for Dauroth. There were parchments that could be gingerly opened that suggested spells that could be altered to fit the more modern arts of the Titans. Other writings revealed details of High Ogre life that Dauroth looked forward to studying and implementing into his future plans.

One of the other Titans used his power to open a small, emerald-tinted box. He peered inside just as Dauroth glanced in his direction.

The lead Titan frowned. "Beware such, Varnin! That has the look of a soul trap there—"

"I sense nothing within, great one! Absolutely—"

His reply turned into a chilling howl that froze the other Titans in the midst of their tasks. Dauroth, however, did not even bother to raise his hand and cast a spell, for it was already too late for Varnin. Instead, he watched and waited—with clinical interest—while the soul trap played itself out.

As the Titan's howl spread through the chamber, something white and gauzy spewed from the hapless figure's mouth then his nose, his ears, and even the tear ducts of his eyes. It struggled as it spread over and around the Titan, its vague outline reminiscent of Varnin himself. At the same time, the spellcaster's physical form became more and more emaciated.

Then the gauzy form shrieked, shrieked as not even Dauroth could have imagined. Even the leader of the Titans felt his heart pound faster.

The ethereal figure was sucked into the box.

The box shut itself immediately after. The physical Varnin, his expression terrifying in its absolute deadness, its emptiness, collapsed then suddenly as if boneless.

Some of the others edged toward the corpse and the box.

"No one goes near!" shouted Dauroth. He alone approached the pedestal. After a brief study of the fallen spellcaster, Dauroth took the box and placed it in a pouch at his waist.

"Varnin has offered a lesson to you all. Open nothing that you cannot identify. Eagerness has its costs." To Safrag and Kallel, he added, "When you are done safely transporting the bones back to the citadel, see to the removal and disposal of his remains."

Safrag bowed. "As you command, great one." The apprentice and his companion had finished setting the bones of the ancient Titan in an organized pile. The shreds of clothing, no longer protected, had become ash. "We are ready to take these away."

"I will assist." Dauroth joined the pair. The three stood facing the bones of the ancient. At the lead Titan's signal, the trio sang the spell.

Black tendrils arose around not only the bones, but Safrag and Kallel as well. The two lesser Titans ceased their singing, enabling Dauroth to seize control of the spell. Safrag placed one hand over the remains.

And he, they, and Kallel vanished.

"It will take them a few minutes to prepare the container for the bones," Dauroth blandly informed Hundjal, who stood nearby. "Now come. I rely on you as much as myself to see that nothing such as Varnin's fate befalls the rest of us."

All but kneeling, the senior apprentice replied, "You may trust in me utterly on this or any other matter, my master. I am and shall always be your most faithful servant."

In that brief moment when Hundjal turned his gaze to the floor, he could not see the dark look that Dauroth flashed at him. All the younger spellcaster saw, when he turned his eyes up again, was the pleased expression that he expected. "I would expect nothing less of you, Hundjal, nothing less at all."

"And to prove myself further, my master, I think in another day I shall give you something far greater than this discovery, something to assure the Titans' guidance over our race."

Dauroth had expected that. His smile widened, the sharp teeth well displayed. "For that, you shall receive a reward such as you would not imagine, good Hundjal . . . such as you would not imagine . . . "

XIX

DAUROTH'S REVENGE

Despite the determination of a ji-baraki stalking an injured amalok, Khleeg could report no progress on the investigation. The ogre officer kept his head low, fully expecting punishment, but all the grand lord did was nod thoughtfully. That only served to make Khleeg more nervous, for not only did his master's favorite meredrake lay chained to the wall near where the warrior stood, but the beast had not yet been fed. Its hunger was surely made the worse by the great copper bowl of raw amalok placed just out of its reach, according to the grand lord's bidding.

"The ogres were said to be loyal, yet they attacked the Solamnic right here in my palace. Strange. The matter will have to be pursued, yes," Golgren finally said, speaking Common, as he was determined to do in private and public from then on. He would prove even to himself that he was properly civilized. "But other matters must not fall neglected because of it."

"Yes, the crowning," Khleeg grunted, grateful for

the change in topic. "The crowning is serious matter. Dangerous time, Grand Lord. Dangerous time. Assassins come then."

"Nay! A glorious time! Grand khan and lord chieftain I will be!" The ogre leader leaped from his seat and snagged some of the raw meat, tossing a gobbet toward the meredrake. The huge lizard strained at the chains as it snapped up the morsel. "And better able then to deal with *Shok G'Ran* and Uruv Suurt."

As the beast swallowed its tidbit and begged for more, Khleeg, too, swallowed. Golgren hesitated. It would not be the first time a ruler of his people had fed a failure to one of its pets. But Golgren let Khleeg fret for a moment then stepped away from the beast. Khleeg breathed a sigh of relief.

"The summer soon gives way to the autumn, Khleeg! All must be in readiness for the glorious occasion! Is it so?"

"The Jaka Hwunar, it readies!" blurted the officer. "The guards, they ready! The slaves, they busy making fine clothes for the grand lord! They carve great faces of him and paint glorious battles he won!" That brought to mind a subject Khleeg wanted to ask about, diplomatically. "Grand Lord, is it true . . . that the elves, they go . . . they go free when the crowning is done?"

Golgren's expression grew veiled. "This none concerns Khleeg! Khleeg should be concerned about the crowning, yes?"

Again, the officer swallowed, glancing at the meredrake. "Yes, Grand Lord! No one will break the walls of warriors! Golgren will be grand khan, lord chieftain of all Kern and Blöde!"

"Golthuu," corrected his lord. "We should both

remember that from now on. When I rule, the ogre lands will be renamed Golthuu, in my honor. No more Kern. No more Blöde."

"Golthuu. Yes, Grand Lord. Golthuu."

"Go! All must be in readiness! You will do it, yes, Khleeg?"

The heavy ogre struck his breastplate. "I swear!"

At that moment, Wargroch entered. The younger warrior repeated Khleeg's breast-beating gesture then announced, "Grand Lord, you wished to practice. Practice is ready."

"Good!" To the departing Khleeg, Golgren growled, "There must be no delay."

The senior officer nodded hurriedly before vanishing from the chamber. A moment later, the grand lord and Wargroch also left. The two marched noisily through the palace, down to the ground level, and through several halls. Soon enough, they came to an inner doorway where two hulking guards stood at attention. One quickly opened the door for Golgren.

The unrelenting light of day rushed over the grand lord. He stepped out into what was almost a miniature version of the floor of the Jaka Hwunar. High walls upon which had long ago been carved an idyllic garden scene—replete with dancing beasts and beautiful High Ogres watching while one of their own played a lyre—surrounded a stone and sand floor. Other than the door through which Golgren had entered—a door immediately sealed from inside the palace by the guards—there was only one other way in, an arched entrance four times as wide as the door and blocked by a toothed, metal gate that could be raised or lowered.

The burning sun illuminated well the many old

crimson stains on the walls. Suspected by Golgren to have originally been a true garden, the area was a kind of brutal playing field; long ago it had been designated as such for the amusement of the ruler during the days when the High Ogres' decline into debauchery and sadism had been in full throttle. There, instead of the onetime garden of peace and music, prisoners fought other prisoners or beasts, or simply fought to survive some insidious torture.

There the grand lord enjoyed a daily practice regimen. With only one hand to use in fighting, he had to keep his reflexes sharp and his mind sharper. Six burly warriors stood watch over the small arena, but they were not there to act as his opponents. Instead, the metal gate squealed open, and two surly figures trod inside. They were low-class prisoners, their crimes varying, but both with tempers more ferocious than most of their kind. Each outweighed Golgren by half again as much, and one was nearly a foot taller than the next largest fighter present.

Both were chained but stood quietly under the watchful eyes of two guards; a third undid their bonds. The two prisoners rubbed their wrists and gazed wearily around at their captors.

"Jaduum!" called Wargroch. *"Hysta i dor—"*

Golgren gestured for silence. "Common. Always speak Common. All must learn it, know it." To the two criminals, he asked, "You know Common?"

The one on the left nodded warily. The second cocked his shaggy head then finally let out a raspy, "Yes."

Golgren beamed with pleasure. The odds were that their understanding of Common was minimal at best, but that would do. "They have been told?"

Wargroch grunted. "Their freedom if the grand lord is beaten or dead."

"*F'han,*" murmured the larger of the prisoners, his blood-shot eyes glinting.

Golgren smiled at him. "Give weapons. Leave fight."

The guards looked distinctly uncomfortable. "Grand Lord," Wargroch protested. "Better I should remain—"

"My command. Obey."

With a shrug of surrender, Wargroch indicated that the captives should be duly armed. A guard handed one of them a long sword and the other a chipped but very serviceable axe with the marking of a Solamnic Kingfisher etched into its face. Golgren made a mental note to have such weapons secreted in the palace while the knight was still his guest. It would not do to remind the human of past hostile encounters between ogres and humans.

The captives wore only kilts and, in one case, not even sandals. The two had obviously led rough lives even in comparison to most of their kind. Partly for that reason, Golgren expected a good fight out of them. The grand lord wore a kilt of much finer make and sandals equally new. Atop he wore a light brown tunic that enabled him to hide what he hung around his neck.

The grand lord patted his tunic once to let his adversaries see that he hid no breastplate or other protection beneath the thin garment. The first prisoner grinned wide, revealing several gaps in his yellowed teeth; the other's eyes narrowed maliciously.

Golgren held up the stump of his arm and Wargroch attached to it a variation of the claw device that the ogre leader used in his battle against rebellious ogre chieftains. There were four claws, banded tightly together. They were also shorter but sharper, and the base was better designed to grip his stump by a series of leather straps rather than the hooks that sometimes ripped his flesh. The new false appendage had been finished that very morning, and Golgren was eager to try it out.

The prisoners shuffled uneasily at the sight of Golgren's arm stump and false claws, but after a moment, both giants recovered their confidence. For Golgren to use the steel talons, he would still have to come well within arm's reach.

In addition to the sword and axe, the prisoners each also received a dagger. The first slipped his into his kilt, while the second gripped the small blade for more immediate use. As for the grand lord, he had hidden away his ancient dagger, replacing it with a serviceable, wooden-handled one designed for more mundane purposes.

At Golgren's signal, Wargroch and the guards retreated through the arched entrance. The criminals were wise enough not to attack Golgren immediately, waiting until the others were well and truly gone and they were alone with the grand lord.

The gate shut again. Golgren raised his talons. "Begin!"

The pair came lumbering at him. With his longer strides, the taller ogre reached the grand lord first. His axe immediately angled toward Golgren's skull, but the half-breed had amazing reflexes. By the time the blade crossed where his head should have been, Golgren was far to the left, taking on his other foe.

His jab to the sword-wielder's waist drew a flash of blood, albeit not enough to slow the prisoner. Baring his teeth, the shorter criminal performed a lunge whose sloppiness nearly enabled him to fumble past Golgren's defenses. The grand lord parried the blow just inches from his throat, then had to turn and contend with the return of his axe-wielding adversary.

Fortunately, the pair didn't think to coordinate their attacks. They fought for position over each other as much as they fought the grand lord. The taller one elbowed aside his partner, eager to kill the grand lord first. A warrior who slew Golgren in battle would gain not only freedom, but an enviable reputation.

But they, like so many others, underestimated Golgren. The prisoner's axe came within a hair's breadth of Golgren's shoulder, and as momentum carried him past, Golgren slashed his wrist with his strapped-on talons.

The huge ogre growled, his weapon dropping and blood pouring from open veins. He gripped the bleeding wound tight, his eyes turning as red as his hand. A berserker fury filled him.

And while that happened, the other prisoner launched another attack, aiming for Golgren's leg. The thrust was an obvious one, however, and the grand lord moved to the side.

Without warning, he felt something clutch at his chest, squeezing it painfully.

That pain was superseded a second later by a more painful slice across his thigh. Golgren hissed and stumbled back, but his attacker followed after him closely. All but smelling his victory, the prisoner threw himself at the smaller figure.

And again, there came the tight and startling clutching of pain in his chest. Stumbling, Golgren dropped to one knee. He gazed up dully as the sword drove for his throat.

Raising his metal talons saved him, but the effort ripped them loose. Golgren immediately dodged underneath the sword and plunged his own weapon into his adversary's thick stomach.

No sooner had he dispatched that prisoner than the second had tackled him from behind and wrestled him to the ground. A bloody hand crushed his face. Ragged breathing filled his ears, and a heavy weight shoved most of the air from his lungs. Blood trickled down Golgren's chest, which still felt tight with pain.

But the giant ogre turned his head briefly, and Golgren saw his opportunity. He raised his own head as best he could and bit at his foe's ear, tearing into it almost with gusto.

His foe howled and pulled away, in the process helping Golgren rip a piece of flesh away from the ear. Spitting out the bloody bit, the grand lord brought his sword up between himself and the prisoner. With as much strength as he could muster, Golgren shoved the sword into the other's chest.

The larger ogre fell back, his life fluids splashing over Golgren in the process. Wasting not a breath, Golgren slashed at the ogre's throat and with pleasure watched the blood pour out.

The prisoner grabbed at the gaping wound, but his struggles were in vain. He flailed for nearly a minute before the grand lord put him out of his misery with a thrust to the heart.

The gate opened and Wargroch and the others trotted forward, relieved grins on their faces. Wargroch started to congratulate his master, but suddenly the grand lord felt that same terrible clutching pain at his chest.

"Away!" he snarled at the others. "Away!"

Before they could react, Golgren turned toward the other door, the one through which he had entered, banging on it. The moment it was open, he barged past, leaving his retinue behind.

The guards stationed at intervals in the corridors were wise enough to say nothing as he staggered past them. Golgren cared for nothing at that moment save reaching his quarters.

To the sentries standing outside his doors, the ogre leader commanded, "No one enters!"

As they quickly shut the doors behind him, Golgren scanned the room for any sign of Idaria. Relieved that she was absent, he immediately took hold of the front of his tunic and tore the garment off in shreds. As he did that, Golgren headed to a gilded mirror whose elegant floral etching marked it as yet another prize from lost Silvanost.

And there, the grand lord eyed the two items dangling by chains over his breast.

The smaller of the pair was the tiny, transparent vial no larger than a pin in which a few small drops of thick red liquid were suspended. Golgren touched the vial with his index finger, feeling the warmth of the contents, aware how they were bound to him. The vial was valuable to him—assuming it worked as the Lady Nephera had said it would—and not the cause of his pain.

That, Golgren knew, fell to his severed hand.

The mummified appendage dangled from a thick chain that was laced through the remnants of his severed wrist. The yellowed fingers were still bent as if ready to grab at something. After the Uruv Suurt Faros had cut his hand off in battle and fled the scene, Golgren had scoured the site of his loss until he had found the precious remains. Using ogre embalming techniques generally reserved for the dead, the grand lord had preserved the hand as a grim reminder of his failure that day.

He had worn the hand over his heart since then, even when sleeping. In a morbid manner, its presence also brought him a measure of comfort and confidence. In addition, the rumors that he carried around his severed hand added to his reputation for fierceness, especially since the severed hand was represented on his banner.

But during the fight . . . but during the fight, the hand had disturbed him.

He prodded the mummified hand. The appendage swung back and forth slightly then stilled. The nails, polished finely, barely grazed the hairs on his chest. The hand was as dead as it seemed. True, death was not always the end of things; his precarious alliance with the late Nephera had proved that. With the powers granted her by her mysterious benefactor—said to be at times either dread Takhisis, foul Morgion, or both—Nephera had controlled the spirits of the dead. Those dead—those *f'hanos*—had wreaked much havoc, and even Golgren had the occasional nightmare concerning one malevolent spirit of hers.

Takyr.

But Nephera was long dead and, as far as Golgren knew, she would remain so.

Perhaps he had been mistaken about the source of his discomfort. The grand lord started to prod the hand one more time when someone dared pound on his door, demanding entrance.

Quickly grabbing the tatters of his tunic and draping them over his hand, Golgren whirled toward the entrance. "Who dares? Enter!"

"Gaho i verizo na!" blabbered a bug-eyed Khleeg. *"Gaho i verizo na iGolgreni!"*

For Khleeg of all his people to forget his master's edict concerning the learning and speaking of Common, with severe punishment for the perpetrator, made the ogre leader instinctively grab at Khleeg and pull him close. "You are forgiven for your intrusion as you ask, Khleeg, if the reason is good."

Trying to keep his composure, the officer blurted, *"F'hanos,* Grand Lord! He says much *f'hanos!"*

Golgren squeezed the hidden, mummified appendage harder as he attempted to understand what Khleeg was saying. Had his thoughts of Nephera brought her creeping back from the beyond? Surely he had heard wrong. "You mean *f'han?* Someone is dead?"

"No! It—may I bring someone in?"

Impatient, Golgren bade him to do so with considerable haste. Khleeg barked a command at the doorway, and a guard ushered in a warrior who was battered, bloody, and beaten and stared with eyes half-insane that darted to every shadow as if expecting to find something terrible lurking within.

"Thraun," Khleeg said by way of hasty introduction. "Rode with Captain Tarkus. Toward the west . . . toward where happened the glorious victory of Golgren over the three."

"And so?" Judging from the addled expression on Thraun's face, something terrible had happened to his captain, as well as the others. "You speak of *f'han?* All dead in the patrol?"

"F'hanos!" shouted Thraun, suddenly flinging himself at Golgren's knee. The huge warrior clung to his lord as if a child. *"F'hanos!"*

The repeated word defied Golgren's comprehension. He looked up at Khleeg. "Explain!"

The officer seized Thraun and pulled him up. Thrusting his face into the shaken warrior's, Khleeg roared, "Tell all!"

"*Bre—*" Thraun swallowed then, seeming to come half out of his panic, said in Common, "Dead. All dead! Only bones! Ogres! Mastarks! Meredrakes! Horses! Saw—saw maybe Trang even!"

"*Trang?*" Khleeg snorted. "No Trang!"

"*Ke!* Yes! Him!" The disheveled ogre made a slicing motion across his neck. "But no head!"

"Forget Trang!" Golgren commanded. "Speak! Bones walking! Is that what you say?"

The rest of the story poured out in incoherent fashion. Thraun had been ordered to deal with the mounts. He had just finished with his duties when the shouts arose and the fighting started. Of Captain Tarkus, there was no sign. Thraun had started to go to the aid of the others, only to witness them quickly slaughtered by voracious undead. Two meredrakes, bits of their dry, scaled hides still clinging to the bones, ripped apart one hapless warrior, he said. Other *f'hanos*—most of them mere bones—surrounded the others like packs of ravenous wolves.

At that point, aware that to stay in place was to die horrifically, Thraun undid the horses' reins and tried to free them. In his clumsiness, he nearly lost all the animals, for the moment that they were free, they panicked and careened into one another.

One failed to make it away, for the *f'hanos* were nearer to Thraun than he had realized. Only the fact that the horse tried to race in the wrong direction likely saved

Thraun from death. Instead, the mount was swarmed by four foul creatures.

However, as the horse went down screaming, another undead tackled the ogre. Empty eye sockets stared down at Thraun; he recalled cold, fleshless fingers clutching his throat. Yet somewhere he managed to find the strength to fight free. He struck the dead skull hard, breaking one of his own fingers. The force of the ogre's blow sent the *f'hanos* stumbling back.

Struggling to his feet, Thraun discovered one horse with its reins tangled. He undid the frantic animal and leaped aboard.

As he rode from the nightmare, he heard a long wail from a comrade who had outlasted the others before silence took command.

The recollection of his ordeal proved too much for the warrior. Thraun collapsed into a trembling heap at Golgren's feet. Ogres were powerful and fearless in battle and lived for their bloodlust, but *f'hanos* represented one of their greatest fears. Death was death; *f'hanos* went against reason and logic.

Khleeg and the others looked to Golgren, who stood silent and impassive. The grand lord was not a believer in coincidence. The horde of undead was marching toward Garantha at just the time when he was about to be crowned ruler of the ogres.

Golgren could think of only one being who could command such peculiar magic, although why he should choose to do so remained a mystery.

"Khleeg! Summon those kept ready! We march when the first embers glow," he ordered, referring to dawn in the phraseology of his people.

"We fight *f'hanos?*" asked Khleeg uncertainly.

"We destroy *f'hanos*," the grand lord corrected him. "Now go!"

His lord's evident confidence brought some of the fighting spirit back to the officer. He saluted sharply then took command over the others. The sentry who had dragged in Thraun managed to get the mad ogre to his feet and out of the chamber.

Golgren stood stone faced until the doors were again sealed. Then he turned to the ceiling and hissed, "Dauroth! Attend me!"

But after far more time than was permissible, Golgren still stood alone. The grand lord called the Titan's name again and again with an equal lack of success.

And that made him finally toss away the ruined tunic again, once more gazing down at the tiny vial. Shoving aside his mummified hand, he gripped the vial tightly, then tighter still. It would take only a little more pressure to destroy it. So the Uruv Suurt witch had said. His hand could do what a hammer or a rock could not; to all else, the vial was said to be impervious. Its fate was entirely and literally in his hand.

And tied to its fate, if Nephera had not lied to him, was Dauroth's. After all, it was his essence—not merely his blood—that the vial contained. Lady Nephera had crafted that little gift for Golgren, albeit at a high price. If Dauroth tried to slay the grand lord, the vial would be his revenge.

As far as Golgren knew, Dauroth was ignorant of the vial. It had been created as a secret weapon. Golgren had always relied on a variety of factors, other magics, to keep the Titans at bay. He understood that, at least until that moment, he had actually performed a vital service for Dauroth, organizing the ogres in such a manner that the Titans could focus on their own desires.

It appeared, though, that Dauroth found his usefulness of diminishing value.

He spit then tried one last summons. "Come, Dauroth. Come."

"I am here, oh Grand Lord."

Golgren cursed, jumping at the suddenness of Dauroth's voice. He turned to face the blue-skinned giant. "At last! I summoned you before this! Where have you been? There is a threat to us all!"

The Titan did not reply at first, instead gliding along the floor in a circle around Golgren. All the while, his golden eyes remained fixed on the grand lord, who turned as the Titan did to keep the towering figure in front of him.

When he had completed his circuit, Dauroth offered a condescending frown. "Such a sorry little mongrel! This is what the ogre race has fallen to! Not even a full-blooded creature, but a miserable half-breed tainted by an elf legacy!"

"You should understand it well, Dauroth. Understand and appreciate."

"I do not appreciate impurity, imperfection, Guyvir."

The grand lord's pulse suddenly pounded. "I am *Golgren*." He gripped the vial again. "You have been warned—"

Dauroth leaned forward, his countenance still utterly disdainful. "Crush it, Guyvir. Shatter it. It matters not. I have known of it for a long time. It is too weak a thing to slay me."

"Impossible!"

"There is magic, I tell you, far more formidable than

that of the Uruv Suurt bitch who made that for you!" Dauroth snapped with abrupt, uncustomary fury. His face immediately relaxed again. "Titan magic . . . the magic that will return the ogre race to its rightful place."

Golgren let the vial drop against him. He recalled the painful clutching at his chest. "Was you, then! You who made this move!" He indicated the mummified appendage. "You who command the army of *f'hanos* marching on Garantha!"

"You are babbling, oh Grand Lord." Dauroth gazed heavenward, a deep frown spreading over his handsome features. "But not about the *f'hanos* evidently. Fascinating! Not me, not me. But who else have you irritated so much, Guyvir, that they would send the very dead after you?"

So it was not the Titans. Golgren hissed. "The *f'hanos* will not stop with me. They will destroy all! The Titans, they must help defend Garantha when I ride to meet these creatures! You shall summon storm and quake and—"

"I will do nothing more for you. You claim the right to be grand khan and lord chieftain in one? Let us see the true cunning and power of Guyvir without the Titans coming to his rescue! Oh, we shall protect Garantha but only when you are outside its gates, dying in a vain attempt to kill those already slain!"

Golgren bared his teeth, wishing that his tusks were long and sharp as he stared up at the smug sorcerer. Dauroth knew his vulnerability. If Golgren waited in the city until the *f'hanos* attacked, he would lose all the prestige he had built up among his kind. With the possible exception of a few diehards such as Khleeg and Wargroch, most of his officers, the khans and chieftains, they would all turn on him.

Yet if Golgren led his army into battle against the dead without the benefit of the Titans' magic, it was highly probable that the greater part of his forces would be routed and the remainder would perish with him in ignoble defeat.

Dauroth folded his arms. "Now our little talk is done. It is time for me to deal with another who thinks himself higher than he is. Then . . . then at last, I can go back to my holy tasks without any more interruptions!" His eyes suddenly glowed. "But first, something to remember me by! You shall wear it to your bitter end."

Golgren bent over in horrific pain. He managed to keep from uttering more than a slight moan. His chest burned.

The agony eased. As the grand lord straightened, he heard a slight clatter on the floor and saw the chain that had held the vial lying there. However, the vial itself was nowhere to be seen.

He shoved aside the mummified hand.

Embedded in his chest was the vial. A thin layer of skin shrouded the sinister container.

"Think of me as you fail, oh Grand Lord."

The Titan vanished amid a swirl of black, smoky tendrils.

Golgren threw himself at where Dauroth had stood but far too late. Panting, the grand lord clawed at the vial, but to touch the area sent spasms of pain coursing through him.

Wargroch called from without, begging permission to enter with some news. Grabbing another tunic, Golgren gave his permission, trying not to gasp as the pain gradually subsided.

The younger ogre was quick with his report. "A scout

from a patrol. Says that there are *f'hanos*—many, many *f'hanos*—near Kubli!"

Kubli was a small, forgettable settlement save for one thing: it was barely more than a day's march from Garantha. What little time Golgren had left had shrunk just like that.

"Khleeg has orders! All must be ready to fight! We ride before the Burning! Make this known to him!"

With a slap to his breastplate, Wargroch fled the chamber.

Golgren's expression shifted to one that was almost passive. He had made his decision. He would face the undead horde and he would defeat it or, at the very least, the ogre race would sing of the legend of the grand lord's great stand.

That was supposing, of course, that there would be anyone left alive to sing it.

Idaria was with Stefan when the news began to spread of some great threat to the city looming on the horizon. The knight, true to his nature, demanded details from the nearest guard, which nearly got him into a fight with the ogre.

The elf managed to calm the situation then took the Solamnic aside. "Let me find out the truth."

"I will follow," he insisted. "If there is a real threat, I must know what it is and how I might play a part against it."

With a shrug, Idaria led him toward Golgren's chambers. On their way, though, they crossed paths with Wargroch.

"What is it?" she asked of the officer, forcing him to

pause and speak to her despite his obvious haste. "What causes such turmoil?"

At first he shook his head, but then, perhaps because he was uncertain as to her influence on the grand lord, he finally rumbled, *"F'hanos,* slave! Army of *f'hanos* marches to Garantha!"

Wargroch said no more, barging past the pair and all but running down the corridor.

"F'hanos?" Stefan muttered, looking perplexed. "What does he mean? I've heard *f'han,* but that means 'death,' doesn't it?"

"In a hundred variations. This is not a word I am familiar with. Golgren will know."

They reached the chambers. Idaria had no trouble gaining entrance, but the guards blocked the knight's path.

"Haroth!" Golgren shouted from within, momentarily lapsing into the tongue of his birth.

"Master," Idaria immediately answered, "forgive me for not being here to attend you."

He glanced past her to the Solamnic. "Sir Stefan Rennert! It is good you came. But it is a shame no alliance yet exists. It is a shame that I must face this threat alone."

The human bowed. "Grand Lord, what trouble threatens this city? An army, I know, but if it is one that is also an enemy of Solamnia, then perhaps I can offer my arm—"

To that, Golgren abruptly laughed. Idaria stared, realizing the desperation behind that laugh. "They are *f'hanos!* I think such as they are enemies of all that live!"

"But what are *f'hanos,* if I may ask?"

The grand lord snarled, as he started walking around, grabbing things that he would need, half talking to himself. "The dead who walk. It is the dead you and your comrades discovered! They are risen and seek vengeance against me, it seems."

His declaration left both the elf and human gaping. There were such stories even among Idaria's people, stories of necromancy.

The knight at last found his voice. "If what you say is true, Grand Lord, then I do indeed offer my assistance! I will not stand by while such abominations walk the mortal plane, for it is true they can mean no good purpose for my people either."

Golgren turned, his face brightening. He grinned. "Good! We shall grind their bones into dust, yes? Or die together!"

Stefan only nodded, his countenance as grim as the ogre's.

The two of them left Idaria in their wake. The slave watched them vanish down the hall, her expression changing from shock to thoughtful calculation. She glanced at the nearest window, then seemed to dismiss that idea. Instead, her hand went to her gown and something she had kept secreted in the folds.

The signet seemed to burn briefly as she pulled it free. Idaria had not given it to Golgren as Tyranos had commanded, for the elf had sensed its latent magic power and had herself sought to probe its secrets . . . sought the secrets and failed.

Idaria glanced again in the direction Golgren had gone.

She replaced the signet in her gown and followed.

XX

DEATH AND THE UNDEAD

The Black Talon had gathered for several reasons, the least of which was to welcome the Titan who would replace the unfortunate Varnin. Dauroth extended his hand into the darkness beyond the ten, singing, "Come forth, chosen one."

It was not entirely a surprise that Morgada entered the light. She bowed deep and sang, "I shall seek to ever prove myself worthy of my place in the Talon."

"You will have sufficient opportunity for that very shortly," replied the lead Titan. "Take your seat next to Safrag."

No one in the inner circle showed any jealousy that Morgada had been rewarded with a place so near Dauroth, but he was aware that envy existed. However, Dauroth looked with indifference on such petty emotions; after all, both the Titans and the Black Talon were his creations. Did he not, then, have the absolute right to do with its members as he pleased?

The second item of business was the disappointing example of Hundjal.

THE BLACK TALON

The athletic apprentice sat proudly at his master's side, bathing in the favor of his master. He had opened the tomb so that all its treasures, especially the precious bones, had remained intact. Hundjal had every reason to be pleased with himself save that, in solving that puzzle—and delving into yet another mystery—he had secretly and without regret broken one of his master's cardinal laws. That Dauroth had manipulated the matter so his senior apprentice would do such a thing was beside the point. Hundjal should have known better.

Then the sudden rise of *f'hanos*—whose origins perplexed Dauroth—presented a perfect opportunity for the leader of the Titans to attack not only Golgren, but also Hundjal.

It was a perfect time to begin.

"Hundjal, summon for us the image of what faces Garantha and the grand lord."

With a cocky smile, the apprentice rose and gestured toward the seated members. A green, spiraling sphere burst into existence then expanded until it was greater than the height of the tallest Titan.

"Serea seloo israya," Hundjal intoned, select words in the beautiful language Dauroth had created only for spells.

The sphere opened and an army as macabre as any witnessed in the history of Krynn wound its way across the landscape. Shambling determined skeletons by the hundreds filled the Titans' view. Meredrakes wrapped only in dried skin weaved their way among the hollow-eyed ogre warriors, plodding along at the silent commands of their ghoulish riders.

That it was dark did not matter, for the sphere illuminated the horrific vision as bright as day. As

Hundjal gestured, the image swerved to show what lay ahead of the fleshless horde.

At the very edge of the horizon, the towers and walls of the capital were just becoming visible.

"Should we not act?" asked Kallel anxiously. "This is surely meant as a threat to all our kind."

"But it risks too much use of our power," argued another Titan. "And we are surely safe here, so many days away and in this hidden valley. Let the grand lord deal with this trouble."

Dauroth raised a hand for silence. "The destruction of an army of bones would be no difficulty for the Talon, with or without the help of the rest of the Titans." He allowed himself a slight smile. "And, as for the grand lord . . . his part in my designs is at an end."

Kallel leaned forward. "So you will let him be taken? After all this time, you will let him be taken?"

"In a manner that will mark his downfall and disgrace. Hundjal . . . " At Dauroth's behest, Hundjal caused the sphere to change to an image of Garantha. The Titans watched as the palace raced into view.

And there they saw hundreds upon hundreds of restless ogre warriors, dressed in the armor of the Grand Lord Golgren, waiting for the order to march. Mastarks with metal helms and body plates trumpeted impatiently, forcing several mounted fighters to struggle to bring their horses under control.

A horn blared. and out from the palace itself appeared their leader. Golgren was dressed as he liked to be when heading into battle, his armor immaculate and shining. He was accompanied by the Solamnic, also dressed in battle gear. Grinning confidently, Golgren saluted his warriors as he and the knight descended to a pair of

THE BLACK TALON

horses with the grand lord's elf slave a few steps behind them.

"The cur even brings his favorite pets along to keep him company in death," Morgada purred. "Should we not at least save that little silver-haired morsel? Her blood must have much strength to have enabled her to survive his hungers."

Dauroth shrugged. One elf more or less was not of any importance at that moment, and he didn't care about the human either. "They will all die together, and the race will see that the great Golgren was less than a *fherkuut* with only one good leg."

Fherkuut were small rodents with long snouts and tiny eyes. They had carved a niche for themselves in inhospitable lands by devouring other animals' excrement and using the few nutrients within. To ogres, they were the lowest of all life.

The others laughed heartily at his clever mockery of the half-breed leader. Dauroth rose. "Come. Let the Talon prepare itself. The grand lord wishes our magic to fall upon the *f'hanos*. We would not want to disappoint him."

Leaving their seats, the eleven spellcasters gathered like eager ghosts around Hundjal's sphere, eyeing the first movements of Golgren's force as it headed out to meet the *f'hanos*. Amusement glinted in the eyes of most Titans. They were finally going to be rid of the half-breed and in a manner that would curse his memory among ogres for all time. They did not know exactly what Dauroth had in mind but trusted in the leader of the Black Talon; he knew many cunning ways to kill his enemies.

And after Golgren was dead, the Titans, led by the

Black Talon, would save the ogre race and take proper control of their destiny.

Dauroth took his place in the center of the group, dismissing the sphere and its image with but a glance. The others took up their appointed positions, creating a pattern with five points and five intersections. Hundjal and Safrag went to their usual places at an intersection opposite their master.

"Nay, my good Hundjal," called the lead Titan. "Your place is close by me for this occasion."

"Great one?" The apprentice could not hide his pleasure at that statement. To stand with Dauroth meant to take a lead in the spellcasting. It not only marked Hundjal as Dauroth's most favored, but also emphasized his likeliness of rising up when the elder Titan stepped down from his hallowed position as their leader. Several of the others looked envious. Safrag merely stared downward. The Titans adjusted their pattern so as to accommodate the alteration that Dauroth's invitation warranted.

Guiding Hundjal to the spot where the sphere had been, Dauroth placed his hands on the apprentice's shoulders. "Dear Hundjal, my Hundjal! Ever daring, ever inquisitive! You hunt secrets with as much determination as you do your prey."

Hundjal beamed proudly. Some of the others nodded their appreciation of the master's assessment of his disciple. Morgada gave the senior apprentice a beguiling smile.

"I seek only to follow in your footsteps, my master. Your teachings are my existence. As you preach, I seek to emulate."

"This will be a spell requiring some sacrifice," Dauroth informed both Hundjal and the others. "And

I think that, Hundjal, you understand the necessity of sacrifice, do you not?"

"Of course."

"I am so gratified to hear that."

Black flames suddenly blazed from Dauroth's hands, enveloping the apprentice with searing heat.

Hundjal let out a gasp but seemed unable to move. The other Titans—with the exception of Safrag—couldn't hide their shock.

"Stay your positions!" Dauroth demanded, his song-voice threatening. He leaned close to Hundjal so his next words would be heard by only his apprentice. "You have touched the forbidden, my pupil, transgressed against me—me!—in an unforgivable manner! I do set the law among us and no one, not even you, dear, precocious Hundjal, may break my rules . . . not even despite my wish and my guidance for you to do so!"

The apprentice's eyes, darting wildly, widened as he understood that he had been manipulated into using the fragment. Hundjal had thought he was cleverer than his master. He was not.

"With you will die any impulse by others to wield that accursed thing! But fear not! You shall serve me and our cause in one last, grand manner and your memory will be honored for it."

Hundjal let out a pathetic gurgle. Dauroth sang three words, three words that would have sent the rest of the Talon recoiling if they had not already been warned to stay in their places. They heard the terrible three words, the ones that condemned those who betrayed the master to a fate worse than even Donnag's.

To become one of the Abominations . . .

Almost. Such a fate was not quite what Dauroth had in

mind for Hundjal, for then his apprentice's tremendous power would not be available to him for the spell against the *f'hanos*.

So there was a slight alteration to the words.

Then a horrified gasp escaped from the mouths of several of the Titans, for Hundjal suddenly and utterly liquefied. The beginnings of a howl issued from his lips and was quickly, mercilessly, cut off. The apprentice, robes and all, poured through Dauroth's fingers onto the stone floor.

But it did not end there, for no sooner had the stomach-wrenching liquid pooled on the floor than it started dissipating into nothingness. As that happened, tendrils of glittering blue energy—a Titan's magic—wafted upward.

And as the tendrils passed over the heads of the Titans, Dauroth opened his mouth wide and inhaled the magic, in the process seeming to swell in size. His body radiated a fearsome azure aura and he looked stronger, more powerful than ever.

His grin wide, the lead Titan casually gestured at the others. They felt their own power, their very essences, surge and bind with his greater power. More than one feared that they would be next to follow the late Hundjal, but Dauroth had merely brought them into the spell in order to take the next step of his plan, dealing with the situation outside Garantha.

And, most important, dealing with the Grand Lord Golgren.

※※◆※※

Mounted on a tall, wide ogre horse, Sir Stefan tested the balance of his sword. Whether or not a blade would work against those fiends was a question that would soon be known. The *f'hanos* had no vital organs, nor even muscle or sinew. Skeletons were all they were, and there must be a way to stop them.

A horn sounded. A rider approached from ahead, his mount moving like a blur. The fear animating both the ogre and his steed was evident long before they reached the grand lord.

The scout barked something to Golgren in the native tongue. Golgren did not order him to repeat everything in Common, as the ogre's transgression was forgettable, understandable, in the face of such calamity.

"They come," explained the grand lord quietly after dismissing the scout.

The sun was only just beginning to rise, but the day looked to be oddly overcast. Many took that as an omen or some evidence of whatever mysterious evil possessed the *f'hanos*.

Golgren's army spread out, deploying according to his instructions. Stefan had been impressed by the grand lord's strategy. Golgren had his foot soldiers, cavalry, and archers arrayed in a manner that would have done any Solamnic commander proud.

But whether or not the most brilliant strategy would deter an undead enemy remained to be seen.

"They must come no farther," Golgren proclaimed loudly, standing in the saddle for all to see and hear him. He adjusted his helmet slightly as he sat again then shouted, "Horn!"

Pulling the curled goat horn to his fat lips, the nearby trumpeter quickly blew the signal to advance. With one ferocious roar, the ogres let out a lusty challenge to any who would face them, then began marching swiftly forward. The banner of the severed hand fluttered everywhere.

Khleeg and Wargroch rode close to their lord, while lesser officers took immediate command of the rear ranks and flank troops. Idaria also rode near the grand lord. The elf still wore chains, and as far as the eye could tell, she didn't carry any weapons but seemed entirely unconcerned about any danger.

Stefan had tried to talk some sense into her as they had mounted up. "You should not be with us! This is no place for you!"

"I go where my master goes," she had replied evenly, her stern glance at him ending any further discussion.

As they rode, the dim, gray light revealed the first hints of something vast pouring over the western landscape. Stefan gripped the pommel of his sword and heard a gasp from Wargroch.

Golgren straightened. Again, he shouted, "Horn!"

The trumpeter let loose once more. Immediately, the ranks shifted, spreading out widely on both sides. The mounted warriors edged forward, preparing for a charge. Archers readied their bows, although of all weapons available to the grand lord, he had the greatest doubt about the efficacy of arrows. What could the missiles accomplish, save bouncing harmlessly off bone?

But then the signal changed and other ogres went over to the archers, bearing small cloth pouches that they bound to the heads of their arrows. Their task complete, those warriors fell back to be replaced by others bearing oiled torches.

"Neeska if'hanosi!" rasped Khleeg suddenly, shaking his head at the size and sound of the dark horde converging on them.

The enemy was coming close enough to be seen clearly,

and some of the individual figures were frightening enough to cause murmurs and hesitation in the ranks.

They were just as the lone scout had described.

Skeletons.

There were ranks and ranks of marching, ghastly skeletons. They headed toward the ogres with a steady rhythm, their empty eyes gazing at the living enemy with what almost seemed jealousy.

Closer and closer the skeleton army advanced, and still Golgren issued no new commands. Several ogres glanced worriedly at their leader. Yet Golgren looked both confident and resolute. There was no sign of any uncertainty, certainly no sign of fear. Despite the superstitious nature of his race, the grand lord seemed unperturbed by facing an enemy of walking dead.

Idaria suddenly leaned close; one hand reached to her gown. "My master—"

He ignored her. "Fire!"

His simple, calm command almost caught the trumpeter by surprise. The warrior swiftly put the gnarled horn to his mouth and blew as hard and long and loud as he could.

The torchbearers lit small wicks dangling from the pouches. The archers immediately aimed high into the air in the direction of their foe.

A vast torrent of flaming arrows shot forth.

At a gesture from Golgren, other ogres began to pound a steady beat on the round copper drums that they carried, held by tanned leather straps reaching to their powerful shoulders. The ranks steadied as training and battle adrenalin took over.

At that point, the arrows descended and began exploding.

Shattered bones and mounds of ravaged dirt flew everywhere into the air. The legions of the undead walked into the explosions as if they did not have the minds to dodge or swerve. Not only were the first ranks utterly decimated, but continual rains of arrows tore asunder many of the skeletal ranks that followed.

An entire fleshless mastark erupted into flames, its scattering pieces taking apart scores of skeletal warriors surrounding it. Everywhere, bits of what had once been monstrous fighters lay strewn like a graveyard upturned by a huge worm.

"Cease!" roared Golgren, eyes flaring with relish. "Cease!"

Alerted again by the horn, the archers lowered their bows.

A victorious shout arose from the grand lord's followers. Even Sir Stefan cheered, he hoped not prematurely. There were still many *f'hanos* marching toward them, though far fewer than before. A good sword or club would undoubtedly shatter the things to harmless bits that could be gathered later and burned.

But then the destroyed skeletons—the pieces of skeletons, the battered and broken pieces that had so cheered the ogres—suddenly whirled back up into the air, gathering here and there and reattaching themselves with ungodly swiftness.

"Kiri-Jolith's horns!" the knight gasped.

The ruined skeletons were becoming whole again. It took barely more than a breath for each of them to reform, some with pieces incorrectly assembled, making them even more monstrous. And after reforming, the skeletons resumed their march, joining the others who were steadily approaching the ogre ranks.

"Not possible!" grunted Khleeg. "Not possible!"

An ogre soldier in the first ranks slipped away. Another followed suit, both of them racing away to the side of the battle. Golgren quickly gestured to the nearest archers. They glanced at him then raised their bows toward the pair.

Two expert shots brought down the fleeing ogres.

Stefan looked horrified. "Grand Lord—"

Golgren glared his way, his eyes so ruthless that the Solamnic immediately shut his mouth, recalling he was still a prisoner there and ogres had their own battle traditions. "There must be order and discipline," the grand lord snarled, "if we are to survive."

As the stunned ogre army stared at their approaching enemy, the *f'hanos* progressed toward them in eerie silence, save perhaps the occasional creak of bone upon bone. The distance separating the skeleton army from the ogres shrank by the minute.

Golgren sat in his saddle, watching the skeletons approach, wondering if they had any possible weaknesses.

Without warning, Idaria grabbed the grand lord's hand and thrust something into it. "Master! Take this!"

Golgren eyed the small object—a sinister-looking ring—then stared at the elf. She stared back at the ogre leader with an expression that was mixed with so many emotions that Sir Stefan, watching, couldn't understand what was transpiring.

The slave murmured in Golgren's ear. "Tyranos! He thought it important to give this to you! It has . . . much ancient power."

The grand lord put the signet into a pouch and, glancing again at the elf slave, pointed back to Garantha. Idaria firmly shook her head, but Golgren summoned a mounted warrior.

"Take this one back to the palace!" Golgren ordered.

Perhaps as eager to be away from the battle as he was to obey his lord, the warrior snagged the reins of the slave's horse and dragged her off. Idaria glanced over her shoulder at the ogre leader, then spared a quick look at Stefan.

Yet the knight agreed with Golgren; the elf slave should be taken away from the battle scene. He rode up to join the grand lord. Golgren was staring at the undead enemy, coming closer and closer.

"What are your orders?" Stefan asked.

Golgren laughed harshly. "Fight, of course."

The grand lord signaled the trumpeter. The horn wailed one last time, sounding both defiant and mournful.

And as the sound washed over his warriors, Golgren let out a bestial war cry that was joined by his army and rode forward.

The ogre army surged toward the undead. On both flanks and in the very center, a gap opened. Through those gaps streamed the mounted forces, including Golgren and Stefan at the lead. Golgren roared louder as he swept past his front lines. Khleeg and others took up his exultant cry, and even Stefan joined in.

The riders—the foot soldiers on their heels—smashed into the enemy.

Stefan swung at the first skeleton within range, throwing his full strength into a blow against its skull. The well-crafted Solamnic blade easily severed the head from the neck and for good measure the knight kicked the creature hard in the rib cage. The skeletal figure tumbled over into pieces.

Coming upon a second, he repeated the attack with equal fervor and success. The *f'hanos* were clumsy fighters at best. As he headed toward a third foe, Stefan cried out,

"For honor and victory! For honor and—"

Something snagged him by his ankle. Looking down, he saw that the second one of his fleshless opponents had already half reconstructed itself. Even lacking its head, the horrifying thing clutched at him, almost dragging the human from his mount. Worse, joining the effort was Stefan's first victim, the skeleton he had beheaded that was again completely whole.

Stefan managed to batter away the one holding onto him, but then the other one seized his leg. The strength of the monsters was incredible; it was all the Solamnic could do to keep in the saddle.

But others were not so successful. Beyond Stefan, two other riders were dragged down. The two vanished under a torrent of grasping, clawlike hands. Even the mounts were not spared, the *f'hanos* dragging them to the ground with equal zeal.

Facing such a chilling fate, Stefan struck out harder and harder. He managed to free his leg, but then pale bony fingers seized his mount by the legs, the tail, and the torso. The frantic animal kicked, shattering more than one of the skeleton figures, yet not only were there too many all around him, but every one that was temporarily broken soon resurrected itself.

With a shriek, the knight's mount at last fell on its side. Stefan tumbled to the ground. He managed to roll into a fighting position just as another of the undead reached for him.

If not for the fact that many of the *f'hanos* were unarmed save for rocks they clutched in their grasping fingers, Stefan would have died on the spot. However, another rider came from out of nowhere and smashed the *f'hanos* threatening him from behind.

Golgren, a thick sword gripped tight, grinned wildly at Stefan.

"My horse, Sir Stefan Rennert! It can carry two, yes?"

Beating away another *f'hanos,* the Solamnic leaped behind Golgren.

"They keep resurrecting!" the human shouted. "I've shattered several and they just instantly reform!"

"Yes!" was all Golgren replied. More and more *f'hanos* swarmed them, as if aware, despite their apparent lack of intelligence, that they had cornered the ogre leader.

"What magic keeps them animated?" the Solamnic cried as he fought wildly from his ungainly perch. "Is there none upon which you can call?"

The grand lord hissed then straightened. "There may be one chance! Sir Stefan Rennert! My Idaria has given me something I do not know how to use, but will try! Pray to your noble gods I succeed!"

Screams filled the air. A giant skeleton trod through the ogres, a fleshless mastark on a rampage. Stefan grimaced as it neared the pair. "Whatever you might be able to do, you'd best try quickly!"

"Guard me!" Golgren sheathed his sword then fumbled inside of a pouch. He pulled something free then held it up. Stefan caught a glimpse of something like a starburst.

"No!" shouted the ogre, sounding utterly disconcerted. "This is not what I sought for! How—"

The unsettlingly overcast sky made it seem almost like night on the battlefield. Yet some small bit of illumination struck the object in Golgren's hand and caused it to glow like fire.

Cursing, the grand lord sought to plunge the item back into the pouch, but it was too late.

A mad light burst to life, blinding both riders and causing their horse to shriek and rear. Golgren let out another curse.

Then the furious, fiery light was all that existed.

XXI

Bedlam And Blood

Golgren's hand burned as if it were utterly consumed by fire, and for a moment the ogre, unable to see, wondered whether he had lost his remaining hand. Yet he still felt the flex of his finger, so, despite the intense pain, he knew his arm was intact.

Of the piece left to him by the gargoyle, he knew nothing. Whether it had been destroyed or simply vanished, the grand lord did not care. He had instead sought the object Idaria had pressed into his hand, the ring with the odd signet. She had been most insistent that he take it and even had said something about Tyranos giving it to her to pass to him. Golgren had been certain because of that that it would help against the *f'hanos*.

How had the other thing found its way into his palm? His fingers had snared the ring. He felt its shape as he pulled it free of the pouch, and yet when he opened his hand, the accursed starburst was there. How had that happened?

"Come, come, Grand Lord," a voice growled in his ear.

THE BLACK TALON

A powerful set of hands dragged him to his feet. "You can't lie around here all day!"

"Tyranos?" Golgren's vision began to clear a little, but what he saw around him made no sense whatsoever.

The area for some distance resembled the aftermath of an inferno. The ground for several yards was baked black and entirely flattened. Pressed deep into the charred soil were the crusted remnants of several skeletons.

The imposing wizard turned him around, forcing him to look in all directions. Tyranos did not appear very pleased to see the ogre, but Golgren did not have to guess why. By coming there, the wizard likely had revealed himself to the Titans and whoever else might be observing the events through magic; that undoubtedly included whoever animated the macabre horde.

"I should've let you die," Tyranos stated bluntly. "But we can't have that yet, can we?"

Though Golgren was dazed, he was finally registering everything that was going on. His warriors were being decimated, just as he had feared and just as Dauroth, no doubt, desired. Thinking of the Titan made him instinctively grab at his chest for the vial.

"Looking for something there?" asked the wizard. He gestured, and the already-damaged breastplate ripped in two, along with the tunic underneath. "Now just where is that vial I've wondered so much about? I have my own use for that vial, not that you'd understand what I have in mind." Tyranos stopped short. "What by the Sea Queen—?"

The leonine human had reached to grab the vial, trying to tear it free. Golgren screamed, the pain eating at him.

Just as suddenly as he had seized the sealed vial,

353

Tyranos let it go. The mage raised his hands angrily, cursing the sky.

"Damned spellcaster!" cried Stefan, coming up from behind Tyranos and standing protectively before Golgren. "Send your dead back to their graves before I oblige you to join them!"

The mage looked over his shoulder. "You blame me for these undead? Are you mad, Solamnic? Are you—stand aside!"

A staff materialized in the spellcaster's left hand. It shot to full length, its bottom tip stretching past the frowning knight's head.

"That'll be your end!" declared Stefan, thrusting his weapon at the spellcaster.

Tyranos grunted in pain as the sword lanced his side. If not for the wizard's quick reflexes, the knight would have run him through.

At the same time, both Golgren and Stefan realized that Tyranos had not been aiming for the Solamnic, but at another *f'hanos* charging toward the Solamnic. The staff struck the undead warrior directly on the breastbone. A silver aura briefly surrounded the skeleton, and the ghoul went flying.

"Damned swift with that weapon of yours, aren't you, you cursed fool?" Tyranos clutched his bleeding wound. "And after I saved both your miserable hides!"

The knight looked chastened and doubtful. "I—you—saved us?"

Tyranos glared at Golgren. "Tell him!"

Golgren rubbed his chest. "I have trouble believing this also."

As Stefan stepped closer to the spellcaster, Tyranos grew furious. "You two are impossible! That starburst

was not supposed to possess any power after it was taken
from its puppet, at least that was what I thought! I had
him leave it as a warning for you, but only—"

"A warning?" Golgren grew cold with distrust. "By a
gargoyle . . . by one of many gargoyles . . . "

Tyranos bared his teeth. "Not all gargoyles serve—"

"Look out!" Stefan shouted.

A huge paw nearly slammed down on the three of
them. The skeletal mastark had moved silently and quickly
sneaked up on them, despite its lack of flesh and muscle.
Even without flesh and muscle, its heavy bones could have
easily crushed them.

Golgren and Tyranos were momentarily thrown
away from Stefan. The grand lord spotted the wizard's
magical staff, an item he had often coveted, which had
fallen to the ground. Grabbing it, Golgren held it over the
spellcaster's throat.

"Traitor!"

"Drop this foolhardy notion, oh Grand Lord. You
think if I controlled these creatures, I'd let one of them
tromp all over me?"

"If not, then why don't you destroy them!"

Tyranos snorted. "You overestimate me, Grand—"

The undead mastark loomed over them again. The
wizard threw himself to one side as the fleshless foot
came crashing down.

Golgren, on the other hand, suddenly clamped his
teeth around the staff and grabbed hold of the bony limb.
He climbed up the creature's leg with a dexterity that was
astonishing. He felt driven by fury, driven by the need to
prove himself.

The mastark tried to jab at him with its long, curled
tusks. When it was clear that Golgren would not let go, the

huge *f'hanos* tried to buck and spin and shake him off.

Golgren wanted to cry out when the creature's tusk tore away what remained of his tunic, painfully scraping his skin, but he held tight to Tyranos's staff.

The scarred tusk came at him once more.

Golgren released his grip, wrapping his good arm around the mastark's tusk and letting it lift him up.

The mastark wildly shook its head back and forth. The ogre reached up for its neck.

Then Golgren noticed a movement to his side. The grand lord scrambled to pull himself up as an undead warrior—possibly the mastark's original handler—also climbed up the side of the beast, trying to reach him. The skeleton wielded the long, hooked bar normally used for guiding the great beasts.

The long iron hook came at Golgren just as he succeeded in getting one leg up around the mastark's neck. He used that leg to push at the hook but only partially fended it off. The hook drew a jagged red line in his leg, and Golgren was wracked by fresh pain.

The ogre leader tried to beat at the skeletal warrior with Tyranos's staff, momentarily stymieing his horrific foe. His arm ached, yet he held on while continuing to stab at the *f'hanos*.

The undead beast continued to shake and sway, but the ogre leader finally managed to get a good grip and reach the top of the mastark.

The moving mastark proved devilish to try to stand upon, though. Golgren satisfied himself with a crouching position, holding the staff while watching the *f'hanos,* which had not given up.

The skeleton lunged at him with the hook again. Golgren caught the hook with the staff and twisted the weapon around. He disarmed the creature, which immediately lunged forward in an obvious attempt to send both of them plummeting over the side.

Golgren swept the staff across, catching the *f'hanos* just above its ankles. It stumbled, then slipped down. One bony hand sought the grand lord, but he kicked it away.

As the creature fell off, Golgren struggled forward. The mastark appeared more determined than ever to shake him off. It was all that he could do to inch his way toward the creature's skull.

Below, the clash of weapons and the screams of the dying told Golgren that his followers were in dire straits. Out of the corner of his eye, he saw Tyranos, moving in a blur, and Sir Stefan, eyeing him. The grand lord swore at Dauroth and the Titans.

The gigantic beast whirled in a circle as it tried to reach or topple its unwanted rider. Golgren inched forward.

At last, he made it to the top of the mastark's skull. The undead giant reared, almost succeeding in shaking off the pest atop it.

Golgren readied Tyranos's staff. He knew the power it contained. That he did not know how to wield that power did not worry the ogre leader. Some sixth sense made him certain that it would do what he ordered it to do.

So Golgren raised up the staff and struck the mastark's skull with the crystal head.

The silver light flashed so bright, he pulled back in startlement. The staff slipped from his hand, and he lost his balance.

At the last moment, Golgren snagged one of the dead beast's ribs. He dangled there, surrounded by the silver light that covered the gargantuan *f'hanos* from tusk to rear. The skeletal giant shivered and creaked, and as the grand lord struggled, parts of the behemoth began breaking off.

Golgren tried to use the rib to slide toward the ground. However, he had only just begun when the beast began to lurch and trip. A heavy bone struck the ogre in the shoulder.

He fell. Golgren was certain of his death, but then the air suddenly thickened beneath him and his descent slowed. Unfortunately, ribs and bones rained down on him from all sides.

"C-consider that another debt that you owe me!" growled Tyranos, shaking the gleaming staff, which had fallen down and was back in his hands again. "And no—no thanks to you! You could have destroyed it! What by the Maelstrom were you thinking?"

Golgren did not bother to answer him, especially because he did not know what to say. The urge had come upon him and he had acted.

With a deep moan, the mastark finally collapsed. Its skull came plummeting down, crashing within a foot of the pair. Ogre and wizard rushed away from the massive crumbling skeleton.

Just as the last parts of the giant *f'hanos* came crashing down around them, more of the ghoulish warriors swarmed at them from all directions. Tyranos battered away two in the lead as Golgren seized a weapon from one of his fallen warriors.

The pair that the wizard had swatted away had already resurrected themselves. Tyranos let out an oath. "Would you mind telling me what you did with my own staff to make them stay dead?"

"The skull! It was the skull I struck, wizard! Atop!"

Tyranos tried again, trying to hit the two skeletal warriors on top of their skulls, and that time the one he managed to hit on top of its head fell down in pieces and stayed down without moving. "Well, that's something, I suppose."

From Golgren's left there came a war cry and the sounds of several weapons clanging. Khleeg, somehow still mounted, was trying to lead a band of warriors to the rescue of the grand lord. The sight would have heartened Golgren if there were not so many *f'hanos* between the loyal officer and his master.

Indeed, the rescuers were blocked; then they began to be forced back. Golgren tried to steer toward Khleeg, but once again they were swarmed by undead who converged on them from everywhere.

"We must be away from here!" Tyranos shouted. He raised the crystal head of his staff to the sky, groaning with pain. Blood still dripped from the wound Sir Stefan had caused.

Reminded of the Solamnic, Golgren searched around for Stefan, wondering what had become of the knight. He saw no sign that he was alive. He regretted the human's passing, if only for the hope that, should they both have survived, there might still be a chance of some sort of alliance between ogres and knights.

Golthuu—and Silvanost—seemed to be dreams that far exceeded his one-handed grasp.

"Be ready, oh Grand Lord!" Tyranos called.

"For what?"

Something huge swooped just above them. With a wingspan far wider than the ogre's height, it circled around for another pass.

Golgren recognized the scaly behemoth: the gargoyle from the palace corridor. Arms outstretched, the winged beast's intention was clear: to grab both figures and take them into the air.

The idea did not sit well with the grand lord, but he accepted it as the only escape. With Tyranos, the ogre fought to clear the area to give the gargoyle proper room to land.

With an evil grin across its wide mouth, the winged fury closed on them. The wizard, closer to the creature than Golgren, raised his arms to reach up to his rescuer.

Golgren did the same.

Then the entire world trembled. The ogre was tossed off his feet just as the gargoyle took hold of Tyranos.

A sound like raging thunder but a thousand times more ear splitting shook Golgren to his very core. He heard cracking and tearing, and realized that the ground just ahead of him was opening up, great chunks of rock collapsing into the huge gap. A *f'hanos* just closing to reach him stumbled and fell back into the swiftly widening crevasse, vanishing from sight.

All around Golgren, the land shook harder and harder. In every direction, huge pieces of earth and stone tore apart or shot up into the air. Ogres and undead alike were tossed about like playthings.

Tyranos and his pet gargoyle had vanished in the sky. Golgren fought to maintain his balance.

He fell to his knees, rose, then almost immediately fell down again. The one thing that the grand lord had accomplished was to achieve a low vantage from which he could see better what was happening all around him, but that view only left him cold.

The entire landscape from the edge of Garantha to

far to the west was caught up in a quake of tremendous magnitude. The legions of *f'hanos* were perishing by the scores, most of them falling into horrific gaps, which opened and suddenly closed again. His own followers fared no better. Golgren witnessed a horse and rider simply sink beneath the land without even the chance for a scream, while other ogres fled in outright panic as relentless rock flows poured over them.

As for the city itself, its walls stood unperturbed, untouched. The towers did not tremble in the least nor were there any plumes of dust and smoke as filled the air about him. Garantha was safe and sound and, strangely, entirely untouched. The citizens surely knew what was going on outside the city, but for them it was merely a monstrous spectacle to watch in awe.

It was a spectacle courtesy of Dauroth.

◆━◆━◆

"The land will be ravaged for mile upon mile!" Kallel declared. "Is this not dangerous?"

Dauroth stared down the other Titan. "It is justice."

"But how long dare we keep this going? It will deplete our energies, risk pushing some of us to collapse. We need more elixir, and there is barely enough for one last round as it is!"

There was less than that, even, if truth be told, but Dauroth was not concerned. After the fight it would be simple enough to gather the elves that Golgren had put in the stone stockade and squeeze from them every drop of necessary blood. That would give the Titans an ample supply of that precious resource until the new sources of rejuvenation could be properly tested.

"We will keep this up until the *f'hanos* and the grand lord share a common grave from which neither shall ever rise again! From this vast destruction will emerge at last the golden age for which we have toiled so long! There will be no further question in the mind of the people that it is the Titans who are their hope, who are their saviors, their teachers."

"But so many will be lost!" pointed out another Titan. "The blame for all of that—"

"The blame for all of that shall fall upon the half-breed, naturally."

The other Titans could not argue. Among ogres, a failed ruler, a dead ruler, was an easy scapegoat for mistakes and catastrophes; such had been the course of things too often in ogre history.

Dauroth focused on the spell again. An exhilaration that he had not experienced in decades filled him. He was thrilled to be destroying Golgren, he finally realized. Until that very moment, the lead spellcaster had not understood just how much he had despised the grand lord.

What a joyous event it shall be! Dauroth thought merrily. I shall make the grand lord's demise a day of celebration!

First he had to finish the task. Like most true vermin, the mongrel was proving adept at hanging on to life. The Black Talon would have to increase its magical efforts. If one or more of the inner circle should suffer fatal consequences from his action, so be it. Dauroth had always preached that to reach the golden age would require sacrifices from many.

With but a single sung word, Dauroth drew more magic from his cohorts. The others let out gasps as they felt the power draining away from them, but there was not even a feeble protest, not that any protest would have changed his decision.

You will be squashed, Grand Lord, the Titan promised. *You will be squashed even if I have to rip apart all of Kern and Blöde to do it.*

∞∞✦∞∞

It should have been Idaria's chance to flee the ogre realm, but still she stayed loyal to Golgren, trying to find and help him, searching through the chaos. Although her thick iron chains yet bound her, she still moved with the grace and perfection for which her race was famous. Where ogres and fleshless undead toppled into chasms and were lost, the elf nimbly shifted from one momentarily stable place to the next.

It was because of the Titans that she was so determined to save Golgren. Only Golgren stood against them. Only Golgren would see that her enslaved people were not herded like cattle to the slaughter, providing more and more blood for the foul elixir of the vampiric spellcasters. She had believed him when he had said that he would release the slaves shortly after his coronation. If Golgren made such a promise, he would fulfill it. Her sacrifice of honor and freedom—of her own body—her spying for the Nerakans would finally be vindicated.

It had been simple to elude her guard, who had been more interested in saving his own hide than in chasing after some mad elf. From there, though, Idaria's mission had proved far more difficult. Her mount she had abandoned far back because the animal was at far greater risk than she under such conditions. Idaria carried only a dagger; any other weapon would have been too unwieldy. The dagger was more for comfort, for it was useless against the undead. Fortunately, she eluded them; the quake was keeping them busy.

How long Dauroth and his followers would—or even *could*—keep up their monumental spell was the question. Even among the most advanced elf mages, such an effort would be highly taxing.

In the distance, she caught a glimpse of Khleeg. The ogre was no longer mounted either. Around him had gathered perhaps half a dozen other warriors. The ogres battled desperately against undead attackers. Yet there was no sign of Golgren, and Idaria moved on. She didn't care about Khleeg's fate.

She alighted on a rock, and that rock sank into the rupturing land with a suddenness for which even the elf could not adjust fast enough. Falling, Idaria got tangled in her chains. Her dagger went bouncing away, disappearing in a new chasm.

As she struggled to free herself, one of the *f'hanos* appeared. Twice it staggered and nearly fell over, thanks to the continuing tremors, but still it lumbered on toward the elf. The hollow areas where its eyes were missing somehow radiated malevolence and, although unarmed, the creature had nails and teeth more than capable of rending her soft flesh to bloody gobbets.

Unable to free herself, Idaria blindly groped for some weapon. Her fingers slipped over something metal and rounded on one side. Without hesitation, she threw it at the undead.

The piece of metal bounced off the skeleton without having any effect on it, and Idaria saw that it was part of a breastplate. The ornate design identified it as having belonged to the highest rank among the ogre army: none but Golgren himself. Despite the menace bearing down on her, her eyes followed the clattering armor, which looked banged and battered as though it had been ripped off the grand lord's body by some terrible force.

Then she heard a labored grunt from the direction of the ghoul. She turned to see a figure in ravaged silver armor barreling into the creature from behind, smashing the *f'hanos* into a wall of rock.

Stefan, his helmet lost and his face scratched and bleeding, seized the half-shattered undead and flung it into the nearest widening hole. He bent down to help Idaria.

"My lady!" he gasped. "I saw the merest glimpse of silver hair, but I couldn't believe that it was you in all this danger! You should be in the city . . . or in flight to some land beyond this one!"

"There is nothing in the capital for me if Golgren dies," the slave retorted, "and there would be even less for my people, whom he has promised to free!" As the Solamnic helped her to her feet, she added, "If there is any chance he lives at all, I must find him. I found a fragment of his armor—"

"Stripped from him by some base mage—Tyrus—Tyron—the name—"

"Tyranos?" Idaria frowned. "What is that one doing here, and why would he choose to slay Golgren?"

"No more talk!" He pushed her against the most stable rock around them then raised his sword. Driven by fury, the blade smashed through the chains binding her wrists. Taking a deep breath, the knight repeated his maneuver on the shackles keeping the movement of her legs limited.

"Only Kiri-Jolith knows how you ever got this far so

bound! My sword may never again be as sharp as before, but it was worth it to finally cut those dreadful chains! I'm only sorry I can do nothing to remove the pieces from your wrists and ankles, my lady!"

"It is all right." She gasped. Then, suddenly, she looked beyond him, a strange light in her eyes. "Then Golgren is still alive?"

"When last I saw him, yes! For an ogre, he has a quick wit, but I can't say how long that'll help him!"

He started to pull her in the direction of the city, but Idaria resisted, pointing at the line of the quake quickly running toward them along the already heaving and buckling ground.

"Not that way!" Idaria warned, tugging at Stefan.

He tried heading in the opposite direction. No sooner had he turned than another roar like thunder erupted and the land in that direction also exploded into boils and rupturing cracks.

"There's nowhere to go!" the Solamnic yelled.

Again, the elf pointed. "To your left! No! Here! Follow me!"

"But, my lady—" But the sure-footed elf had started off in a zigzagging path, and he allowed her to pull him along.

"Wait! Why do we not go there?" Stefan abruptly demanded, tugging at her to stop and pointing ahead. "Look! It could take us to Garantha! To continue in your direction leads us away—"

"I must find Golgren!" the slave insisted, tugging at him.

"There is nothing you can do for him, my lady! There is nothing even I can do! You think I'd abandon a comrade of any sort? I—"

His words cut off with a gasp that startled Idaria. She

looked where the Solamnic was gaping and shaking his head.

She followed his gaze to see a pair of *f'hanos* converging on them. They even had bits of loose armor dangling from their bony bodies, but other than that, Idaria could not see that they were any different from the other undead that surrounded them.

Yet the knight muttered the same thing over and over as he stood, slack jawed, his sword hanging limply in his hand. Idaria finally made out his words, which only puzzled her more.

"Forgive me," the Solamnic repeated. "Forgive me . . . I couldn't do anything . . . forgive me . . . "

The two horrors were nearly upon the bedraggled duo. Idaria did not want to abandon the human, but he stood there as if frozen in place. "Sir Stefan! Come! Sir Stefan! Why do you—?"

Then she realized that there was indeed something different about that pair of *f'hanos*. Not only were they shorter of stature than any of the others, but their skulls were differently shaped and lacked any hint of the tusks of ogres. The skulls of those two were much closer to those of elves.

Except they were human.

"Willum . . . Hector . . . please forgive me," the Solamnic pleaded.

The slaughtered humans had once been Stefan's comrades.

XXII

TERROR OF THE BLACK TALON

It was not how it should have gone. Tyranos had put together scenario after scenario, but none of them had accounted for that . . . nothing, unless . . .

He shook his head. All that mattered was salvaging the situation as best he could and preserving his relationship with the Grand Lord Golgren if that was still possible.

"Chasm!" he shouted, calling the broad-shouldered gargoyle's name. "Find the ogre!"

Chasm did not have to ask which ogre his master meant. There was only one that concerned them both. The huge gargoyle banked, swooping down closer to the devastation. High above it, the winged creature was not overly concerned about the tremendous quake, save that it stank of foul magic. Gargoyles could smell the magic to a degree, but even if he didn't have the nose for it, Chasm would have recognized spell work in the madness below.

Still gripped tightly by his servant, Tyranos, whose hood was off and whose hair was whipping about, pointed the tip of his staff toward the ground. Whether or not he could successfully locate Golgren was another question. The remarkable energies organized by the Titans made it difficult to ferret out anything amid the chaos and destruction, but the wizard thought he might have a chance. Golgren was unique; even he did not understand just how unique he was. That very uniqueness was in part why Tyranos had chosen him in the first place.

As they descended, a dust storm assailed the pair. Tyranos covered his face as best he could and prayed that his masking spell would hold. Of all of his spells, it was the most vital.

The staff detected something. "Bring me down over there! Quickly!"

Chasm did so, his massive, leathery wings beating hard against the air. The gargoyle could cover a mile in less than a minute, but still Tyranos felt he was moving too slowly. Whatever it was the staff had sensed, it was already fading away.

That might very well mean that Golgren had just died.

But suddenly the staff detected something else, and instantly the wizard discarded any concern for his "ally."

"Up! Up! Hurry!"

Gritting his sharp teeth, the gargoyle strained as he abruptly shifted direction and flew up. His breath came in heaving gasps, and for the first time, he faltered slightly.

Tyranos eyed the turbulent scene below him, cursing the arrogance of all spellcasters, himself included.

"Those damned fools! Those damned Titans!"

❧⊰✿⊱❧

The Black Talon sustained the spell, but the great effort was beginning to tell on many of them. Sweat covered most, causing the fine silken garments they wore to cling to their bodies unceremoniously. One Titan already was breathing raggedly and weaving back and forth, the pain distorting his usually handsome features. Others were holding on by sheer grit.

But Dauroth paid no mind to the strain on his followers. His glowing eyes still gazed triumphantly into the ether, and his mouth wore its widest, most predatory smile.

He imagined the wonderful era that would follow once the Black Talon reestablished the true course of ogre destiny. Dauroth relived the dream of the golden city. The lead Titan saw himself finally gaining entrance into the vision and viewing the wonders aplenty within those walls, wonders that he would make real and for which he would be immortalized.

But again Golgren refused to die. Somehow, the half-breed managed to scamper over the rising and falling earth, avoiding the huge ravines that opened up to swallow both living and dead by the scores. Dauroth's optimism turned to frustration, and he ripped more power from the others for his awe-inspiring spell.

"G-great one!" sputtered Kallel, betraying his fear. "Surely this is enough! S-surely the *f'hanos* have been returned to their graves and the grand lord shamed beyond redemption!"

"He is not dead," Dauroth responded tonelessly. "He is not dead."

No other protests were uttered, only sighs of exhaustion

and resignation. The inner circle of the Titans steeled themselves for whatever their leader demanded of them next. They had no other choice. They would obey unto death.

"If it is not enough," Dauroth said aloud to himself. "Then there will be more. Let us see how long you can dance, Guyvir."

The other Titans trembled as he extended the spell. Spittle stained the mouths and chins of several of the spellcasters. Kallel looked ready to say something else, but Safrag quickly shook his head. Mouth set, the apprentice studied his master closely then declared, "Take from deeper within me, great one! Bind my full power to yours! If you guide me so, I can help amplify your strength yet more!"

Dauroth eyed the younger Titan approvingly. "Good, loyal Safrag, you shall be rewarded."

A tendril of black energy darted out from Dauroth's chest and struck Safrag. The apprentice let out a brief moan then steadied himself. His eyes flared bright with loyalty.

The elder spellcaster nodded. "Now. You and I shall see that no crumb of dirt remains untouched."

With the other Titans to fuel them, the two combined their wills, multiplying Dauroth's earlier efforts several times over.

"Garantha may feel some of this," he admitted to the others. "But in the end, they will rejoice because of it."

⋄⋄✧⋄⋄

And in the capital of Kern, where hundreds lined the sturdy walls and towering gates and where many stared in awe and shock at the most violent quake ever wit-

371

nessed in their lives, the ground shifted for the first time. Suddenly, the awe gave way to panic, for no club, no axe or sword was powerful enough to stop a tremor. Against such, ogres could only pray and die.

That the landscape beyond shook even harder than around Garantha itself did not in any manner assuage the populace. What rattled the city seemed powerful enough to level it.

Fragments of the outer wall broke off and fell into Garantha and outside its perimeter. Two guards lost their balance and plunged below. The towers swayed, and in one, cracks began to appear. A massive crack opened up near the gates and began racing with dreadful swiftness through the capital, regardless of what streets or buildings stood in its path.

And with each passing second, the tremors grew worse.

⊶⊷⊙⊶⊷

They would destroy everything. They would bring down all of Garantha and sacrifice all its people just to kill him, Golgren realized.

No, the grand lord corrected himself. Not they, but rather he! It was Dauroth's doing only. He was who demanded of the Titans such monstrous use of their power, even though surely it would risk the lives of more than one of his brethren.

Golgren cursed both the master Titan and the useless vial sealed to his chest. Twice he had pounded on the latter without any success. And even if the vial could be shattered, Dauroth had stated quite bluntly how useless it would be.

The ogre leader had managed to find a massive rock formation to cling to, a wide, flat formation that thus far had not fallen away. But it was surely only a matter of time before he was lost. Golgren eyed the heavens; the overcast sky was filled with red-tinged clouds. Not only did the quake continue, a fierce wind also began to assail him.

In the face of all that, Golgren suddenly laughed his defiance. He raised the stump that had been his hand and shook it at the sky.

"Come, Sargas! Come, all you gods! If you would have Golgren, you must teach Dauroth to strike harder!"

And as if the gods had heard him, the land shook more terribly than before. As the stone suddenly twisted, spinning him around, Golgren saw one of Garantha's mighty towers fall. A mushroom cloud of dust blossomed above the city walls moments later.

Then his view cartwheeled as the rock he clung to began to sink into a freshly deepening ravine. Golgren looked up and, bracing himself, he searched for some-where—anywhere—to jump.

There was only one choice, no other. Bracing as best he could, Golgren hurled himself forward just as the vast stone tipped and dropped into the gap, completely disappearing.

The grand lord landed safely. Without warning, a skeletal warrior came from behind, seizing him. Surprised that any of the undead foes were still on their feet, Golgren was nearly throttled to death by the bony fingers before he reacted. Then he struck the *f'hanos* hard in the jaw, which only battered his own hand. The undead creature's ragged nails tore at his throat. Golgren reached for his waist, seeking the dagger secured in his kilt—the dagger he had slain the ji-baraki with so long ago—and instead grasped the belt pouch. Feeling a weight within, Golgren tore the pouch free and swung it at the side of the *f'hanos's* skull.

A crackle of fiery energy engulfed his fleshless adversary the moment the small bag touched bone. The *f'hanos* released Golgren. Flailing wildly, the skeleton began to fall apart, the pieces flying in every direction.

Heart pounding, Golgren grabbed for the pouch. His searching fingers plucked out that which he had earlier sought—the mysterious ring Idaria had thrust upon him. He still had no idea as to its origins or what it actually was supposed to do.

But surely there was enough power to help him. Golgren was no spellcaster, tutored for years by some bearded master. He could not explain his odd certainty that Tyranos's staff would save him against the ghoulish mastark, and yet it had. Nor could he explain why he had such faith in Idaria's ring.

Then the grand lord lost his footing again. Golgren banged his shoulder as he collided with the shifting ground. He nearly lost his hold on the ring but kept it between two fingers.

Golgren did the best he could to slide the piece of jewelry onto his fourth finger. For the first time, he got a good look at the signet, with its double-bladed sword turned downward. What that symbol or the others represented meant nothing to him, but Golgren was filled with a renewed determination. Surely, somehow the signet would aid him against Dauroth's spell.

And even as he thought that, the signet flared a searing orange color. He was suddenly ringed by a brief, intense fire that shot several hundred feet up from the ground.

Then the fire dwindled, and all around him changed. It happened so abruptly that the grand lord could not at first believe it. He lay on the ground for a moment, staring at everything, then staring at the signet once more.

Then Golgren smiled.

Dauroth felt the opposite emotion. He felt the sudden surge of incredible magical forces around the mongrel just before he saw the astounding results. The lead Titan glared in disbelief.

"The power of the ancients!" he roared, eyes burning as bright as the sun. "How is it that he commands the power of the ancients?"

Kallel let out a hacking cough then called, "Great Dauroth! E-end this now! We h-have destroyed Golgren's army and proven that only the Titans have the might to rule the ogre race! We have proven we are the masters of destiny! If we keep this up, we will only destroy Garantha and possibly our—"

"From the ruins we will be better able to rebuild the city and our kind! Now cease your whining!" Dauroth stared beyond the room, thinking furiously. "A signet! The half-breed must possess a signet of the High Ogres . . . and he even *wields* it!"

"How is that possible?" asked Safrag, sweat pouring down his face. Yet of all the others besides Dauroth, he looked the most determined, the most willing to push on with the spell.

"A moot question! Even the signet will not save him! In the end we shall salvage it from his crushed and buried body! Safrag, I must ask for more power from you and the others!"

No one dared protest. Dauroth was pulling all of them, including himself, beyond their known limits. Under his command, the robed spellcasters concentrated their willpower, their essences, into the task. Some no longer looked so handsome, so perfect. Instead, they appeared old and emaciated, in more than one case so withered that they seemed almost like *f'hanos* themselves. Their expressions, so pained, were horrific to behold. Yet they told themselves that all of that would be remedied when their work was finished . . . if it could be finished soon.

Only Dauroth did not care. If he had to sacrifice everyone else, he would see it through. Then not only would there be no more grand lord, but this new prize, the signet—however it had been acquired by the mongrel—would be added to his collection.

❧❀❧

The two human *f'hanos* converged on Stefan and the elf, who were having trouble standing, much less preparing to fight.

Stefan eyed the pair regretfully. How he knew which of his comrades had become those fleshless fiends was beyond his ken, but he recognized the duo as easily as if they were alive and standing before him. Once again he condemned himself for failing to save them somehow, preventing their terrible fate.

"Sir Stefan!" Idaria shouted. She had been shouting his name repeatedly, trying to jar him out of his seemingly dazed state. "Sir Stefan! You cannot just stand there! Please!"

Forced to take action on her own, the elf slave picked up a large stone and tossed it at the nearest of the undead. However, the stone bounced off without doing any harm.

Her attempt managed to stir Stefan to action. He gave a start, struggling forward and lunging at the one he knew was once Willum. If the *f'hanos* retained any of their memories or abilities after death, Willum would be the most dangerous.

Indeed, the larger ghoul dodged Stefan's awkward attack and continued to close on them. Willum carried no weapon, but one bony hand was folded into a fist and the other reached for the knight, likely with the intention of ripping out his throat.

The Solamnic swatted away the grasping hand then swung. His blade rebounded off the figure's bones with such force that Stefan nearly dropped his weapon. At the same time, the thing that had once been Hector tried to seize his sword arm, but Idaria grabbed the bony limb, then tried to twist it around.

"Keep back!" Stefan cautioned, but Idaria did not heed his warning. Hector turned on the elf woman, seizing her forearm and holding it tight. She slammed her hand into his rib cage, but the *f'hanos,* moving swiftly, grabbed hold of her wrist.

"No!" Stefan made a desperate lunge with his sword at the other undead man's nearest limb. However, Willum seized *his* arm, keeping the sword from being a threat to either creature. "Let her go!" Stefan pleaded, for Willum was eyeing Idaria hungrily. "She has nothing to do with us! Take me as you will, but let her be, Willum!"

The skeletal figure with Hector's features, hearing the familiar voice of his old comrade, suddenly stilled.

Willum, too, paused but then jerkily brought his fist forward.

Stefan started to react, but halted as the skeletal Willum opened his fist. In Willum's bony palm lay a triangular pendant. The setting was forged from steel, and the center had a pair of arching horns made from brass.

It was a medallion of the god of just cause, Kiri-Jolith.

As Stefan stared in bewilderment, dead Willum offered it to him again.

Staring at the empty eye sockets, Stefan gingerly plucked the medallion from the *f'hanos's* palm. A warmth began to wash over the knight.

Hector suddenly released the elf woman. The two undead warriors stood motionless for a moment, then collapsed together in a pile of bones.

At that point, the ground beneath them suddenly cracked and heaved worse than before.

Secreting the medallion in his armor, Stefan seized Idaria's hand just as the two of them started to sink into a fresh chasm. Together, they jumped up to a nearby rise.

Idaria abruptly tugged him. "It is him! He is there!"

"Who?" No sooner had he asked the question than the Solamnic caught sight of the Grand Lord Golgren in the distance. The ogre leader looked crazy, his hair flowing wildly around his grinning face as he sought to climb up a high jumble of massive stones.

The elf cried Golgren's name, but the ogre did not hear her. Golgren finally reached the top of his little mountain and stood straight. He laughed and held up his fist, shaking it at the sky and everything, as though taunting the forces assailing him.

And those forces responded in kind, for the sky, which had turned to fire, suddenly unleashed a dozen bolts of black lightning. They shot toward the grand lord, battering and burning around where he stood, dancing on the roiling land and dodging the bolts. The black lightning bolts churned up so much earth and dust that the pair quickly lost their view of him.

Idaria let out a gasp of fear. Stefan shook his head. "He can't have survived that."

But though the lightning continued unabated, through glimpses here and there they saw the half-breed *still* standing and laughing defiantly. His garments were ruined, his skin was black and bruised, but he retained an air of invincibility.

"We must reach him!" Idaria tried to move forward, but in doing so nearly fell into a ravine opening up on one side of them.

The knight pulled her back. "We can do nothing for him and likely nothing for ourselves but pray!" He touched a hand to the medallion. "If there is a way, great Kiri-Jolith . . . if there is a way to guide us—even *him*," Stefan added, referring to Golgren, "—through this, then I ask humbly for your aid. Or else what is lost here may lead to a dread darkness spreading beyond the ogre realms."

But their own position remained precarious, and the heavens assailed Golgren as the ground sought to devour him. Black lightning bolts peppered the ogre like monstrous spears.

Then one of the deadly bolts struck.

A rush of dirt and stone filled the air. Stefan and Idaria were blinded. The knight pressed his companion close, using his armor to shield her from the massive rush of debris that was certain to fall upon them. Stefan Rennert prayed over and over to Kiri-Jolith, in the end merely chanting the god's name.

Huge chunks began pelting them. They clattered against the knight's armor, battering and denting it. Stefan clutched Idaria closer. He wasn't wearing a helmet, and raised one arm over his head to try to ward off the deadly rain.

Several heavy rocks struck the knight on his back. Then he was smacked on the back of the head. Pain jolted Stefan, and Idaria let out a muffled exclamation.

Then there was nothing.

XXIII

DOWNFALL OF A TITAN

The signet did not protect him completely. Golgren had brutally discovered that reality. Yet the signet had kept him from severe harm when the one bolt had struck him—no small miracle in itself. The ogre had been shocked and tossed about, and his right shoulder still felt painful and numb, but he lived.

How much longer that would be the case was difficult to say.

He held up the ring and wished for some sort of all-encompassing shield, but in fact there was a new barrage of bolts, none of the bolts coming as close as that first one, thankfully.

Yet he couldn't stand awaiting the inevitable. Again he shouted, personally addressing the leader of the Titans. "Come, Dauroth! I spit upon your efforts! Never will I kneel to you! Come!"

The air was inundated with dust. Golgren's pronouncement ended in an unimpressive hacking cough. His lungs felt as if they were filled with acid. He pressed his hand against his chest, shoving aside the mummified appendage that somehow still hung around his neck.

His fingers grazed the cursed vial. Its uselessness bothered him even more than the fact it was sealed to his flesh.

Then his harried thoughts flitted to a face, an elf face.

The face was not that of Idaria, but of a female who, although no older than the slave, looked as though she had lived twice as long. Weathered lines that should have never graced such a delicate face had run rampant over his mother's visage. Despite everything that she had suffered, her eyes spoke of life and energy. She had stayed alive rather than kill herself because of her child, the misfit half-breed she had been forced to bring into the world and yet had loved more than herself.

The image in his mind lasted but a second, yet it filled him with not only a deep longing and regret, but also a rage that reminded him of what he was and what he sought to achieve.

His hand drifted to the ancient dagger, gripping it tightly. It had been meant for another deed, but better to end his life and gain a small satisfaction that Dauroth would be annoyed.

He brought the point up to his throat.

A new, far more intense tremor ripped through his surroundings. The shining dagger fell from his grasp, tumbling among the rocks. Golgren let out a frantic cry, and the lord of Kern and Blöde snatched at the weapon. His mother's face and the struggle with the ji-baraki in the old temple momentarily overwhelmed him. The dagger had become, in his eyes, a gift from his mother's spirit, always to remind Golgren of her and of how she had helped him to survive after her own death.

To lose it recalled to him how he had lost her.

As the tremor increased in magnitude, Golgren pushed back the memories and tried to focus. He found no hope, though. Destruction lay everywhere. The ogre glanced around at what would soon become his grave, aware there would not be enough scraps for anyone to bury or burn should his former subjects decide it was even worth their trouble. More likely, whoever found him would strip whatever of value remained then spit upon his ruined body. That was the fate for a failed leader.

Then, as he looked off to one side, Golgren beheld two tiny figures. One was the Solamnic knight, Sir Stefan Rennert, who appeared either unconscious or, more likely, dead. The armored fighter lay sprawled on his back across a small outcropping.

Idaria stood over the man, her left hand on his shoulder, trying to pull him up to safety with her other arm. Yet the elf's gaze was not on her companion, but fixed on Golgren.

The grand lord tore his eyes from her. It was bad enough he had to die, but to have the elf slave as his final witness . . .

The chain that held his withered hand seemed to be suffocating him. Swearing, Golgren nearly tore off the lost appendage as he loosened the chain. Again his fingers touched the vial that Dauroth had insisted was of no danger to him. In his desperation, the grand lord wondered: Was there a chance?

Had the Titan lied?

A bolt rocketed down. It tore up the soil just ahead of him. A new torrent of rock and dirt assailed Golgren as he fell back.

He slammed his fist against the vial.

RICHARD A. KNAAK

It did not break. Worse, the heavens exploded, and the ground churned as if it had turned liquid. Golgren had only a moment to note that it all took place in his immediate vicinity and nowhere else. Dauroth wanted him and only him, and it looked as if he might be successful.

Golgren was lost.

And yet some mysterious force still protected him, or else the first moment of the new upheaval would have seen him crushed under tons of stone. However, that protection was weak, and was weakening further. It would not last long.

Again his harried thoughts returned to the vial. Golgren could not explain why, but he felt certain that it was his best hope. Unfortunately, he could not seem to pry it loose.

Wrapping his maimed arm around a jutting piece of rock, the grand lord rubbed the side of his scarred and bleeding face with his hand, trying to think even as he fought to keep his balance with the ground shifting beneath him. Another bolt struck, barely missing him. He felt a sharp pain across his face. Adding insult to injury, he had added to his multitude of wounds by somehow cutting himself. As the blood trickled down his face, Golgren saw why. The edge of the signet had scraped against his skin. Some blood even splashed across the signet.

And suddenly the symbols flared a fiery orange again.

That orange glow was reflected in his widening eyes. Teeth bared in a fatalistic grin, Golgren twisted his hand around so the ring faced inward, toward himself and the vial.

"Perhaps we go together yet, eh, Dauroth?" the grand

lord hissed. "That would not be so bad an end, then, for me."

It was a final, crazy notion, yet just as when Golgren had figured out how to wield Tyranos's staff against the skeletal meredrake, it seemed the right—the *only*—thing to do.

As hard as he could, Golgren smashed the bloody signet into the vial. He heard the tinkle of breaking glass, and suddenly he felt as though all the air had been ripped from his lungs. Golgren cursed his naïveté, cursed having failed so utterly.

The ground rushed up at him from all sides. The sky vanished under a hail of earth.

✖✖✦✖✖

Dauroth gasped.

He had lost control of the spell; the quake had lessened, and the lightning ceased altogether. The other Titans darted glances his way, but he ignored them, allowing only Safrag, through his deeper connection, to understand even the least bit of what was happening. The apprentice wisely kept silent.

But the pain did not pass as he might have wished. Rather, it grew and swelled. The immense effort had finally begun to take its toll on him. He had to finish it. Then, while the others awaited him there, he would go to his sanctum and be the first to imbibe again from the dwindling supply of elixir.

Yes, that was what was left to do; in spite of the pain, he had to finish Golgren. The rest would fall into place.

Fighting to concentrate, Dauroth located Golgren. A final thrust of magical power, and the grand lord would be no more than a blot of red on the ruined landscape.

Just a final thrust—

His entire body suddenly flinched, feeling as if on fire. Dauroth could not hold back a roar of agony. The pain was everywhere; it was inside him and surrounding him. Only his incredible willpower kept everything from falling apart.

Kallel made things worse by interrupting his struggling thoughts. "Great Dauroth! You must stop! This is taking from you too much—"

"Taking from *you*. Is that not what you mean?" countered Safrag emphatically. "The master is not so weak of will as you! His strength of mind is more powerful than anything!"

Safrag's declaration pushed Dauroth to try and overcome his agony. It must pass. Surely it would pass.

Dauroth screamed as his body was wracked with worse pain. He felt as though he were being torn apart. He felt . . . only pain.

And in that moment, clarity came to him. He understood the cause of his struggles. The vial was not powerful enough to hurt him! The minotaur priestess's spell work was inadequate! Dauroth had tested the vial several times and proved that he was immune. Her enchantment had been too weak. At the most, it should have caused him a mere twinge, not the abject horror he was experiencing.

Yet . . . what other explanation was there?

The *signet!* The ancient signet that somehow had found its way to Golgren. The mongrel must have learned how to use the signet to amplify the enchantment on the vial, actually make the Uruv Suurt priestess's spell function as originally intended.

But Golgren was no master of High Ogre artifacts and magic. It would take a true scholar of the arts, such as a Titan, to make it function properly.

And not just any Titan . . . such knowledge, such casting of spells, required a member who belonged to Dauroth's inner circle.

The Black Talon.

And with that realization, he turned his torturous gaze upon those standing with him, his eyes focusing first and foremost upon Kallel. Kallel, who had protested ever Dauroth's demand upon the rest for power, who constantly worried about whether there was enough elixir or whether the other sources they had gathered would ever be enough to replace the blood of elves. Kallel . . . Kallel . . . the name played over and over in his head, in condemning fashion. Dauroth's skull pounded.

"Betrayer!" he shouted at last, the shocking denunciation fortified by the torture Dauroth was undergoing. "Betrayer!"

Taken aback, the rest of the Black Talon broke from the pattern, not caring that in doing so they shattered the spell. Kallel, gaping, sought to hide among his comrades. However, they shoved him away, leaving him to face the master alone.

Something had begun to gnaw at Dauroth, a terrible gnawing that grew with each labored breath. "Betrayer!" he managed to gasp again. One hand twisted into a fist. He felt Safrag strengthen him for what he was about to do. "Kallel, you are condemned!"

"Nay, great one! I know not even what you speak of! I did nothing!" Kallel's eyes were bright with fear. "Nay! Do not—"

"You are an Abomination to me."

Kallel howled. His body seemed to lose all solidity, as if his bones had turned to butter. His blue skin paled, turning a foul, decaying green. Hideous boils erupted all over his body. Kallel's face distorted, the eyes seeming to slide to random positions. His mouth deformed. A stench arose from him, one of corruption. His limbs twisted into tentacles.

His own insides twisting, Dauroth let out a sharp cry of his own. With a commanding gesture, he cast the transforming Kallel from the sight of the rest of the Black Talon, sending him to that remote place to which all Abominations were condemned.

At the same time, Dauroth felt Safrag sever the link between master and apprentice.

"Safrag!" The elder Titan spoke in a grating voice, startled by the development. Safrag he counted on as his key to survival. "Safrag! Attend me! Attend me now!"

But his apprentice, staring stonily, merely shook his head. "There is nothing I can do for you, my master."

The gnawing sensation had been moving up Dauroth's body, yet he retained enough presence of mind to cast a keen glance at Safrag, and at last he understood. For one of the very few times in his existence, Dauroth knew he had been played for the fool.

Kallel had not been the culprit. Safrag had merely fostered that idea in his master's mind, just as he had fed so much distrust of Hundjal before, Dauroth realized.

"Safrag! You—"

But it was too late to punish the traitor. The curse upon the vial's contents took its final toll. It was as if someone were peeling Dauroth apart from the inside. His chest folded open—his ribs, organs, and beating heart were momentarily revealed, to the horror of the others—

and from inside of him burst a green-tinged energy that further ate away at the Titan.

In the end, it was not hatred for Golgren or anger over the betrayal by one of his own that was Dauroth's last thought; rather it was the long-held dream. He beheld the ancient spirit from his first vision, then the golden city from the more recent. The city stretched out before him, the gates open and inviting. The gleaming figure was there too, and at first Dauroth believed he beckoned the spellcaster toward those gates.

But then the guardian transformed into the robed spirit. The beautiful male/female shook its head in sorrow. It waved a slim hand, and the gates shut tight.

You have failed to earn it, the guardian sang. *You have failed . . .*

As the rest of the Black Talon watched, Dauroth reached a shaking hand toward empty air, and the last of him was peeled away until *nothing* remained but dissipating wisps of smoke.

❦

In Garantha, the quake came to such an abrupt halt that nobody could question its supernatural origins. The remaining towers, still teetering, very quickly stilled. Dust drifted over everything, so thick as to be blinding.

Certain the catastrophe would return, Garantha's inhabitants remained frozen, and the only sounds heard throughout the city were those of the injured and dying calling out unheeded for aid. Only as more time passed and the land remained quiet did more normal signs of life gradually return. Only then did help begin to come to those in dire need.

With the return of normal life came the shock of awareness of the death and destruction that had engulfed the city. The cries and weeping began anew, for even ogres can stand only so much before their spirits break. Yet for all the violence within the city, an even greater menace, encroaching from the west, had been met in battle. Guards peeking over the walls caught their first glimpses of the ruined land beyond, making them thankful the city had not suffered as much by comparison.

The call went out for those who ruled to take command of the emergency and issue instructions for relief and aid, but of the self-proclaimed master of all Kern and Blöde, the only signs were the mangled and ruined banners and the cracked images.

⚬⚬⚬

Idaria woke first; it was she who first discovered that she was alive. She lay half buried in silt and stone, her body bruised and slashed, but miraculously not badly harmed.

No, it was not so miraculous. Recalling her rescuer, she looked around hopefully. Yet there was no evidence of any silver armor nearby, no hint of a human hand or limb.

"Sir Stefan!" she rasped, her wracked voice sounding like it'd be more suitable for a goblin. "Sir Stefan!"

The elf bent down and started digging frantically, tossing aside loose dirt and small debris. When the first hole she dug did not satisfy her, Idaria tried a second and a third and more. The knight had saved her life. He must be buried there somewhere, crushed by dirt and rocks. She had to find him.

But each shallow hole ended in sheets of solid rock. Whether that rock was ancient or the result of the quake was impossible to say. Stefan could lay buried yards away or right under her feet. Never had she felt so defeated.

"Sir Stefan," the elf rasped again. "Sir Stefan . . . "

Then her fingers scraped against something. Desperate, Idaria scrabbled at the object, finally uncovering it.

It was the medallion. She recognized both the medallion and the revered symbol decorating it. That drove her to prayer. "Kiri-Jolith! Lord of Just Cause! I call you in the name of one of your own! Help me find him if there is still any hope."

What she expected in response, Idaria did not know. The medallion did not flare bright, however, and no ghostly image of the good god appeared, pointing the way to the buried knight.

But then a clatter of rock to her right made her straighten expectantly. To her astonishment, she saw the armored figure she sought, off in the distance, stumbling away from her over the ravaged landscape. Stefan kept his head turned away from the elf, as if something before him held his utmost attention.

Confused, Idaria took a step after the human. Stefan was heading toward neither Garantha nor in the direction of distant Solamnia. If anything, he was heading toward the more mountainous regions of Kern and, for that matter, Blöde.

"Sir Stefan!" she shouted after him. "Sir Stefan!" Although her voice was strained, her cry was loud; yet the human did not give any sign of hearing her, nor did he turn around. He continued to stumble determinedly along on his path.

Idaria hesitated. Golgren's face formed in her mind.

She remembered all she had struggled for in her mission as an ogre slave. And she fought against feelings that had nothing to do with that mission, having only to do with herself.

Looking back, the elf saw not only Garantha, but the great waste that stretched from its walls to as far as the eye could see. Golgren lay out there somewhere, surely dead. Idaria had no more need to stay, no more need to concern herself over his machinations. As for his enemies, the Titans, she could do nothing about them. Only Golgren had been able to keep them at bay . . . until then. It was best that she follow after the knight and leave Kern behind.

Her eyes shifted to the Solamnic's dwindling figure then back to the ruined landscape that had to be Golgren's grave.

Squeezing the medallion tight, Idaria murmured, "Forgive me, Kiri-Jolith."

She rushed toward where she had last seen the ogre.

❦

His lungs burned, yearning for air. He tried to inhale, but dirt filled his mouth and squeezed his lungs.

He wasn't breathing; he was hacking. The urge to breathe, to live, fought with the temptation to die. He flailed in the direction he thought was up, seeking anything that would tell him he was making the right choice. It was hard to think. His brain and his heart pounded; his chest felt as if it were about to collapse.

Golgren's head broke the surface.

He coughed up more dirt, then madly gulped air. That brought about another hacking fit, but at least something other than the dust and soil finally was entering his lungs.

The ogre forced his eyes open. They teared painfully, creating a murky effect that reminded him of being under water.

Then through his tortured gaze, he beheld a gleaming figure of gold, a figure with no countenance, no telling detail. However, though the golden figure had no eyes to speak of, Golgren knew that it was studying him intently.

A powerful heat radiated from the shining being. Eyes stinging, the grand lord blinked, and in that blink, the golden figure vanished.

His strength spent, Golgren sagged, his head dropping down, face slamming into the ground. He did not black out, although he wished that he might if only to be momentarily free of pain.

Then a sound burrowed through the haze of his thoughts: a voice, a familiar voice.

An elf voice . . .

XXIV

Masters Of Death

What remained of the Black Talon stood in a circle. The center of that circle was where they had last glimpsed the prophet of their dream, their leader and founder, Dauroth.

The Titans were also spent, some dangerously so, but they dared not rest. What had happened only hours earlier still rattled them to the core. Those who were not members of the Talon could not be informed that Dauroth had perished. That unthinkable thing would spread chaos among the spellcasters. It might mean not only the end of the dream, but the end of all of them too.

"The elixir!" snapped a Titan called Yatilun. His pale, haggard face was the mirror of most others in the room. "Before anything else, we must partake of the elixir!"

"Then I should be first!" interjected another.

"Nay! I!" called a third. Arguments began to break out.

Morgada shook her head, her long, black hair flowing wildly. "We are lost! Without Dauroth, we are lost."

"Nay."

They looked to Safrag, who stood straighter than the rest, looking less weary than the rest.

He stood far more confidently than the rest.

Unlike the others, Safrag was resplendent, handsome, and in perfect command of himself. He glided among them, and they could not but help but be impressed and calm down slightly. "Dauroth's passing will be known and it will be mourned, but the Titans—and the Black Talon, especially—do not live and die with him. The dream that the master sought is still attainable. Another must merely guide our efforts."

"But who?" demanded Yatilun. "There is no other like Dauroth!"

"Perhaps at one time Hundjal might have led us," the Titan next to him suggested. "But Dauroth found some terrible, inexplicable fault in him . . . just as he did with Kallel."

Safrag nodded in agreement then, bowing with taloned hands spread, bluntly replied, "I would humbly put forth myself."

Morgada had watched Safrag closely from the moment he had begun speaking. The hint of a smile appeared and began to spread across her face. "Yes! Safrag was Dauroth's apprentice also! Safrag would know all the master's secrets!"

"You are correct in your last statement, Morgada. No one knew the master better than I, perhaps not even Hundjal."

There were those among the Talon who might have protested such a declaration, but as each one of the Titans stared at Safrag, comprehension dawned. He was not the servile toady many had thought Safrag to be. They all knew they were seeing a new side of the apprentice, a Safrag revealed as never before.

"The elixir?" Yatilun prodded almost gingerly.

Safrag smiled broadly, his teeth perfect and so perfectly sharp. "There is enough for now . . . for the Black Talon. A bit more can be made for others who most urgently require it. We also have the many bones. They will help us for a time."

The gathered sorcerers murmured among themselves, reassured about their welfare, their future, and happy to be reminded that the bones would still be of use. Without casting a vote, with little more than nods and glances, they accepted Safrag as their leader.

"I will be taking over the master's sanctum. At the midnight hour, you shall come to me one by one to receive the elixir." Safrag's gaze flitted among the Titans, finally settling upon one. "Morgada, you shall be first, and thereafter, you will assist me."

"I am at your command," she murmured, curtseying. Her eyes glowed with eagerness. Safrag had as much as declared her his chief apprentice.

"We must rebuild much and recuperate more," he informed the others. "The dream will be fulfilled . . . in the name of the master, of course."

The other members of the Black Talon bowed before Safrag, cementing his role as their leader, their new master. As he straightened, Yatilun cautiously brought up a subject thorny but familiar to the spellcasters. "What about the Grand Lord Golgren? What if, by fate or luck, he lives? He will wish vengeance! We cannot permit that, and yet we are weakened."

"The mongrel *does* live," Safrag informed them, startling more than one there with the new depth of his knowledge. "I sensed it. Whether he retains control for very long, though, is a question. For the time being, while we recuperate, we shall let him live and let him play at ruler. The dream is our ultimate goal and our ultimate destiny. The Grand Lord Golgren may continue to be a useful tool. When we are ready, he shall pass as all grand khans and lord chieftains have passed."

"When we are ready . . ." repeated a Titan. "When we are ready . . ."

"Dauroth promised it would be soon, but he never said how he would finally accomplish it!" said a second. "The signets and other artifacts from the tomb were to assist, but that was all! He never told us how he would forever liberate all Titans from the continual need of elixir. The bones are a temporary solution! He never told—"

"He told me," the former apprentice turned master replied with a gracious smile, displaying all his teeth.

As the others stared at Safrag with fresh interest, Morgada shifted her position nearer to the new leader. Safrag steepled his fingers in contemplation then expounded, "He told me his intentions only a day ago. The dream finally revealed to him the necessary path. It will take more sacrifice, more determination, but it will at last lead us to fulfilling all!"

"Pray, good Safrag," the Titaness asked demurely. "What information did Dauroth relay to you? Can you give the rest of us some hope, some clue? Is that permitted?"

"I would not leave my fellow Titans wandering in the dark like the rest of our fallen race, dear Morgada. All shall know our course, for all shall be needed for the hunt."

Yatilun frowned. " 'Hunt'? You almost sound like Hundjal when you speak so, Safrag! What are we hunting this time?"

The former apprentice smiled in a manner very much like that of his late mentor. He spread his arms wide again, as if to embrace all those present. "A dream in itself, a legend that has been determined at last to be fact. We owe Dauroth a debt for revealing to us the final piece." His smile widened even more. "We hunt the resting place of the Fire Rose."

That brought renewed gasps and gaping from the Black Talon. "The Fire Rose?" someone shouted. "But it is only reckless myth!"

"A myth Dauroth forbade us even to research," reminded another, "for all the tales of it, he said, had endings most dire."

"I ever found that strange," Yatilun admitted. "Why forbid seeking something that supposedly did not exist?"

Safrag waved away all their doubts and superstitions. "The master sought only to protect those too eager to be of assistance. The Fire Rose is our key. You may trust me on that point."

Yatilun shook his head skeptically. "But how can we find this thing so long lost? How do we track a legend so ancient?"

"Like calls to like. Dauroth taught us all that lesson. We can and will find it."

"But to do that, we would need—"

"A part of the legend. A minute piece of the myth. Yes, Yatilun. Yes, all of you . . . Dauroth and I managed to discover a small fragment of the Fire Rose." Safrag's eyes burned with ambition, though he spoke modestly. "A thing in itself very powerful. We shall use it to find that to which it belongs." He bowed his head at the empty space where his master had last stood, last stood staring at Safrag. "As Dauroth wished us to do."

◦◦◦⬥◦◦◦

Idaria tended to Golgren, who had passed out just as the slave reached him, as best she could. She kept his head up, scanning the carnage for another living being who might help them. It was more than an hour before three warriors in breastplates came across the pair. Under her guidance, they carried the grand lord as carefully as they could toward the capital.

Golgren awoke during his journey and, despite his injuries, commanded the pair to set him down so he could walk. When they protested, he muttered, "It would not show strength to be carried through the gates like an infant."

He accepted a supporting arm from two of the warriors out of necessity but kept his head high and his expression defiant. As they wended their way toward Garantha, survivors began to collect behind Golgren. Their numbers were small, but he hailed each. Most welcome was the survival of Khleeg. The officer, ugly even for an ogre, was even less appealing of face, bruised and bloodied and scraped. Khleeg was a ghastly sight. His toadlike mouth was still bleeding, and one tooth was gone. A huge bulge over his left eye made it nearly impossible for him to see out of that orb. His nose was also broken. Yet he silently took up a position near his master and, armed with an axe not his own, marched as if leading a parade of victory.

By the time they reached Garantha's gates, a little

399

more than a hundred warriors—many of them limping and even, in some cases, dragging wounded legs—marched with the grand lord. It was a sorry lot, admittedly, but at the same time one that set Golgren's blood stirring with pride.

Another familiar figure met them at the gate. Wargroch, fairly untouched and mounted, leaped down from his horse and dropped to one knee. "Grand Lord, I thought all dead! I search and search then return here! When I hear of your living, I bring you this!"

He turned the horse so Golgren could mount. Golgren couldn't suppress a grin, in spite of the pain, as he mounted. He looked back to survey the survivors of his force, nodding at Idaria nearby, then raised his hand and clenched his fist.

The beaten, broken soldiers shouted out his name. "Golgren! Golgren!"

Seeing one trumpeter among the guards still manning the ruined walls, the grand lord gestured. The trumpeter hastily put the goat horn to his mouth and blew hard. Another trumpeter farther away picked up the note and joined in. As Golgren started to ride, the capital resounded with one blast after another.

Khleeg renewed the shouting. "Golgren! Golgren!"

The other warriors followed suit and, within a minute, many onlookers did too.

And as the small party rode deeper into the devastated city, more and more ogres came out to line the cracked streets or halted their cleanup efforts to stare at the return of the grand lord. Many joined in the cheers and shouting.

At they turned toward the palace, Golgren's eyes narrowed. He suddenly guided his horse in a different direction. Khleeg, Idaria, and the others did their best to keep up, not knowing what he had in mind. But Golgren did nothing by chance or accident.

As word continued to spread ahead of the march, ogres from various sectors of Garantha joined in the grand lord's wake. Many were warriors left to defend the city, overjoyed to find their leader alive, even if so badly battered. But many ordinary citizens, in growing numbers, swelled the parade.

At last, Golgren arrived at his chosen destination. It was not the Jaka Hwunar, where he had once intended his glorious climax to take place, but rather the temple of Garantha's patron spirit. The ancient edifice was intact—minus one column that had broken free and tumbled down the steps—and the area was clear enough of debris to enable a crowd of citizens to surround the grand lord as he rode the horse up the steps.At the top, Golgren leaped down as if full of fresh energy and entirely unharmed from his ordeal. Not even Khleeg or Idaria were allowed to know the pain that made him wince, the jarring of his bones when he landed on the stone steps. Golgren bound his mount's reins to one of the columns then turned and stood before the many assembled ogres. Over his chest he still wore his mummified hand, and that he suddenly held high.

"Kee yo if'hanosi uth if'hani dakar!" he roared so all present would hear his claim. Golgren then repeated the words in Common. "I have brought death back to the undead!"

His followers barked and, lacking clubs, slapped one fist into the other over and over. Their enthusiasm spread among the ordinary folk. To the people, Golgren was alive and the undead were no more. The people were amazed, and they were proud.

"*Dakar iGaranthi uld iGolgreni ne iGolgreni uld iGaranthi!* Garantha is Golgren just as Golgren is Garantha!"

There was more clamor from the crowd and especially the grand lord's warriors, with Khleeg leading the shouts, "*Kala i iF'hanosi il aF'hanari Faluum iGolgreni!* All praise to the Final Death of the Undead That is Golgren! All praise!"

"*Kala i iF'hanosi il aF'hanari Faluum iGolgreni! Kala i iF'hanosi il aF'hanari Faluum iGolgreni!*" the crowd repeated in an awkward chant. To ogres, any title was prestigious, and the more titles, no matter how ungainly they tripped off the tongue, the more prestige.

Golgren looked at Khleeg, who understood immediately what was asked of him next. The officer rushed halfway up the temple steps then turned and yelled in Common, "All praise the *grand khan* of all ogres! All praise the grand khan of Golthuu!"

The crowd immediately cheered his bold, new pronouncement; those whose grasp of Common was not good enough to understand all the words caught the gist and simply mouthed the Common chant, "All praise the grand khan of Golthuu!" Caught up in the excitement, all accepted the momentous proclamation, for it would bring a semblance of order and sanity to a devastating situation.

"All praise the grand khan of all ogres!" Khleeg shouted over and over at the top of his voice. As the rest assembled joined his effort, their thunderous chant flowed out over the rest of Garantha and became truth throughout the ogre realms.

It was not the extravagant traditional ceremony

Golgren had intended, but in the end, it served him as well . . . at least for the time being. For he was the grand khan of all. When there came an accounting for all the tragedy, he knew there would be controversies and questions focused on his leadership.

There would be many repercussions from the disaster. News of the ruination would reach the Uruv Suurt, whose emperor would smile at the thought of so many dead ogres and who might think to add to their numbers. It would also reach the Solamnics, who, with the knight Sir Stefan Rennert lost—the dream of an alliance lost— might also cause future problems for the ogres.

And there were others whose fate was in question.

Golgren did not glance at her, but he felt Idaria's gaze strong upon him. The elves beyond the realms, who sought to free their kind from slavery, might take the opportunity to create trouble. There were older enemies yet in Neraka and among his own kind. Not for a moment did the new grand khan believe he had won any clear victory. Not for a moment did he think that he would not soon face opposition from other ambitious ogre warriors. Even if seen as a victory, the day had drained the numbers of his supporters and loyalists.

There was also the mysterious force watching him— trying to manipulate him—through the eyes of gargoyles. Golgren had not rejected the notion that Tyranos guided the gargoyles. Tyranos no doubt had survived. But it was more likely that someone else steered the foul creatures, someone even more insidious.

Yet of all threats, of all his enemies, there existed only one that he considered of immediate danger. They might be leaderless and in disarray—for surely Dauroth *was* no more—but the Titans were in a power struggle to the death with him. The reins would be taken up, and they would seek Golgren's blood anew.

He grinned wider and while the throngs assumed the grin was meant for them and his own pleasure, the half-breed ogre leader smiled in anticipation of the great fight ahead of him. In his life, Golgren had endured ridicule, beatings, enslavement, and sufferings that made the loss of his hand a minor inconvenience. He had endured those tribulations and grown the stronger. They had molded his ambition, his ruthlessness.

Guided by Khleeg and his other supporters, the ogres continued to cheer and shout his name. Golgren turned in every direction, waving and acknowledging the crowd. He knew he stood straight and tall and looked powerful, despite his slighter stature.

Yes, the Titans were welcome to betray him again.

The Uruv Suurt, the dark knights—all his adversaries —were welcome to try their best too. Golgren laughed, and his subjects, thinking he was savoring his triumph, laughed with him.

No, he was savoring his future triumphs. He was surrounded by enemies who wanted to unseat or kill him. That was why Golgren laughed. No sane person would wish to be surrounded by enemies . . . no one.

"Come to me," Golgren murmured to those distant foes. "Come to me . . . and I will teach you fear."

And as if hearing his taunt, something fluttered away from a building in the distance, something the new grand khan realized had to have been there all that time, watching.

Barely had he focused on the ugly thing than a second one rose from the west, joining the first in flight. A third was added to their ranks from the northern section of the capital. The three hovered in the sky, hovered just long enough for Golgren to understand they *wanted* him to see them; then, with a sudden, intense flapping of wings, the three gargoyles rose high into the yet overcast heavens . . . and vanished.

THE END

JEAN RABE

THE STONETELLERS

"Jean Rabe is adept at weaving a web of deceit and lies, mixed with adventure, magic, and mystery."
—sffworld.com on *Betrayal*

Jean Rabe returns to the DRAGONLANCE® world with a tale of slavery, rebellion, and the struggle for freedom.

VOLUME ONE
THE REBELLION

After decades of service, nature has dealt the goblins a stroke of luck. Earthquakes strike the Dark Knights' camp and mines, crippling the Knights and giving the goblins their best chance to escape. But their freedom will not be easy to win.

August 2007

VOLUME TWO
DEATH MARCH

The escaped slaves—led by the hobgoblin Direfang—embark on a journey fraught with danger as they leave Neraka to cross the ocean and enter the Qualinesti Forest, where they believe themselves free. . . .

August 2008

VOLUME THREE
GOBLIN NATION

A goblin nation rises in the old forest, building fortresses and fighting to hold onto their new homeland, while the sorcerers among them search for powerful magic cradled far beneath the trees.

August 2009

RaVenLoft™
the covenant

RaVenLoft's Lords of darkness have always waited for the unwary to find them.

Six classic tales of horror set in the RAVENLOFT™ world have returned to print in all-new editions.

From the autocratic vampire who wrote the memoirs found in *I, Strahd* to the demon lord and his son whose story is told in *Tapestry of Dark Souls*, some of the finest horror characters created by some of the most influential authors of horror and dark fantasy have found their way to RAVENLOFT, to be trapped there forever.

LaureLL K. HamiLton
Death of a Darklord

christie golden
Vampire of the Mists

P.N. eLrod
I, Strahd: The Memoirs of a Vampire

andria cardareLLe
To Sleep With Evil

eLaine bergstrom
Tapestry of Dark Souls

tanya huff
Scholar of Decay
October 2007

FORGOTTEN REALMS

R.A. SALVATORE

The *New York Times* best-selling author and one of fantasy's most powerful voices.

DRIZZT DO'URDEN

The renegade dark elf who's captured the imagination of a generation.

THE LEGEND OF DRIZZT

Updated editions of the FORGOTTEN REALMS® classics finally in their proper chronological order.

FORGOTTEN REALMS®

You cannot escape them, you cannot conquer them,
you can only hope to survive . . .

THE DUNGEONS

DEPTHS OF MADNESS
Erik Scott de Bie
Twilight awakes in the dungeon of a deranged wizard surrounded by strangers as
lost as she is. Twisted magic and deadly traps stand between her and escape, and
threaten to drive Twilight mad—if she lives long enough. . . .

THE HOWLING DELVE
Jaleigh Johnson
Meisha returns to find her former master insane, and sealed in his dungeon home
by Shadow Thieves. She must escape, but her survival isn't enough: she must also
rescue the mentor she left behind.

STARDEEP
Bruce R. Cordell
The seals that imprison an eldritch wizard within his prison are breaking
down, and the elves scramble to find the reason before the wizard's
nightmarish revolution begins.

November 2007

CRYPT OF THE MOANING DIAMOND
Rosemary Jones
When an avalanche of stone traps siegebreakers undermining the walls of a
captured city, their only hope lies deep within the tunnels. With water rising around
them, and an occupying army waiting above them, will they be able to escape alive?

December 2007

Wizards

SEMBIA:
GATEWAY TO THE REALMS

A powerful family, where everyone from the maid to the matriarch is hiding something . . .

BOOK I
THE HALLS OF STORMWEATHER
Edited by Philip Athans

Sembia is a land of wealth and power, where rival families buy and sell everything imaginable—even life itself. In that unforgiving realm, the Uskevren family may hold the rarest commodity of all: honor.

BOOK II
SHADOW'S WITNESS
Paul S. Kemp

To protect the family from the horrors of the Abyss, Erevis Cale must return to the shadowy life he left behind. The first FORGOTTEN REALMS® novel from *The New York Times* best-selling author Paul S. Kemp!

BOOK III
THE SHATTERED MASK
Richard Lee Byers

Shamur Uskevren must reveal her true identity to gain her vengeance. But in her anger the matriarch has forgotten that few things in Selgaunt are exactly as they seem, and the Uskevren have many dangerous enemies.

BOOK IV
BLACK WOLF
Dave Gross

A "hunting accident" with the Beastlord of Malar leaves Talbot Uskevren infected with lycanthropy. The priests of two gods offer him solutions—for a price—and every night Tal delays may cost more lives.

August 2007

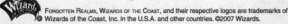